THE THRILLING LIBRARY:

The Best of Thrilling Adventures

The Black Bat Archives, Volume 1

The Black Bat Archives, Volume 2

The Black Bat Archives, Volume 3

The Black Bat Archives, Volume 4

The Black Bat Archives, Volume 5

The Black Bat Archives, Volume 6

The Crimson Mask Archives, Volume 1

The Crimson Mask Archives, Volume 2

Diamondstone Archives

Dr. Zeng Archives

The Eagle Archives

George Chance—The Ghost Archives, Volume 1

The Masked Detective Archives, Volume 1

The Purple Scar Archives

VOLUME 1

BY
NORMAN A. DANIELS

INTRODUCTION BY
TOM JOHNSON

THRILLING PUBLICATIONS
2017

© 2017 THRILLING PUBLICATIONS. ORIGINALLY PUBLISHED IN 1939.

NO PART OF THIS BOOK MAY BE REPRODUCED OR UTILIZED IN ANY FORM OR BY ANY MEANS WITHOUT PERMISSION IN WRITING FROM THE PUBLISHER.

VISIT US AT WWW.THRILLINGPUBLICATIONS.COM.

TABLE OF CONTENTS

	INTRODUCTION i
I	BRAND OF THE BLACK BAT 1
II	MURDER CALLS THE BLACK BAT 117
III	THE BLACK BAT STRIKES AGAIN 239

INTRODUCTION

TOM JOHNSON

THE THRILLING Group kicked off their second round of pulp hero heavyweights in 1939. In June of that year, the Candid Camera Kid popped up in *Detective Novels* and in July we found the Black Bat in the pages of *Black Book Detective*. More heroes would follow in 1940 and '41. Standard's wordsmith, Norman Daniels, created many of the new series.

Daniels' original idea was for Tony Quinn to fight crime as The Tiger. Blinded in the courtroom by acid, the damage left scars around his eyes, giving him the moniker. The story was accepted, but Leo Margulies, head editor for Standard at the time, wanted something that would coincide with a magazine they'd recently picked up, *Black Book Detective*. A short story series that ran in a previous title, The Bat, in *Popular Detective*, may have influenced their final decision. The Tiger was changed to The Black Bat, and became one of the most popular of the late edition heroes for Ned Pines' Thrilling Group. It was merely coincidence that The Black Bat and Batman started during the same period.

Standard slapped their house name, G. Wayman Jones, on the stories to let Norman know the character belonged to them, but he became the main author for the series throughout its long run. He told me that Leo wanted the character to have the feel of The Shadow, and that every time Walter Gibson got a raise, so did he. In "Markets of Treason," Winter 1944, the Black Bat does drop the ribbed cape, and now merely wears black to blend into the shadows. The stories continued to be top notch. However, the bat regalia was now missed by most readers.

The July 1940 entry, "The Black Bat's Flame Trail" is the first unknown author assigned to the series. Will Murray believes this author is Whitney Elsworth, but I lean more towards Prentice Winchell (most familiar to readers under his pen name, Stewart Sterling). Two more stories, "The Black Bat's Dragon Trail," January 1941, and "The Black Bat's Summons,"

July 1941 are also unknowns. Perhaps the three are by the same author. I suspect at least two of them are.

There is no question on the next ghost author. Laurence Donovan writes three non-Daniels entries, "The Murder Prophet," September 1942, "Millions for a Murderer," March 1943, and "Without Blood They Die," Summer '43. The rest of the stories are by Norman Daniels until the end of the series. Daniels told me that a new editor had been assigned to the series, replacing long-time editorial head, Leo Margulies. Who this new editor was, he couldn't remember, but said it was a woman, and she wanted more adult content to the stories. Norman didn't feel comfortable writing sex scenes, so she brought in another author.

"The Eyes of Death" is promised for Spring '52, but does not appear. Instead, the next novel to appear is Prentice Winchell's "Hot, Willing, and Deadly," Winter '53. A little research does turn up an old novel titled, "The Eyes of Death" by Stewart Sterling. It was a Dan Fowler story published in November 1941, and involved Nazis. My guess is that Sterling planned on rewriting the Fowler story into a Black Bat entry, but was having trouble replacing the Nazis. Or else the new editor rejected the rewritten story, skipping an issue, until Sterling/Winchell could come up with another story. "Hot, Willing, and Deadly" was probably more in keeping with what the editor wanted. Another story is promised, "The Lady of Death" by Prentice Winchell. It doesn't appear. The series is ended. Winchell/Sterling rewrites "The Lady of Death" as "The Lady's Out for Blood," and sells it to *Triple Detective*, Spring '53. Tony Quinn has been replaced. Norman Daniels had written an unpublished Black Bat story, "The Celebrity Murders," but it never appeared.

Stewart Sterling was a good writer, and had worked in the pulps for years. I'm sure he was writing Phantom Detectives, early Dan Fowlers, and probably those early Black Bats. I wish we could find his records, as I'm sure we would uncover some interesting facts, as well as possibly some unpublished manuscripts. But those final Black Bat stories were an incredible jump from a good series, to mediocre stories. The sex and rough language the editor wanted just didn't work well on Norman Daniels' 1939 creation. Personally, I think they should have left it alone.

As with all of the single character pulps, the early stories were the best in the series. So it was with the Black Bat. At least up through the end of the World War, we had some exciting stories of Nazis and sabotage, and even some super criminals. After the war years, the stories tended to tone down, becoming more simple crimes, especially the "long ago crimes," where something happens years before that now surfaces into some new crime. Until the end, when we are given drug or juvenile gang-related criminal activity, or, as with Prentice Winchell, prostitution and crimes of passion. Good stories perhaps, but I missed the super criminals and foreign agents bent on the destruction of America.

I often wonder how the series would have fared had it began in the early Thirties, as a companion to *The Phantom Detective*. There is a possibility it would have been more popular, and even outlasted the great Phantom. Unfortunately, it would have been created by someone else, and ended up with an even more chaotic authorship. Perhaps it's best the series waited until 1939 after all.

Happy reading!

Tom Johnson
Seymour, Texas

BRAND OF
THE BLACK BAT

CHAPTER I

VISIT BY NIGHT

TONY QUINN stirred restlessly in his sleep as a man's form moved silently across the room. The intruder was in a hurry, but he made not the slightest sound. Moonlight brought him into relief a moment, showing him to be about forty with a high, bald forehead, pointed, narrow nose and a small mouth. While there was nothing sinister or evil looking about him, he did exude one specific quality—that of being slippery.

He touched the sleeping man's shoulder and shook him slightly. In a flash Tony Quinn was awake. His brain oriented itself immediately and one hand darted beneath his pillow to come forth with a .38 automatic.

"Wait, sir," the intruder whispered. "I'm doing you a great favor. Hear me out—please."

"Go ahead," Tony Quinn said softly. "Explain what you're doing in the house of the District Attorney."

"Are you the D.A.?" the intruder gasped. Then, without waiting for an answer, he went on. "That settles a lot of things. I'm not the only man in this house, sir. There's another, searching the rooms, and he's carrying a gun. Oh, I admit I came here to rob, but I don't relish being made a part of murder, sir."

"In the closet with you," Quinn said quickly. "Close the door and make no sound. If you're telling the truth, you won't be sorry. If this should be a trick, I'll riddle that closet door with slugs."

The intruder seemed to float across the room, so little noise did he make. Quinn lay down again, shoved the gun beneath the covers and slowly released the safety. His mind was fully awake now. He even grinned a little.

Then, through slitted eyes, he saw his bedroom door open. A man's chunky frame was silhouetted against the moonlight for a second. Lights flashed on. Quinn turned nervously, sat up and blinked. The man who had entered held a gun pointed straight at Quinn's chest and he was not more than ten feet from the bed.

"Take it easy, D.A.," the second intruder warned. Quinn studied him. He saw a short, pudgy man with a wide, cruel face and eyes that were narrowed tensely.

"All I want to do is talk," the man said. "You're alone in the house so I know I won't be interrupted. Just don't make any fast moves because I don't want to kill you."

"Now just a moment," Tony Quinn said calmly. "Who are you and why did Oliver Snate send you here?"

The intruder grinned. "You guessed it. Smart—ain't you? That's right—Snate sent me. Never mind who I am. Now listen—today court was adjourned to give you time to produce a surprise witness against Snate. He's on trial for intimidation and conspiracy. So far he's way ahead, according to the way we look at it, but you said something about a witness and recordings of Snate's voice. I came to make a deal."

Quinn never moved a muscle. "My life—against the recordings and the name of the witness—so's you can murder said witness. Don't bother to tell me—I know. The answer is—nothing doing."

THE KILLER made a wry face. "You're making it tough, D.A. I got my orders—either the recordings and the witness' name, or I put a slug in you where it'll do the most good. Think it over—for five minutes. Don't do anything rash because I've got the drop and I'm ready to shoot."

Tony Quinn glanced at the closet door and wondered if this stealthy intruder who had warned him, was no more than an agent of Snate's also. Mentally he damned himself for being so cocksure. Police Commissioner Warner had wanted to provide a guard, but Quinn had laughed that off. Now he seemed to be in a spot with death as the only exit.

True, with the automatic concealed beneath the bed covers, Quinn had a trump card to play, but he shuddered as he thought of what his predicament might have been if he hadn't been warned.

His finger tightened against the trigger of his gun. He looked squarely at the killer.

"I want this clearly established in my mind," he said slowly. "Snate sent you here with orders to get the recordings I mentioned—and also the name of my witness. Unless I produce them, I die. Is that correct?"

"You heard me, the first time," the killer rasped. He was getting a bit jittery. A man in Quinn's precarious position should be trembling, quaking under the threat of sudden death. Yet Quinn was as cool as though he were addressing a jury on an open and shut case. It wasn't natural and the killer sensed that Quinn had something up his sleeve.

The killer licked his lips and primed himself for the murder. If he killed Quinn, Snate couldn't complain. Maybe the witness wouldn't dare come forward then—and the recordings might be in the house and easily found. The killer's finger tightened on the trigger.

The Black Bat

Quinn saw the gleam in the man's eyes. He prepared to raise his own gun, still beneath the covers. It all depended upon who could shoot the fastest now. Then Quinn's heart stopped beating a moment. The gun was caught in the covers—

At that moment the closet door opened and a shoe came hurtling out, straight for the gunman. He turned his head, swept the gun toward the closet and fired once. Quinn's automatic came free and the bang of his shot almost merged with that of the killer.

For a second or two, the thug stood perfectly still, gun still pointed at the closet. Then he gave a long sigh, his body sagged, hit the floor and rolled over into a heap. Quinn was out of the bed in a flash. On his way to the closet, he kicked the gun out of the thug's hand.

The intruder who had warned him was holding onto a hook with one hand while blood streamed down his face. He attempted a grin, but it failed because he was on the verge of unconsciousness. Quinn seized him just as he was about to take a header to the floor. He carried the man to the bed, placed him on it and then secured towels from the bathroom. He hastily wiped the blood from the man's face and saw that the bullet had inflicted only a scalp wound. Unless there was a concussion, the intruder would be on his feet within ten minutes.

QUINN POURED raw brandy down the man's throat and nodded in satisfaction when the eyelids fluttered. Quinn left him for a moment and examined the gunman. He was quite dead.

"You—you're all right, sir?" the man on the bed asked. Quinn straightened up from his grim task, walked over to the bed and sat down.

"Thanks to you, I'm quite all right," he said. "You have a scalp wound that doesn't look serious. Can you talk now?"

"Yes sir, I can talk all right, but there isn't much to say. I—I entered your house with full intentions of robbing you. I—I have a police record and—well—I suppose it's all up with me now."

Quinn poured another pony of brandy and helped the man prop himself up against the pillows. "Not by any means," he said. "You saved my life. Your act of burglary is wiped out by your act of courage. You practically gave yourself up to warn me and then you deliberately brought down that killer's bullets on yourself so I'd have a chance to shoot. Tell me more about yourself."

"My name is Kirby—Norton Kirby. I—I'm known on the records as Silk Kirby. I'm a confidence man. Burglary is out of my line, but I was hungry and desperate. I opened your front door with a master key and got inside just in time to see this other man open a window and crawl in. I knew he wasn't on the prowl and I figured he intended to murder you, sir. I reached you first—that's all."

"Silk Kirby," Quinn smiled a little. "I've never heard of you. I'm going to get you some food and coffee—if you can stand the stuff I call coffee."

"Let me, sir." Kirby raised himself and swung both feet to the floor. "I used to be a valet, sir. I can do it."

Quinn believed him, twenty minutes later, while he sipped some of the coffee Silk had made. The confidence man talked eagerly, as if he wanted to get things off his chest.

"I've never been vicious, sir. Whatever I did was against people who deserved to be—ah—clipped. Breaking into your home was the first act of violence I've ever attempted."

"It will be your last," Quinn said, and then as Silk grew pale he added hastily, "I'm not going to turn you in, Silk. You see, I need a man like you. I'm not married, I've plenty of money and I am also the District Attorney with any number of enemies. One in particular would like to see me wiped off the earth. He sent the thug I killed. How would you like to work for me—act as sort of a bodyguard."

Silk's eyes lighted up with an eagerness that couldn't have been assumed. "I'd like it, sir," he said simply. "I won't be so much of a bodyguard, but I could help you, sir."

Quinn grinned. "You're hired. I can judge men and I know you'll be honest with me. Now about this attempt at murder. You see, I'm trying Oliver Snate—a racketeer—for conspiracy. As with every other one of his tribe, it looked like a farce with witnesses who became tongue-tied, alibis for Snate that cropped up and couldn't be broken down by any amount of questioning. Snate thought he'd be free soon, but—I had a trump card.

Silk

"A LITTLE old man named Brophy who runs a store on the west side. He refused to knuckle under to Snate's men and Snate himself paid Brophy a visit. Brophy was no fool. He knew Snate would come so he arranged to have their conversation recorded. He turned the records over to me and they are in my safe now. Tomorrow Brophy will mount the witness stand, testify and the recordings will break Snate's alibis and protests of innocence, wide open. I've got him on the run."

"I have heard of Snate, sir," Silk said and tried desperately not to wolf the sandwich he had made. "He's a dangerous man and I don't think he's finished yet. I'll remain up the rest of the night, sir, and guard the safe. You get some sleep. You'll need to be refreshed in the morning, sir."

Quinn walked over to a wall phone in the kitchen and dialed a number.

"You forget, Silk, there's a dead man in my bedroom. Even a District Attorney has to report sudden and violent death. Now remember, you're my valet. I hired you yesterday. No one will ask questions because the only servant I have had is a woman who cleans during the day."

Silk filled up on sandwiches while Quinn talked over the phone. Twenty minutes later a coroner's assistant appeared on the heels of a score of police. The body was removed. Silk prepared another room and Quinn retired. Silk found a gun in a library table drawer, sat down on a straight backed chair, tilted it against the wall safe and sat there until morning.

When Quinn came down, breakfast was ready.

CHAPTER II

SEARING ACID

PROBABLY THE tensest man in the courtroom was Oliver Snate. Attired in a two hundred dollar suit and a twenty dollar shirt with accessories to match, he sat on the edge of his chair and nervously chewed on the tips of his fingers. He knew that Quinn was the ablest District Attorney to operate in years and he knew also that the man he had sent to kill Quinn, had himself died. Snate was scared and dangerously desperate.

He looked over his shoulder and some measure of confidence returned. Mingled with the onlookers in the courtroom were five men, imported from a distant city so that detectives on guard wouldn't know them. These men had specific instructions. If they failed, Snate was doomed—not to a term in prison but to the electric chair. He didn't know these men either for an assistant had hired them, but he was a judge of such things and could pick them out.

Quinn entered the court room followed by Silk, who carried a bulging brief case and two heavy law books. Silk set these down, whispered to Quinn and then took a seat at the reporter's table.

Court opened. Quinn addressed the judge and jury briefly. "Your Honor and Gentlemen of the jury, court was adjourned yesterday in order that I might produce irrefutable evidence that Oliver Snate is guilty of intimidation and conspiracy. My witness has been carefully hidden. Recordings that will prove Snate's guilt have been kept in my own home. I alone know exactly what those records will reveal and to what my witness will testify. These precautions are necessary because Oliver Snate is a ruthless, vicious beast. He—"

"I object," Snate's lawyer howled. "Bring on the evidence. Never mind the accusations. The District Attorney is trying to defame my client before the jury. My client, who is innocent and happens to be as upright a man as the eminent District Attorney himself."

Quinn faced Snate and inquired mildly, "Would an innocent man send one of his paid assassins to murder me during the night?"

Snate turned his head away quickly. His lawyer gulped and sat down. Quinn stepped up to the witness stand, turned and motioned to a white haired old man who sat in the front row of the gallery.

"I call Joseph Brophy to the stand," Quinn said.

Brophy got up, looked around and all but tottered to the witness chair. He was sworn and sat down, tapping his fingertips together nervously. Quinn opened his brief case, drew out two recording disks and placed them on the table. Then he faced the witness.

"You will tell, in your own words, exactly how you met the accused. You will point him out and testify to everything you know concerning him. When you have finished, I will play back the recordings you took and then allow the learned counsel for the defense to see if he can discredit cold, mechanical testimony from a phonograph."

BROPHY BEGAN talking.

"It was three months ago tomorrow. Two of Snate's men came into my store and told me I had to buy insurance. I didn't need any and I told them so. Then they broke my show case. Two days later they came back and assaulted me. I—I had to go to the hospital for a week. They came again and I told them to get out. This time they smashed my plate glass window. After that I got ready for the next visit. I prepared a recording machine with a sensitive microphone. I was in luck, because Snate himself came. I let him think I was ready to knuckle under and he talked. Every word is inscribed on those records."

"Tell us what he said," Quinn asked and watched the jury lean forward. These twelve men were eager to convict Snate. The super-racketeer had gotten away with every crime from murder down to simple assault and battery. All the jury needed was evidence enough.

Snate saw the jury too. He nervously drew a silk handkerchief from his pocket and wiped his forehead. Behind him, five men tensed. It was the signal. One casually dropped a hand into his pocket, yanked the pin on a specially created smoke bomb and suddenly he jumped up, hurled the missile and then whipped out a gun. His four companions followed. The bomb burst the moment it landed just outside the jury box. The court room was thrown into an almost impenetrable fog. Working in unison, the five men pushed their way through the gates. Two of them jumped for the recordings on the table. One held a bottle of powerful acid in his hand. He dumped part of the contents on the disks.

Quinn, fighting his way to the table, saw the act. He lunged for the man with the acid. He drove a hard blow to the face, missed and stumbled. He fell heavily, but was up in an instant. The courtroom was in a frenzy. Women screamed and men cursed. Police and guards tried to distinguish the men who had started the riot, but the smoke fumes were too thick.

Quinn spotted the man with the acid and this time he wound both arms around him, trying to pin him down to the floor for a knockout blow. The thug, realizing his danger, used the only weapon handy. He hurled the remaining contents of the acid bottle over his shoulder. The searing liquid struck Quinn full in the face. He felt it bite into his flesh; felt it burn his eyes until the white fog was displaced by an inky blackness. He stumbled around, clawing at his face. Tears ran down his cheeks. The agony was almost more than human nerves could stand.

Carol Baldwin

He reeled, clutched at the table, dabbed his eyes again and as the acid bit deeper and deeper he gave vent to a scream. Someone took his arm. Dimly he heard two quick shots and then blessed unconsciousness wiped out the torture that throbbed through his body.

Silk was at Quinn's side. A gun gleamed in his hand. Someone stepped up beside Quinn. Silk peered through the haze, raised his gun and fired once. A man, with an automatic in his fist, toppled to the floor, shot through the center of his forehead.

THAT SHOT seemed to be a signal. More guns barked. Someone smashed windows and air rushed in to displace the smoke. As the fog gradually cleared away, two men were seen elbowing their way through the milling crowd in the courtroom. They reached the heavy swinging doors.

Someone shouted, "Stop them! Stop those killers!"

The gunmen whirled and pumped half a dozen bullets in the direction of the bench. Then they burst into the corridor to be met by a hail of hot lead from a rapid fire rifle in the hands of a policeman. The two men went down, riddled.

It was almost half an hour later before a semblance of order was restored. Ambulances and squad cars packed the curb in front of the court building. A horde of police filled the corridors, searching and questioning everyone. Snate sat between two guards, both wrists cuffed. Doctors worked frantically over half a dozen men.

Police Commissioner Jerome Warner came in. He surveyed the courtroom and swore softly. Outside, in the corridor, lay two gunmen, killed by a score of bullets. Within the courtroom itself, lay the other three men who had been hired by Snate. All three were dead. One, accounted for by Silk, the other two killed under a withering fire from a dozen policemen's guns.

Brophy, the sole witness to Snate's act of conspiracy, still sat in the witness chair, but his body sagged forward and a knife was driven to the hilt in his chest. Quinn lay on one of the long tables while two doctors swabbed his eyes. He knew nothing of what went on. Silk hovered nearby, sweat running down his cheeks.

The commissioner mounted the bench and sat down beside the still pale jurist.

"An act which should make the people of this country blush with shame," the judge said, his voice trembling. "Despite all the precautions which I ordered, this ghastly thing has happened. The witness is dead, his recordings are destroyed by acid and the District Attorney probably blinded for life. Mr. Commissioner—why can't you do something about this?"

The commissioner mopped his perspiring face. "What can I do that I haven't already tried? If we can pin this on Snate—we'll send him to the chair, but don't be too certain that we can. Snate has been in prison and has a perfect alibi. Unless we can establish the identity of these five killers—who can't talk—we're licked. We must tie them up with Snate and his mob or there is no evidence."

"I'll hold Snate," the judge snapped. "I'll hold him just as long as I can. Get your men to work, Commissioner. Tie those five killers to Snate's gang and you'll have him. Show the public we have a police force—not a bunch of blue uniformed morons."

But Commissioner Warner soon learned that this was impossible. The five dead thugs were identified by finger-prints. They were strangers in town and in no way could they be linked to either Snate or even the most obscure member of his gang. It was the old story of the ruthless destruction of evidence and witnesses that couldn't be otherwise suppressed. The case against Snate had collapsed. What people thought, or assumed, had no material effect on the letter of the law. There was absolutely no evidence against the sneering racketeer.

THREE HUNDRED especially picked detectives worked frantically, night and day, to uncover some scrap of evidence which might hold Snate, but no such piece of evidence existed. Snate's attorneys were clever, too. They protested that their client could never have conceived this hideous plan. They proved that he had been allowed no visitors and could in no way send out word to his men. Whatever had happened was not of his doing, Snate's high-priced attorneys protested cynically.

Butch

They spoke of theories by which some man whom Tony Quinn had sent away had exacted his vengeance. The theory was plausible for Quinn had made many enemies during his three years' term as a crime buster. Theories, conjectures and suppositions filled the air, but there was no meat to them. In the end, Snate was released by the same judge who had been forced to duck bullets dealt out by Snate's hirelings. Not even the intruder who had been killed by Quinn could be connected with Snate's mob. In fact, the dead killer had been identified as a man with good cause to hate Quinn. His brother had died in the electric chair as a result of Quinn's work.

Newspapers took up the challenge. They called for everything from a complete change of administration to the arrest of Snate on no charges at all. Commissioner Warner lost fifteen pounds in two weeks. His face grew haggard, his eyes became puffed and bloodshot from lack of sleep and physical exhaustion.

Only one man offered no suggestions, made no statements. Tony Quinn lay on a davenport in the library of his home. He spoke rarely and to no one but faithful Silk, and then only when necessary.

For Tony Quinn's heart was filled with a rage. His mind sought vainly to find some solution to it all, but there seemed to be none. And what sent Quinn deep into the blackness of despair was a new affliction which filled every waking hour with agony.

Tony Quinn was stone blind!

CHAPTER III

GIRL OF MYSTERY

TONY QUINN, no longer district attorney lived on in darkness. The days grew into weeks, the weeks into months.

"I'm blind, Silk," he said for the thousandth time. "Blind as a bat, Silk. I'm doomed to live the rest of my life in a world of darkness so that an inhuman monster like Snate can flourish. What are the latest reports about him?"

Silk shook his head slowly. "I won't hold back anything, sir. You're clever enough to know when I do. Snate is back where he was before you arrested him a year ago. He's growing more powerful than ever. I—I didn't tell you this before, sir. Snate sent a box of flowers to the hospital when you were there—with a note of sympathy. I threw them into the trash can, sir."

Quinn laughed hollowly. "You did quite right. I only wish it had been Snate himself. Well, Silk, I don't suppose you'll be around much longer. I've recovered as much as I ever will. My face is scarred for life, I'm blind with absolutely no hope of recovery according to the best doctors that money can hire. I'm washed up and above all I want no sympathy, so if you wish to leave—it's all right with me."

Silk straightened out the covers on Quinn's shoulders. "If you don't mind, sir, I'll stay on. You need me now and I—I've grown to need you, sir. Perhaps one day we will meet a doctor—one who may give us some hope. As for your scars—they are hardly worth mentioning. One can scarcely notice them, sir."

Quinn laughed again cynically.

"You're a cheerful liar, Silk. Why, I can even feel them with my hands. Odd, Silk, how strange my sense of touch has become. It's a year since I became blind, yet already I can distinguish things by merely passing my hands over them. A recompense, in part, for my lack of sight. What about some of that good coffee, Silk? In one thing at least I'm fortunate—having you."

Commissioner Warner listened to the frantic appeal.

Silk swallowed hard. "I'll make the coffee, sir. It won't take but a few moments. Don't try to move."

Quinn arose, threw off the blanket about his shoulders and walked rapidly toward a table in one corner of the room. He sidestepped a chair, stopped an inch from the table and put his hands on it.

"No need to worry about me, Silk," he said with a smile. "That's another thing I've learned. Objects I cannot see tend to warn me in some way. I know they are in front of me and I can avoid them. I'm quite all right. Get busy with the coffee."

Silk moved to the door. "It's almost midnight, sir. I'll have it ready at a quarter after."

HE HURRIED to the kitchen with a slow shaking of his head. Silk was grateful that Quinn couldn't see the livid scars that made a mockery of a face once handsome. The acid had eaten deeply, etching a hideous mask around Quinn's eyes that now were dead and blank.

Quinn made his way back to the davenport and sat down. His mind was spinning. What could he do? He couldn't even read. The radio had long since grown to be a bore and Quinn refused to see any of his friends with the exception of Police Commissioner Warner.

Quinn's fingers worked in and out, as though he had Snate's fat neck between them. Once Quinn had even considered sending for Snate and shooting him down. He gave up that idea when he went looking for a gun. Silk had removed every weapon—to guard against suicide.

Suddenly Quinn raised his head and turned it to one side, like a listening dog. He reached out and curled his hand around a heavy cigarette container.

"Who is there?" he demanded in a whisper. "Speak up. I know there is someone in this room. I can hear the wind rustling through the curtains and every window was closed when Silk left me."

There was no reply but Quinn's highly sensitive ears caught the rustle of silk and his nostrils dilated as they sniffed a perfume. Then a cool, soft hand touched his wrist.

"Please," a woman's voice said softly, "I'm here to help you, Tony Quinn. I'm sorry I had to do it this way, but it was necessary."

"Who are you?" Quinn's hands rose and touched her face. Eagerly the fingers traced every curve and outline. "You're pretty," he went on. "Very pretty. Your hair is soft and silken. You have warm, well shaped lips and I'm betting your eyes are blue."

"You win the bet," the girl said softly and sat down beside him. "What I have to say will not take long, Tony Quinn. I know how you lost your eyesight—I know everything about you. The doctors all said there was no hope, but I am here to give you that hope. Will you accept my suggestions no matter how strange they may seem?"

"Who are you?" Quinn asked. "And how can you give me hope?"

"You will wait exactly three days," the girl said, paying no heed to his questions. "Then go to a little town in Illinois—Springville by name. You will consult a doctor named Harrington. Everyone knows him in Springville. He knows you are coming and he is ready. He alone can cure you."

"How?" Quinn demanded in a hoarse whisper. "How can some country doctor do what world famous surgeons say is impossible? Why are you so interested?"

"I'll tell you—some day," the girl said. "You will do this for me, Tony Quinn? For yourself?"

He nodded and tried to find her hand. She pulled them both out of his reach and arose.

"Come back." Quinn was on his feet. "Come back—please."

But there was no answer. Silk ran into the room with a broad bladed kitchen knife in his hand.

"What is it, sir? Was there someone here?"

Quinn sat down slowly. "An angel, Silk. She must have been an angel because she has given me hope."

Silk gaped and edged toward the phone. What he had so long feared was now an actuality. Quinn's tortured mind had snapped.

"No," Quinn laughed, sensing Silk's actions. "I'm quite sane. There was a girl here. She came through one of the French windows and she told me where to go and get my sight back again. In three days, Silk, we leave for Springville, Illinois. No one is to know where we have gone. No one, understand, Silk?"

"Yes sir, but—"

"NO BUTS. If you so much as whisper this to the canary, I'll skin you alive. Look here, Silk, I've got faith. I have visions of a new life beginning for me. I *know* that some day I'll see again and when that day comes Oliver Snate is going to wish he had never been born. He's going to be broken—mentally and financially. I'll wear him down until he's on his knees. And I won't use the weapons I had at my command as District Attorney. I'll use highly unorthodox ones. I'll fight him with his own methods. I'll—"

"*We* will do that," Silk put in. "*We*, sir."

Quinn smiled. "Right. In my enthusiasm I forgot you, Silk. You'll be of tremendous help to me. Together we'll twist the coyote's tail until he howls. Perhaps all this is false hope, but that girl sounded so real, so sincere. Find out where Springville is, Silk. We won't charter a plan because I want this whole affair kept a secret. Make reservations on a train, under assumed names."

The buzz of the door bell put an end to further conversation. Silk escorted three men into the room. Quinn nodded in their direction.

"I can't say the usual thing—that I'm glad to see you, Commissioner Warner, because I can't see. Rather, I'll say I'm happy you're here. You and your friends."

Commissioner Warner sat down and twirled his hat. His iron grey hair and mustache seemed to have taken on a lighter shade recently. The lines of worry under his eyes had become permanent. His companions ranged themselves on either aide of him.

Warner introduced them. Paul Stewart was a robust type with a short, fat neck and squinty little eyes. He was none the less Commissioner of

Correction for the entire State. The second man was Otto Fox, head of the nation's largest armored car service. He was thin, mild looking and even more nervous than Warner.

The Commissioner said: "We've come to you for advice. When you were District Attorney, you could place your finger on the authors of crime faster than any dozen detectives. I wonder if that trait still holds good?"

"It's about armored cars, Commissioner?" Quinn asked. "Go ahead, fire away. If I can help you, I certainly will."

Warner looked a little startled. "I suppose you guess it was armored cars because Otto Fox is with me. You're right. We've run up against the strangest thing, Quinn. Armored cars are sent out over their routes. They start with a full crew of men known to be perfectly honest. They make their regular calls and then drop off the face of the earth. Somehow they are being spirited away with their entire crews and, of course, every cent they've picked up along their route."

"They vanish like some of the things a magician waves his wand over," Otto Fox broke in with a reedy voice. "I tell you it's supernatural. How could anybody steal an armored car—full of armed guards with orders to shoot? It can't be done, I tell you. It's not possible."

"How many have vanished?" Quinn asked.

"Three—so far," Warner said. "There isn't a trace of them. I've a hunch your friend Oliver Snate might lie securely behind this little plan. Does this look like his work?"

QUINN SHOOK his head. "It may be his work, but not his brains. Snate couldn't think that deeply. I'm sorry, gentlemen—I can't help you. A year ago I'd have joined in as eagerly as possible, but—I'm a blind man. I can no longer move without a man at my side. I stumble over things and I can't step outside my home except for a short breath of air."

Warner put a hand on Quinn's shoulder. "I know that, old man, but your brain isn't impaired. I thought, perhaps, you might recognize the methods behind this new racket. I'll tell you what, Tony. If there are any new developments, I'll drop in again. You might solve the whole problem for us."

Otto Fox, faintly drumming his finger-tips on the arm of his chair, nodded assent. Paul Stewart looked a little bored. Quinn shook hands with them and Silk ushered them to the door.

Silk returned, frowning. "I don't understand it, sir. The Commissioner comes out here with his problems and expects you to solve them instantly—without even an investigation."

Quinn laughed. "He's not fooling me, Silk. Warner only drops in to pretend he needs my help. That serves to give me an idea I'm still in the running. It's a colossal bluff and I might seem to fall for it, but there's only Commissioner Warner's good heart in all this. Mind you now—not a word of our intended trip."

Silk served the coffee and sat down to drink a cup with Quinn. The blind man stared straight ahead.

"You know, Silk, Warner had an interesting problem. Imagine, three armored cars, staffed by reliable men, disappearing in broad daylight? In the face of that this enforced inactivity is enough to drive a man mad."

In the following four months, eleven more armored cars vanished from sight while police ran themselves ragged striving to uncover the slightest clue. Commissioner Warner listened to frantic appeals for help.

The relatives of the armored car guards clamored for some news of their loved ones. Newspapers took up the cry.

And all the while Tony Quinn sat in a darkened room with bandages across his eyes. His visit to the little rural town in Illinois had been brief—barely two weeks. He had undergone an operation, the nature of which an old, brittle-tongued, family doctor had refused to discuss, but Tony Quinn knew one thing—*he could see.*

True, there had been only vague shadows, but those were sufficient to bring his courage and hope up to a maximum. As to the girl, he had learned absolutely nothing. The one stipulation under which the doctor had consented to treat him was that he must ask no questions.

Silk finished reading the latest newspaper and threw it on a table. Quinn leaned back in his chair, gently massaging his eyes.

"In a few days, Silk, I'll see again. I know I will. I must because there is so much work to do. You and I are going to find out what has happened to those armored cars. We're going to pin something on Oliver Snate and see that he pays a suitable penalty for the suffering he has caused."

"I don't see how you'll be able to do it, sir," Silk put in. "You're well known. Of course everyone thinks you are blind and there is no hope of ever recovering your sight. You could wander around without arousing suspicion."

"SILK, WHAT do you suppose I've been planning all this time?" Quinn spoke passionately and exultantly. "Wander around?" Quinn laughed and there was no longer a hollow tone to his laughter. "We won't wander, Silk. We'll go out—with smoking guns in our hands if necessary. We'll use whatever means we think best in our fight against

Snate and others of his kind. We'll fight them with their own weapons—with treachery, intimidation, theft—and draw the line only at murder. If we kill, it will be in self defense. We'll take every nickel of their stolen loot. We'll worry them until they are as jittery as a one legged man on a tightrope. We'll work with the police or against them if need be. We'll make our own laws and we'll enact our own judgments. Silk—this is the opportunity I've waited for during long weeks of darkness. Every moment when I was blind, Silk, I planned for this."

Silk's eyes flashed eagerly. "So have I, sir. I've hoped—almost as strongly as you. I've even thought of quitting your service and going after Snate myself. I can still see him, so smug and domineering, in a courtroom filled with man-made fog and spitting guns. I wanted to shoot him that day. I almost did."

"Good," Quinn approved. "Not about shooting Snate. That's too easy for him. It's your attitude I like. You see—I'll need a man like you—one who knows the underworld and has a few connections."

"But how are you going to handle it, sir?" Silk wanted to know. "Your face, if you'll pardon me, is disfigured. It won't be a pleasant sight when you first see it. You'll be recognized."

"My face?" Quinn leaned back and compressed his lips. "That can be taken care of. Plastic surgery can make it over. But not now, Silk. Not now! I want people to think I'm helpless and that I haven't enough interest in life to even have my features mended. We'll operate anonymously. No one must know who we are. I'll have to wear a mask, of course—a complete hood, I suppose, if my features are as bad as that doctor said they were."

"Yes sir," Silk nodded, "it will have to be a hood. I'll make one, sir, of silk. Black silk, that can't be seen in the night. You can dress in black also and be nothing more than a dim shadow in the darkness."

"But there must be some means of identification," Quinn pursed his lips. "Something by which men can recognize me. An insignia—a name, Silk—I have it! I've been blind—as blind as a bat. I still am so far as anyone knows. I shall prowl during the night. Bats are blind and fly by night also. I'll be the bat, Silk. *The Black Bat!*"

CHAPTER IV

THE LIGHT AGAIN

EACH DAY Silk read the newspapers aloud while Quinn mentally filed away whatever information they offered. Another armored car had vanished. Even the increased staff of guards hadn't prevented it from disappearing.

The papers traced it carefully. Under sealed orders, the contents of which were known only to a trusted employee, the car had first visited two big banks and carried away heavy payrolls. Then they had picked up more money at busy department stores and restaurants. The previous day's receipts of prominent theatres were collected until it was estimated that two hundred thousand dollars rested within its steel lined walls.

It had visited a small manufacturing plant where ten thousand dollars was dispensed to meet a payroll. After that the car had been seen heading north along a busy boulevard and from that moment on it had never been seen again. Somewhere, along an important street where thousands of people walked and rode, where police cars and patrolmen were on active duty, the car had vanished as completely as if swallowed up in the middle of the road.

There was other news too—of Oliver Snate. His connections had grown during the months of Quinn's blindness. He was now the recognized overlord of crime. His influence reached into political offices, delved deeply into private businesses and touched the very bottom of the underworld. No crook, no matter how big or small, would dare to operate without sharing a portion of his profits with Snate. His power had increased until even the newspapers were afraid of him. Only one dared print the real truth, and that paper had suffered a bomb explosion in its linotyping rooms.

"Peter Gage is trying to do his job," Quinn told Silk. "He owns the *News-Record* and he's certainly thrown down the gauntlet to Snate. But there is someone else behind Snate. He's just a front—a man to take the rap if anything happens. Snate is ruthless, but he can't think. There are brains behind all this and I'm banking that those same brains have concocted a way to make armored cars vanish from the face of the earth. One of these days we'll know, Silk. We'll know and Snate will be unpleasantly surprised."

"You'll remove the bandages tomorrow, sir?" Silk asked.

"Tomorrow," Quinn repeated. "Yes, Silk. Then I must remain in a darkened room for thirty days. They'll be the longest of my life even though I shall be able to see a little. That's all, Silk. I won't require anything more tonight."

Silk withdrew silently, his lean face aglow with enthusiasm. Quinn wanted to be alone—in these last few hours of his blindness, for with the morning he would know whether or not he might really see again.

Oddly enough, Quinn's mind wasn't on his affliction or the possibility of its cure. As he sat before a glowing fireplace he thought of the soft spoken girl with the silken hair and the blue eyes, hair and eyes he hadn't been able to see. Yet somehow he felt as though she was always near him, watching over him much as Silk did. A clock intoned midnight. Quinn raised his hands to the bandage around his eyes. Slowly he began unwinding it and he knew that his heart never missed a beat.

The confidence which the country doctor had exuded served to give Quinn part of its measure. The last folds of the gauze fell away and two thick pads dropped from his eyes.

THERE WAS a searing flash of light and Quinn uttered a cry of pain. He turned away swiftly. He had been facing the fireplace and had forgotten that its light might harm his vision.

One thing he did know. His eyes reacted! There had been a flash of light! He could see! How much, he didn't know—yet. But he was satisfied. He could really see. A hymn of thanksgiving rose in his soul. He turned his back on the fire and then slowly and carefully opened his eyes again.

There was a chair. Dim, yes, but still a chair. He could see it! A mirror on the further wall reflected some of the light from the fireplace. Quinn gasped. He could see that.

Then he stiffened. There was something else. A dim shape—there in the dark corner of the room. It was moving. Moving out toward him, like a grim spectre. Quinn blinked and tried to penetrate the haze. He moved his head to one side and closed his eyes tightly. There was a pad of feet, a swish of silk. And Quinn knew. The girl of mystery had returned.

"You," he cried. "You!"

"Yes, Tony Quinn. I knew that when midnight passed, you'd no longer be able to restrain yourself. But you must not expose your eyes to light—not yet. It might harm them. Walk into the next room and I shall follow. It is darker there—and better for your eyes."

Quinn obeyed, keeping his lids tightly closed as he passed the fireplace, but basking in the knowledge that some of the light penetrated the lids. He was going to see again!

He sat down and opened his eyes. Faint moonlight streamed in through the tall French windows. Then he saw the girl move across his range of vision and to his amazement he could see her plainly. Far more clearly than it had been possible before he had been blinded. Even the colors of her face, her hair and her eyes were visible to him in this room of almost absolute darkness. He started up, involuntarily, with one hand reached out toward her.

"No," she said sternly. "You must remain just where you are, Tony Quinn. I have come to talk and ask a favor."

Walker closed his fingers around the gun.

"Favor?" Quinn said. "All the favors within my power could never fill the appreciation I feel for you. And you are lovely—your hair is so golden, your cheeks so red and your eyes so blue."

"You—can—see that?" she asked incredulously.

"I can. Somehow that operation has given me hyper-sensitive eyes enabling me to see in the darkness. You're as clear to me as if the lights were on. I—I hardly understand it myself."

"I do," the girl said quickly, breathlessly. "I know the anatomy of the human eye, Tony Quinn. Within the cornea are the aqueous humor and the iris. The iris is a colored muscular membrane with the pupil in the center. The pupil is, actually, a hole for the transmission of light and in your eyes this pupil is exceptionally large and therefore much more sensitive. A cat's eyes are the same. Just behind the pupil lies a crystalline lens which acts the same as the lens of a camera. Yours is much larger than that of a normal eye because of the enlarged pupil. Your range as well as your sharpness of vision is greater and—you are enabled to see in darkness. I tell you this, Tony Quinn, so you will know for yourself. I won't talk about it again until you hear my complete story."

SHE SAT down, ten feet across the room from him. "I did all this for you with one idea in mind, Tony Quinn. Now that you can see again, you are ready to fight back against the forces that blinded you. I want to join that fight."

"You?" Quinn gasped. "But how did you know that? No one knows—except Silk, and he certainly hasn't talked."

"He hasn't," the girl answered. "Yet I do know that you plan to fight evil and crime with their own weapons. That you hope to force Oliver Snate to pay for his crimes. Don't ask me how I know. The fact that I do will suffice for the moment. You will let me help you?"

Quinn shook his head. "No. That is one thing I cannot do. From tonight on I am no longer Tony Quinn but the Black Bat! There will be danger where I go—and sudden death. It is no place for a girl."

"That is final?" she asked.

"It is final," Quinn answered. "Anything else in the world I will more than gladly do. I owe you the return of my sight, but I can't repay that debt by exposing you to death. There is no place for a girl in my operations.

"I tell you all this because I know you are to be trusted. But—why not tell me who you are? Why you did this and what lies behind your request to join the forces of the Black Bat?"

"Close your eyes, Tony Quinn," she said with something that sounded like a choked sob. "You must not keep them open more than a few moments at a time until several days have passed."

Quinn closed his eyes slowly. It seemed a very natural thing to obey the girl. He heard a rustling sound, the click of a window lock and she was gone. He started up, walking rapidly toward the window through which she had escaped. A light laugh came from the darkness outside.

"Tony Quinn," her voice drifted in to him, "I'll join your forces whether you like it or not, and one day you'll *ask* me to work with you. No—don't interrupt me. I have one thing more to say. On the first of next month—after your eyes are quite recovered—Oliver Snate plans to start a campaign of bank robbery. You must prevent it."

Then she was gone. Dimly, Quinn heard a car's motor whine into life. He walked slowly back to his chair and sat down to think. How had this girl learned of his plans to rid the city of crime in all its vicious forms? Silk hadn't talked. Quinn knew him too well to suspect that. Yet not another soul knew of these plans. Her mysterious knowledge spelled clairvoyancy, even though Quinn believed in none of the occult sciences.

It was daybreak when he went to bed—with his eyes covered by pads and adhesive.

The days passed quickly after that. By night, Quinn worked furiously. A sound proofed target range in the cellar of his spacious home, echoed to the roar of exploding guns. Targets that were mere blobs in the darkness, were shattered by Quinn's expert marksmanship. Not until he could hit a playing card, tossed into the air by Silk, did he cease his pistol practice. And that card had been used as the target in a range as dark as pitch.

"IT'S A sort of payment for the months you couldn't see at all," Silk offered happily. "I can't even see a regulation size target three feet away, but you put two bullets through the deuce of spades at thirty feet."

"Darkness is almost like daylight to me," Quinn said. "But there is no time for talk. In two days I can face daylight. When that happens, Silk, we shall begin to create furrows of worry on Snate's placid brow. Is everything lined up?"

"Yes sir. Two or three of Snate's men have been systematically robbing jewelry houses and the loot runs into many thousands of dollars. They haven't fenced it yet because none of the local fences will handle the stuff. It's too hot."

"So?" Tony Quinn pursed his lips. "You have something else on your mind, Silk?"

Silk parted his lips in a cold grin. "Yes sir. A new fence—with plenty of money—might suddenly appear and be willing to buy up all kinds of hot goods. I think it could be arranged, sir."

"It is arranged," Quinn said happily. "Draw enough money, Silk. Work quickly and get things all set. Have every bit of that stolen jewelry concentrated in one spot. Begin—now!"

CHAPTER V

VOICE ON THE WIRE

SILK KIRBY presented a wholly new appearance when he walked into the expensive cafe ten hours later. He couldn't disguise his narrow face, nor the thin nose and slanting forehead, but he looked anything but a valet. His clothing was obviously expensive and loud. He smoked dollar cigars and kept his vest pocket stuffed with them. A two carat diamond flashed iridescent rays from the ring finger of his right hand and he wore a diamond-studded watch low on his wrist where it was constantly in sight.

"Brandy," he informed the bartender. "The very best—Napoleon '96."

There were half a dozen men at the bar and they eyed Silk with interest. That interest grew when he paid the dollar and a half check for the sip of brandy. Silk's purse was crammed with bills of big denomination. He drank slowly, relishing each drop. Then he went out.

One man followed him very carefully, but Silk was aware of that. The men at the bar had been of Snate's tribe and they accepted him immediately as either a positive sucker—or a man who might be valuable to Snate. Silk didn't care which idea they assumed.

He took no pains to conceal his movements and once he stopped at a jewelry store where he had a whispered consultation with the manager. Watching eyes saw the manager shake his head violently and Silk put something back into his pocket. When he had gone, the man who had followed him, entered the store.

He flashed a badge, stolen from a detective many months before. "That guy who was just in here. What did he want?"

The store manager looked around quickly and dropped his voice to a whisper. "He had an emerald—a perfect specimen—and he wanted to sell it. Somehow that stone looked familiar. I don't want anything to do with crooks. I put him out."

"You should have called headquarters," the pseudo-detective growled.

He left and headed up the street in the direction Silk had taken. Much to his surprise, Silk was loitering along the avenue, gazing into store windows. When Silk turned into a swanky hotel, his shadow heaved a sigh of relief. Snate would pay well for this information. His organization allowed no poaching and this flashily dressed man was definitely engaged in some kind of crooked work, else where had he secured a valuable emerald—and the wad of cash that filled his purse?

A discreet question to a bell captain and Snate's man had everything he needed.

"That man?" the bell captain slipped the two dollar bill into his pocket. "His name is Alexander Green, sir. He came here from Los Angeles. A perfect gentleman, sir."

Upstairs Silk watched through parted curtains as his shadow stepped into a taxi. He grinned, stripped off his loud suit and donned a bathrobe. Then he placed two guns in different parts of the room, both of them concealed, yet quickly accessible. After that he read newspapers for the better part of two hours. When his phone rang, he betrayed no surprise. A Mr. Walker wanted to see him. Silk had Mr. Walker sent up.

WHEN HE opened the door, two men stepped in. One closed the door, put his back against it and kept one hand deep in his coat pocket. The other, who had been Silk's shadow, sat down and offered Silk a cigarette.

"Being a stranger here," he began, "I suppose you are surprised to receive visitors. I'll be perfectly frank with you. A few hours ago you tried to pass a certain kind of rock in a certain kind of store. Maybe you could interest me in it."

"Could I?" Silk asked mildly. "Perhaps if you asked that gorilla by the door to let go of his gun, I might feel more in the mood. Personally I hate guns. They have no place in my business."

"Okay, Joe," Walker said. "You can relax."

The gunman eyed Silk fishily, but he sat down and folded his arms. Silk had a notion that a second gun rested only a few inches from the thug's right hand.

"That's better," Silk grinned. "Now, Mr. Walker, I'm listening most intently. By way of introduction my name is—"

"Green," Walker put in. "From Los Angeles. We've checked, you see. First of all I want to warn you. Taking it for granted that you are a right guy, get this straight. Nobody operates in this town without permission from a certain man. This town is all sewed up. You either work with the organization—or you don't work at all."

Silk puffed contentedly on his cigarette and crossed his legs. "I see," be said quietly. "You're a bit off the trail though. I'm no hood. My specialty is the discreet handling of gems. I'm an artist when it comes to jewels. I feel the warmth of them, glory in their allure and sparkle and, very incidentally, I like the profits they sometimes produce."

"That rock you showed a jeweler downtown," Walker narrowed his eyes. "Where'd you get it?"

Silk looked into space. "I don't violate confidences. Enough that I paid a fancy price for it and I expect to get about fifty thousand for the gem. It's quite perfect. Here—look for yourself."

He reached into his pocket and the thug instantly moved to action. His right hand vanished under his coat and half pulled a gun from a spring holster. Silk regarded him with a mild grin and dropped the flashing emerald on the table top. Walker scooped it up and whistled.

"Some rock! Sure you can get rid of this?"

"I certainly would not have purchased it if I thought I might have a white elephant on my hands. Don't be a fool—of course I can sell it. Why?"

"Would about fifty or sixty stones like this interest you?" Walker asked cautiously. "Not all emeralds, of course. There are diamonds, a matched string of pearls and a few other doodads. You know what I mean."

"How hot?" Silk arose and walked the floor, hands clasped behind his back. He paused at the side of the thug and put a hand on his shoulder. "Please don't bother with the cannons. You'll tire your shooting hand always keeping it tense."

The thug scowled and muttered something, but he did relax. Silk faced Walker again.

"I asked you—how hot are those rocks?"

WALKER SHRUGGED. "Not very. They've been out of circulation about three months. Maybe you'd like to see them, huh?"

"Perhaps. Will you bring them here?"

"Smart, aren't you?" Walker laughed. "We're no saps, Green. No—you'll come with us, and blindfolded at that. You'll see a few samples and we'll dicker."

"I'll get my hat," Silk suggested. "We'll go at once."

Ten minutes later Silk was inside a sedan. He felt a gun shoved into his side and Walker pressed adhesive over his eyes. They rode that way for almost an hour. Then Silk was led out of the car, across a cement driveway and up five steps. He sat down when a chair was shoved under him and blinked when the blindfolds were removed.

He found himself in an expensively furnished library. There were four men lined up against the wall and they wore the surly looks of professional killers. Behind a huge desk sat Oliver Snate. He hadn't changed much during the months since Silk had seen him in court. He was still tall, angular and his patent leather hair was slicked down on his scalp. His closely cropped mustache was jet black and he kept rubbing his hands together.

But Snate's eyes were narrow. "I've seen you somewhere before," he said suspiciously. "I rarely forget a face."

Silk's lips parted in a smile. "I heard that of you, Mr. Snate. You did see me. Once, three years ago, you came to Folsom Prison to visit a man named Mandell who was doing the book. You were trying to spring him, but the screws caught on. Mandell was transferred to Alcatraz. I was the trusty who led Mandell into the visitors' room. He told me about your plan after you had gone. We were pals."

Snate nodded. "You must be on the level or you wouldn't have known that. All right, I'm convinced, although I might warn you that if I'm crossed you'll join a lot of other saps at the bottom of the bay where they're resting in a bed of cement. Now, what's your racket?"

"I buy—and I sell," Silk answered readily. "Which means we can help one another and I'm in no way infringing on your own rackets, Snate. I've got cash and I'm ready to buy."

"To the tune of a hundred and fifty grand?" Snate asked.

Silk nodded. "I'll give you an even hundred thousand for the stuff you say is worth a hundred and fifty grand. Don't play me for a sucker, Snate. I know what hot stuff is worth."

"Okay," Snate grinned. "We understand one another, I see. You'll be taken back to your hotel. Wait there. Tonight some of my men will show. Look over the stuff they offer and give them your best price. They'll phone me and if it's all right, we trade. You might also give me the name of one or two right guys on the coast. I'll phone them and get an okay on you—just to be sure."

"Of course," Silk agreed. "Call Jerry Monohan—at the Club Elite. You know Monohan even if you are three thousand miles away. Ask him about Alex Green. That's the name I went under out there."

An hour later Silk was escorted into his hotel suite by Walker and the same pug who had acted as guard.

"You," Silk indicated the pug, "come here." He dropped a hand into his pocket and withdrew a short barreled pistol. With a grin he passed it over, butt first, to the gunman. "I took this out of your pocket before we went to Snate's place. Take my advice and always keep your guns in holsters. And beware of pickpockets."

THE THUG took the gun with a stunned look. Walker guffawed.

"You must be okay," he said. "Imagine—seeing Snate with a gun in your pocket! That never happened before. We'll see you about ten-thirty tonight. Have the dough ready."

Silk waited more than an hour after they had departed. Then he went down to the lobby, studied the faces of the men and women who lounged there and entered a phone booth. He dialed a number.

"This is Green," he reported. "At ten-thirty tonight we do business. Everything looks okay."

Then he hung up and went back to his room. He felt confident that he had put the deal across nicely. If Snate did contact the coast, Jerry Monohan would identify Alexander Green. Silk had once deemed it wise to assume another identity now and then.

But Silk might not have been so sure of himself had he been able to listen to a conversation in a taxi just outside the hotel. While Silk surveyed the people in the lobby, an ugly face was almost pressed against one of the big plate glass windows that overlooked the entire lounge of the hotel. The man who watched nodded his head emphatically, as if to emphasize to his own mind that he had been right.

Walker was in the taxi. "Well," he asked eagerly, "were you right?"

The thug grimaced, "Was I? Say—that guy is made up plenty and he dresses different, but take it from me—that's the same mug who followed Quinn, the old D. A., into the court room the day he got the acid in the face. I know because I was close to him. He came outa the same car with Quinn and carried his brief case and books. Then, later on, this same mug bumped one of them hoods Snate hired to take care of things in court. We gotta see Snate—quick."

Walker shook his head and smiled wisely. "Not so fast. Look—if this guy is really a stooge, we'll make him talk so we can prove it to Snate later on. But what nobody but you and I will know is where that hundred grand has gone. We'll give the jewels back to Snate, tell him it was a plant and this guy didn't bring any dough."

"Okay," the other man growled, "but how do we work this?"

"Snate doesn't know that Green is a stooge of Quinn. He wouldn't even know the guy was in court that day because Snate wasn't watching anybody but himself. So what do we do? We take Green for a little buggy ride and see if he's got a tongue in his head. I know treatments to make stubborn men talk. What's more, we don't tell anybody else because if we do, they'll try to horn in. Soon as this punk tells us enough to convince Snate, we bump him. I'll have the dough and the boys who are to help us won't know it."

The cab drove away quickly and Walker plotted the procedure of the evening.

Snate, meanwhile, waited until he was alone in the study. Then he carefully locked each door, pulled open the lower drawer of his desk and removed a telephone. He simply lifted the receiver and the connection was automatically completed.

"I GOT something," Snate reported without the preamble of introducing himself. "A guy blew in here from the coast. Says his name is Green and he's looking for rocks. How about getting rid of that stuff? I can get a hundred grand for it—in cash."

The voice that answered him was steady, monotonous and obviously disguised by turning the tonal qualities into a hiss.

"Be sure you're right, Snate. The price seems too good to be true. Have you checked up on him?"

Snate answered, "I'm trying to now. But he must be okay because one of the boys saw him try to get rid of a nice big rock just a couple of hours ago."

"Very well," the hissing voice agreed. "Do business with him and keep him handy for more. Just be certain he's no police spy."

"You bet," Snate answered cheerfully. "I'll take care of things."

"Yes," the voice purred, "you will, Snate—or I'll take care of you. Oh—one more thing. Tony Quinn, the ex-D. A., is getting active. I want to be positive he is really blind. See to it."

Snate hung up and shivered. Odd how that voice affected him. Snate possessed no doubts as to the caliber of this man who directed his every move. There was cold blooded murder in that voice and a ruthlessness which even surpassed that which Snate packed in his so-called heart.

Snate tapped the top of his desk a moment, replaced the phone and then growled. Why should he waste his time trying to contact the coast for confirmation? If this Green was a stool, he'd pay for it!

CHAPTER VI

BRAND OF THE BLACK BAT

AT TEN-THIRTY Silk opened the door to let Walker and his pug into the hotel room. Instantly, Silk sensed danger. Walker was too smug, his gunman too eager.

"You have the stuff?" Silk inquired and edged over toward a chair under the cushion of which he had a gun concealed.

"What kind of a sap do you think I am?" Walker demanded irascibly. "Show us the dough and I'll take you to where the stuff is waiting. We don't take chances, see?"

Silk shrugged, removed a wallet from his pocket and threw it on the table. Walker flipped over the sheaf of big denomination notes, closed the wallet and nodded.

"It's okay. Now just come with us. It's about a ten minute ride and we'll turn over the stuff to you."

Silk started to rise, but the gunman shoved him back on the chair and carefully searched him. "This time," he said flatly, "you ain't gonna pack no rod and don't try grabbing mine because I'll bust you one in the jaw if you do."

He stepped back. Silk put his hands against the chair to arise. Neither man saw the small gun moved from the chair into Silk's pocket. He felt better with it, for more and more Silk sensed the fact that things weren't going just right.

He preceded the two men out of the hotel and into a car driven by a third thug who leered openly at him. No blindfold was placed over his eyes and Silk felt a sinking sensation in his stomach. Was Quinn's plan to fail when it was only beginning? Would Snate get the upper hand at once?

The car headed due east toward the river and stopped in front of a darkened warehouse. Silk climbed out and now the gunman deliberately shoved an exposed automatic into the small of his back. Silk marched into the warehouse, through its damp, spacious interior until he reached a small office where two more men were waiting. Five against one! He wondered just what he could do about it, but he savagely determined to take as many of them in death with him as possible.

"Sit down, Green," Walker motioned to a rickety chair. "Take a load off your feet and off your mind too. Before you get the rocks, we want to know something."

"Yes?" Silk sat down warily. Two men stood directly behind him. Out of the corner of his eye he saw a blow torch resting on the top of the scarred old desk in a corner. A blow torch had no business here—not a shiny new one.

"We checked with the coast," Walker explained suavely. "Everything is okay, but there's just one thing we don't understand. What were you doing in the court room the day that Tony Quinn got his?"

Silk's face never moved a muscle. He sighed and folded his arms across his chest. "Sorry—I don't know anyone named Tony Quinn and I've never been in a court room in this city—yet."

Walker stepped close and slapped him across the face. "You're a damned liar. You even plugged one of the hoods who started the rumpus there. Tell the truth."

"I don't know what you're talking about," Silk insisted and while he spoke, little beads of perspiration formed on the back of his neck.

WALKER GESTURED and one of the men picked up the blow torch. He pumped air into it, primed it and then applied a match. He turned the flame down until it was light blue and almost invisible. He stepped up to Silk and ripped his vest and shirt open. Silk felt the heat of the torch and shuddered.

Walker said, "Going to talk—or do you want to be roasted alive? The torch will make you open up eventually. Why not save yourself a lot of worry and pain by talking now?"

Silk averted his eyes from the stabbing flame. He looked directly over Walker's shoulder and, for a moment, doubted his own senses. Just inside the door he saw a black object pasted against the wall.

It was the figure of a Black Bat with wings outspread!

"What do you want to know?" he asked stonily and then delivered a message to whoever had applied that eerie sticker to the wall. "There are five of you—all armed. I don't see how I can fight that many. Not even if I had help."

"You're getting smart," Walker said. "Tony Quinn hired you, didn't he? He paid you to set a trap for us so you could lay your hooks on the rocks we lifted. Didn't he?"

Silk made no reply. He didn't know what to say. If he admitted it, Quinn would be given away. If he didn't speak, that damned torch would sear his flesh. The thug who held it seemed to relish his job. There would be no mercy from this quintette of killers.

The torch advanced a couple of inches and Silk winced at the terrific heat. Walker slapped him again and motioned to the torch bearer. "Give him a good taste of it."

The torch moved forward again and then the two lights in the room went out. Walker yelled an imprecation. The thug who held the torch decided to go through with his deed anyway. He pressed the flame closer and closer, but now Silk was able to move without being seen. His hand darted into his pocket and came away with the gun. He fired once. The man with the torch lost the sadistic grin around his face and doubled up like a small boy who had eaten too many green apples.

That happened in a split second and then hell really broke loose. Walker yelled orders to shoot. Silk was out of his chair in a flash. A bullet smashed into the wall beside his head. He snapped two quick shots in the direction from which the flash of gunfire had originated and he heard a man sigh deeply, as if exhaling a long breath of despair. There was a crash as a chair smashed to bits.

"Stand where you are!" The voice was low, ominous. It came from the direction of the doorway. "The first one of you who moves will die. Walker—you're leaning back against the desk. Stay there! Your two men are lined up by the east wall. All of you are covered."

Walker gasped. "How—how did you know that? I can't see you. You're guessing. Take him!"

THE LAST two words were directed at his men. They jumped forward, guns racking the vicinity of the doorway. Mingled with the roar of their weapons came two quick blasts of powerful automatics. The two gunmen stopped in their tracks. Their weapons dangled from lifeless fingers and they slowly sagged toward the floor.

Walker was smarter. As his men acted, he leaped in the direction where he figured Silk would be standing. Silk fired at the dark blob that loomed up, but he delayed a fraction of a second too long. Silk wasn't entirely sure of the identity of this figure that came for him.

Walker luckily found Silk's gun hand and turned the wrist cruelly. The gun banged against the floor. Walker seized Silk, whirled him around and held him as a shield.

"Okay—wise guy," he snarled. "If you can see so damned good in this darkness, maybe you'll know the spot your stooge is in."

"He is no stooge of mine," the voice had absolutely no expression. "You are holding him as a shield and your gun is thrust out ready to shoot. Walker, you have one last chance for your life. Drop the gun and let him go."

For answer Walker fired two rapid shots in the direction of the voice. He heard the bullets crash into the wall and a shiver racked his body. What manner of man could move so fast? What sort of a devil could penetrate inky darkness and know the instant when his finger tightened against the trigger?

Suddenly Silk moved. His right foot kicked out and rapped against Walker's shin. Walker howled in pain and his grip loosened a trifle. With a lurch, Silk pulled himself free, but he faced a new menace now for he was very close to Walker and the gun covered him. Silk didn't hesitate. With one hand outstretched, he leaped straight toward Walker. The extended hand reached his throat and closed around it. At the same time Silk threw his body sideways and the bullet only ripped through the tail of his coat. Walker stumbled and fell heavily. Like a flash, Silk was upon him. Walker nudged his gun up until it covered Silk—the muzzle resting against his side.

Something slapped against Walker's skull and he vaguely felt the muzzle of his gun turned forcibly outward as he pressed the trigger. After that Walker lost all interest in things.

When he opened his eyes, the office was flooded with light. Silk sat on the edge of the desk, but Walker didn't see him. His eyes were riveted upon a weird form that loomed up half a dozen feet away. The man was tall, very well built and there was a shining black hood and winglike cape encasing his head and shoulders. Merciless eyes watched Walker's movements. The killer shivered. Those eyes got him. With an effort he tore his gaze away. He saw the four men who had been a part of his trap. They were lying side by side and the floor around them was smeared with blood. Upon the forehead of each man was the insignia of a tiny black bat.

"Who—who are you?" Walker found his voice after a moment. He sat up, bracing himself with his hands. As he did so, he felt the cool butt of a pistol beneath him. Walker closed his fingers around the gun and confidence surged through him once more.

THE EERIE figure, dressed entirely in black, moved like some grim shadow. The voice made Walker shiver again.

"I am new to men like you," the voice intoned. "You might call me the Black Bat. Fools like you have brought me into existence. So long as your breed lives, the Black Bat will work to crush you. No—don't move!"

"What's your racket?" Walker asked. Inwardly he forced himself to remain calm. He wanted to know all this hooded creature had to offer. Snate would pay plenty for the information and Walker had few doubts but that he could deliver it. The gun which he held behind him was his own and there were bullets in the firing chamber. He knew this.

"Racket?" the Black Bat asked and behind the mask lips smiled grimly. "The extermination of rats. My methods are as ruthless as yours, Walker. Not many minutes ago you threatened a man with a hideous death unless he talked. Now, perhaps you face the same fate. A blow torch can be a ghastly means of killing a man and you ought to know it. Snate is planning to start a campaign of bank robberies. Which bank is he starting with?"

Walker gasped. Only two or three men knew of that intended campaign. Yet this hooded man knew it also. Walker decided this had to end swiftly. His eyes narrowed and his crafty brain formulated a plan. If he could get the Black Bat close enough, he could fire quickly and be protected by the Bat's own body. Then, before Silk could swing into action, Walker would have a bead on him.

"I'll talk," he declared sullenly. "Only I ain't going to yell the news. Come closer and I'll whisper it. If Snate ever finds out I sang, he'll tear me apart. You got to promise you won't spill this to anybody else."

The Bat made a surreptitious motion with his left hand. Silk saw it and thrust one hand into his coat pocket where his fingers curled around a gun. He pointed the weapon at Walker and half pulled the trigger.

The Bat moved toward Walker. He held no gun, but Walker saw the butt of an automatic protruding from The Bat's belt.

In his mad desire to wreak vengeance upon this man, Walker lost his head for a moment. He told the truth, figuring it would sound more authentic than some trumped up story and anyway The Bat would never live to repeat it.

"He's going to tackle the Security National," he said hoarsely. "It's all set for tomorrow morning at ten o'clock sharp. This is the way it's to be worked."

Walker's voice dropped to a mumble and The Bat stepped closer, bending down to hear better. At that moment Walker twisted his body, brought the gun into view and compressed the trigger. Something smashed into his shoulder, sending him sprawling. He knew he had missed The Bat, but Walker was on his feet and shooting again.

This time he saw The Bat's gun come up. With a yell of terror Walker lunged for him, gun extended. The Bat's gun barked. The bullet, ranging upward, smashed a button on Walker's coat, ricocheted and ended by crashing full into his face. Walker swayed drunkenly, fell to his knees and tried to speak. Words turned into a bubbling scream as he fell forward.

THE BLACK BAT rubbed a hand over his forehead. Silk was at his side in a second.

"You hurt?" he asked.

The Bat shook his head. "He missed me—by a fraction of an inch the last time. I knew Walker had that gun and I gave him a chance—to talk and surrender, or fight—and die. When I followed him here, saw him and his men carry a blow torch inside, I knew he planned to bring you here and apply his own brand of torture. I know why too. You were recognized. Some of Snate's men watched everyone who entered court the day his hirelings threw the acid around. They remembered you. I hadn't planned on that. So I slipped into this warehouse and arranged things. I cut the electric light wires at the crucial moment."

"Then we're sunk," Silk said sadly. "They'll know I work for you—Quinn the lawyer. They'll connect me with The Bat too."

But The Bat shook his head. "Every man who could have known is dead. I slipped into Walker's so-called office and overheard a brilliant conversation. Snate didn't recognize you and he doesn't know you are working for me—either as Tony Quinn—or The Black Bat. These pleasant mugs were set to take your money and double-cross Snate. They told him nothing."

"But we didn't get the jewels," Silk groaned. "I figured we could lay our hands on them."

The Black Bat laughed and threw a chamois sack on the table. "I said I watched Walker all day. The jewels were kept in that office where I was hiding. Getting them out of the safe was very simple, Silk. I've studied a few things about safes and Walker's was no treasury vault by any means. You take charge of the gems. Send them back to the insurance company that paid the losses on them. There's a reward for almost every one. Drop them an anonymous note saying that the reward is to be paid to a good charitable organization. Sign it with one of my stickers—the image of a Black Bat."

"Yes sir," Silk agreed. "That's a good idea."

"And now," The Bat went on, "this is only the beginning. I'm certain Walker told the truth about the bank holdups because what he said compares favorably with scraps of conversation I overheard in his office.

Tomorrow we'll stick our heads into danger. We'll try to stop the holdup by calling the police in. If that doesn't work, we'll stop it ourselves. Now one more thing. I want Snate to have a shock tonight. It's bad for his nerves."

CHAPTER VII

THE TEST

OLIVER SNATE, attired in pajamas and bath robe, heard the door bell buzz. He yanked open a drawer, thrust a gun into the pocket of his robe and hurried to the door, motioning a stolid faced servant away. This should be Walker, with news. Snate yanked the door open. There was no one on the porch. He frowned and tightened his grip on the gun. Then he shrugged and turned back. Something squeaked. He glanced down the length of the porch and saw a rocking chair, back toward him, rocking slowly. Snate stepped back, turned on the porch light and cautiously made his way along the porch.

"Don't move," he called softly. "You're covered! Stand up!"

But the chair only kept on rocking. Snate made a lunge along the rail until he was in front of the chair. His gun hand sagged and his eyes grew wide in horror and amazement.

Walker sat in the chair. His head hung down over a bloody chest, his arms rested against the arms of the rocker. Snate raised the head and then stepped back with a yelp.

In the middle of the forehead was the image of a Black Bat!

With a supreme effort, Snate recovered his wits. He dashed back into the house and made two hasty phone calls. First, a light delivery truck pulled up in the driveway and Walker's corpse was transferred into it. Then a car, filled with armed men, appeared. Snate got into that himself. He was driven far outside the city limits, directly to the house which he had made his headquarters. Assembled in the big library were Snate's lieutenants—ten in number.

Snate sat down importantly.

"Now listen, every one of you. Walker is dead. I don't know what happened to the four boys who went along to dicker with this fence, Alex Green. I checked on Green by calling the coast and he is okay. I think he's dead, along with everybody else who was in on the deal. I found Walker on my porch with some silly piece of paper pasted on his forehead. It looks like a bat with wings spread way out. The guy who pasted that on Walker, also killed him, killed Alex Green and the men I sent with Walker. He hijacked the stuff Green was going to buy. I don't know who this guy is or what his racket can be, but you men get out and find him. Contact everybody you know. Put out a dragnet for this killer who pastes a bat on his victims. Find out who he is and why he's bucking me. Then kill him! Pump him so full of lead they'll need a wrecker to lift his body. Smash him—do you hear me?"

"What's he look like?" one of the men asked.

Snate made an impatient gesture. "How do I know? But you mugs find him. And another thing—tomorrow morning the job at the Security National goes through an hour earlier at nine instead of ten. You've studied the blue prints, you know the whole layout of the bank. You who have been assigned, be there when the doors open and the time-lock goes off. Have your guns ready and shoot down any fool who tries to resist. Be sure all of you are masked. That's all—except for Grogan. He is to remain."

The others filed out. Grogan lit a cigarette and dropped into a chair. Snate leaned across his desk and spoke very earnestly.

"YOUR JOB is to check on that ex-D. A., Tony Quinn. Find out if he's blind. You're not known, so go right into his house. Fake some papers so you'll seem to represent a home for the blind. Tell him he's a rich man and you want a donation. All the while watch him—test him—and be damned sure he can't see. Report back the minute you know one way or the other."

Grogan arose. "As good as done, boss. What about the armored cars?"

"You'll get your orders," Snate snapped. "Now get busy with Quinn."

Grogan drove directly to Quinn's house, walked boldly to the door and rang the bell. He heard slow, faltering steps move across the hallway and the door was opened. Grogan winced at the sight of the man who stood before him. The deep, acid burned scars, were vividly clear. Quinn's eyes stared blankly ahead, seeing nothing.

"Mr. Quinn?" Grogan asked. "My name is Blackwell—from the Home for the Aged Blind. May I come in?"

"Of course," Quinn answered. "Follow me."

Quinn became tangled in heavy drapes that hung across one doorway. He extricated himself, smiled in an embarrassed way and then stumbled over a footstool.

"Careless of my servant to leave that stool around," he said. "Of course you know how dangerous such things can be to a blind man. Won't you find yourself a chair?"

Grogan pushed a chair toward Quinn and as the blind man began to sit down, he threw his hat on the seat. Grogan knew that if a man was only pretending to be blind, he would hesitate the barest fraction of a second if there was something on his chair. But Quinn sat down heavily and the hat flattened while Grogan groaned. That hat cost him sixteen bucks and he liked it.

Quinn half arose, fumbled beneath him and extricated the hat, "Is this yours?" he asked. "I'm so sorry. I didn't know it was on the chair."

"It's okay," Grogan fumbled. "My fault. Now—we'd like a little donation, Mr. Quinn. You know how dependent blind people can be and you are independently wealthy."

"Of course," Quinn said. "Just leave me your card and I'll be happy to send something. I'll even run up and talk to your directors. Being blind is a terrible calamity, Mr. Blackwell, but if one is blind and destitute also—that must be infinitely worse."

Grogan stuck a cigarette into his mouth, struck a match and then leaned forward very silently. He brought the match closer and closer to Quinn's eyes, but they never flickered. Yet inwardly, Quinn's nerves shrieked aloud. It took every ounce of will power he possessed not to blink. The slowly approaching light was bright enough to hurt and had his visitor made any quick movements with the flaming match, Quinn would certainly have blinked despite himself. But the match moved forward slowly enough not to induce winking. Suddenly Quinn jumped.

"What was that?" he asked. "It felt as though fire was brought toward me. I distinctly felt heat."

GROGAN MADE a clucking sound with his tongue. "Sorry—I just lit a cigarette and I guess I got the match too close to you. I'll be going now. Be as generous as you can, Mr. Quinn. You, of all people, must know how it feels to be blind."

Quinn fumbled around until he found a cane. He accompanied his visitor to the door, opened it for him and as Grogan stepped out, Quinn's cane flicked sideways. Grogan tripped over it and went sprawling on the porch. He emitted a curse that didn't jibe with his alleged profession of seeking funds for the blind. But he recovered his wits quickly enough and got up.

Quinn was apologetic. "I'm terribly sorry. My cane must have tripped you. You're not hurt?"

"I'm okay," Grogan snapped as he brushed himself off. "Maybe I'll see you again, Mr. Quinn. Next year, shall we say?"

"Shall we?" Quinn asked innocently.

Grogan jammed on his battered hat and hurried to his car. He stepped on the starter with an oath.

"He's blind as a bat. Snate must be going nuts if he thinks that guy is trying to muscle in."

But as the front door closed, Silk stepped out of the dining room. He stowed away the gun he held and grinned at Quinn.

"Perfect, sir. I couldn't have done it better myself."

Quinn threw his cane across a chair and frowned. "He came from Snate all right. The fool didn't even leave a card to back up his statements. What worried me is this—who in the world would suspect I'm not blind? Who would want my sight tested? Snate couldn't possibly know, so there must be someone who suspects. Someone who is the real power behind Snate and gives him his orders. Silk—three men visited me this morning. Otto Fox, Stewart and Commissioner Warner. I offered my services and one of those three men believes I may take a more active part in the game than I pretend. One of those men, or somebody very closely connected with them, is the real leader of Snate's mob."

"Yes sir," Silk was worried too. "It would seem that way. This man knows your record as a prosecutor, sir, and he fears you. He knows that if you could see, he'd never get away with it."

Quinn nodded. "Right. We've learned to be careful, Silk—and to suspect Stewart, Fox or Warner. Now to work. Run outside and take a quick look around. There may be another man watching and we can't take chances."

Silk drove Quinn's car out of the garage. To all appearances he was alone at the wheel. But deep within the shadowy tonneau another figure was hunched up against the corner. There was an ebony black hood over his head and his clothes were jet black. A pair of rubber soled shoes covered his feet and deadly automatics hung from shoulder holsters concealed beneath his coat.

The car pulled up to the curb directly across the street from the Security National Bank. It was almost two in the morning and except for a private patrolman, the street was deserted. From the parked car, a shadowy form flitted toward an alley and vanished the moment darkness closed around him.

THE BLACK BAT had a bulky object under his arm and he moved deftly through the inky night until he stood in front of the rear entrance to the big office building. He laid his burden down carefully, drew a small leather kit from his pocket and went to work on the lock. In less than a moment the door swung open and he stepped inside. He closed and locked the door again and then moved noiselessly along the corridor until he was in the lobby.

He found the superintendent's office, let himself in by the use of the same kit of thin tools. He examined the register of the building, consulted floor plans pinned to the wall and found that one front office was vacant. He slipped back to the lobby, climbed the stairs to the third floor and entered the office designated. He peered out of the window and nodded in satisfaction. The entire front of the Security National Bank was before his gaze.

Working with amazing speed, yet making not the slightest sound, he set up an automatic motion picture camera equipped with a long range lens. He sighted it, arranged a time clock so that the shutters would begin clicking at five minutes of nine the next morning and then he departed. Three watchmen in the building had no inkling of his presence.

"That's taken care of," he said from the depths of the car. "The next job is yours, Silk. You know what to do."

CHAPTER VIII

BANK ROBBERY

AT EIGHT-FORTY the next morning, a heavy sedan pulled up to the curb directly in front of the bank. Silk climbed out, left the keys in the switch and only partly closed the door of the car.

He walked hurriedly up the street and turned into a doorway of a store not yet opened for business. After a two minute wait he saw another sedan roll slowly along and stop. Quinn was behind the wheel with a slouch hat pulled very low and his coat collar turned up around his face. Silk approached the car, slid behind the wheel abandoned by Quinn and then parked across the street from the bank.

"Everything set, Silk?" Quinn asked from the folds of his coat collar.

"All set, sir," Silk replied. "You don't think you're biting off too big a chunk this time, do you? You'll appear in broad daylight."

"The mask will take care of everything," Quinn answered. "I'm climbing into the back of the car. You duck beneath the dash and stay there. This car must appear empty. I'll pull down the curtains in back."

"Will the police be here?" Silk asked anxiously.

Quinn shrugged. "I don't know. They have an hour yet and they probably will appear by ten, but I talked to some stupid, pig-headed fool called Lieutenant McGrath. Commissioner Warner wasn't to be found. McGrath, first of all, said he wasn't in the habit of accepting anonymous tips. I told him the bank would be held up at ten o'clock, but to get his men here before nine—just in case the bandits changed their minds and decided to strike earlier. I have no hunches about the matter, but it seems to me that the minute the bank opens its doors is the best time to stage a robbery."

"Yes sir," Silk replied quickly. "I've talked to a dozen bank robbers and they all say the same thing. No customers to fool with then and the dough is all in one place—not scattered around to a dozen tellers."

They were silent for a moment, but The Bat was alert.

Eyes, framed behind a black hood, watched another car draw up as a clock struck nine. The bank guard swung the doors wide, tested the revolving doors and then walked back into the building. From the car that stopped and double parked in front of the bank, stepped six men, all masked and openly armed with submachine guns. They worked with the precision born of long practice. So quickly were they inside that not one of the bank employees, nor the few clients, knew where they had come from.

One man raised his gun and yanked the trigger. A clerk went down with his face a blob of blood.

"That's a sample," the killer yelled. "Open the vaults and haul out the cash. Snap into it before my finger gets itchy again."

The bank guard had more courage than sense. All his mind clicked on was the fact that he was paid to protect the bank. He reached for his gun. The blast from two Tommy guns almost cut him in half. Tellers had the big door open and under the menacing muzzles of the machine guns they hauled out thousands of dollars in currency. These were stowed into a big sack, slung over one man's shoulder and the bandits backed out of the bank.

Outside, two others stood guard with Tommy guns at a ready position, a third with a menacing revolver. The latter suddenly dropped and triggered. An advancing plainclothesman fired a single shot before his life was blasted away. The four men inside emerged and raced for the parked car.

AT THAT moment things happened. From another sedan, across the street, stepped an eerie figure. The bandits had struck an hour earlier than expected and The Bat was being forced to show his hand. There were no signs of the police yet, but The Bat, taking no chances, was fully prepared.

Under one arm The Bat held a long barreled rapid-fire rifle. It sang a deadly song and the slugs smashed into the hood of the bandit's getaway car. The driver shoved a gun through the open window. The rapid-fire rifle raised its curtain of fire and the driver slumped over the wheel.

But The Bat was handicapped. Crowds packed the streets at this hour. They stood in a dense throng, held by fear and the threat of flying bullets. The escaping bandits were directly in front of a score of pedestrians. The Bat couldn't shoot or he'd mow down innocent people.

"Grab another car," one of the masked bandits shouted when he saw the driver of their own sedan, dead at the wheel and the motor stalled. A group of stunned pedestrians were in the way. One of the thugs snarled a curse and raised his automatic rifle to clear a path. Berserk with rage, he was ready to slaughter any number of them so long as his own warped life would be saved. In another second a score of people would go down under the curtain of lead.

But before that second had elapsed, one man made a wild dive out of the crowd. He was poorly dressed and his hat was knocked off as he moved. His skull was smooth shaven and he had a stumpy, muscular neck. His features were crude and wide; his jaw undershot and aggressive.

He reached the killer before the spattering rifle could get working right. One hand ripped off the mask from the gunman's face and revealed him as a pimply, pasty-faced thug.

At that moment the crowd sensed the danger and scampered for safety. It left a clear path for The Bat's gun. He raised it, but the unmasked thug saw him and acted quickly. He slugged the husky looking man who had prevented the wholesale slaughter, wound his arms around him and with the strength born of desperation, pulled and pushed his human shield toward the getaway car. Eager hands pulled them both inside. The Bat lowered his gun, backed up and suddenly darted away. No one in the crowd saw where he went.

The bandits sent a warning hail of lead over the heads of the crowd and the car started away from the curb. A radio car shrieked toward them and the Tommy guns went to work again. The radio car piled up against a wall, its driver dead and the second patrolman badly wounded.

The third gunman dropped and triggered.

Someone in the crowd shrieked and pointed to the spot where The Black Bat had been standing. "There's another one of them over there."

But there was no sign of The Bat. Police arrived in droves and began a methodical search of the neighborhood. Commissioner Warner appeared, shouting orders and paling as he saw the havoc wrought inside the bank. Four men were dead, several others badly wounded. Outside, a traffic cop lay in a welter of his own blood and a radio patrolman was crushed behind the wheel of his wrecked car.

"THERE WERE seven of them—and another at the wheel of the getaway car," one of the bank officials told Warner excitedly. "The seventh man stood across the street. He was a weird looking figure—all dressed in black and he had a hood over his face—not just a simple mask. And he did a very strange thing. As the bandits raced for their car, he opened fire, riddled the getaway car and killed the driver. If there hadn't been another car parked at the curb, God knows what would have happened. The bandits appropriated it and ran."

"What's this about one of them being unmasked?" Warner queried.

A detective hove into sight with a frightened young man at his side. The young man talked—a rush of words that fell over one another.

"Big guy—grabbed one of them crooks—just in time or we'd all have been shot—pulled mask offa one man's face. They cracked him—with gun—flung him in car before they ran—"

"What did the unmasked man look like?" Warner asked.

The young man gulped. "I—I dunno. Honest I was so excited he coulda been colored pink for all I know. Say—that guy was ready to mow all of us down."

"Who is the man behind the wheel of the stalled car?" Warner asked.

A uniformed lieutenant answered that one. "We don't know, sir. His prints are on their way to headquarters now. Looks to me like that hooded man we've heard so much about wasn't a member of this outfit. He tried to prevent the bandits from getting away as I see it."

"You're right," Warner agreed. "But we'll go into that later on. Call headquarters and broadcast an order for all suspicious cars to be stopped. Cover every road, even the country lanes. How much did those rats get?"

"Almost half a million," a bank official proclaimed sadly. "But the money is nothing. They killed half a dozen people. Shot them down ruthlessly. Commissioner, why isn't this sort of thing stopped? The entire city is seething with crime. No man or woman is safe on the streets. Not even a great bank such as this can open its doors in the morning without a prayer that none of these killers will appear."

"We're doing all we can," Warner replied. "I"—he was looking through the big plate glass windows—"Stop him, somebody! Quinn—look out!"

For Tony Quinn, tapping his cane, progressed slowly across the road. A car was bearing down on him. The driver swerved the wheel crazily, cursed and rammed into a parked truck. Warner raced out of the bank, elbowed his way to Quinn's aide and took his arm.

"What's happened?" Quinn asked blankly. "There are many people around. I can hear them. And sirens!"

"You gave me an awful scare," Warner exhaled violently. "This is Warner, Tony. There's been a bank robbery with several people murdered. You blundered across the street and the fool drivers traveling along had their heads stuck out looking at the bank. One of them almost knocked you over."

QUINN SHRUGGED his dropped shoulders. "Would there have been much lost, Commissioner? No—I'm sorry I said that. You've tried to help me, saved my life just now, in fact. I'm very grateful."

"Get into my car," Warner suggested. "I've got to go to headquarters for a few minutes and then I'll have you driven home."

Quinn was assisted into the big police car and he relaxed against the cushions. His stony eyes stared straight ahead, but something of a smile crossed his lips. Silk was elbowing his way through the crowd. Under his arm he held a bulky package.

Commissioner Warner gave further orders and the crowd was pushed back. Warner walked toward the getaway car, looked at the dead man behind the wheel and then casually raised his eyes. They jerked wide open. Plastered against the windshield was the image of a Black Bat with wings outspread.

"That wasn't there five minutes ago," Warner yelled. "Who put it on the windshield?"

No one seemed to know, but inside Warner's car, Quinn idly rubbed his gloved hands until a smear of glue vanished from the tip of the right index finger.

Warner piled into the car beside Quinn and the driver headed back toward the office. Warner pushed his hat to the back of his head and swore.

"Those damned black bats," he said aloud. "I don't understand them. We found four dead men in an abandoned warehouse this morning and each one had a black bat pasted to his forehead. Now another of those insignias has appeared—on the windshield of the getaway car that the bandits left. I can't understand it."

"Probably one of Snate's pleasant gestures," Quinn offered without enthusiasm. "He might be putting those things on the men he kills."

"Would he paste one on a car his men intended to use in getting clear?" Warner asked irritably. "No, Tony—there's someone else operating recently. I can't make up my mind whether he's on the side of the law or against it. Those four mugs were of Snate's tribe. We can't find a possible motivation for their deaths. Only the Black Bat insignias. I wouldn't be surprised if such a creature existed. The Black Bat! I only hope, if it's true, that he's working against Snate. We can't do a thing to him legally."

"Why?" Quinn asked, but there was no particular interest in his tone.

"Why? Because he's become clever lately. Devilishly clever—almost as if he possessed a new set of brains. He sits back like an octopus and flings out his tentacles, but not once does he show himself. He has every crook from shop lifter to murderer lined up behind him as solidly as an attacking army. Snate does nothing but plan and give the orders. We can't pin a thing on him. Damn it, Tony—if you were the D.A., we'd get some action. You never did bother much with technicalities."

"But I'm not," Quinn said sadly. "I'm just a helpless, blind man. I wish I could be of assistance, Commissioner. I'll tell you what. Perhaps I can't see, but—I can think. The acid didn't sear into my brain. Sometimes a blind man can think even deeper than one with healthy sight. If I mull these things over long enough, I might reach some kind of a logical conclusion. At least it will give me something to do—make me think I'm of some little use in the world."

"EXCELLENT," WARNER cried. "I've been trying to get you to do just that for weeks. You always had a knack for thinking out puzzles. See what you can do with this one. Explain the Black Bat business. Tell me how I can corner Snate. Tell me just how eleven armored cars, filled with cash, can vanish in broad daylight."

"You're asking for a lot," Quinn seemed to have acquired a new interest in life. "But I'll do my best. When you have a spare moment, drop into my home and tell me all you know. I've an idea I might be of help."

The radio under the dashboard squealed.

"Calling Commissioner Warner. Commissioner Warner. Getaway car used in Security National stickup, found abandoned fifteen miles north on Route 4. Waiting your orders. Please contact dispatcher."

Quinn said, "You can let me out here, Commissioner. I'll only be in the way. Just call me a taxi."

The police car's siren shrilled and a taxi pulled up at the command of the police driver. Quinn was helped into it by Warner. They clasped hands a moment and Warner was off. Quinn settled back.

"Drive me to the park," he told the chauffeur. "I need more exercise."

When the taxi stopped at the entrance to the park, another car pulled up behind it. Silk raised a newspaper to cover his features, but he watched Quinn alight clumsily, pay off the driver and then head for the park.

Once the taxi was gone, Quinn turned, tapped his stick and approached the curb. Silk jumped out and helped him into the tonneau. Then he got behind the wheel and headed north.

"I caught the broadcast too," he said excitedly. "We're going after the bus, eh?"

"Right," Quinn said from the back seat. "And you'll have to lay on the whip, Silk, old man. Fifty police cars will head there within three minutes."

Quinn was busy as he talked. He removed his topcoat and grey suit. In their place he donned a black outfit. He covered his white shirt front with a piece of black silk, pulled his hood over his head and from a specially constructed compartment in the tonneau removed two automatics. He gloved his hands again and leaned back.

"We're making headway, Silk," he said. "You got the camera safely, I see. Now to reach the car before the police. Then we'll know our bandits and be in a position to deal out some rather high handed justice. They'll hole up for days before they dare show their faces again."

"Did you see that little episode where a man jumped out of the crowd and tackled that killer?" Silk asked.

"I saw," Quinn answered. "That man would be a decided asset to our little group, Silk. But I suppose he's been thrown into some ditch by now. Can't you make this car roll faster?"

SILK HUNCHED over the wheel and brought his foot down hard. The sedan raced at ninety along the highway, guided by Silk's expert hands.

Then Silk suddenly slowed up. Ahead of them they could see two cars pulled off the highway and a uniformed man standing on the shoulders of the road. One car was a state police patrol, the other a city detective cruiser.

"Someone came out without waiting for Warner's orders," Quinn said. "I hope there's not too many there. Slow up, Silk. You turn around and run for it. I'll handle the police. Meet me back on the fourth lane to your right."

CHAPTER IX

THE TRAP

DETECTIVE LIEUTENANT McGRATH had one foot on the running board of the car which Snate's men had stolen for their getaway. He wore a puzzled frown on his face.

"It's so damned odd it can't be coincidence," he maintained to his driver and the two state troopers who listened silently. "This bus was stolen last night. It was left in front of the Security National with the door half open and the keys in the ignition. Nobody can tell me it wasn't planted just in case something happened. Those killers were smarter than usual by having two cars ready."

One of the state troopers walked over to the sedan and peered through the window into the tonneau. He nudged Lieutenant McGrath.

"Take a look at the upholstery—along the back seat I mean. Looks like part of it had been cut out and then sewed back. Now, why would anybody want to carve a chunk out of the seat?"

McGrath looked too and grunted. "I know what it means," he said. "That seat was carved up and there's a sort of hidden compartment behind it. See how that spot is directly over the trunk at the rear? Maybe those hoods passed their guns into the trunk—or got them by shoving their arms through the hole in the seat. In case of a quick frisk the roscoes wouldn't be found."

McGrath was chunky, beefy-faced and he had been a policeman for more years than he liked to brag about. He had risen to his present position by hard, long hours of work. There wasn't a spark of mercy in his makeup. If a crime was committed, someone had to pay and McGrath didn't give a hoot if that person happened to be his brother, the mayor or even the governor of the state. Thoroughly honest, no criticism had ever come his way and his record stood positively clean.

McGrath turned away from the car and jerked erect. Ten feet behind the car stood a lone figure of a man dressed entirely in black with a hood covering his head and neck. There were two automatics in his hands and by the way this masked man held them, McGrath got the idea he knew how to shoot.

"Gentlemen," the hooded figure spoke politely enough, "you've examined that car sufficiently for the present. Will you stand away from it now—with your hands up?"

Slowly the four men obeyed. "Just keep right on backing up," The Black Bat said cheerfully. "And don't become so foolish as to think you might reach those holstered guns before I can open fire. I'm rather good with a thirty-eight automatic, but I'd hate to prove it—right now."

McGrath leaned forward slightly. "You're the masked man who polished off the bandits' driver this morning. You're the mug who pastes black bats all over the victims you leave behind."

"Not all over them, Lieutenant," The Bat said. "Just upon their foreheads. I have two reasons for doing that. I don't want the crime pinned on anyone else—nor do I wish to have the friends of those men who shoot it out with me kept in the dark as to who was the victor. Killing those four men in the warehouse simply saved the state the expense of four executions later on."

"You can brag now," McGrath snapped, "but some day I'll do the bragging. You're a murderer and you'll pay the penalty, even if the men you killed deserved to die."

"MY," THE BAT said laughingly, "you do have a sense of duty. But you really ought to exercise more, Lieutenant. When the day comes that you will find the chance of chasing me, I'm afraid you wouldn't run far. Anyway it's bad for the heart. Now there are all sorts of contrivances to help you thin down that waist line.

"I could name them—"

"Shut up," McGrath yelled, for The Black Bat had touched a sore spot. "And how long do we stand here with our hands in the air, listening to your crazy jabbering?"

"Turn around—all of you," The Bat warned. "I want this car. I have a liking for it. You see—I stole it last night."

The Bat climbed behind the wheel, stepped on the starter and slowly backed up. Every moment, one gun covered the quartette. He had no doubts as to what would happen the moment he drove on to the highway. Bullets would fly fast and thick. Furthermore, the State Troopers had a reputation for accurate shooting. Yet The Bat had no time to disarm

The Bat saw four men, with pointing guns, as the lights flashed on.

them. By now a dozen police cars would be racing from the city toward this spot.

The rear wheels rolled to the pavement. The Bat straightened the car out, raised his gun a few inches and yanked the trigger four times. The bullets whined over the heads of the four men and they dropped quickly. The Bat tramped on the gas pedal and shot away.

McGrath didn't stop to shoot. Instead he ran over to the detective cruiser and jumped into it. The troopers stepped into the road and emptied their guns at the speeding sedan. Then they raced for their own car. Two minutes later four disgruntled men stared at the motors of the two cars. The wires had been ripped away so that there was no spark.

"That guy," McGrath said, "thinks of everything, but some day he'll slip and that same day I'll slip—cuffs on his wrists."

The Bat turned off the road four miles from the spot where McGrath worked on the cruiser. Halfway up a lane he saw Silk waiting. He stopped and instantly Silk flung himself into the tonneau. He ripped away the sewed portion of the seat and extracted a heavy recording machine. He stowed this into the other car and jumped in to find The Bat already at the wheel.

They left the stolen car parked across the lane so that no pursuit was possible until after it was moved.

There would be some difficulty there too, for The Bat had ripped wires away again and tall trees on either side of the lane prevented any attempts at pushing the car off the road.

They struck another highway two miles east. The Bat stopped, turned the wheel over to Silk and got into the tonneau. He worked quickly now. He changed his black clothing for the conservative grey suit that he wore as Tony Quinn, the blind man. The black outfit, hood, guns and all went into a hidden compartment which locked securely and gave no evidence of its existence.

When they reached the State Police barrier, Silk Kirby, gentleman's gentleman, was taking his blind master for a ride. The State Police all knew Quinn. They called greetings to him and passed the car along.

"Neat, Silk," Quinn grinned. "Now back to the house as fast as possible. I want to develop the films and run off the recordings I hope we picked up."

THERE WERE recordings all right. Plenty of them inscribed on the thin disk. Quinn could identify the men only by their voices. Two men took up the brunt of the conversations and they were apparently the leaders. One had a hoarse bellow of a voice, the other a reedy tone.

The hoarse voice came through clearly. "I just slugged this bozo who pulled the mask offa Whitey. What're we gonna do with the guy?"

"Bump him—whaddya think?" Reedy Voice snapped. "Only we gotta wait until we get the orders from the big boy. Anyway, I think this guy was planted an' maybe he knows somethin'."

"Okay," the first man agreed. "I hope he knows about that Black Bat guy. Did you see him mow down Joey? I still wonder why he didn't turn that gat on us. Hey Slim, you know the way okay?"

A third voice, muffled, came through. It was the driver. "Yeah—ditch the bus and pick up the other buggy. Then about four miles north, right turn, second left and first left after that, until we hit a red farmhouse. Think I'm so dumb I can't remember them directions?"

Gruff Voice snarled a curse. "You wasn't supposed to drive, so I figured maybe you forgot where the hideout is. Don't get wise, Slim. It don't pay with guys like me."

There was more conversation but nothing of interest. Quinn turned off the play back machine.

"Silk—our fondest hopes have come true. They did talk about where they were going. I figured that with a new driver, orders might have to be re-issued. They were and we know where these bandits are holed up. Now for the film. Get the quick drying apparatus ready. I want to run these right off."

It took more than an hour before the film was dry enough to use. Then Quinn and Silk watched the bank robbery unfold itself again. They saw the shooting, for the telescopic lens had picked up every detail. They saw the burly man dart out from the crowd to grapple with the crazy killer, saw him slugged and thrown into the getaway car. Quinn shut the projector off.

"You'll need two guns and a mask, Silk," he said quietly. "Be ready in ten minutes. We haven't much time to lose."

"They're going to be there for days, sir," Silk reminded him.

"But not that ugly looking gorilla who was willing to die if he could save other people's lives. I want to make an attempt at rescuing him—if it's not too late."

Quinn pulled down the shades in the library and stepped up to the fireplace. He touched one of the massive stones and a portion of the wall receded. He entered a compact, white tiled laboratory equipped with every chemical and piece of apparatus necessary to fight crime. He filled two thin vials with a yellowish fluid, rolled them in cotton and carefully tucked them away in his pocket. He donned a black suit and shirt, slipped his hood in place and hurried out the rear door. Silk had a sleek roadster purring sweetly.

THEY TOOK it easy until they reached the highway. Then Silk opened her up. They were taking chances with motor cops, but such risks were necessary now, for Quinn had firmly made up his mind to save the gorilla-like man who had risked his life to prevent wholesale slaughter.

They passed the spot where The Black Bat had taken the getaway car from Lieutenant McGrath, and Quinn grinned a little at the memory.

"Look out for a detective lieutenant named McGrath," he warned Silk. "He's not exactly on our side and I rather aggravated him when I took the car away. Furthermore, McGrath is a human bloodhound. When his nose finds the scent, he'll never give up."

Silk grunted something, but kept his eyes and attention glued to the road. They found the turns described by the driver of the bandit's car. Silk rolled to a stop, left the roadster well hidden by brush and with The Black Bat at his side, he carefully maneuvered his way through the darkness.

"Hold my arm," The Bat whispered. "I can see the farmhouse plainly—even see that it's painted red. There's a door at the rear, but no lights are showing anywhere, so unless some of the windows on the opposite side are boarded up, the bandits will be hiding in the cellar. Remember—there are six of them and they are well heeled."

Silk mumbled a reply, took The Bat's arm and let himself be led through darkness that defied his keenest stare. Yet the Bat moved quietly and avoided every pitfall.

"Maybe we'll find a trace of those vanished armored cars," Silk whispered. "Maybe McGrath wouldn't be sore if we exposed that racket. He's head of the squad working on the case."

"I doubt they'll be here," The Bat answered. "Armored cars would be spotted this far out of the city—and remembered. The moment we've cleaned up this mess and annoyed Snate a little more—then we'll find out what has happened to those cars. Careful now—no more talking. They've got heavy painted canvas drawn over the cellar windows, but I can see traces of light through some of the chinks in the framework around each section of glass."

They dropped flat and wriggled on their bellies across the newly mown grass. Both men were garbed in black. Had a guard been standing five feet away, watching intently, he would still have seen no trace of these two figures.

They reached one of the windows and The Bat pressed an ear against the glass. His sense of hearing, perfectly attuned during his months of blindness, functioned just as efficiently now.

The bandit with the gruff voice was talking.

"Take that big stiff and put him up against the wall. We're ten miles from no place so we don't have to worry about the noise our roscoes will make. Tie him up and we take pot shots at him. The guy who kills him loses. The stake is a grand apiece payable to the sharpshooter who can put the most dents in the mug's hide and still let him squeal."

There came the sound of hoarse laughter and a struggle. Then The Bat heard a thud.

"Too bad," Gruff Voice said. "We'll have to wait until he wakes up now. Throw some water in his face, slap him around a little. What the hell—you can't hurt a guy who is ready to croak anyway."

QUINN TOUCHED Silk's hand. Carefully both men drew their guns and wriggled toward the back porch.

"I'll go in," The Bat whispered, "because I can find my way through the darkness. You park outside that window. Break it down if you hear any shooting. And Silk—take these two glass vials. Throw them into the cellar if things get too hot. Then hurry down and drag me out if I can't make it under my own steam."

Silk tapped The Bat's hand twice in a signal that he understood, He took the glass vials and crept back to the window. The Bat approached the rear door, tried it and found it locked. His small kit of instruments opened the way for him and he walked across a kitchen. Two chairs in the middle of the floor were as plain to his eyes as beacons. Mentally he blessed the surgeon who had so miraculously cured him. And then The Bat thought of the girl. She had sworn to force him to accept her as a member of his organization. Odd that he hadn't heard from her yet.

A board creaked and The Bat stiffened. He cocked his head to one side, but he heard nothing more. He took another step forward. A man's form flitted across his range of vision. The gun in The Bat's right hand exploded. The form stopped and slumped to the floor. The Bat moved forward a step. He heard a rush of many feet. He pumped four more bullets as fast as he could and then a mighty blow crashed against his temple. He reeled until he struck the wall. Lights flashed on. The Bat saw four men, all armed, with their guns pointed at him. His own weapons were on the floor, fallen from nerveless fingers.

And standing off to one side was a girl. Her hair was black instead of golden. She used too much makeup and she had a hard sort of look, but The Bat wasn't deceived. This was the girl who had done so much to restore his sight!

CHAPTER X

NEW RECRUITS

GRUFF VOICE was stocky, had cold, fishy eyes and a leering grin around his thick lips. His appearance matched his harsh tones.

"Well, if it ain't the big shot who tried to trip us up this morning? Are we glad to see you! Lucky, ain't it, that Slim came upstairs to get some water? He heard you pick the lock and we got here before you knew what happened."

"Extremely fortunate," The Bat said almost pleasantly, but his spirits were low. He was trapped, facing guns in the hands of four men. A fifth he had killed—the sixth was undoubtedly still in the cellar guarding the prisoner. Those facts, in themselves, were serious enough, but to the Bat's astounded senses the presence of this girl, working closely with the band of killers, was even more of a blow.

Gruff Voice twirled his gun carelessly. "We just lined up a nice finish for a sucker who tried to stop us this morning. You'll get the same medicine—after we pull that mask off your face and see who you really are."

He moved toward the Bat, but the girl's hand touched his shoulder and he stopped. She simply reached for the gun he held, examined it to be sure a cartridge was pumped into the firing chamber and then motioned the four men back.

"This man," she said very quietly, "killed Joey this morning. Joey and I were in love although you dopes probably didn't know it. I want the first crack at his murderer."

"But we gotta contact the boss," Gruff Voice protested. "We can't just knock him off. The boss will be sore."

"I'm not going to kill him," the girl said calmly. "All I'll do is plant a bullet in his hide where it will hurt the most. I want him to suffer—as he made Joey suffer—as he has made me suffer. Stand back—I need plenty of room."

The four thugs moved away, giving the girl every opportunity. She sighted the gun and smiled tightly.

"You're a very brave man," she told The Bat. "You're clever too—the way you handled things and found this hideaway. Why don't you show how clever you are by catching the bullet I'm going to shoot? Why don't you just reach out, seize the slug and throw it back to me?"

The four thugs laughed uproariously. Then the girl stepped just a trifle closer and lifted the gun once more. Suddenly the weapon came hurtling toward The Bat. He caught it deftly and before the thugs could recover from their astonishment, the gun was spitting. Gruff Voice went down with a hole in the middle of his forehead. The other three sprang toward The Bat. He sent one reeling backward. The other two fired rapidly, but The Bat was dancing lightly from right to left while his own weapon swung with comforting speed.

The reedy-voiced man, screaming in rage all the while, suddenly changed his tactics. He headed straight for the girl who had drawn off into a corner. She shoved a chair toward him and he tripped over it, went sprawling on the floor.

INSTANTLY SHE pounced upon him and wrenched his gun away. It spoke and one of the thugs who threatened The Bat, suddenly let go of his gun and looked with amazement upon a bleeding, numbed hand.

"Good work," The Bat called out to the girl. "We've got them now."

He moved toward the reedy-faced man, but suddenly stopped in his tracks. From the doorway behind him came a harsh voice.

"You got who, wise guy? Elevate your mitts or I'll blow your backbone in half."

It was the one thug left to guard their prisoner in the cellar. During the excitement, The Bat had forgotten him. He raised his hands slowly.

"The same goes for you, Helen—I always figured you were a rat."

The girl was pale and a bit unsteady on her feet. She dropped the gun and backed up toward the wall.

"That's better," the thug approved. "Now Mister Hooded Guy—let go of that roscoe, walk over beside the dame and claw at the wall paper. Remember—I've got ten shots in this gat and I'll pump all of 'em but one into your hide. The last one is for the dame—the dirty, doublecrossing little rat."

The Bat dropped his gun and walked carefully toward the further wall where he stood, facing the girl.

"You were splendid," he said quietly. "But what did I tell you about horning in on dangerous business like this?"

"You'd have been unmasked and killed long ago if it hadn't been for me," she answered with a catch in her voice. "Now I—I don't know what will happen."

"Turn around, you," the thug ordered. "Turn around and rip that mask off your face. I want to see what you look like before I change that expression with lead."

The Bat turned very slowly, keeping his hands shoulder high. The thug was, perhaps, the smartest looking one of the lot. His gun was held as steady as a rock. Reedy Voice was trying to get up off the floor. The thug whom Helen had wounded sat in a chair, white as paper while he tried to stem the flow of blood from his wrist.

"Take off the hood," the gunman snapped. "Take it off or I'll blow it off."

The Bat's eyes narrowed behind the mask. There seemed but one thing to do—charge straight into the face of the spitting gun. He was doomed anyway and his only chance lay in forcing the killer to shoot too fast for accuracy. It looked like deliberate suicide, but The Bat's mind was made up. He'd rather die trying, than merely standing there to face the inevitable stream of slugs. He tensed his muscles for the leaping charge.

Then a hand appeared behind the gunman. Something flew into the middle of the room, dropped with a slight crash and instantly the air was filled with a yellowish smoke. The gunman yanked the trigger wildly, but as he did so, The Bat moved fast. Bullets slammed into the wall behind the spot where he had been standing. That is, two of them did. The last one struck the ceiling and sent a shower of plaster down. For at that moment Silk had jumped with an inverted gun.

"RUN FOR it," The Bat shouted. "In the cellar—get the prisoner out, Silk. Helen—where are you?"

He tried to penetrate the yellow haze, but it was almost impossible. Here The Bat's abnormal eyes were no better than those of an average man. Already he could feel the effects of that stupefying gas. Two more minutes and he'd drop too. Then he heard a moan. He whirled in the direction of it and took half a dozen long steps before he found the girl slumped against the wall.

He lifted her with great effort, for his muscles were beginning to react to the narcotic influence of the gas. Staggering, he reached the door, kicked it open and ran into the kitchen where the fumes were less thick. He picked up a pan and hurled it at a window, smashing the glass and allowing cool air to enter. He sucked in lungs full, hurriedly unlocked the door and went out into the night.

Silk was kneeling beside a prone figure, chafing his wrists and trying to bring him back to consciousness.

"Are you all right, sir?" Silk asked anxiously. "And the girl?"

"We're both okay," The Bat answered. "What of the prisoner? Is that he?"

"Yes—one of them struck him quite hard, I think. I can't seem to bring him to."

"Run for the car," The Bat ordered. "Drive it here and lose no time. Take the adhesive out of the compartment in back and bring it to me. Hurry!"

The Bat eased the girl to the ground, ripped off his coat and made a pillow of it. Before Silk returned, she had opened her eyes and smiled wanly up at him.

"I hoped to show you I was worthy of joining your forces," she whispered. "I—I guess I bungled things."

"Bungled them?" The Bat held both her hands tightly. "You saved my life, Helen. Your name is Helen?"

"No—it's Carol—Carol Baldwin. Oh, Tony Quinn, I—"

"No names," The Bat whispered quickly. "Tony Quinn doesn't exist so far as you know. There may be ears."

"I'm sorry. If you'll let me go, now, I'll just drop out of sight."

"Let you go?" The Bat chuckled. "Oh no! Once you warned me I'd beg you to join my forces. I'm doing just that. I need a girl like you and I owe you so much besides."

She sat up and blinked dizzily. But her lips were parted in a warm smile. Then Silk roared up in the roadster and The Bat went to work. He smashed other windows in the farm house, let the gas seep out and then entered, before any of the thugs awakened. He applied the adhesive scientifically until each man looked like a mummy. He rolled them as far apart as possible, stood up and surveyed his work with relish.

Silk came rushing out of a back room with two big valises in his hands. "Here is the money," he enthused. "What a haul they made!"

"So Snate didn't get it," The Bat laughed. "Put it in the roadster. Pile the unconscious man in the front seat, help the girl in and you ride the rumble. I'll be out in a moment."

For the Bat had one more duty to perform. Methodically he applied his trademark to the foreheads of each thug—the tiny black bat that portrayed his handiwork.

FIVE MINUTES later he sent the roadster heading for the highway. The girl spoke in a low voice.

"I joined Snate's forces weeks ago—just to lay my own plans to destroy him. Some day I'll tell you why."

Carol turned to the unconscious man at her side and gently wiped some of the blood from his face.

"You may not know it," The Bat said, "but that man saved the lives of a number of innocent people. One of Snate's gunmen decided to send a burst of machine gun bullets into the onlookers at the bank stickup. This man jumped the gun."

"I know," she replied. "They were talking about him and if you had been only a few minutes later, he'd be dead now. Snate gave the orders to murder him."

CHAPTER XI

THE COMMISSIONER'S VISITOR

NOT LONG after midnight, a figure, dressed completely in black, climbed silently up a porch pillar at the rear of Police Commissioner Warner's residence. He crawled to the top of the porch roof and then carefully pulled up several heavy objects at the end of thin, yet strong ropes. He carried these to the window of the room where the Commissioner was asleep.

A patrolman, on special detail, sauntered through the back yard and The Bat lay prone, watching the man in the darkness. After he had gone, The Bat crept to the partly opened window, raised it and slipped inside. He drew a gun, walked over to the bed and turned on the light.

The Commissioner sat erect, rubbing his eyes and trying to get his bearings. He saw the menacing gun first, raised his head and stared at the black hooded figure of the intruder.

"The Black Bat!" he said hoarsely

"Right you are," The Bat replied. "Don't speak loudly and if anyone approaches, tell him you simply can't sleep and that's why the light is on. I'm not here to harm you, Commissioner. My work will enable you to put a much wanted man behind bars—where he belongs."

"Go ahead," Warner nodded. "You have my word that I won't try to get help or reach for the gun under my pillow."

The Bat chuckled. "The gun is no longer there. I removed it in case you acted before I had a chance to explain. Furthermore—your word of honor goes a long way with me."

The Bat stuffed his gun back into its holster. He walked to the window and picked up the bulky objects he had carried into the room. He set up a motion picture camera first.

"This was operating from a vacant office across the street from the Security National Bank," he explained. "It will show you just what happened and enable you to make a still of the man whose mask was ripped off."

"Great," Warner approved. "I'd give a lot to lay my hands on him."

"That," The Bat said, "will be very simple. Phone headquarters and have them send a detail of men to a red painted farmhouse along Spring Lane—just off Route 4. Every member of the holdup gang is there, either dead, wounded or securely tied up."

The Commissioner seized the phone and gave cryptic orders. Then leaned back against the pillows and watched the camera unreel the pictorial history of the holdup. After that The Bat played the recording.

"May I have those?" the Commissioner asked. "If you wish, I'll say they were delivered to me anonymously. There is evidence enough here to send every member of that gang to the chair."

"It's yours," The Bat nodded. "The recordings were taken from conversations of the gang as they fled. I purposely crippled their getaway car so they'd steal the handiest means of escape—another sedan I had planted in front of the bank. The recording device was hidden behind the rear seat. Your Lieutenant McGrath will appreciate knowing that, Commissioner. I'm afraid he's just a little put out with me."

THE COMMISSIONER growled, "He even went so far as to demand that I give him a permanent assignment to run you down. I had to comply. You have broken laws, you know—and killed men. Necessary, of course, but still you are not an accredited officer. Just who are you?"

"A man—with a mission. I trust you, Commissioner, but if you don't know who I am, it will never be necessary for you to explain away something that might prove dangerous to your career. Now—in return for all this—I want full news of Oliver Snate. Have you any suspicion as to who is behind him?"

Warner showed his surprise. "You think that too, eh? Well, so do I, although I've been laughed at for it. No, I haven't the slightest idea who is behind him, but I do know that Snate is probably the most powerful crook ever to rise out of the garbage heap he must have come from. He's a crawling maggot. He preys upon everyone, crook and honest man alike. He murders at will, laughs at the police and our puny efforts. Snate must be crushed and—I hate to admit it, but I think you are the one man to do that job."

The Bat retreated toward the window. "Thank you, Commissioner. Oh yes, the money stolen from the bank. Don't bother to search for it. I—"

The Commissioner sat bolt upright. "Then you're a crook, too?"

"Why not? You stated that I'm far outside the law. I might as well go the whole way. But you interrupted me. The money is just inside the door of your garage. And remember—I still have your word of honor not to try and stop me."

He stood for a moment, outlined starkly against the window. Then he was gone. The Commissioner lay back against his pillows, rubbed his chin thoughtfully and made a sudden decision. He jumped out of bed, hastily donned his clothes and phoned for his car.

Twenty minutes later he pushed the door bell of Tony Quinn's house. Quinn, tapping his cane methodically, opened the door.

"Tony, it's Warner," the Commissioner said and tried not to put any of his chagrin into his voice. "I—I was just going by and—and I thought I'd drop in. I saw the lights on."

Quinn laughed. "Come in. Lights? Oh yes, Silk leaves them on, unconsciously, I suppose. He thinks I need them. Something on your mind, Commissioner? You're out very late."

The Commissioner sat down and twirled his hat nervously. "I've got too much on my mind. The Black Bat for one thing. Frankly, I thought this mysterious, hooded figure might be you, but I—I know how wrong I am now. Forgive me, Tony."

"It's an honor even to be suspected," Quinn chuckled. "I've heard of The Bat and I appreciate the work he's doing. What made you think I might be he?"

"He is built like you, Tony, and he has a somewhat similar voice. But you—you're a—"

"BLIND MAN? Don't be afraid to say it. I'm used to that now. Commissioner, remember what you told me today? About cooperating with you? I've been thinking things over and I may be able to help. Snate is the man we must get first, but in getting him we must force him to reveal the identity of the man behind him. That man is far more important than Snate and in my mind there is no question of his existence. If he lives, or goes free, he will start a new gang, put another dummy like Snate at their head and carry on as before. That must be prevented. The angle to work from is that of the disappearing armored cars. How long since one dropped out of sight?"

"Three weeks to the day. It's almost time for another to vanish. I've assigned detectives to ride every car in the city. What good they can do I don't know. Sometimes I think it's like sending a man to his grave."

"Tomorrow morning," Quinn suggested, "why not call a conference of interested parties? Mr. Otto Fox, for instance. He owns the largest armored car concern in the country. Then there is Paul Stewart, the Commissioner of Correction. I understand he's not quite so popular of late. Many of Snate's gang seem to be paroled convicts whom Stewart was instrumental in releasing."

"That's right, but Stewart is honest," Warner insisted. "He's working with me, trying to pin enough on those paroled men to drag them back to a cell. So far the score is blank."

"Also," Quinn went on, "bring with you Peter Gage, who runs the *News-Record*. Snate has been hammering away at him and he has the courage to retaliate. I think he might help."

"We'll meet at your house," Warner approved the idea. "Ten o'clock, shall we say? I'll be going now, Tony. And watch out for Lieutenant McGrath."

"McGrath?" Quinn frowned. "Why?"

The Commissioner smiled tolerantly. "Oh—just an idea of mine. You see, McGrath received a phone call tipping him off about the bank holdup, but before he could get into action, the thing was done. McGrath, however, was on the scene not long after and he is sure he saw your man Kirby acting suspiciously. Then he saw you crossing the street. McGrath has an idea you might be this new character who has come into life. The Black Bat."

For long minutes after the Commissioner departed, Quinn sat quietly staring into space with his apparently sightless eyes. A slow smile played around his lips. Silk entered with a tray.

"It's all right to send in Carol and our new found friend," Quinn said. "Do you think he can be trusted, Silk?"

"Yes sir. Very much so. His name is Jack O'Leary, sir, and he is commonly known as Butch. He once had pugilistic aspirations, but it seems he was framed into a faked bout and thrown out by the boxing commission. A little slow witted, perhaps, but he's as strong as a bull."

Butch marched into the room behind Carol. His head was neatly bandaged and in his eyes was the look that a St. Bernard might give its mistress after its life had been saved. Carol sat down while Butch clumsily arranged pillows at her back. Then he stepped before Quinn.

"Say—you look like you can't see. I figured you was this Black Bat guy."

"And if I am?" Quinn asked him.

BUTCH LICKED dry lips. "Well—maybe I ain't so bright, but if you need a door or somebody's face pushed in, I'm right there with my dukes. I was framed by a gang of hoods like these mugs that belong to Snate. I hate 'em and I'd work for nothin' if you'd give me a crack at mussin' 'em up." He gulped and moved one foot awkwardly. "That is—if you are The Black Bat."

"I am," Quinn answered quietly, "and I'm glad you asked to join forces with me. I would not have asked you because your life will be in constant danger from now on. I'll arrange a means of contact. Meanwhile you must never be seen with me—as Tony Quinn. Nor as The Bat if we can manage it. You'll be my left hand, Butch. Silk happens to be my right."

"You can count on me," Butch said very seriously. "Boy, are those hoods of Snate's scared of you. That's all they talked about. You want any good muscle work done, I'm your man."

"Thanks," Quinn nodded. "I knew you'd help."

"And I?" Carol asked with a smile.

"You," Quinn turned toward her, "are my eyes. You gave them back to me."

"But those pictures?" Silk put in quickly. "You gave the film to Warner. He'll spot Butch in a second."

"That portion of the film has been destroyed," Quinn said. "And—I think Warner has his suspicions anyway. Not definite ones," he added hastily, "but he more or less expressed himself tonight. We can trust him and he will never really know I am The Bat. Now, before we retire, there is work to be planned. Tomorrow we begin to really wear Snate down. Butch, I want you to wangle a job with the Star Express Service. That's Otto Fox's armored car company. We'll prepare false recommendations. Ride those trucks and keep your eyes open. It's a dangerous job. You may be aboard one of them when it vanishes." Butch nodded tersely.

"Silk," Quinn went on, "you will remain here. I may need you in a hurry."

Carol walked over to the davenport and sat down beside Quinn.

"I'm speaking for myself," she said. "First of all I'll wash this dye out of my hair and remove some of this awful makeup. I have a small apartment not far from here. You can reach me at any time, Tony Quinn."

"Good," Quinn smiled. "It's better that you are never seen with me—nor with The Black Bat either. You'll work in disguise, as Silk will be forced to do. There must be no way by which either crooks or police can tie any of you to The Bat. Tony Quinn, being stone blind, wouldn't make new friends so you won't be able to come to my house except secretly. Quinn is supposed to be too disgusted with life to be interested in anyone. Perhaps you won't understand how that could be, Carol, but I do. I was really blind long enough to find out for myself."

She nodded and he thought her eyes were a little sad.

"Yes—I do understand," she murmured softly, "You see—my father was—blind."

CHAPTER XII

NIGHT BATTLE

ERSTWHILE DISTRICT Attorney Quinn got no sleep that night. Butch departed for his rooming house with cleverly forged recommendations prepared by Silk. Carol, safely under Silk's watchful eye, returned to her apartment. And Tony Quinn went forth into the sight as The Black Bat.

He had followed Silk and his captors to Snate's private hideout, so no time was wasted in finding the place again. Quinn parked his car well away from the address, walked toward the place through underbrush and soggy marsh. He donned his hood, made sure his guns were ready and then slipped up to the rear of the mansion-like dwelling.

It took him but a few moments to secure entrance through the cellar, and walking softly through the intense darkness of the house, he reached the door to Snate's study.

One of Snate's men was half asleep behind the big desk. The Bat saw him as plainly as though the lights were on. His presence signified that Snate needed a guard in this room at all times. Therefore something of either great value or an incriminating bit of evidence was kept there.

The Bat reversed one of his guns, smashed it down on the sleepy guard's skull and quickly bound him with adhesive. He carried the man to a supply closet, stowed him away inside and locked the door. Then he returned to Snate's desk and began searching the drawers. Nothing of interest showed up until The Bat tried to open the large lower drawer. It was locked. He fell to work on the lock and to his surprise discovered that it was a modern tumbler type. But his tools soon turned the latch. He pulled open the drawer and gazed thoughtfully at the telephone that lay inside.

He left the drawer partly open, arose and methodically unscrewed every electric light bulb in the study. Then he made a rapid investigation of the rest of the house. Two men, ostensibly servants, slept in an upper room. The Bat slugged one into unconsciousness and used his gun butt on the other.

Now he had the entire house at his command without undue danger of being surprised.

Returning to the study he sat down back of the desk, picked up the phone and held it to his ear. There was a click and a surly, hissing voice made him hold his breath.

"What the devil now, Snate?" the voice asked. "Didn't I tell you not to wake me up in the middle of the night unless something important turned up?"

The Bat took a bold chance. Speaking rapidly, as if badly agitated, he imitated Snate's tones as best he could, depending on the Unknown's sleepy brain to discount any slight difference in the tone.

"It's the boys, they're getting restless. We got to do something."

"Damn you, Snate," the man at the other end snapped, "you're getting more jittery by the day. Tell them we're going to pull another armored car job within the next forty-eight hours. I'm getting things set now—and if you waken me again with such a trivial excuse, I'll take steps to punish you. If the men won't obey, shoot one or two. The rest will toe the mark then."

The phone at the other end slammed down. The Bat carefully restored the instrument to its drawer, closed and locked it and then eyed a huge wall safe with considerable interest.

HE HAD a well founded hunch that Snate's accumulated wealth lay behind that great steel door. For now The Bat was positive that Snate was only a puppet and his master would hardly allow Snate to dispose of the huge profits of their joint reign of crime. Safe deposit boxes had grown unpopular with crooks of late because authorities had a habit of locating them and getting court orders to have them opened.

The Bat had tried to place the voice of Snate's master, but it was impossible. Obviously the voice was disguised until it became nothing more than a kind of hissing without tonal qualities. The Bat laughed to himself as he thought of the next time when Snate spoke over that phone and received a warning as to how the men should be handled.

The safe door intrigued The Bat, but he had no aspirations about opening it. Nothing less than a diamond pointed drill, plenty of soup and hours in which to work would break down that barrier.

Then a door slammed shut with a bang and The Bat jerked up. His two guns appeared with the ease and speed of a magician's feat. Backing quickly, he selected a dark spot and crouched there waiting. It was too dangerous to attempt a rushing escape for he had no idea as to how many men had entered the house.

"Hey!" That was Snate's voice raised in anger when no one came to receive him. "Something's happened," Snate went on, speaking to his men. "Two of you get at the doors. The others watch every room, especially the windows."

The door of the study opened and The Bat saw Snate and one wizen faced crook outlined against the light from the hallway. Snate snapped the switch on the wall and bit off a curse when no lights came on. He moved toward the desk. The Bat moved too, sidling toward the door. He closed it very gently until Snate and his thug noticed that the light from the hall was being cut off.

Both spun around, reaching for their guns.

"You're about to commit suicide." The Bat's voice came brittle as thin ice. "Don't move and don't call out."

"The Black Bat!" Snate gulped.

That name seemed to do something to the warped brain of Snate's undersized thug. Either fear or drug-impelled bravado made him go for his gun. He was swift, too, and the gun was ejected from its holster by a spring. But the hammer never fell against the cartridge. The Bat's gun barked once and the thug spun completely around before he struck the floor.

That shot started things. Snate, half mad in fear of his own life, charged The Bat. His men were running toward the study. Snate dragged his gun out, tried to aim it in the darkness, but he had no target. The Bat, moving on rubber soled shoes, was no longer near the door. Snate turned around, swept out his free hand reaching for The Bat, and ran squarely into a teeth rattling punch on the mouth. At the same moment a hand that felt like steel, twisted his wrist until the gun dropped. That same hand moved again with amazing rapidity until it clutched Snate by the throat.

"I COULD kill you now," The Bat hissed, "and the world would be the better for it, but the time is not yet ripe, Snate. So I'll compromise with the urgings of my heart and only knock you stiff."

Snate whimpered, tried to scream, but those fingers were too tight against his windpipe. He heard the rush of air made by The Bat's fist, felt a pile driver of a punch strike him squarely in the face and then Snate's interest in things animate ceased.

The Bat let him collapse to the floor. Someone shoved open the door of the study and for a second The Bat stood revealed. Two men at the door cried a warning and at the same time opened fire. A bullet whistled past The Bat's ear. His two guns pumped lead with a fury. One thug clutched at his stomach and fell. The other decided he might live longer if he beat a retreat and he did so—very hastily.

The Bat surveyed the study, saw that it had no windows and that ventilation was provided by a grilled ventilator. He had to leave through the door. Darting forward, he reached the hallway before any of the other gunmen responded to the shouts for help and the firing. The Bat's gun spoke and the light in the hallway went out. He sped to a small table lamp, hastily unscrewed the bulb and inserted a bit of metal into the socket. He felt a slight shock, saw the blue flash as the power was short circuited—all over the house, the lights went out.

Now The Bat was in his element. Here, in the darkness, he could see plainly while his enemies blundered around, not knowing which way to turn. One was coming down the stairs. The Bat quietly seized a small chair and placed it on the stairs several steps from the landing. The descending thug tripped, fell headlong and when he tried to scramble to his feet, a gun butt put him out of the running.

The Bat headed toward the front door, opened it and then slammed it shut again as two bullets smashed into the heavy oak. There was a car in the driveway, its headlights on and flooding the porch. Those same lights would illuminate the rear of the house also. Another man was coming down the steps as quietly as possible. The Bat moved sideways, heard a board squeak and drew down the fire of the man on the stairs. The Bat shot once and missed. When the thug started back upstairs, he fired a second bullet that stopped the fight.

There were at least two men outside. The Bat could hear them talking. They'd expect him to emerge through the rear door and take his chances in reaching the thick brush that surrounded the house. Therefore The Bat did the exact opposite thing. He turned the knob of the front door, flung it wide and raced out into the night.

Guns cracked and he saw a burly man raise from the protection of a thick bush. The ground at The Bat's feet spurted dirt as another bullet hammered into it. In desperation The Bat jumped and went into a nose dive that carried him across the ground and behind a hedge.

"I winged him," the thug yelled. "I put a slug in his carcass. Careful now—he may still be able to shoot."

THE BAT'S nose dive to safety had been mistaken for the antics of a badly wounded man. He smiled tightly, rolled over and over until he was a dozen yards from the spot where he had vanished, and then lay prone, gun arm resting on elbow and weapon pointed straight out.

He saw one man move into his range of vision. The Bat's gun flashed. His aim was accurate, but the flame from the muzzle of the weapon drew down the fire of the last crook. There was nothing to do now but shoot it out. The Bat waited, tensely. He had one advantage. If the killer showed himself even slightly, he would see him. The headlights of the car streamed in a direction away from the two men and both were operating in total darkness.

Something dropped to the ground about twenty feet to The Bat's right, but he wasn't fooled by that trick. His gun swung left. He saw, as clearly as though a spotlight focussed on the subject, the stealthy movements of the last crook. The Bat fired twice, heard a scream of agony and waited until the flailing of limbs in the brush died away. He approached the wounded man, saw that his slug had inflicted a deep scalp wound and he knew the battle was over.

He paused long enough to attach one of his tokens that emblazoned the image of a black bat on the man's forehead. Then he hurried to the parked car, got behind the wheel and backed to the road. He roared up the highway to the spot where he had parked his own car. There he disabled the sedan he had temporarily appropriated, climbed into his own sedan and drove away.

He left it parked ten blocks from his own home, slipped through neighbors' yards as quietly as a cat and reached his own back door. Silk was waiting anxiously. There was a smear of blood on The Bat's hand.

"You're hurt, sir," Silk gasped.

The Bat stripped off his hood, glanced at the hand and shook his head. "That's the blood of one of Snate's men. I must have got it when I pasted a black bat on his forehead. Tonight, Silk, my slippery one, I gave Snate a token of my respect. Unless I'm badly mistaken, I broke his nose—at least that's what I intended to do."

"I hope it was his neck," Silk grimaced. "Everything is quiet here. Butch left, as you know. Carol is safely in her apartment and you can contact her by phone whenever you wish. A lovely girl, sir, and clever as they come."

"Right you are," Tony Quinn picked up his cane, stared straight ahead and began tapping his way out of the kitchen. "Come along, Silk, I've something to discuss."

"One moment, sir," Silk said. "I'll phone Miss Carol you are back. Unless you need her, sir."

Tony Quinn shook his head. When Silk returned, he was sitting in the chair before the fireplace, eyes staring blankly at nothing and they seemed dead—like the eyes of a blind man, Tony Quinn took no chances that his secret might be discovered. Lieutenant McGrath might have ideas and come snooping.

"**SIT DOWN,** Silk," Quinn said. "We're in something of a jam right now. Butch can operate perfectly without anyone knowing he works for me. The crooks who might recognize him are either dead or behind bars. Carol can readily change her appearance. But you—Silk—I don't wonder you turned to house breaking. Any police officer could pick you out in a crowd of ten thousand. We've got to remedy that."

"But I have already arranged it," Silk broke in eagerly. "I haven't talked about myself much, sir, but when I operated during my prime, I took over quite a few rather intelligent people. I assumed a disguise that I worked on for years. I have small porcelain cups that fit to my molars and puff out my cheeks. A little color rubbed into the right spots on my face and a trick beard of the Van Dyke type, make me look quite distinguished, sir. Then a conservative suit, nose glasses suspended by a silken ribbon around my neck and I'm the very essence of a college professor. In fact, I was once known as The Professor."

"Great," Quinn cheered. "Have you any other accomplishments, Silk?"

Silk flushed a trifle embarrassedly.

"Well, sir, I have been known to put out some rather fancy kites—forged checks. I also possess the knack of imitating a person's voice. That used to be quite handy when I made phone calls in some other man's name."

"Silk," Quinn said, "you're going to be a priceless asset. Now to bed with you. I need rest also, because tomorrow Commissioner Warner is bringing three men here to confer with Tony Quinn, the blind man. Shortly after that, there is to be another armored car disappearance and then, my dear Silk, Snate is really going to get a headache. Tonight I talked to Snate's master and through Snate, I'll land him too!"

CHAPTER XIII

THE DISAPPEARING TRUCK

WHEN COMMISSIONER Warner swept the nose of the big departmental limousine into the driveway of Tony Quinn's home, he saw the blind man slowly making his way along the drive.

Warner stepped on the brakes and the tires grated against the gravel. Instantly Quinn made a crazy jump for the bank. It was rounded upward and he fell on the slippery grass until he sprawled on his stomach. With a cry of fear he pulled himself along the turf until he was out of the drive.

Warner reached his side and helped him to his feet. "Tony, I'm terribly sorry that I frightened you."

Tony Quinn exhaled a long breath of relief. "I'm acting like a child, Commissioner. But the sound of brakes seems to get me. Every time I hear them squeal, I expect to feel the radiator of a car smash against me."

"Let me help you inside," Warner suggested, and swore at himself for being such a fool as to suspect Tony Quinn of being The Black Bat. "Fox, Stewart and Gage are already on the porch. Feel well enough to confer with us?"

"Oh yes, of course." Quinn flashed a quick smile. "Using my brain in trying to figure this thing out is all that seems to make living worthwhile. I have an idea, Commissioner, and it may work."

Quinn shook hands with the three men who waited on the porch. His eyes stared straight over their shoulders, but Tony Quinn's grip sized up each man as he held their hands in turn.

Gage had a plump, warm fist. His clothing seemed to smell of printer's ink, for Gage wasn't one to be content as an executive. He practically lived beside the great presses that pounded out his newspaper. Gage was big, rough, and ready.

Stewart was big, too, but in a different sort of way. There was no surplus strength in his muscles and the flesh on his face hung down in jowls. His handclasp was limp.

Otto Fox typified the go-getter type, slender, immaculately dressed and always nervous. His hand felt moist and cold, Quinn thought.

Silk served highballs and discreetly withdrew. Quinn took the floor.

"Gentlemen, the Commissioner has been good enough to ask my help. I've thought about this armored car disappearing act for many hours. I haven't solved the manner by which it is done, but—I think we might forestall any further attempts."

"Yes," Otto Fox leaned forward and clicked the ice cubes in his glass. "Tell me how you will do that."

"It looks to me like an inside job," Quinn offered. "Therefore the men who control it must be circumvented. There is a way. Each morning your crews, assigned to each truck, are given sealed orders. They don't know where they are going until the trucks start out. All armored car services operate that way. Therefore, instead of allowing regular employees to handle those sealed orders it is my suggestion that you, Mr. Fox, handle every detail yourself. You route the jobs, you issue the orders direct to the men."

"NOT ME," Fox shook his head. "If anything happens, then I will be instantly blamed. You forget, these losses are not mine. Those shipments are insured and I do not care to draw down insurance company detectives on me."

"Let me handle it," Stewart spoke up. "I've an interest in this case. I'm being publicly censured for letting criminals out on parole, but I'm powerless to stop their release. All I can do is send them back. Doubtless many of them are helping this man Snate, and if I help to prevent these robberies I at least interfere with their plans a little."

"Why, of course," Commissioner Warner broke in. "Stewart is quite impartial and if anything happens, the blame cannot be thrown upon Otto Fox."

"I think it's damned foolish," Gage snapped. "If there are inside men, don't you think they'll get wise?"

"Let them," Quinn interrupted.

"What can they do? Stewart is to be given a list of the places where the trucks are to be sent. He will sort these clients under Otto Fox's direction and route the trucks secretly."

"Fool proof," Stewart exulted. "Quinn, Warner is right. You have got a brain in that skull of yours. Now tell us how we can pick up Snate and put him behind bars."

Quinn smiled wanly. "I can't do that, gentlemen. My thinking powers don't go quite that far. Some day I may have an idea, though, and I'll certainly expose it. I have no love for Snate."

When they were gone, Silk entered. "I thought you were going to trap those armored car thieves," he protested mildly. "But as I see it, sir, you've simply stopped them."

Quinn lit a cigarette. "I've laid the groundwork for the plan that will trap the master crook of this age, Silk. Do you think my puny little ideas will stop him? Oh no. You see, the man who owns Snate was in this room just now. He is one of those four men."

"What?" Silk gaped. "Are you sure?"

"The master crook knows everything that goes on. Those three men stick with Warner as much as possible and one of them does so simply to gain knowledge and pass it on to Snate. In that angle lies his defeat, although he doesn't sense it. Prepare the car, Silk. Carol and I are going for a ride."

"It's quite ready, sir. And so is Miss Carol. She arrived a few moments ago."

Quinn took both her hands as she met him. He didn't speak, for words seemed unnecessary. Instead he picked up his cane, tucked her arm under his and permitted her to lead him out the door and into the roadster. It was hard to pretend blindness on a morning like this, and with a beautiful girl beside him.

She parked the car along a road that overlooked the bay. They sat staring at the water.

"You never know how blue the sky and the water can be, Carol," he said quietly, "until you've lived in darkness for months."

SHE TURNED to him. "That's why I drove here, Tony Quinn. It's time I told you who I am. My father was a police officer—a detective sergeant. Eight years ago Oliver Snate ruled a small midwestern town—not very far from Springville where Dr. Harrington brought back your sight. Dad fought Snate—and lost. Snate cornered him one night and put two bullets into his back. They paralyzed him for life. Another smashed through his temple, severing the optic nerves—blinding him. He was too weak for an operation.

"Dad heard of your fight against crime and followed you through every phase. Followed you with my eyes for I read him every scrap of information we could get from the newspapers. But Dad was doomed and he knew it. When the time came, he bound me by a promise to obey his instructions. I was to contact you, and through Dr. Harrington present you with new corneas for your eyes, if such an operation would be successful."

Quinn's face was strained, his eyes gaunt and starkly clear now. "Other doctors told me such an operation would be useless," he said, "How did Harrington do it?"

"Harrington could be as famous an eye surgeon as any of those you consulted. But he chooses to live quietly in a country town. No one but Dad could have persuaded him to operate on you—and Dr. Harrington used more than the corneas. He took entire sections of the eyes.

"Furthermore he performed a delicate experiment which had been successful on animal subjects. Dr. Harrington made the pupil larger and exposed more of the eye lens. He asked me to report the results and I did, immediately after the night when you saw me for the first time. You not only have new eyes, Tony Quinn, but exceptional eyes in the manner by which they function. The change which Dr. Harrington made cannot be seen by others, so there is no fear of their abnormality being discovered."

"You were there," Quinn said tensely. "You watched the operation and while I was under anesthesia I talked of what I hoped to do to Snate."

She nodded mutely. "It made Dad's death easier when I told him. He didn't live long after that. Now do you understand why I must be with you—must help you against men such as Snate? Oh, I know he won't be the last one, and those of his kind cannot be fought with fair means. Dad discovered that. So did I."

Quinn said nothing on the drive back. When the car stopped, he took her hand and held it tightly.

"Of course I could never do without you now, Carol, even if you hadn't told me any of this. You proved yourself when you had the courage and tact to enter Snate's mob and then save me from being unmasked and killed. And what you have told me makes me more resolved to fulfill my mission than ever before. No one is safe so long as men like Snate exist. They build themselves up until every boy with the slightest criminal tendency idolizes them, imitates them. Such a thing must stop and there is but one way. To crush those men and in crushing them make them humble. Show them up for what they are—stupid, vain, selfish killers."

"And you are going to do that?" she asked.

"Exactly. Snate's days of freedom, perhaps of life itself, are numbered. Tonight The Black Bat flies again and this time there is a trap to be baited and set. Snate may spring it and jump clear, but one day its jaws will close and that day is at hand."

QUINN WAITED until almost midnight before he ventured out of the house. He slipped through the back door, garbed entirely in black, with twin guns strapped in place and his black hood concealed in a specially constructed pocket.

Keeping the brim of his hat low, he stepped into a street two blocks from his home, hailed a taxi and had himself driven into the heart of the business section. There he became most cautious, for the scars around his eyes would be a dead giveaway if he were observed. He used dark sidestreets to reach the huge garage where Otto Fox maintained his armored car fleet and his general offices.

There were watchmen on duty, but they were old men, retired from the more arduous duties of guarding cash. Quinn fitted his hood in place, sidled through a small delivery door and found himself in a dark, oily smelling room. He walked across this, as sure footed as though every light were turned on. There were winding, steel stairs leading upward. He made his way softly around these until he reached the top, and his goal—the entrance to the offices.

The iron barred door was locked and it took him ten minutes to open the twin locks. From this vaulted room the orders for each car were passed out, and, sometimes, sacks of currency.

Once a guard walked by the door, tested it and passed on, satisfied. There was a small grill set high in the door. No light streamed from it and had there been light, it would have illuminated an entire section of the corridor. Therefore the guard was satisfied, for what manner of intruder could work in pitch darkness? Even the ray of a flashlight could be easily observed.

The Bat soon found what he was looking for. Neatly stacked under the locked cover of a roll top desk, he discovered the orders for the following day. They were in large envelopes, all sealed with wax and impressed with the firm's seal. It was impossible to open the flaps without detection, but The Bat had other methods. From his pocket he took a small round silver bar with a slit running along it. He carefully inserted this through the flap, above the seal where the envelope came together loosely. Maneuvering the bar, he engaged the edge of the paper in the slit. Turning the bar slowly he rolled the paper tightly around the bar until he could pull it out.

One by one he treated each sealed envelope in the same manner, copying the contents until he had a complete list of every truck's destination. Next he consulted record books which he removed from a steel, fireproof cabinet that gave way easily to his set of tools.

It was almost dawn when his work was completed. A difficult task that often threatened to be without result, yet it finally yielded the one item The Bat required.

The careful check he had made of the instructions and the record books revealed that there was one stop—to be made by one truck only—that wasn't recorded except on the sealed orders to the truck itself. The client was not listed on any billing or order accounts. It was the Triton Garage, a huge storage and repair place far uptown.

The Bat made his stealthy way out of the building, just as he had entered. The four guards who patrolled every portion of the grounds, except the record rooms, had no inkling that a hooded man had spent half the night in a room where even they were not permitted.

SILK RAISED the shades just before noon the next morning.

"You were late last night," he said diffidently. "I hope you were successful. And Butch phoned. He secured his job with the armored car concern and is assigned to Truck M. They letter, instead of number, their trucks, sir."

Tony Quinn whistled softly. Truck M was the one with the superfluous call. Things were shaping up nicely, yet if The Black Bat failed, Butch might lose his life. Not one of the armored car guards who had vanished with their rolling vaults had ever been heard from again.

"Work for you, Silk," Quinn said. "You might begin by stealing a set of marker plates—from a car whose owner won't miss them for a day or two. Then go to a used car exchange and buy the fastest job on the floor. Nothing flashy, but be certain there is plenty of power under the hood. After that, it will be best if you prepare yourself as The Professor and keep the disguise on until you hear from me. Should anyone call, let Carol answer the door and make our regrets."

"Yes sir," Silk replied simply, but his eyes were shining brightly. Silk had been idle too long to suit his nature.

Quinn decided to go for a walk in the middle of the afternoon. With his cane tapping a path, he strolled out of the house, walked a dozen blocks slowly. He seemed to be worried about his health for he kept a muffler tied well up around his throat. As always he wore a wide brimmed hat pulled low, for Tony Quinn was known to be sensitive about those scars that marred his features.

Once he paused and turned deliberately around, as if hesitating whether or not to retrace his steps. But in reality he looked carefully up and down the street. There was no one about and it was beginning to grow dark with the early dusk of winter.

Then he turned down a side street, sauntered up to a black coupé parked at the curb. When he was certain he was unobserved, he slipped behind the wheel and sent the coupé racing out into the highway. He parked, in a deserted section, peeled off his grey topcoat and revealed his black outfit beneath. He changed to a black slouch hat that had been thrown on the seat of the car. From a concealed pocket he drew his hood and made it ready. He tested his two guns—and was off.

It took him only a few moments to reach the busy center of the city, but he went straight through, rolled uptown and finally selected a parking place which he could pull out of easily. He waited there for more than half an hour until he saw one of Fox's armored cars comng along. He trailed it, very carefully, for he knew that police might also have the car under observation. It made two quick stops.

Each time Quinn saw Butch emerge from the back with an exposed gun in his fist. Another man climbed out and the two of them entered the designated place of business while a third took up a station beside the truck. Butch usually heaved into sight first, holding heavy bags of money while his companion guarded every step they made. As they approached the truck, the rear door opened. Butch and his guard got in while the third man hurried to the front seat.

THEN THE BAT raced ahead of the truck to avoid being spotted and parked just outside of the mouth of an alley that led to the big Triton Garage. When the armored car entered this alley, The Bat watched very carefully. He saw it roll into the garage and stop. Two minutes later it came out again.

The Bat saw the two uniformed drivers at the wheel and there seemed to be nothing wrong. He noticed also that there was a V-shaped crack in the window beside the driver. But instead of turning south and heading toward the banking sections where the deposits were to be made, the truck turned north, speeding up.

The Bat followed, at a safe distance. He saw the truck swerve sharply and turn onto a narrow little street. Three minutes later The Bat reached the corner and suddenly reached for the hand brake. Another car, with weak headlights, was approaching and taking up more than its share of the road. It pulled over finally and The Bat watched it pass by. It was a florist truck of the light delivery type. He snapped off the emergency, started down the street again and found that it was blind!

And there was absolutely no sign of the armored truck!

Leaping from his car The Bat made a swift inspection of the few garages on the residential street. There was none in which the armored truck might have been hidden. He returned to his own car and sat behind the wheel trying to puzzle it out. His eyes were extraordinarily good and there were no kinks in his brain. He had seen that armored car turn down this street. It was impossible for it to have driven out again without his seeing it. Yet—the earth might just as well have swallowed the truck for all The Bat could figure out.

He backed his car out of the street and headed back to the Triton Garage. Somehow he knew the secret to all this lay at that point.

CHAPTER XIV

BUTCH FINDS TROUBLE

JACK "BUTCH" O'LEARY found that working for The Bat was a simple process. Everything seemed arranged for him. The forged papers he carried were accepted as genuine and he was instantly given a job as an armored car guard, just as Quinn planned.

Not long afterward, Butch knew why. The guards working for Fox's service were quitting rapidly. Their sole conversation was of the permanent disappearance of more than thirty men and eleven trucks. Moat of the guards were new, attracted by the double wages being paid.

Butch got himself rigged up in one of the green uniforms used by the service, buckled on the forty-five automatic and began to feel important.

"Lemme see the guy who tries to hijack the truck I'm on," he told the three men who were to ride with him. "Trouble with this whole set-up is that the mugs who went out and never came back, couldn't take it. Hell, why didn't they put up a fight? All they had to do was fire their guns a few times and draw down a raft of cops. But did they do it? No, because they were too damned scared to shoot."

Loomis, a white-haired employee of the company for more than twelve years, was doubtful.

"You didn't know those others—who have disappeared. They were competent guys. We have target practice twice a week and all those men could knock the head off a match at thirty paces. They weren't scared easy either. No sir, whatever happened to 'em happened so fast they just didn't know what to do. And I been lucky too long. One of these days it'll get me too."

"Stick around," Butch snorted. "Me—I'll take care of you. Only keep your eyes open, see? Maybe if we do that, we'll get the jump on the guys who been taking the cars."

At nine, the armored truck rolled out. There was a weary detective riding with the two guards in back. Two more were up front. At a tiny desk inside the rolling vault, Butch broke the seal of the first route order.

"Alston Trust to pick up payroll for Esquire Shoe Company. Twenty grand for delivery at six bells tonight. That's a funny time to deliver a payroll."

"They make it up first thing in the morning," the detective explained disgustedly. "Don't ask me how I know. I been checking these things for weeks. They got a safe over there that nobody could crack."

They made the pickup and Butch turned to the second sealed order. All day long they followed that procedure. It grew hot inside the truck; the detective peeled off his coat. Then Butch picked up the last order of the day.

"Triton Garage to pick up day's receipts and then home, boys, without the boogy man laying his mitts on us. That's on account of I was along. He musta saw me and got scared."

The driver took the order, drove uptown and turned down a narrow alley leading to the garage. The great doors opened as the truck hove into sight. It stopped inside the garage and Butch climbed out, drawn gun in his hand.

There was an office directly across the wide floor and he hurried there. He heard something of a swish, heard a motor start at the same moment and began to turn around. Something whizzed down and collided with his skull. He dropped to his knees and a grinning thug brought down the short iron bar again, almost cracking Butch's thick skull.

BUT BUTCH was tough. At least Butch wasn't completely out as he fell. He had his eyes slitted and was conscious of what went on. He saw that the armored car he had worked in all day, was now covered with a huge canvas. There was a pungent, choking odor in the air. He saw also an armored car, the counterpart of his own truck, even to the letter M painted on the door, rolling out.

Even Butch's slow witted brain caught the idea. The real armored car stopped when it entered the garage. The huge piece of tarpaulin, held in position and out of sight dropped down and as it struck the truck, deadly gas bombs broke. The crew had no time to shoot. Then a duplicate truck rolled out to provide an alibi for the Triton Garage. Plenty of witnesses could swear that the armored car left the garage all right.

"Will I slit this big ape's throat?" a voice asked, and Butch promptly closed his eyes and fought to recover his strength.

"He's out stiff—damned near dead from those socks you handed him," another voice rejected the idea. "Drag him into the empty stock room. We'll take care of him when we cart the others away. There'll be blood stains if you bump him here and we can't take chances."

Someone grabbed Butch's feet and pulled him across the floor. Butch remained as limp and passive as he could. His life depended upon the way he played possum. He was in a serious predicament, but Butch felt no fear. He remembered a cold-eyed man with a scarred face, and if Butch needed assurance, it lay with that calm person. The Black Bat wouldn't rest long now. Butch had a well confirmed hunch that The Bat wasn't very far away.

He was thrown into a corner. Someone slapped him across the face. Butch didn't move a muscle.

"He ain't dead yet, but I think the big lug is breathin' his last. How about the guys in the truck?"

"All dead," another man reported and Butch had to restrain a shiver from running up and down his spine. "That gas don't fool, Limpy. Remember that last guard we socked? When he didn't die, the boss tested the stuff on him and he was dead in less than three minutes."

"Sure—why not? Ain't it the same stuff they feed the poor death house chumps out west? That's where Snate got the idea. Boy, was there a haul in that truck! A hundred and fifty grand if there was a cent."

"Yeah," the other thug mumbled, "and what do we get out of it? A measly hundred bucks a week with a promise of a big cut later on. If you should ask me, it's too damn much later on. We get about two or three hundred grand apiece coming to us and all Snate hands out is promises."

"*Shh*—Limpy. You wanna have that gas tried on you? Snate don't take no back talk from nobody—'specially lately. Somethin's got in his hair. You know what? He's scared. Scared stiff!"

"Who wouldn't be?" the first thug asked. "That Black Bat is got himself nine or ten lives. Ain't no bullet made with his number on it. If he gets just a little closer to this racket, I'm pullin' out—cut or no cut."

THERE WAS silence after that. Then Butch took a chance and opened his eyes a crack. He shuddered. The bodies of the truck guards were being carried into this small room. Their faces were suffused with a peculiar greenish tinge. Loomis was there, and the weary detective who rode the truck. Snate's batting average was running a hundred percent—except for Butch.

Perhaps thirty minutes crawled by. Butch wasn't sure, for it seemed like a year to him. He was alone in the little room, alone with four dead men. Carefully he crawled over toward the bodies and groaned a little when he saw that they had been stripped of their guns. He heard someone approach and tried desperately to get back to the side of the room where they had flung him. He was too late.

"Hey, look at that big guy," someone hissed. "He's alive. Get busy with that knife."

That was enough for Butch. He suddenly arose, looking as big as a mountainside to the two men in the room. He reached out one mighty paw and the fingers closed around the knife man's throat. They squeezed—once—and bone cracked. Butch flung a lifeless body from him and looked around for the second thug. He was gone, but as Butch headed toward the door, a menacing gun stopped him. Three men backed him into the little room. Only one had a gun. The others looked on with obvious interest.

"So," it was the man called Limpy who spoke, "you're a tough guy, huh? You rubbed out Slim, did you? Well, you were gonna die anyway—only nice and easy—with some swell gas—but now you're gonna take it in the belly—every damn slug in my gun."

Butch's eyes protruded and his vast body shook with rage. Yet even his slow witted brain told him there was no hope. He couldn't jump the gun. There wasn't room enough. Slowly he backed away until he felt the cold wall at his back. The trio advanced, step by step, glorying in their new found control over life and death.

Then Butch saw the door behind the men silently open. A black gloved hand emerged and it held a gun. There was a single shot. Limpy gave a scream, whirled around and fell headlong. The other two men reached for their weapons, but their hands froze. Standing in the doorway was a figure that had grown to be the nemesis of the underworld. The Black Bat faced them, two guns at a ready angle.

"Back up," he ordered. "You," he indicated Butch, "get out of here."

"Sure, sure," Butch grinned happily. Then he used his head. "I dunno who you are and you look like a crook to me, but thanks anyway. Just lemme take care of these two mugs in my own way. Then, if you wants, you can plug me. I'll die happy."

He received a curt nod of that hooded head. Butch spat into the palms of his hands, hunched his shoulders and then spread his arms wide. The two thugs cowered, bleating in terror. Butch grasped each one by the scruff of the neck, lifted them completely off the floor and brought their heads together twice. Then he dropped them, wiped his hands on his thighs and faced The Bat inquiringly.

"Run for it," The Bat whispered. "This place is full of Snate's men and they'll be down here like flies."

BUTCH MADE a line for the door, racing across the huge empty space of the garage. He heard someone shout. A gun barked. Butch felt a mighty blow against his forehead. He reeled, clutched at the air in a vain effort to find something by which he might support himself, and then his huge body collapsed like an empty sack.

The Bat leaped out of the small room, fired half a dozen quick shots toward the ramp that led to the upper floors of the garage and drew a squeal of pain from one of the thugs who hid there. The others ducked. Then a siren cut loose.

The Bat glanced out of the nearest window. Two cruisers, crammed with detectives, were pulling into the areaway before the garage. Other things happened so fast they seemed amazing. A heavy car came rumbling down the ramp. It braked to a stop beside Butch. Two men jumped out, picked up Butch's limp form and threw him inside. The Bat snapped a pair of hasty shots, missed and raced toward the rear of the garage seeking an exit. There was none!

He saw the bandits' car speed by the detective cruisers with an exchange of shots. One of the cruisers turned to take up the chase while five detectives raced toward the doors of the garage. At their head was Detective Lieutenant McGrath.

The Bat surveyed the garage quickly. There was no sign of the real armored truck and The Bat possessed no idea that it had remained inside the garage while a ringer rolled out. Powerful elevators had raised the truck to a dismantling room where it was already beyond recognition.

There was one thing The Bat wanted to do before he beat his retreat. The armored car guards lay in that empty stock room, mysteriously dead and showing no signs of violence. While Lieutenant McGrath and his men cautiously approached the building, The Bat hurried to the stock room. Using one of his sharply pointed tools, he deftly made a small incision on the arm of a dead guard. The blood, still warm, flowed under pressure of his fingers and he mopped up a quantity on a clean handkerchief.

As he turned away his eyes passed over the two unconscious thugs. They wore regulation overalls and mechanic's smocks on the back of which were emblazoned "TRITON GARAGE" in bold sewed-on letters. Just above these were faint marks in the cloth where other letters had been previously sewed. The Bat spelled out AJAX AUTO REPAIR. He made a mental note of this.

Then he set to work formulating a plan to escape McGrath. Watching carefully he waited until McGrath and his men entered the building. They were bunched together, and started an extensive search of the place. McGrath motioned toward the ramp and they headed that way. The Bat selected that auspicious moment and stepped into the open with both guns drawn.

"Don't move," he called out. "This is The Bat! Remain exactly where you are and drop your guns to the floor. Drop them!"

The Bat's guns barked in unison and the bullets slammed into the wall above the heads of the detectives. That was warning enough. Their guns clattered to the cement floor.

"Turn to the right," The Bat commanded, "and walk straight ahead until I tell you to stop."

McGRATH OBEYED, but he shouted a warning. "You may think you're some kind of a tin god, but one of these days I'll run into you first, Bat. That's the day you'll roost in a cell."

"I'll be looking forward to it," The Bat answered gayly. "Now—all of you stand just where you are. McGrath—I'll give you the honor of removing yourself and your men from my presence. All of you are now standing on the platform of an elevator. Pull that rope at your left and take a ride."

McGrath ground out an oath, but he glanced over his shoulder at the eerie figure in black, took firm cognizance of the two menacing guns and shivered. McGrath was too wise to resist. He possessed a good trait of biding his time. He manipulated the rope and the lift began moving slowly upward.

The Bat sped toward the door. He raced around the garage, cut through an alley, removing his hood as he ran. He vaulted a fence with ease, reached the street and headed directly to the spot where he had parked his car. Two minutes later he drove north.

CHAPTER XV

THE BAT'S DILEMMA

BUT THE BAT was intensely worried over Butch. The fact that the fleeing bandits had stopped long enough to pick him up meant but one thing to The Bat's agile mind. Butch had learned something of extreme importance. Yet The Bat knew that he was powerless for the moment. McGrath might test out a theory that Tony Quinn was The Bat by hurrying to Quinn's home and demanding an explanation if Quinn didn't happen to be there to receive him.

The Bat stopped at a busy corner, drew his collar up and his hat brim down. He stepped into a drug store, reached a phone booth and dialed Police Headquarters.

"Commissioner," he said when Warner was on the wire, "this is Tony Quinn. I've been sitting in front of my fireplace thinking, since dinner, and I need your help on one detail. Will you check your records and call me back? I want to know the last port of call that each of those vanished armored cars made the day of their disappearance."

"Of course, Tony," the Commissioner assented. "I've bad news for you though. There has been another one of those jobs pulled. McGrath is working on the case now. Stewart prepared the sealed orders and swears no one knew what was in them but himself. It is impossible for any other person to have known the route of any truck and prepared the trap by which this latest one vanished."

"You suspect Stewart then?" Quinn asked.

"What else can I do?" Warner answered. "Yet I simply cannot persuade myself that he is our man. But I'll call you back in a few moments, Tony."

He hung up and The Bat sped back to his car. He reached his home and was inside his study just as the phone rang. He was breathing hard, but he governed his voice well as he answered.

"It didn't take me long to find them," Warner said. "And I have still more news for you. First, the armored cars used to make different stops at the end of their day's run. Usually it was at some bank where deposits were made. We checked carefully and there is nothing significant there. Now—this last truck to vanish: it must have either driven into, or been near the Triton Garage, because Lieutenant McGrath was investigating some shooting there and found the murdered armored car guards. They died of some violent poison."

"Are you sure the truck visited the Triton?" Quinn asked. "Did it have orders to go there?"

"We don't know yet," Warner answered. "Have to check with Otto Fox first. Two mechanics disclaim any knowledge of the truck and simply said a car drove in, dumped out the dead guards and got away after a lot of shooting. The mechanics were badly injured and couldn't tell us much. They weren't with the Triton very long. Came from one of that garage's branch plants known as the Ajax Auto Repair up on Lenox Street."

"Someone," Quinn offered, "was close to the crooks and they were forced to get rid of their death cargo fast. There is no other solution."

THE COMMISSIONER chuckled dryly. "Someone was close all right. Those mechanics didn't know it, but The Bat was there. That's what all the shooting was about. McGrath is running down some idea of his now. One of the men with him reported all this to me just a minute ago."

"Thanks," Quinn answered. "That may help me."

He hung up and slowly turned away from the phone. Then he jerked erect and one hand darted for a gun. It levelled at the man who stood not a dozen feet away.

"Who are you?" Quinn snapped. "And keep your hands right where they are."

The man was about fifty with hair grey at the temples, a fat, round face and nose glasses fastened securely in place with a flowing black ribbon hanging loosely around his neck. He wore a wide, black, loose flowing bow tie, a morning coat and grey striped trousers. To Quinn's momentary amazement the man smiled broadly.

"I'll be certain not to move, sir, until you've put the gun away. Fooled you, didn't I?"

"Silk," Quinn gaped. "You're perfect! No wonder the suckers fell for your line. You reek importance and money."

"Thank you, sir," Silk answered and he was highly pleased. "I'm quite ready to begin work."

"Great. Drive at once to the Ajax Garage and Repair Plant on Lenox Street. Investigate the place carefully and if you value your life, don't give your identity away. That garage may prove to be a mare's nest of spies and cutthroats. Butch has been snatched from the Triton Garage and the Ajax may be another hideout for the mob."

"I'll be careful, sir," Silk said. "And might I suggest that I stop and pick up Miss Carol? She's rather champing at the bit, sir. Wants something to do. Perhaps we can satisfy her desire for action by letting her drive me. The mission is comparatively tame, sir."

Quinn had no time to discourage the idea. A car had stopped outside with a squeal of hastily applied brakes.

"Run for it," Quinn cried and donned a grey tweed smoking jacket as he spoke. "The back way, Silk. The car is parked at the usual place."

"But you, sir?" Silk protested.

"I'm going to have company. Lieutenant McGrath is coming to call. Now will you hurry?"

Silk was out the back door as the front doorbell buzzed. Quinn quieted his nerves, picked up his cane and slowly tapped his way to the door. He opened it and his attitude was one of expectancy.

"Yes? You'll have to announce yourself. I'm blind."

McGrath narrowed his eyes. "I'm a detective lieutenant—sent here by the Commissioner. May I come in?"

Quinn moved aside and indicated the direction of the study with his cane. "Certainly, Lieutenant. I suppose your visit is about the armored car guards who were found dead at the Triton Garage. I talked to Commissioner Warner about five or ten minutes ago concerning them."

McGRATH STOPPED in his tracks and Quinn, fumbling his way along, bumped into him head on. "Oh—I'm terribly sorry," he apologized.

"Wait a minute." McGrath gripped Quinn's arm. "Did you say you talked to Warner ten minutes ago?"

Quinn nodded assent. "Is there anything so peculiar in that? I phoned him fully fifteen minutes ago and he called right back with the information I wanted."

McGrath walked over to the phone and got the Commissioner on the wire. Full confirmation of Quinn's statement was followed by an irate order from Warner.

"McGrath, you fool, if you pester Quinn, I'll have you broken. You're going a little mad with this idea of the Black Bat. Listen to me now—never mind talking. You talk too much anyway. I thought Quinn was The Bat myself, but I changed my mind. You change yours, do you hear?"

"Yes, sir," McGrath gulped. "But you can't blame a guy for thinking. This Bat is clever and so is—the other person we referred to. The Bat acts just the way I'd expect this other man to act and they are precisely the same build. I'm wrong though and I admit it. He simply couldn't have been at the Triton and reached this house fifteen minutes ago. Sorry, Commissioner."

Quinn was staring somewhat to McGrath's left. "I really don't get the gist of all this," he complained in the annoyed tone of a blind man, helpless to determine things for himself.

"It doesn't concern you, Mr. Quinn," McGrath said in an abashed voice. "All I wanted was to phone the Commissioner from some place where I knew my words wouldn't be overheard by anyone we couldn't trust. Thanks for the use of the phone."

"Not at all," Quinn followed him to the door. "I have few callers and I'm even delighted to see you, Lieutenant."

McGrath didn't grasp the significance of the remark until he was in his car. Then he snapped off the tip of a cigar so violently that he tore the wrapper. He hurled the cigar away and swore vigorously.

Quinn made his slow way back to the study and sat down. For fully twenty minutes he remained immovable. Then he arose and stood, apparently looking at nothing, but in reality he studied each window. If anyone lurked in the darkness outside, he could have seen them. Certain he was unobserved, Quinn moved toward the fireplace and entered the small laboratory he had constructed behind it with his own hands.

He went to work swiftly now. First he took the blood-stained handkerchief from his pocket, put the stain into a solution and divided the fluid into five equal parts. Methodically he tested each portion with reagents. In the third test tube he obtained a precipitate and he set it down, satisfied.

"The armored car guards were killed with cyanogen gas," he told himself. "Somehow it was administered to them very effectively and in a well enclosed area where it could work so fast they had no time either to draw guns or call out."

HE TOOK the time to reload his guns before he removed his jacket and revealed the somber garb of The Bat. This time he was forced to use one of his own cars, but he took the precaution of removing the marker plates and substituting ones stolen by Silk. All this took time that he hated to lose. For one thing, he knew that Silk had accepted his silence as consent and stopped to pick up Carol. Silk might run into almost any kind of high danger at the Ajax Garage if it was infested with Snate's rats. Mentally Quinn damned McGrath and his suspicions.

He drove slowly out of the garage, turned up the street in front of his house and made certain McGrath had placed no shadowers on his trail. Then he opened the car wide and roared north toward the Ajax Garage.

It was early morning now and it was easier for him to prowl unrecognized, yet he took no chances. He parked the car and walked briskly along until he reached the entrance to the garage. He looked vainly for signs of Silk's car. Something gleamed brilliantly in the gutter. He picked it up and for the first time since he had gone blind, Quinn felt the full pangs of fear.

What he had picked up was a vanity and on its cover were emblazoned Carol's initials!

Butch was gone—kidnapped by Snate's men! Carol and Silk had disappeared as mysteriously and thoroughly as those vanished armored cars. The Bat was stymied completely. There seemed to be no way in which to turn. Snate would be clever enough now to shift his headquarters and there was no doubt that he had several other hideouts.

CHAPTER XVI

THREE PRISONERS

CAROL AND Silk parked half a block from the entrance to the Ajax Garage.

"The orders were explicit," Silk lied honorably. "This is a job for one person, Miss Carol. Two of us would make too much noise. You will have to remain in the car. Keep the motor going in case I make a hasty exit. I don't know what I'm going to find in this garage, but since The Bat has sent me, I'm sure there must be something of consequence."

"But I'm only being a chauffeur," Carol protested. "I want an active part in this work. It is as much my fight as it is The Bat's. I even dyed my hair again."

Silk was agreeable to the idea, but Silk was also smooth. "Supposing you went into the garage and were accosted? What would a girl be doing in a garage at almost midnight? No, Miss Carol, it's my job alone."

He smiled at her, straightened his cutaway and drew himself up pompously. He marched straight into the garage, spotted an attendant who looked more like a ruthless killer than a mechanic and walked up to him.

"I," Silk announced, "am Professor Calkins of the University. My car has broken down several blocks away. I want a wrecker and prompt service for which I will readily pay—"

"Go away," the pseudo-mechanic growled. "We're full up and we don't work nights."

"But I'm in trouble," Silk went on.

"Will you beat it?" the thug barked. "Or do I heave you out on your ear?"

"That," Silk said angrily, "is quite enough. I'll see about this matter later on. Good night!"

He walked toward the door, glanced over his shoulder and saw the thug sauntering toward the ramp. Silk stepped quietly into a small office and crouched there, waiting. After five minutes he emerged again, scurried across the wide garage until he reached the base of the ramp. He crept up this very cautiously and halfway to the top paused long enough to remove a gun from a hip holster.

He heard someone descending and he ducked into the second floor where he knelt behind a car in dead storage. The thug who had received him was hurrying down the ramp with two men in tow. Silk smiled grimly. The gang was holed up somewhere on either of the two floors above. It took him fifteen minutes to investigate the third floor and be certain there were no concealed rooms. On the fourth he stood gazing thoughtfully at the east wall. There was one corner which ended too abruptly and left a considerable space unaccounted for. Unless one looked for a hidden portion of the garage, it would hardly have been noticed, but Silk's eyes and wits were sharp.

He tiptoed to the farther wall and gradually approached this cubicle in the corner. He knew that Carol would be growing both impatient and worried, but Silk dared not hurry his movements. There was too much at stake now.

WITH HIS back flat against the wall he put an ear to the cubicle and listened intently. No sound reached him. He studied the blank wall again and smiled tightly as he saw minute cracks in the shape of a narrow door. Gun ready, he moved toward it. Somehow Silk had a hunch this was too easy. A mob like Snate's would naturally have alarms set, yet he saw no trace of them.

There was a box-like arrangement about waist high on the wall. Silk had passed it already. He stopped abruptly and squinted in the faint light to make out a similar box-like arrangement on a pillar directly opposite. He knew what it meant. He had passed through an invisible ray of light and set off an alarm.

He was in for it now and wisdom told him a quick retreat was in order. He started for the ramp.

"Hold it!" a harsh voice snapped. "One more step and I'll bury lead in your back."

Silk sighed, dropped his gun and raised his hands. He turned around and saw two thugs approach him. One held a sub-machine gun at a ready angle. He was done this time. There was no bucking one of those fast shooting babies.

The second thug drew a heavy pistol, clubbed it and moved in rapidly. The gun butt swung twice and Silk hit the floor with a thump. The lights spun in a galaxy of motion until unconsciousness swept him into temporary oblivion.

Two more men came running up the ramp. The pseudo-mechanic indicated Silk.

"That's him—he called hisself a Professor. I thought he was a phoney. Joe says there ain't no crippled car within ten blocks. But there is a buggy down the street with a girl in it."

"Okay. Bring 'er in."

The thug moved Silk's limp body with his foot and then grinned.

"We got something this time. I'm betting my share in the last armored car job that this guy is The Bat. Put him in the bus. We'll grab the girl—she must be in on this or she wouldn't be hanging around—and scram before somebody else shows."

Carol saw nothing suspicious in the two men who sauntered up the street. They separated just before they reached her car, one crossing the street. The other walked directly toward her and as he drew opposite the car, he sprang for the door. Carol quickly snapped the lock on the door, but while her attentions were centered on this man, the second had approached quietly. He yanked open the door, clapped a huge paw over her mouth and threw her into the rear seat. He climbed over himself and held her so that she could neither move nor scream.

The car pulled away from the curb, slowed as it approached the garage and allowed another sedan to precede it. Then both cars were off. In the first, Silk lay stunned into insensibility. In the second, Carol fought vainly against a strength five times her own.

Silk listened intently.

Her eyes were covered by a handkerchief after a few moments and the thug at her side gave a growled warning.

"I can't hang onto a wildcat like you forever, so unless you are good, I'll knock you stiff."

CAROL KNEW he meant it and estimated that her chances of escape were far better if she remained conscious. She gave her assent with a nod of her head. The thug let go of her, but he kept his right fist curled and ready to swing if she attempted to reach the door of the speeding car.

"You're making a mistake," she said. "I'm not worth kidnapping. Nobody cares enough about me to pay any ransom—even if my friends could raise the money."

"Now listen, baby," the thug smiled crookedly, "don't stall with me. You're workin' for The Bat and we know it. So just be nice and quiet because I'm tellin' you I wouldn't care if I slugged you so hard you'd never wake up."

Carol made no reply. She didn't attempt to move the handkerchief around her eyes for she sensed such an action would bring a prompt reprisal. She tried, instead, to visualize the path of the car, but she had started this angle too late. Carol hadn't the slightest idea of where she was.

An hour later the car rolled over gravel and came to a crunching stop. Carol was helped out, firmly gripped by the forearm and propelled into a house. Then the bandage was yanked from her eyes. She saw two things simultaneously. Silk, who was sprawled, half dazed, in a big chair—and Snate, who regarded her with a contemptuous sneer.

She paid no attention to Snate, but hurried to Silk's side. "Are you hurt?" she asked.

"Who," Silk asked with a quick wink, "could hurt The Bat?"

Carol grasped the situation at once. Snate thought Silk was The Bat. So long as he assumed that, Quinn would have a good chance to prowl.

"I—I never thought they'd get you," she said slowly.

"That's enough gab," Snate barked. "Take the man into the next room and leave him there. I'm going to have a little talk with this dame. Maybe she can tell me a few things I'm curious to know."

Silk put up no fight as he was led into a room that was plunged in pitch darkness. He was thrown into a chair about five feet from a small table. Silk barely made out the lines of the furniture in the room. He settled back to think.

He had awakened from his coma half way to this place and overheard the men talking of their great capture of The Bat. At once Silk decided to act out the part. Snate would be less on guard if he believed The Bat was dispensed with. The thought that Snate might work fast and murder the man he believed responsible for his troubles, occurred to Silk, but he dismissed it with a shrug. Tony Quinn was in this game wagering his life against the outcome. Then why shouldn't The Bat's right hand man take the same attitude?

Minutes passed and Silk worried about Carol, worried about Butch and The Bat also. Suddenly the lights were turned on. Snate entered with a swagger and a malicious grin. For the first time Silk noticed that an automatic had been lying on the small table, almost within reach of his right hand. Snate picked it up.

"YOU," HE announced triumphantly, "are a cock-eyed liar. You're not The Black Bat because if you were, you'd have grabbed that gun long ago. I know The Bat can see in the dark—you can't. Now—either you talk or I'll have the boys pistol whip you until your face is ribbons. Who are you? Where is The Bat and who is he?"

Silk's lips compressed themselves into a thin line. Defeat made him more bitter than hopeless. He should have suspected something of this kind when he was left apparently alone in a pitch dark room.

"Now listen," Snate went on. "You think you're a tough guy. Well, so am I. You'll tell us how to contact The Bat or—I'll have the boys work on you and I'll personally put a slug in that dame's skull. Which is it?"

Silk's eyes flashed around the room. There was no doubt in his mind but that Snate was telling the truth and he was fully capable of carrying out his vicious threats.

There was nothing to do but stall—and hope.

"You win," Silk said. "But I can't tell you how to contact The Bat because I don't know how myself. He contacts me. The girl also. He's no fool, Snate. He knows we were always in danger of being captured and he knows your methods of making people talk too. If we don't know any thing, we can't talk, can we?"

"There's a way for you to reach him," Snate thundered. "How?"

Silk heaved a mock sigh of resignation. "Okay—I'm licked. His instructions were to write a letter to the *News-Record* and he'd come to whatever place I designated."

Snate showed smug satisfaction.

"He'll come, all right, because he won't get a letter from you, wise guy. It'll be from me—and if he don't show, you and the dame get knocked off. I'll prove both of you are here by sending him a little token. This time The Bat is done. He's a sap—like cops and all guys who call themselves 'right.' He'll give up his life to save yours and the girl's. That's what he'll think. And when he finds out what he's got himself into—well, now, won't that be just too bad!" Snate, sneered.

Silk glared at him wordlessly.

CHAPTER XVII

THE TRUCK DOUBLE

THE BAT didn't wait to puzzle out his next move. He swung into action at once. Stowing the broken vanity case into his pocket, he stepped into an alley, slipped his hood into place and made his way to the back of the big garage. There was a small door at the rear and it gave way to his tools. Inside he heard no sound and no one lurked in the darkness waiting to pounce on him.

His sensitive eyes saw a folded piece of paper lying in the middle of the floor. He estimated the chances of its being a trap, rejected the idea when his abnormally keen sense of hearing detected no sounds of the breathing of men who might lie in wait. The garage was empty and The Bat knew it.

He picked up the object, found that it was a newspaper and spread the sheet wide open. He looked at the date line, the paper's masthead and the edition. It was a copy of Gage's *News-Record* and this particular edition wasn't due to be released to the newsstands for almost half an hour yet. The print itself was still moist!

The Bat's eyes narrowed beneath his hood. He selected the first likely looking car in the garage, started the motor and shot out to the street. It didn't take long to reach Gage's newspaper building, but the main difficulty now lay in securing admittance without being seen.

He found, after a full half hour's prowling, a small elevator that ran directly up to where he knew Gage's offices to be. The Bat stepped into the lift and sent it moving upwards. It stopped automatically and without making a sound. The doors parted in the middle and they were very well oiled. He opened them a crack and looked into Gage's private office.

Gage was sitting behind his desk, feet propped up on the edge. Otto Fox was pacing the floor, hands clasped behind his back, chin resting against his chest.

"I tell you Stewart is the man," Fox stated with finality. "He must be. No one else could have known where that armored truck was being dispatched. He sealed those orders."

"But Stewart insists he told no one. He left the orders in your office," Gage argued. "And he'd be a complete fool if he was responsible for the truck's disappearance. The blame was certain to be shoved right down his throat."

"That's just it," Fox put in irritably. "He's smart enough to realize that a vast amount of suspicion also creates doubts as to its authenticity. He hopes that no one would believe he could possibly be foolish enough to go ahead with his plans after he was made solely responsible for the safety of the truck. Did you know, Gage, that the truck carried an extra heavy load this afternoon? One bank shipped two hundred and fifty thousand dollars in notes of hundred dollar denomination. The rest of it brought the total up to almost half a million."

Gage whistled in astonishment. "I didn't know that, but it still makes little difference to my way of thinking. Oh, I realize that even Commissioner Warner suspects Stewart. It is true that plenty of mugs slipped through his fingers from the various prisons of this state. It's true that he may not have tried to prevent this, but he has his side also. He insists he did try to stop it and was powerless."

FOX RUMPLED his thinning hair. "Then in heaven's name, who is it? You, Gage? Or me? That's silly, of course. I stand to lose more than anyone from these damned thefts. In fact my business is completely ruined. And you—what interest could you have in piling up money when you've more than enough now?"

Gage nodded. "I see your point. Say—that suit of yours is soiled—did you know it?"

Fox dabbed at some black spots near the right coat pocket.

"Damn the suit," he raged. "What's a suit compared to the losses the banks and insurance companies are suffering? And mark me, Gage, this isn't the finish. I can sense greater and more atrocious crimes ready to burst wide open. Something must be done and I'm going to suggest that Stewart be arrested."

He banged the door on his way out. Gage sat immobile for a moment or two. Then he furtively looked around the office, reached for the lower drawer in his desk and pulled out a heavy manila envelope. He dumped the contents on the desk top and The Bat, who watched every move, gave an almost audible gasp.

That manila envelope had contained a necklace of emeralds and jade. Nothing extremely expensive or particularly significant to one who did not know, but The Bat had last seen the necklace around Carol Baldwin's lovely throat!

He drew a gun, parted the elevator doors and stepped into the office. "Keep your hands on the desk," he ordered brusquely. Then he moved to the doors and locked them from the inside. "Gage—where did you get that necklace?"

"The Black Bat!" Gage drew a sharp breath. "I—I'm glad you came. I—I was trying to formulate a plan to reach you without actually advertising for you."

"Why?" The Bat asked.

Gage shoved the necklace and the envelops across the desk. "You don't have to keep that gun pointed at me. I'm your friend—I hope. Anyway, I've tried to work with the police on this cast and I've fought Snate to a standstill. That proves I'm on your side."

"It proves nothing," The Bat snapped. He scooped up the necklace, jammed it into his pocket and then extracted a letter from the envelope. He read this, but his eyes also watched Gage. The note was very brief.

> "The Black Bat: Either you show up before morning at the last house down Strawberry Lane or two people will croak—slow. Stay away or bring the cops and you'll see how we do it."

There was no signature and the note had been typewritten. The Bat felt the texture of the notepaper by gently rubbing it between his fingers and then picked up similar looking sheets from Gage's desk. His sensitive touch told him the paper was of the same quality. He held both sheets to the light. They were similarly watermarked.

"Get up!" he ordered Gage. "Walk over against that wall where I can watch you while I experiment a bit."

GAGE OBEYED and The Bat sat down at a typewriter—the only one in the office. With one hand he copied the note from Snate's mob. It took him but a moment to compare some of the printed letters. There was no question in his mind now. This note had been typed on Gage's own paper and on Gage's own machine.

"How did you get this letter?" he demanded.

Gage shrugged. "I can tell by the way you're acting that you believe I wrote the letter. I didn't! I was called out about an hour ago. Someone wanted to see me about an exclusive story he wouldn't trust a regular reporter with. Of course I went—and was tricked. Nobody met me. When I returned, the letter was lying on my desk."

"Not a very convincing story, Gage. In fact it smells to high heaven. You've read this—written it too—unless I miss my guess. Two of my people are being held prisoners. They must have been forced to state how their captors could get in touch with me. I have no arrangements made for such an emergency and certainly if I had, it wouldn't be through the medium of a newspaper. Do you think I want my business blasted over every front page in the country? Those people of mine never talked because they had nothing to say. You wrote this letter to me, placed it on your own desk and pretended you found it there."

"I told the truth," Gage said. "So help me."

The Bat's hand moved to his pocket and threw the newspaper he had found in the Ajax Garage upon Gage's desk.

"That edition of your paper—when did it come off the presses?"

Gage glanced at the edition banner. "About three quarters of an hour ago. You must have got that somewhere in the plant. That edition hasn't been distributed yet."

"That's what I thought." The Bat picked up the paper again. "Stay just where you are, Gage. I may change my mind about you—I hope so—because I've admired the way you've fought Snate, but if you send out any alarm for me, I'll shoot. That's a warning."

He stepped back into the lift and sent it down. At the bottom he listened a moment. Gage certainly wasn't creating a rumpus. The Bat smiled a little and ran to the spot where he had parked his car. He stripped off his hood before he reached the street and made his way back to his home without detection.

There he sat down, glanced at a clock and saw that he had but a few hours to deadline. At dawn Snate would murder Silk and Carol. Butch hadn't been mentioned in the letter, therefore Snate didn't know that Butch also was a member of The Bat's ring.

He took out the necklace, laid it on the table and his nostrils twitched for it smelled faintly of the perfume that Carol used. Then he looked startled. The necklace was composed of large and small beads. As he recalled it, they were systematically strung, first a large bead and then a small bead. Now their positions were changed. Several small beads and then a larger one, followed time after time by similar arrangements and between each set a firm knot.

He gasped as he realized their true significance. The small beads represented dots, the large ones dashes and the knots the end of a word. Carol had restrung her necklace so that it spelled a message in code.

QUINN CHARGED into his library, found a book on codes and hurried to decipher her message. Gradually his pencil marked out letters until a sentence was created.

AJAX TONIGHT
LOOT HIDDEN THERE

Quinn was up and out of the house within a minute. It was clear that Carol had heard Snate's men talking and knew that they intended to remove the hidden loot from the Ajax Garage before morning. It was likewise certain they would bring their treasure to the same hideout where Carol, Silk and Butch were held prisoners. Carol was telling him in the only way she knew how that the trail was still wide open.

He drove his car into an alley, donned his hood and proceeded to make his way to the big garage. Lurking in the darkness outside, he saw a car pull up before the closed doors and stop. A man got out and entered the garage through a small door set in the huge roller type one. He emerged after a few moments and walked down the street. The Bat maneuvered his way to the parked car, crawled into the tonneau and crouched there, hard against the back of the front seat.

As he had expected and hoped, a mechanic emerged after a few moments and drove the car into the garage, up the ramp to the third floor and left it there. The Bat got out, listened intently for a few moments and then began his prowl.

A cold horror possessed him, for if he was too late and the loot had already been removed, his chances of reaching Carol and Silk were practically ruined. To obey the orders of that note meant instant death, for Snate's men would be lying in wait, ready to blast the life out of him at the first opportunity. The Bat could do them no good alive and they had suffered enough humiliating experiences at his hands already not to withhold their fire when the chance to exterminate him arose.

There was nothing on the third floor and The Bat was torn between the problem of searching the second or fourth floor first. He decided to go higher and climbed the ramp to the top. A weak light cast a yellowish shadow of light over the parked cars. The third floor had not been lighted. To The Bat's mind this was significant. If men of Snate's mob were in the habit of coming here, they would need light enough to see their way between the cars.

As Silk had done, The Bat carefully studied the architecture of the place. He spotted the cubicle setting off one corner of the floor, remembered that the building itself presented a square appearance from the outside and knew that a secret room was located behind those jutting walls. But unlike Silk, The Bat moved warily. He saw the apparatus used to create an invisible beam of light and avoided it. His eyes, efficient as they were, quickly made out the lines of the hidden door. He approached it softly, guns ready.

Then he heard the whine of a motor in first gear. A car was coming up the ramp.

HE DUCKED hastily and watched a light delivery truck bearing the name "Campbell The Florist" on its panels, stop at the top of the ramp. Two men alighted, leaving the cab doors open. The Bat watched them rap smartly against the hidden door, saw it open and they vanished inside. Before he could get into action, the two men emerged again, this time carrying heavy valises which they threw into the back of the truck. When they disappeared, The Bat made his catlike way to the truck. As he passed the front of it, he paused. There was a V-like crack in the window beside the wheel.

Instantly his mind clicked. He had seen that odd shaped crack before—on the window of the armored car that rolled out of the Triton Garage.

"A confounded jackass," he berated himself. "That's what I've been. An armored car window wouldn't be cracked. They're bullet proofed and they'd cobweb instead of cracking."

He hurried to the rear of the truck, opened the door and got inside. There he squatted, pursing his lips in a noiseless whistle of amazement. He had solved the mystery of the disappearing armored car. It was vividly clear to him now.

The real armored car had never left the Triton. Instead, this truck had rolled out, looking exactly like the armored car. It had turned into that dead end street and there it had undergone an astonishingly quick and efficient change. The truck was so constructed that the sides of the body could be literally turned inside out. What had looked like the formidable steel sides of an armored car became only the exterior of a florist's truck. No wonder the disappearance of Fox's armored cars had been so mysterious and complete.

For the inside, this florist delivery wagon was the counterpart of the outside of the vanished truck. It occurred to The Bat then, that the small cab was also the same color as the armored car. Undoubtedly provisions had been made to remove all identifying marks so that not the slightest trace remained to give any suspicion that this florist delivery wagon could possibly resemble anything like an armored car.

CHAPTER XVIII

THE BAT TAKES A RIDE

HEARING THE two men come out of the hidden room, The Bat lay prone on the bottom of the truck. Wisely, he had moved the valises of money to the far end of the vehicle so that when one of the thugs glanced in to see that it was safe, his eyes didn't wander far. The Bat was pressed against the panel separating the truck from the small cab. His black clothes merged with the darkness and he was unseen.

He remained in that position while the truck moved down the ramp, through the big garage doors and finally turned into the street, heading north. It traveled sedately along, obeying every traffic regulation even at this hour of the morning. The thugs were taking no chances on being stopped.

The driver turned sharply after half an hour of that and headed for the river. They were far uptown, where the estates of wealthy people formed the landscape of the river's bank. The truck turned into a driveway, rolled straight through the doors of a five car private garage and stopped. The Bat tensed now, for what happened from this moment on depended solely upon his prowess.

He softly opened the rear door, stepped out and made a nosedive from the garage to behind a hedge that bordered a path leading to the big house.

"Hey!" one of the thugs whispered softly, "the rear door of the truck is open. You damned nit-wit, we might have spilled all that dough out in the road."

"I closed it," the second man snapped. "And what's more, I think I heard a funny noise just now, like somebody runnin'. What if it's the—Black Bat? I wouldn't want to meet that guy now. Not after the boss snatched his pals. Between you and me, that guy's scared me outa this racket. I'm ready to pull my freight the second I'm handed my cut."

"Me too," the other man agreed. "Remember what he did at the boss's other hideout? He killed three men and wounded three others. That bird can shoot like he's got telescope lenses in his eyes. I ain't afraid of the cops—not any part of 'em—but this Black Bat—I don't like him at all."

Each man picked up a valise and walked quickly toward the back door of the mansion, as though they feared the darkness. The Bat followed along, slightly behind them and well protected by the hedge.

"But what we got to be afraid of?" one of them assured himself. "The Bat ain't gonna let the boss polish off his pals. He'll give himself up—wait and see. He's that kind of a guy."

"Yeah—he'll give himself up," the other snorted, "with a couple of spitting roscoes in his mitts. If that guy shows, I blow, cut or no cut. And I got a funny feelin' about him—like he ain't licked yet."

They looked up as the rear porch light was snapped on. The Bat, crouched in the darkness, saw Snate himself step out to greet the men. But the greeting wasn't pleasant.

"Where you tramps been? We got work to do and you mugs hold up the parade. Get that stuff inside and count it. And no chiseling. I know just how much is in that haul. Leave them hundred dollar bills alone, hear me? Take just one and I'll know it. Now scram!"

THE DOOR closed and darkness surrounded The Bat again. He lost no time now. The house was provided with a cellar hatchway through which entrance was gained by opening a set of slanting doors. There was a huge padlock closed by some competent looking brass staples. The Bat drew out his kit of tools, selected a pair of small but very sharp cutting pliers, and in half a minute the hasps were cut. He opened the hatchway doors very gently lest they squeak.

Closing them over his head, he knelt beside another door barring the entrance to the cellar itself. This door was also well sealed, but he forced his way through it quickly.

There were no lights on in the cellar, but that hindered The Bat not at all. He avoided empty ash cans that were strategically placed around the cellar floor in what seemed to be an arrangement indicative of a crude alarm system.

Then The Bat hesitated. To his exceptionally keen ears came the sound of steady scraping, like the claws of a giant rat digging its way through cement and stone. He traced the origin of the sound and was confronted by a solid steel door with only a small closed trap set high in the center of it. Someone was behind that door, someone who was evidently a prisoner. The scraping was very clear now.

The Bat's hopes mounted high. Could this be Carol and Silk trying to dig their way out? Was his mission to be accomplished so easily? The Bat tapped on the steel panels.

"Who is it?" The voice came from within and to ordinary ears would never have been distinguishable.

"Butch," the Bat whispered. He knew the imprisoned man couldn't hear him and the word came involuntarily. He heard Butch yelling inside, but The Bat was at work. He examined the lock and groaned. It was practically pick-proof and no key that he possessed would fit it. He stood erect and tried the little trap door set in the steel. It opened by pressing a spring latch.

"The Bat!" Butch was peering out. "I can see the outlines of your hood. Boy, you didn't come too soon. Those babies are getting ready to knock me off."

"I can't open this door," The Bat whispered. "There isn't time enough for that. Take this gun and use it if I'm not around when they come for you. Silk and Carol are prisoners in this house too."

"So that's who it is," Butch gasped. "I heard the mugs talkin' about two more saps they're gonna experiment on. I'm first and I know what they mean. It's a poison gas they use on the armored cars—to kill the men inside. Thanks for the gat. Will I polish off them babies when they show!"

Someone walked across the floor upstairs and The Bat quickly closed the small door, scurried through the cellar and merged with the inky darkness behind the staircase leading to the first floor. A weak electric light bulb turned on.

A door opened and three men came down, talking audibly. One said, "You handle the stop watch, Rocky. I'll heave the bomb through the little door and Ted watches the guy croak. You sure that gas mask is okay, Ted? If It ain't, you'll hear the angels singin'."

"IT'S OKAY," a muffled voice came from behind a gas mask. The three men strode toward the steel behind which Butch waited eagerly. He didn't know that there wasn't a chance for him. He'd have no opportunity to shoot before that tiny bomb of deadly gas would smash against the floor at his feet.

The thug with the stop watch carefully set the hands, nodded and a second man opened a small wooden box, removed the tiny glass bomb packed in cotton and carefully held it between two fingers. He took a step toward the door and stopped—very quickly.

"The first one of you who makes a sound will die," The Bat stood directly behind them, a gun covering the trio. "You have the keys to that door. Open it!"

The thug with the gas bomb turned slowly and his jaw sagged. He gasped, "The Black Bat!" Then he realized the import of that small bomb he held. "No you don't, Bat. This little thing I got in my hand will kill you in one minute flat. Put down that rod or I'll throw it."

"And kill yourself?" The Bat asked contemptuously. "If you have that much nerve, go ahead and throw it. You'll die during that same minute too."

"D-don't throw it," the crook with the stop watch quavered. "He's right. That gas will polish off all of us."

"Open the door," The Bat warned. "And do it quietly. Not another sound out of any of you."

One of them drew out the key, inserted it in the lock and swung the door wide. Butch, looking up like some monstrous shadow, emerged, blinking his eyes against the weak yellow light from a single overhead bulb. He held The Bat's gun in his fist and started for the trio of crooks aggressively.

"No," The Bat hissed. "There is no time for that. You three men get into the cell. See how you like being cooped up in darkness for awhile."

They obeyed, but as they marched through the door, The Bat's extraordinary ears picked up a few words of a mumbled conversation. The thugs seemed almost willing to obey him, but as the last one stepped well into the cell, he swung around suddenly and drew back his right hand.

"See if you can scare this," he howled and the glass bomb started its fatal flight through the air.

But The Bat was prepared for this. With his foot he gave the iron door a quick shove and it slammed shut. The glass bomb struck it, burst and the thugs inside screamed in terror. They fought for possession of the one gas mask. Those screams died away within a single minute.

"They asked for it," The Bat told Butch in a whisper. "Now to get Carol and Silk out of this place. Walk softly, Butch. We don't know how many are upstairs."

"But I got lots to tell you," Butch gripped The Bat's arm. "I know how them armored cars disappeared. I was gonna tell you back in that garage, but things happened too fast."

"I know how they vanished. Follow me, Butch, and you'd better remove your shoes. They squeak."

BUTCH OBEYED quickly and they stole up the stairs, paused at the door while The Bat listened and then he gave the signal to proceed. He opened the door a crack and looked into a spacious kitchen. No one was in sight, but some kind of a stew bubbled aromatically on an electric range.

"Remain at the back door!" The Bat ordered. "Open it quietly and be ready for a quick getaway! Don't use your gun unless absolutely necessary."

"Right," Butch replied. "I'll just bust their necks with my bare hands."

The Bat swung open the door leading into a serving pantry and peered through a small serving window. He looked out into a handsomely furnished dining room. Now voices came quite clearly and one of them was Snate's hoarse bellow.

"We're all set," he gloated. "Before dawn The Bat walks down that road to Strawberry Lane. He won't think anything will happen until he reaches the house I told him to enter, but he'll get his belly full of lead before he even gets within a quarter of a mile of that place. There are four guys waiting—with sawed off shot guns. They can't miss him."

"Gosh, boss," another man breathed in admiration, "you're a smart guy."

"Sure I am," Snate patted himself on the back with words. "Don't the papers play me up big? Listen, the other day I saw a bunch of kids playing cops and robbers. The cops were getting the worst of it and gave up to the crooks. What do you think the leader of them kid crooks called himself? Oliver Snate! Ain't that somethin'?"

The Bat's eyes grew hard and his lips compressed firmly. It was something! The glory that the press had placed over Snate's head was bearing fruit. Snate was becoming something of an idol to the boys who lived in the slums.

Snate spoke again. "Joey—you better go up and see how them two birds are getting along. I ain't heard a squawk out of the man in an hour and before that he yelled his head off until I slugged him."

"Gonna give them two the works, boss?" someone asked eagerly. "The dame too?"

Snate emitted a sigh. "Sure. She's tied up with the Black Bat, that dame, so she's poison, even if she is a looker. Both of 'em get the gas—just as soon as the boys report in that The Bat has been blown in half."

One man emerged from a room opposite the dining hall. He scampered up a flight of stairs. The Bat set his finger firmly against the trigger of his gun and edged his way along the wall until he reached the hallway.

If Snate or one of his men happened to come out while he went up the steps, it would be all over.

But luck was on The Bat's side now. He reached the staircase without detection, went up the steps three at a time as noiselessly as though he were a ghost. There was a long corridor at the head of the stairs and The Bat was just in time to see a man backing out of a room. The man closed the door, locked it and started for the stairs.

SUDDENLY HIS face drained of color and his hands shot high above his head.

"Go back in there," The Bat hissed, "and don't make a sound."

The thug's knees quaked, his lips moved in terror and his eyes bulged. This hooded figure in somber black was the very essence of defeat and death to him. He made no attempt at tricks.

Carol, tied to a chair in the middle of the room, strained against her bonds and at the gag that was inserted between her lips. Silk lay in a corner savagely trying to extricate himself from the folds of several strong leather straps that pinned him with cruel tightness. He rolled over, saw The Bat and actually shivered in delight.

"Untie them," The Bat whispered to his prisoner. "Work fast if you want to live."

The thug freed Carol first and she hurried to the protection of The Bat's free arm. He held her closely and whispered, "Don't talk. Don't move unless necessary."

Silk stood erect in a moment. His disguise was still intact, but he looked badly worn. There was an ugly gash on his temple near the hairline and a bruise discolored one eye. But Silk remained riveted to the spot. He knew that undue walking could be heard downstairs. The Bat nodded in approval. He stepped up to the thug, indicated that he was to turn around, and then smashed down with his gun butt. Silk caught the man before he hit the floor. He eased him down so that no noise was created.

"The window," The Bat whispered. "Out that way."

Carol shook her head. "Barred," her lips formed the word.

"Then follow me," The Bat hissed. "The slightest sound will give away the party. If anything happens, run for the kitchen. Butch is there—waiting."

They both nodded mutely and The Bat led the way to the head of the staircase. There he stopped and signaled the others to stand back. A man was coming up.

He reached the top, turned right and a hand suddenly clapped across his mouth. At the same moment a fist slugged him under the chin, snapping his head back. He went limp. Silk laid him down gently and The Bat nursed bruised knuckles. Silk hastily searched the man and stood up with a gun proudly flashing in his fist.

"You first," The Bat whispered to Carol. "Go straight to the kitchen. We'll cover you."

She hesitated, as though she didn't want to obey the order. The Bat jerked his head toward the steps and she went down slowly and softly. She reached the bottom, turned toward the dining room—and then all hell broke loose!

One of Snate's men glanced out of the library and saw her. He shouted a warning and jumped for the girl. The Bat's automatic slammed once and the bullet found a vulnerable mark. The thug dropped in his tracks.

"You next," The Bat told Silk, "I'll cover you."

"Sorry, sir," Silk said quietly. "You're more important than I."

"Get on with you," The Bat snapped. "Hurry!"

SILK COULD do nothing but obey.

He poised at the top of the steps and then launched himself down them at a terrific speed. A crook loomed up in the doorway of the library. The Bat fired and he drew back with a curse. Silk was getting ready to run for it, exposing himself to the gun fire from inside the library. It was a risky business, but he never hesitated a moment. As he went into the lurch that carried him past the range of gun fire, The Bat's automatic blasted seven fast shots. Silk made it safely.

The Bat whirled, streaked for the nearest room and scooped up a chair as he crossed it. He could hear the thugs running up the steps. He swung the chair against the window, smashed it and shattered the remaining glass with the flat of his gun. He turned toward the doorway and pulled the trigger to send a warning shot out. The gun clicked. There were no more bullets in the magazine and no time to insert a fresh clip.

He was on the second floor and the drop was dangerously high. If he miscalculated, there would be at least a broken leg and now the slightest delay meant instant death whether it was within the house or just outside it.

Suddenly a blast of firing sounded. Men screamed and the shooting increased as new guns added to the din. Downstairs, Butch and Silk were firing rapidly. The Bat wormed his way through the window, hung by his finger-tips a moment and then let go. He landed in a clump of bushes that scratched him, ripped his clothes and knocked the wind out of him for a moment. Then someone helped him to his feet. It was Carol.

"I have a car ready," she whispered tensely. "Oh—if only Silk and Butch make it!"

They did. Both of them appeared a moment later. Carol signaled by blinking the lights of the car she had rolled out of the garage. They jumped in and The Bat, who was at the wheel, sent the sedan rolling at top speed in second gear, toward the road in front of the house.

As he turned into the street, he saw a man running madly from the front porch. There was a coupé parked at the curb and he ran directly across the range of the headlights.

"Stewart!" Silk gasped. "He must have been in there!"

"Never mind him now," The Bat said hoarsely. He stripped off his hood with one hand. "Silk, load your gun and hand it to me. I'm going to stop this car soon. You take over and go straight back to the house. Straight back—understand?"

"We ain't gonna be in on no more fun?" Butch asked disappointedly.

"There's going to be plenty of it—later on. Right now I have a job that is a solo. Wait for me."

The Bat slowed, pulled into the curb and stopped. He climbed out, grinned a farewell and vanished into the darkness.

The Bat watched Silk, Butch and Carol disappear down the road. Then he made his way to an all night drug store and stepped into the phone booth. He dialed Commissioner Warner's home.

"I'm sorry to awaken you at this hour, Commissioner," he said cheerfully. "This is The Bat!"

HE HEARD Warner's quick gasp of astonishment and then went on talking. "If you want to help me solve the mystery of the vanished armored cars and trap Snate and his real master, there is one thing you must do immediately."

"Yes," Warner said softly. "Anything you say. But I warn you—no matter how much help you are in this case, if you're caught it's a cell and, perhaps, the electric chair for you."

The Bat chuckled. "Let me worry about that, Commissioner. Now phone headquarters and have cars sent for Otto Fox, Paul Stewart and Peter Gage. Have them taken to your office and hold them there for an hour and a half. Don't, under any circumstances, allow any one of them to use a phone, communicate with any person other than yourself, or leave your office. It's vitally important that they be held and yet not realize the fact."

"I'll do it," Warner agreed, "because I am so certain you are trying to help the side of the law—even if you smash every doggone law that's ever been enacted in so doing. They'll be with me until"—he glanced at a clock beside his bed—"three-forty."

"Just long enough," The Bat answered. "Lie like the devil to them and don't even mention my name. Before dawn you'll have Snate and his real master as well."

The Bat hung up, paused to check three addresses and made notes of them. Then he spent almost all the allotted time in making a very discreet search of three homes—those of the suspects whom Warner now had closeted in his office at headquarters. At the last one, The Bat found what he wanted, yet so quietly done were all his operations that no servants were awakened, nor the slightest alarm raised.

CHAPTER XIX

MASTER OF CRIME

IN THE mansion once more, Snate wiped the blood off a light wound along his left forearm. His face was a mask of intense hatred.

"Listen, all you guys," he snapped.

"Get out of here—fast. The cops will come like flies in a minute. We'll meet again—at the river hideaway. It's time for a split pretty soon, but I got to contact a guy I know to see if the land lies clear. Scram—all of you."

Snate himself beat a hasty retreat for the garage and piled into a coupé. He heard sirens in the distance and took the first road to the left. His anger was subsiding for he knew he was safe for the moment. Then Snate began to think seriously about all this. The Bat hadn't fallen for his trap, had in fact secured the release of his friends. To Snate it smacked of the near supernatural. How had The Bat ever discovered this hideout, so securely nestled among the estates of wealthy people? Besides seeing in utter darkness, did The Bat also possess some abnormal powers of magic? More and more Snate thought of dumping the whole business, taking his share of the loot and running for it.

In twelve years of law breaking he had never met a policeman he feared a fraction as much as he feared The Bat. It was time to clear out—with a whole skin and a fortune that would keep him for life.

Snate doubled back over several highways, crossed town twice and finally headed straight for the only remaining spot where he considered himself safe. It was a small, dilapidated dwelling in a poor section of the city. To this place Snate had transferred all his business, even to the contents of the vault. A smaller safe guarded the accumulation of loot now.

He drove his car into a ramshackle old shed at the rear of the place, entered cautiously, with a gun in his fist until he was satisfied that The Bat hadn't preceded him. Snate sped directly upstairs and opened another locked door. Inside the room was his big desk. He unlocked the lower drawer, removed the telephone secreted therein and picked up the receiver.

There was a click from the other end. "Chief," Snate breathed the word. "I got a lot of bad news. The Bat didn't fall for my little plan. He got away, damn him, and he took that dame and her pal along."

"You utter fool," the hissing voice of his master made Snate shiver. "I told you to be careful. The Bat won't stop now. We must get clear before he reaches us. We're ready for that anyway—after one more job is pulled. Your organization is breaking up fast, Snate. Three of your men have written affidavits exposing your whole setup."

"What?" Snate half screeched. "Tell me who the dirty rats are. Tell me where I can find them. I'll—"

"Silence," the voice rasped sternly. "I'm talking now. Here is what you must do—and without the slightest delay. Once, Snate, you were a safe cracker—a rotten one perhaps, but you can still open a box. You've got nitro, so take along a bottle of the stuff. Go to the offices numbered 501 in the Carlton Building. There you will find a small safe that should be simple to open. Inside it is the letter which the three traitors signed. Take that—and whatever else there is of value to give the job an appearance of being just routine burglary. Then get together every cent of cash we have. Have it as compact as possible and come to me. Do you hear that?"

"COME—TO—YOU?" SNATE asked doubtfully. "Ain't that dangerous?"

"Of course it is. Our whole business is dangerous. Are you becoming frightened, Snate? Are you turning rat too? Remember this—if you cross me, you'll die a slow, miserable death. We'll share that money between us. You've got to come here."

"Okay," Snate licked his lips. "I was going to suggest we let the boys cool their heels anyway. It took our brains to think up this racket and we ought to get all the profits."

"It took my brains, Snate," the voice hissed. "Now get busy. I'll be waiting here so don't delay."

Snate checked a heavy automatic to be certain it was loaded. Then he went to the vault, but hesitated before opening it. Somehow Snate didn't feel quite right about this business. Cheating his own men formed no part of his problem. It was The Bat who worried him. That hooded figure in black seemed to be everywhere at once. Snate was going to be glad when there were many miles between him and this city. He secreted a small electric diamond-pointed drill under his coat. That would be essential for the work at hand.

He spun the combination, opened the vault and quickly stowed the sacks of currency and the small boxes of gems into two huge suitcases. He locked these, slipped downstairs and out the back door. There were no neighbors and he was quite unobserved. He got into his car and headed back to town.

He parked it, directly outside the Carlton Building, locked it with some misgivings, for he might need a quick getaway. The cash inside the car convinced him the doors should be secured however. He sauntered toward the entrance to the building and found the big doors open. The lobby was dimly lighted.

He went up the stairs, disdaining the elevator lest its motor attract the watchman. Snate found 501 quickly and opened the door with a set of master keys. There was something written on the glass panel, but he paid no attention to it, since the hallway was in darkness and he dared not use a flashlight.

Closing the door softly, he moved across the small reception room. He drew his flashlight now, placed his hand over the lens and parted his fingers a trifle to emit only a slender beam of light. The only door he saw was marked "Private." He grinned sardonically, stepped into the main office and saw the safe.

"Cheese box," he muttered triumphantly and went to work. He drilled the holes with practiced skill, poured in his soup and covered the safe with rugs that he took from the floor. He set the fuse, lit it and then ran for cover. The explosion was well muffled—Snate knew his business. He crouched in the darkness waiting to see if the rumble attracted any attention. When no one came, he approached the safe, removed the carpets and threw the ray of his flash into the yawning box. There was no sign of an envelope, but he did see a neatly stacked wad of currency—all brand new. He flipped part of it through his fingers.

"Two hundred grand in five hundred dollar notes," he exulted. "To hell with the letter. I don't see it and I'll be miles away from here if it's ever found."

HE STUFFED the money under his shirt and tiptoed to the outer door. He stepped into the corridor, saw no one and reached the lobby without detection. He was gloating inwardly. Why tell the Chief about the haul? He'd simply say that the safe was empty. It never occurred to Snate that he might get away with all the loot. Memory of that hissing voice gave him no doubts as to the nature of the man who possessed it.

He inserted his key in the door of the car, had it partly open when a man moved into his range of vision. Snate's stomach took a bad turn. It was Detective Lieutenant McGrath and he looked as though he meant business.

"Snate—I want you," McGrath yelled.

But Snate plied into the car, tramped on the starter and was off. He raced madly along the deserted street and groaned when he spotted headlights in the mirror. He turned corners wildly, pushed the gas pedal to the floor along the avenues and finally there were no longer any signs of a pursuing car. He breathed in relief and pointed the hood of the car toward his real destination.

He stopped a block down the street, looked up and down carefully, and when he saw no one, dragged out the heavy valises and began running toward a brownstone front house.

He pressed the door bell and cursed his mentor for not being there to receive him. At any minute a patrolman might come along and grow suspicious at the sight of a man carrying two valises at this hour of the morning. Also there was a better than even chance that McGrath had sent out an alarm.

He heard burglar chains rattle, locks pulled back, and finally the door opened. Snate stepped in, set the bags down and mopped his forehead. His host stood in the darkness of the hallway, a gun in his hand.

"I almost didn't make it," Snate gasped. "We ain't got no time to lose, Chief. Lieutenant McGrath nearly nabbed me and he'll have the whole damned police force looking for me now. You all ready to blow?"

"Snate!"

The man who was his master no longer bothered with a disguised voice. The time for that was over. He had played safe only in case one of Snate's men might stumble on the phone and hear his voice. Now he surveyed Snate angrily.

"Have you gone crazy?"

"Me—crazy? Say—I just did what you told me. I opened that box easy, but there wasn't anything inside. I got all the dough from the last few jobs in these bags. You got the rest of it, ain't you?"

"Snate—what's this about? Who told you to come here?"

Snate's jaw fell. "You did."

"You fool. I've been home only a few moments. The Police Commissioner sent for me—with some trumped up excuse that held me in his office. I thought this might happen. It's the work of The Black Bat! Didn't you kill him?"

SNATE WRINKLED his face into questioning lines. "I told you he got away, didn't I? Listen—I'm not crazy. You asked me to come here with your own lips. I phoned—on the special wire—to get instructions. I—"

"I never talked to you, Snate! It's all up now! That was The Bat you talked to! There's but one thing to do. Run for it! Come upstairs—to my study. I'll get the rest of the swag, we'll divide it and travel."

Snate raced up the steps behind the man. In an elaborately furnished study, the real leader of Snate's men opened the valises, examined the contents quickly and then faced Snate angrily.

"You're holding out," he snapped. "There's something under your vest. It bulges. Come clean, Snate. You know better than to trick me."

Snate licked his lips. "I—I wasn't holding out, chief. It was like this, see? I opened the safe you told me about and found two hundred grand in there. So I copped it. Ain't that okay?"

"I didn't tell you about any safe, but if you have two hundred thousand dollars, it's quite all right. Let me see it."

Snate dumped the loot on top of the desk. He stepped away, waiting for further orders. Snate was ill at ease in the presence of this man. Somehow he reminded him of a snake—a crawling thing ready to strike a man in the back. Snate surreptitiously patted the gun under his armpit.

"Get my hat and coat from the rack in the corner," Snate's master ordered brusquely. "We're leaving at once."

Snate then made the greatest mistake of his life. He turned his back on a man he didn't trust. Snate was halfway toward the clothes rack when he sensed the danger. He swung around, but much too late. The man from whom he had taken orders, held a gun. It exploded and the bullet plowed through Snate's fat back, rasped against his spine and he spun around like a top gone wild. He plunged to the floor unconscious.

The man who had betrayed him smiled thinly, opened one of the valises and began hurling Snate's latest haul into it. He paused, gasped and held one of the packets of money under the light. It was banded and upon each band was the insignia of The Bat.

"Damn him," the Unknown almost shrieked. "I should have emptied my gun into his stomach so he'd die slowly. He even planted counterfeit money for Snate to steal."

He hurled the worthless money to the floor, closed the bag and picked up both of them. He raced down the steps, opened the front door and stopped.

METHODICALLY, AS though his life depended upon it, he counted twelve husky detectives and twelve sub-machine guns all pointed squarely at him. The valises thudded to the porch and he raised both hands. Commissioner Warner and Lieutenant McGrath seized his arms. Handcuffs clicked. Warner stepped back with a dubious shake of his head.

"Otto Fox—you very nearly got away with it."

As the cavalcade of police cars pulled away from Otto Fox's house and two ambulance orderlies carried out Snate, a shadowy form watching from a thick shrub across the street smiled contentedly.

CHAPTER XX

THE BAT EXPLAINS

QUINN, SILK, Butch and Carol sat around the fireplace. There was a peaceful, satisfied grin on Quinn's face.

"Thanks to Carol we finished up the case quickly," he said. "Sending your necklace in the form of a coded message saved the day."

Carol laughed. "It wasn't hard to convince Snate that you'd recognize my necklace. I overheard them talking about the Ajax Garage. And after all my part was so very small."

"Your part," Quinn reminded her, "began long ago—with the restoration of my sight. Now to get on with the story. You know how the armored cars vanished. The drivers are entombed in thick slabs of cement and dropped somewhere at sea. I'm reasonably certain of that because Snate maintained a launch that used to put out to sea quite frequently."

"But I don't see how you got wise to Otto Fox," Butch broke in. "I don't see nothing that shows he was the real big shot."

"There wasn't much," Quinn admitted. "I knew the brains behind Snate lay within the skull of one of three men. Stewart, Gage or Fox. Fox seemed to stand the greatest loss because his business was vanishing almost as fast as his armored cars, but—the loot he obtained more than repaid him. Fox tried to pin the guilt of Stewart with voiced suspicions and upon Gage by planted evidence.

"When his men captured you and Carol, Silk, he suspected you were friends of The Bat. Therefore he also believed that I'd begin looking for you by starting at the garage. Under ordinary circumstances he might have planted his men there to shoot me down, but it was more advantageous to plant evidence that might convict another person—Peter Gage.

"So when Fox slipped into Gage's private office after luring him away by a trick, he stole one of Gage's newspapers, not yet released. He dropped this in the garage. The ink was still wet, but Fox became careless there. He thrust that wet newspaper into his coat pocket. Later on I saw how the ink had stained the cloth. Gage noticed it also!"

He stopped and lit a cigarette before he went on. "I had Commissioner Warner get Fox, Gage and Stewart out of their respective homes. After they had gone, I slipped inside by committing a little fancy burglary. I looked for one thing—a private telephone on a private line that connected with Snate. I found this—in Fox's bedroom. Then fortunately, Snate phoned. I acted out the part of Fox and gave Snate some instructions which he followed to a tee.

"Snate broke into the offices of the United States District Attorney and robbed the safe of a number of counterfeit bills that were to be used as evidence against a crooked engraver. By so doing Snate violated federal laws. You see—it might have been hard to pin much on him because he remained in the background. But a federal offense—with Snate's reputation and record—meant Alcatraz. Fox too would have been difficult to convict so I let him reveal himself. Warner and Lieutenant McGrath were warned to be on the lookout. McGrath even tried to accost Snate as he left the offices of the federal attorney. That was to scare Snate so he'd run immediately to Fox's house. Fox also tried to pin suspicion on Gage by writing me a note on Gage's paper and with his typewriter."

SOMEONE RANG the front door bell and Silk jumped up. Quinn's eyes, sparkling brightly as he reviewed the case, assumed the dead expression of a blind man. Butch and Carol quickly vanished into another room.

Commissioner Warner, Stewart, Gage and Lieutenant McGrath came in, faces aglow in victory.

"We got them," Warner sat down with a sigh of relief. "Fox was our man. He shot Snate and tried to make away with all the loot. Snate won't die and he is charged with robbing the Federal Attorney's office and what do you think he got? Counterfeit money! You should see the way the newspapers played it up. Made a stupid fool of him."

"I wrote an editorial about it," Gage broke in eagerly. "I made it quite plain that all crooks of Snate's type are arrogant fools without the brains of a two hour old mouse. If Snate ever built up an aura of glory, it's dashed to pieces now. The whole country is laughing at him."

"Very good work," Quinn said quietly. "Did you handle it, Lieutenant McGrath?"

McGrath looked slightly confused. "Well, I got the credit, but it isn't really mine. The Black Bat prepared the traps and he sprung them too, I suppose. But how are you going to give credit to a man you can't identify—a man who commits every crime on the books to gain his own ends? You know, I don't understand that guy. I don't get his point—unless he's looking for revenge. Just like you might, Mr. Quinn. Why, if you weren't blind, I'd swear you were The Bat."

Stewart contained himself no longer. "I almost laid my hands on Snate not many hours ago. I actually tracked him to his hideout, but The Bat was there ahead of me and making a target range of the place. I ran for it, knowing I'd be of no help."

"What of my idea—about the armored cars' sealed orders?" Quinn asked. "Didn't that help at all?"

"Help?" Stewart cried. "No—I'm sorry, Quinn, it didn't. In fact that idea placed me in a very embarrassing position. I made up and sealed the orders as you suggested, but Fox threw them away and had a clever forger make up new ones—in my handwriting. If Fox hadn't confessed to that, I really think Commissioner Warner would have arrested me. Incidentally the racket of paroling unworthy convicts is broken up. Fox was behind it."

Quinn folded his arms. "Then I guess the case is closed. I'm only sorry I didn't have an active part in it. Still, Snate is behind bars and that gives me a lot of satisfaction."

Lieutenant McGrath eyed Quinn askance as the four men arose and went to the front door.

"Just the same," McGrath said, "The Black Bat reminds me of you, Quinn. If he ever looks you up, tell him for me that what he's done means nothing—nothing at all. If I can throw him into a cell, I'll do it—so fast he won't know how he got there."

Quinn smiled. "But really, Lieutenant, I don't know The Bat. He wouldn't contact me. I'm helplessly blind and I could be of no value to his work."

"Yes," McGrath grated, "if you are blind. But no offense, Quinn. I'm just suspicious of everyone."

SIMULTANEOUSLY, WARNER and McGrath extended their hands.

Quinn took Warner's and shook it warmly.

"Everything is forgiven, Lieutenant McGrath. Being suspected of acting as The Black Bat is an honor, I assure you."

"Aw, what's the use," McGrath said disgustedly. "That's Warner's hand you're shaking, Quinn. I'm over here."

They trooped away. From another room Carol's merry laughter broke the stillness and Butch joined in. Silk seemed a little despondent.

"I'm sorry it's over," he said. "Now what are we going to do?"

"Do?" Quinn chuckled. "Silk, before another hour has passed, someone will rise up to take Snate's place—Otto Fox's too. Crime doesn't stop, but we won't stop either. The Black Bat isn't dead, Silk. He's just asleep, roosting on the rafters until someone gets the idea he is greater than all law and order."

Carol put her hand on Quinn's arm. He looked down at her, covered her hand with his own, and they walked back into the library to sit before the cheerful fire.

II

MURDER CALLS THE BLACK BAT

CHAPTER I

DEATH BY THE GUN

THE GRAHAM COMPANY wore the expensively modest front that might be expected of one of the world's most famous jewelry shops. Within its doors were consultation rooms and never a sign of such plebeian objects as show cases. Gems were brought directly from the huge vaults to the customers who were served in those private rooms. Buying a diamond from the Graham Company was like purchasing currency at the United States Mint. Graham's diamonds were just as negotiable.

Perhaps that was why the clerks looked up in utter amazement as Mrs. Van den Killan swept into the shop with fire in her eye and acid on her tongue.

Clarence Graham, head of the firm and fifth in a long line of antecedents who had carried on, heard her voice even above that of his secretary as she switched on the inter-office phone.

"What's all the excitement?" Graham inquired mildly. "By all means send Mrs. Van den Killan in."

She came, slamming the door behind her. She deposited a wrapped package on Graham's desk.

"And this," she shrilled, "is what the name of Graham means! I bought a tiara here seven weeks ago. I paid one hundred and thirty thousand dollars for it. It's incredible! Most incredible!"

"My dear madam,"—Graham arose and helped her into a chair—"please calm yourself. If there is anything wrong with the tiara, we shall certainly remedy the condition."

"Wrong with it?" she half screamed. "Wrong with it? You have the complacency to sit there and ask me what's wrong with it! The whole thing is a fake. It's paste! Paste I tell you! Worth about one thousand dollars."

Graham smiled. "There is, of course, some error. Perhaps if we—"

"My husband is ready to go to the police!" the woman snapped. "I purchased the tiara, believing it was the original once worn by the czarina. I took it abroad with me, to wear at an important function in Amsterdam."

She leaned forward and banged the flat of her hand against the desk, "You can imagine my utter embarrassment when the Belgian Ambassador's wife swept through the ball room wearing an identical tiara."

Dr. Wohl

"What?" Graham arose. "But that is impossible. There is only one tiara like that which I sold you. The other must have been false."

Mrs. Van den Killan screwed up her face in distaste.

"Of course I thought that too. I removed mine and later on I learned that the Belgian woman had purchased her tiara just three days before, especially for the occasion. Therefore I took steps to find out whether or not the one you sold me was false. I am quite certain that I was the one who was cheated, Mr. Graham."

WITH FINGERS that shook, Graham unwrapped the package, exposed a large plush case and touched the spring controlling the lid. It flew back and the tiara gleamed warmly under the light of a desk lamp. Graham lifted the flashing collection of gems from the box, placed it on the desk and put a jeweler's loupe to his eye. The magnifying glass brought each finely cut gem into bold prominence. Graham heaved a sigh of relief.

Then he touched a button on his desk. Two minutes later a short, round-shouldered man with a closely trimmed beard, entered the office with a hobble that appeared to be characteristic.

"*Ja, Herr* Graham," he said and looked over his thick glasses. "You sent for me, *nein?*"

"Dr. Wohl," Graham said, "I want you to look at this tiara and tell me its worth. Mrs. Van den Killan wishes a new appraisal of the piece."

Wohl picked up the tiara, glanced at it critically, and brought it close to his eye.

"Dr. Wohl," Graham told Mrs. Van den Killan, "is one of the most famous jewel experts in the world. He will reassure you as to the genuineness of this tiara, for I am sure you are mistaken, madam. Graham sells nothing but perfect stones."

A moment of tense silence passed. Then Graham looked at the gem expert.

"Well?" he asked impatiently.

Wohl set the tiara back in its plush case and drew himself fairly erect. "This tiara," he said in a matter-of-fact voice, "is worth about one thousand dollars. It is of the finest paste, created by an expert—but it is worth no more than a thousand dollars, *mein Herr.*"

"But that's the tiara we sold Mrs. Van den Killan seven weeks ago!" Graham cried. "It was perfect then—had been appraised at a hundred and fifty thousand dollars! How can it have changed to paste?"

Wohl shrugged indifferently. "That I do not know. There are many ways—perhaps a substitution was made by someone in the family. Perhaps by clever thieves. Who knows? I am not a policeman—*nein*. Only a gem expert, and I say this piece is a lie, a fake."

Graham dismissed the expert with a wave of his hand.

"Mrs. Van den Killan," he said slowly, "I don't know what happened. Frankly, I cannot imagine. We sold you this tiara as a genuine bill of goods. You must have been tricked somehow and this paste replica substituted. I cannot say as to that. But in view of the prestige of Graham's and the value of your account, I shall make good your loss at once. I hope that will be satisfactory."

"Thank you," the woman said. "I don't know what happened, but that tiara is exactly as it came from your shop, Mr. Graham. I took it to Europe the day after it was delivered. It was in the custody of the ship's purser on the way over and then was placed in a Paris bank vault. Upon my return yesterday, I brought the tiara to Harriman's Jewelry Store for appraisal—after what had happened abroad. He insisted it was a fake."

"I shall try to determine what happened," Graham said suavely. "At the earliest opportunity you will be called back and told what we are able to discover. Thank you for your patience, Mrs. Van den Killan, and I assure you that this has all been most unfortunate."

WHEN HE closed the door behind her, Graham almost staggered back to his desk and slumped in the chair. He looked keenly at the tiara. Even to his trained eyes it looked like the real thing.

Or did it? Weren't some of the stones lacking in warmth? Didn't their glow reflect a certain coldness? Of course Wohl was right. No one could dispute his word.

Graham arose suddenly, walked over to a wall safe and opened it. He drew out three steel trays of cut diamonds, opened them and gazed intently at the stones. He fastened the loupe to his eye and examined some of them. His face grew as pale as the whiteness of a pearl. His breath came in rasping gasps. With a trembling finger he pushed the buzzer for Wohl.

The expert shuffled into the office, his bald pate glistening, his watery eyes regarding Graham suspiciously.

"Wohl," Graham said, "look at these. We've had them in the store for the past six months. They were brought here and passed by you as perfect gems. They don't look right to me. In heaven's name, man, tell me—are they phonies too?"

Methodically Wohl went to work. While Graham paced the floor, he examined each stone and made two separate piles of them. One was twice as large as the other and it was to this pile that Wohl pointed.

"Mein herr," he said, "those are fakes. Pure fakes, worth a fair sum as excellent replicas—but not diamonds, *nein.* Not diamonds!"

"But they haven't been out of my safe since you passed them as genuine!" Graham roared. "Wohl, are you slipping? Did somebody pass these fakes over on us as the real goods?"

Dr. Wohl drew himself up. "I," he stated pompously, "have worked with diamonds for thirty years, *ja!* Not once have I been accused of carelessness. When those diamonds came to me for appraisal, they were genuine. What happened to them after they left my hands, I do not know or care."

"Yes—yes, of course," Graham groaned. "You're one of the world's greatest experts. You worked in Amsterdam for many years, in a position of great trust. But it's incredible! Approximately two-thirds of these gems are paste. Wohl—the rest of the stock! Maybe it's been tampered with too! Listen—go back to your office. I'll send in the stock, tray by tray. Examine it all. Work as you've never worked before. We carry millions of dollars' worth of gems here. If two-thirds of them are fakes, I'm bankrupt! Insurance companies won't pay. They'll claim these gems were fakes when they were insured. They'll be in the right too, for how could such substitution be made?"

For two hours Graham sweated profusely, locked in his private office. Every ten minutes Wohl shuffled into the room and made two piles of stones. Opals, emeralds, rubies and sapphires. Out of each tray, two-thirds were phonies—masterly reproductions of the real thing, but fakes just the same.

"Not a word of this," Graham told Wohl. "We have a few hours to see if we can find out what has happened. Keep on sorting the stock. Don't talk to anyone."

Graham's phone buzzed. He answered it in a curt voice and his shoulders drooped as he listened.

"All right. Send him in."

A MAN of about thirty entered the office, carrying a three-carat diamond in the palm of his hand. His face was almost as pale as Graham's.

"Yes, Mr. McFayden," Graham snapped at his chief clerk. "What is it?"

McFayden swallowed hard. "I—I really can't account for it, sir. Mr. Philip Mitchell purchased this stone yesterday, as an engagement ring for his fiancée. He paid us three thousand dollars. And—and now he maintains this stone is a fake."

Graham seized the gem and held it under the light. Then he motioned McFayden away angrily.

"Tell Mr. Mitchell there was an error. Tell him we'll replace this stone at once—within two or three hours. Tell him anything, man, but get out of here. Get out, I say!"

McFayden backed hastily out of the office. Graham took a drink of water, passed a hand across his tired face and groaned aloud.

"Tricked! Fooled completely. A million dollars' worth of stock stolen right under my eyes and replaced with fakes. I must be dreaming! Such a thing couldn't possibly happen!"

He sank weakly back into his chair....

Perhaps half an hour more had passed, when in the outer office McFayden looked up from his desk with an air of irritation as an under clerk approached.

"Mr. Graham wants you—at once," the clerk told him. "His secretary just called to say you are to go to his office."

"More of this mysterious business," McFayden grumbled to himself. "Next he'll be accusing me of planting that phony chunk of paste in stock."

Passing from his desk into the anteroom of Graham's private office he nodded to Graham's secretary and walked over to the door of his employer's private sanctum. He tapped on the panels and waited for Graham's voice to bid him enter. Nothing happened so he rapped harder.

"Are you positive he's in there?" McFayden asked the secretary.

"Positive," she answered. "Wait—I'll get him on the inter-office phone."

She flicked down the button and called Graham's name. There was no reply. She jumped to her feet.

"Something has happened—I know it! McFayden—open the door!"

McFayden turned the knob slowly and eased the door open. The secretary looked over his shoulder—and a terrible sight met their eyes. Graham was seated behind his desk. His head hung limply against his chest and in the solid, high backed chair, he looked like a gnome. They saw his right hand slowly dip into the drawer of the desk and remove a gun. Slowly he raised it until the muzzle almost touched his temple.

"No!" McFayden yelled. "No! Don't shoot, Mr. Graham! Don't shoot!"

BUT GRAHAM paid no attention. He acted as if he were already living in another world. His finger squeezed the trigger. His head jerked to one side and blood spurted, staining the chair arm and seeping to the rug. The hand holding the gun dropped from sight. The gun hit the floor with a thump.

Graham's secretary gave a long-drawn-out sob that welled into a scream of horror. She and McFayden backed out of the office and McFayden closed the door.

"Stay here," he told the secretary grimly. "Don't let anyone in."

McFayden dashed out of the office. The secretary glanced at the closed door of the death room.

"Me stay here with—that?" she screamed, and rushed after McFayden.

He had stopped dramatically in the center of the store.

"Mr. Graham just shot himself!" he yelled. "Committed suicide! I saw him shoot! Get the police! Get a doctor! Hurry!"

CHAPTER II

MURDER CALLS

THE EXPENSIVE sedan stopped in front of a neat, smartly appointed home in one of the better sections of the great city. Oaks and elms, scores of years old, shrouded the house. Shrubs, well trimmed, and flowers of myriad colors, made a show place of the estate. A plain oak plank fastened to the gate bore the owner's name:

TONY QUINN.

A man got out of the sedan and hurried up the path to the house. Philip Harriman had reason to be in a hurry. His usually polished, suave exterior, known well to his best customers, was missing. It was difficult to realize that he was a prosperous, much-envied man who owned one of the three greatest jewelry firms in the country, for he looked more like a worried, distraught man who had been caught short in a market crash.

He pressed the bell and the door opened almost immediately, as if the servant who answered had been watching. Harriman knew "Silk" Kirby, Tony Quinn's butler. Silk nodded in recognition also.

In appearance Silk was little like the preconceived idea of a butler in a wealthy man's home. He was too slippery-looking and his eyes were cold as ice. His forehead was high, above a pointed, narrow nose, and a mouth too small.

"I'll announce you, Mr. Harriman," he said.

"Let me go right in," Harriman begged "It's terribly important."

Silk's hand checked the jeweler.

"Sorry, sir. But Mr. Quinn doesn't receive many guests since—since he became blind. He's rather sensitive, you know."

"But this is vitally important—means millions!" Harriman exploded. "Tony is still my attorney. What difference does it make if he's blind? I still need his advice."

Silk's expression didn't change, but he seemed to take cognizance of Harriman's anxiety. He gestured and led the jeweler into a huge living room. Before the fireplace there, in a big leather chair, sat a slender, well built man. He sat erect, his head cocked to one side as if he had heard the voices in the reception hall. But his eyes stared straight ahead—the lifeless, glassy eyes of the blind.

His face was not pleasant to look upon. Deep, ugly scars had been burned in the flesh, especially about the eyes. It gave him a sinister appearance.

Harriman stepped forward. "Tony," he cried eagerly. "Tony Quinn! It's me—Phil Harriman. I've got to talk to you."

Tony Quinn's voice was flat, a hollow mockery of the ringing tones that once had stirred juries and made criminals writhe in fear. Something seemed to have gone out of Tony Quinn when he became blind. There was defeat and desolation in his voice.

"Come in, Phil. Sit over there. The green chair. I can hear you best there."

Harriman sat down and Silk quietly withdrew. Harriman lit a cigarette and tried to compose himself.

"You're a wonder, Tony," he said. "Every time I come to see you, I'm told exactly where to sit and what my chair looks like."

TONY QUINN smiled ruefully.

"I keep track of the furniture," he said slowly. "When a blind man moves about, he must know where every article that may trip him is located. Now Phil—what's worrying you? I recognize the note of excitement in your voice."

"I need advice," Phil Harriman said quickly. "You were in private practice before you became the best D.A. we ever had. I was one of your clients and I still consider you my attorney. Oh, don't hold up your hand to stop me. You're blind, but that hasn't affected that keen legal mind of yours.

"Listen, Tony! There's something downright hellish going on. This morning Mrs. Van den Killan—yes, *the* Mrs. Van den Killan—came into my office with a tiara she'd purchased from the Graham Company about two months ago. She wanted me to look it over. Well, I looked it over and I even had Anghis Khan—my gem expert and one of the best in the world—do the same. The tiara was paste! The most perfect reproduction I've ever seen in my career—but paste nevertheless. I—I had to tell her."

"So?" Tony Quinn tapped his fingertips together and looked mildly interested.

"That," Harriman went on with a groan, "is only half of it. Anghis Khan and I couldn't believe our own eyes. The tiara is composed mostly of diamonds with a few rubies and emeralds sprinkled through it for color. To assure ourselves that our eyes were still good, we got some of our own gems out of stock for purposes of comparison. That, Tony, is when I received the greatest shock of my life. My own gems were paste! Reproductions of the originals. Like Mrs. Van den Killan's tiara, they were superlative work and could pass any casual inspection. Khan and I examined every stone in my stock—and three-quarters of them are phonies!"

Tony Quinn leaned forward. He gripped the cane he held and the knuckles of his hands gleamed whitely. That was his only outward show of interest.

"An inside job, Phil," he said flatly. "Must be!"

Harriman groaned again. "Yes, yes, of course. I thought the same thing. But every one of my employees has been with me for years—more than half were employed by my father as well. They can't be dishonest. And—well, because of that paste tiara I've been wondering if Graham has suffered a similar loss. I'm going to see him as soon as I leave you... Tony, I'm virtually bankrupt. I need an attorney. I need you. There will be all kinds of legal angles to this. Will you help? Will you tell me what to do?"

"One thing right now," Tony Quinn said quietly. "Go to the police. Then, if you take your insurance papers to any reliable attorney, he'll tell you if you are covered. It's an odd case, Phil. I'd enjoy handling it if—well, if I was worth anything to anybody, including myself. But go to the police at once before the man or men responsible get clear."

Harriman stood up and jammed his hat down hard.

"Exactly. I just wanted to be certain I was right. And consider yourself still my attorney, Tony. I won't take no for an answer. Now I'm going to see Graham and then to the police. Thanks, old man."

SILK LET Harriman out and closed the door quietly. He heard Harriman's car start away from the curb, then he walked briskly into the living room. Tony Quinn still faced the fireplace, unseeing eyes as blank as ever.

"Silk," he said slowly, "you heard Harriman's story?"

"I heard it," Silk answered. "Sounds like the screwiest set-up ever."

"There's more than appears on the surface, Silk. Graham wouldn't sell a fake tiara, or even a fake quarter-carat diamond. He's like Harriman—completely honest and operating his business on that principle. They carry tremendous stocks of gems, the finest in existence. If someone has been clever enough to appropriate three-fourths of Harriman's stock, he has probably also taken as many from Graham. It may be the police will find themselves stumped. It may also be, Silk, that the Black Bat will take a hand in this. The case sounds interesting."

"Yeah," Silk said eagerly, "it does at that. And we've been laying low, boss. Much too low for me."

The phone buzzed and Silk sped away to answer it.

Harriman's voice game over the wire, trembling and high-pitched.

"Let me talk to Tony Quinn, Silk. Hurry!"

"Sorry, sir," Silk said. "Mr. Quinn doesn't answer the phone any more. I'll take any message."

"Oh, damn it, why does he have to be so sensitive about his blindness!" Harriman rapped out nervously. "I tell you—"

"I'm sorry," Silk broke in. "Mr. Quinn doesn't like to move about too much, sir. It's rather difficult for him. If there is a message—"

"Yes—yes, there is. Tell him that Graham just committed suicide! They won't let me into his place of business—it's full of police. McFayden, Graham's clerk, saw Graham shoot himself through the head. There was some kind of a suicide note, I hear. I'm going to Police Headquarters at once. Quinn will understand what I mean."

"Thank you, sir," Silk said and hung up. As the connection was cut off, his face lighted up. He hurried back to the living room.

"It was Harriman," he reported. "Says Graham just bumped himself off. Harriman's going to the cops right now."

Tony Quinn's lips pursed and he whistled softly. For a moment the blankness in his eyes faded and they became alive and real.

"Something is brewing, Silk," he said softly. "But it's Harriman's battle right now. We'd better get to bed."

CHAPTER III

THE BLACK BAT

BUT AT one a.m. Tony Quinn was not asleep although all the lights in his room were out. Silk, in his own quarters on the first floor, also had too much on his mind for slumber. Too many things had happened to let sleep come easily.

More and more Tony Quinn sensed that this was no more an ordinary case than he was an ordinary man.

As had been the case when he had heard of Graham's suicide, Tony Quinn's eyes were again eager and alive; not blank and staring. In his face, also, was none of the persistent inquiring look of a blind man. The room was black as midnight, but Tony Quinn could distinguish each object as clearly as if a beam of sunlight were fastened upon it. Not only could Tony Quinn see, but his eyes were exceptionally acute!

His pose of a blind man was one so perfect that only a period of actual blindness could have schooled him. And that was true! Once a promising young district attorney, Quinn had fought bitterly against all crime. He fought physically too, one day in open court. Certain phonograph records, containing evidence enough to convict an important crook, were destroyed by acid flung by the hands of this crook's band of criminals.

Tony Quinn had stepped directly in front of the records as he sought to save them. The acid had struck his face and burned deep, ugly scars. It ate away his sight and made horrible mockery of those eyes.

Totally blind, with no hope of a cure, Tony Quinn had resigned and settled down for a life of darkness with no hope of release save in death. But when his sight failed, his other senses grew so acute that he acquired the hearing of a jungle beast on the prowl. His fingertips, resting against an object, could form in his mind every feature, of its shape. Only actual color escaped his senses. But his instincts were quickened until he could acutely feel the presence of anyone in a room.

Then, on a night of darkest despair, had come a girl—a girl whom he could not see. She called herself Carol Baldwin and through her he had met an unknown country doctor many miles from the city. Under his hands Tony Quinn had undergone an operation which not only restored his sight but even added to it. By some miracle of that surgery he was enabled to see as plainly in darkness as in daylight.

He had returned home from that obscure country place presumably from a vacation trip, apparently as blind as ever. But with such a firm purpose fixed in his mind that only three people shared his secret besides the surgeon, who has since died.

Carol Baldwin knew. She lived quietly just a few blocks away and was prepared to take an active part in Quinn's work at any time. Then there was Silk Kirby, who had come to rob Quinn and remained to become his most trusted assistant. And Silk had become invaluable to Quinn, since not only was he a reformed burglar whose loyalty to Tony Quinn now approached fanaticism, but he was also an ex-confidence man, glib as the best in that racket.

And finally there was "Butch" O'Leary, a tremendous hulk of a man who had attracted Tony Quinn's notice during a bank robbery when Butch had leaped at a machine-gun armed thug who was in the act of mowing down a score of bystanders. Quinn had known at once that Butch was a man he could trust.

ALL THREE were faithful, willing and anxious to help. For Tony Quinn had created for himself an utterly new life. Because the underworld in general secretly gloated over the blindness of the ex-D.A. and called him "blind as a bat," Tony Quinn had become a "bat." The "Black Bat" who prowled by night and matched his wits against the keenest in the world of crime.

He had become a Nemesis, a dark blot of shadow soon feared by every man who lived by violence or by his wits, and now was a scourge of the underworld of crime. For each time the Black Bat acted, he left a vivid token of his work. His victims bore the brand of the Bat—a miniature black bat, with wings outstretched—stamped on their foreheads.

Financially independent, Tony Quinn had resolved to devote his whole life to an endless fight against crime in all its rotten, lecherous phases. Yet on the surface he remained the old Tony Quinn, scarred and blind for life. His secret was carefully guarded.

Now Tony Quinn propped a pillow against the head of his bed and reached for a cigarette. He could clearly see the pack in the darkness, even its coloring. Suddenly his hand paused and stiffened. His head turned slightly, like that of a listening dog. From downstairs he heard a soft thump and a muffled groan.

Silk heard things too. Someone had raised a window in the dining room. Raised it very softly and with all the skill of a trained burglar. Silk took a gun from his bureau, walked in bare feet to the hall and then moved silently toward the dining room. A gust of cool night air swept in on him and he shivered. The window was open.

Silk passed by the portieres draped artistically at the side of the door. Something swished. A gun butt cracked against his skull and at the same time an arm encircled him, keeping his limp body from crashing to the floor. His lips were sealed by a hand clapped across his mouth.

The intruder laid the stunned Silk carefully on the floor and then, with a grin, started up the steps. Killing a blind man was the easiest stunt he'd ever had to do. He'd wake the poor sucker first, give the fool a chance to act, so it would seem as though the burglar had shot to create an avenue of escape for himself.

The killer reached the landing at the head of the stairs and stood listening. He could hear the rhythmic breathing of a man in a sound sleep. His lips curled sardonically. He'd make that sleep permanent. Wasn't this blind guy an ex-D.A. and was anything sweeter than polishing off one of his breed?

The killer stepped into the bedroom, saw the recumbent form under the covers and crept forward, gun carelessly held in his hand. He smiled confidently and prepared to awaken the sleeping man. His mouth opened and stayed that way. For a hand had dropped on his shoulder. A hand with fingers of steel. He was spun around as easily as though he were a top in the hands of a child.

He tried to raise his gun, but it was wrenched from him.

With a savage oath he ducked and twisted, finally tearing himself free of the restraining grasp. All thoughts of murder left him.

Only one idea was in his mind now—escape!

HE JOLTED a quick blow to the face of the towering man who held him, missed and squirmed until a whole side of his suit tore loose. Like a deer, he bolted out of the room. Behind him rushed Tony Quinn.

He reached out and touched the fleeing man's shoulder.

The killer gave a howl of dismay and took a flying dive down the staircase. He tripped, a quarter of the way down, and tumbled over and over. But when he hit the bottom, he bounded up again like a rubber ball, racing along the hallway toward the front door.

Quinn, hurrying down the stairs, hesitated to shoot. But with the quick realization that his midnight visitor might have some mysterious knowledge that Tony Quinn was the Bat, Quinn raised his gun to put a slug through the intruder's leg. But the killer carried a spare weapon. As he reached the door, he jerked this out of a shoulder clip and flung it up toward the man on the stairs.

From the dining room came a single shot. The killer's sadistic leer changed to a look of mingled agony and surprise.

He turned about methodically, as if undecided what to do, took one step toward the door and then pitched forward on his face.

"Good shooting, Silk," Quinn called softly. "Turn on the lights and watch yourself. He went down like a dead man but you never can tell."

The lights flashed on. Silk, nursing a bump on his head, came cautiously into the hallway, his still smoking gun gripped in a steady hand. He approached the still form of the killer and nudged him with his foot. Then he calmly stowed the gun and knelt.

"Got him through the heart," he told Quinn. "A damn easy way for a mug like this to die. They got electric chairs for his kind."

"Odd," Quinn said. "What made him come here? Not mere chance, because he made no attempt to rifle drawers. He came straight upstairs and when I grabbed him he was ready to fire at the blankets I'd rolled up beneath the bedspread. He came to kill, Silk."

Quinn turned the dead man over and calmly searched his clothing. From an inner pocket he drew out ten one-hundred-dollar bills.

"Blood money. This man is probably a hired killer. And what's this?"

He turned a sealed envelope over and over in his hands. It was labelled, "TO THE POLICE" in bold, flowing handwriting that was somehow familiar. Quinn walked over to the desk in the study and sat down.

"Maybe we oughta call in the cops," Silk suggested doubtfully. "Or should I dump the guy some place and forget all about this?"

"Silk"—Tony Quinn laid down the letter he had extracted from the envelope—"we will notify the police that a burglar entered the house and when he pulled a gun, you shot him. The whole affair was staged to look as if a burglar had broken in, and it will remain so. Your gun did the killing. You take the responsibility. There won't be many questions. The whole thing is much too clear cut. Then, after the police have gone, we notify Carol and Butch to come here at once."

"Y'mean—" Silk asked eagerly.

"I mean the Black Bat is taking a hand in something that's pretty vicious, Silk. Harriman was a friend of mine. I liked him and he trusted me. Harriman—is dead!"

"But how'd you know?"

"Read the letter, Silk."

SILK PICKED up the letter carefully, holding it by the edges. His face grew grim and somber as he read the brief contents.

> TO THE POLICE:
> This is the only way out. For four years I have steadily appropriated stock from my own store and substituted for it certain paste replicas of the original gems. I never intended these to be sold and used them only to keep up my inventory. Now I am revealed. Though these people I have served for many years will never forgive me and my friends be unable to grant me forgiveness in their minds, I pray that my God will forgive. I take the only way out.
>
> Philip Harriman

"Poor guy!" Silk shook his head sadly.

"Your sympathies are cockeyed," Quinn said. "If Harriman wrote that note, what is it doing in this mug's pocket? Why did he come here to kill me anyway? We don't even know if Harriman is dead."

"He seemed okay when he phoned about Graham bumping himself," Silk offered. "A little excited maybe, but he didn't sound like a guy who was going to knock himself off. Say—" Silk was suddenly assailed by a horrible idea. "You don't think maybe this killer was sent here by someone who knows you are the Bat?"

"No. There was an entirely different reason. I was to be killed because the man who directs these crimes believed Harriman may have told me something—as an attorney, of course. Something he didn't want revealed. To work, Silk. First we must dispose of this shooting affair. Remember—this crook is just a burglar who pulled a gun and you were forced to kill him. Call Sergeant McGrath."

"McGrath?" Silk gaped. "But that heel will suspect you did it. He'll suspect all kinds of things. He already thinks you are the Bat, boss. Sure, I know he ain't got a thing to go on, but just the same McGrath is a square cop and he's sworn to get the Bat. No use letting him stick his mug in on this business."

Quinn smiled a little. He well knew what Silk Kirby meant. He was referring to a case not long past when Tony Quinn had come closer to being unmasked than at any time since he had undertaken his self-appointed mission to do his share to clear the world of crime. And by that same Sergeant McGrath. Quinn had at last managed to slide out, and in his rightful character innocently plead ignorance, stressing his blindness.

But it had been a close call, and because McGrath had a one-track mind he had stubbornly refused to give up his idea that Tony Quinn was the Bat—and that he was not blind. His trouble was that he could prove neither assertion. Still he refused to admit he was wrong, and had become rather annoying to the former district attorney.

Quinn was remembering all that as Silk made his remonstrance.

"If we don't call him"—Quinn's smile grew a little wry—"his suspicions will grow still greater because he will believe I am afraid of him. Afraid he might learn something to prove his accusations. No, call him and get it over with. And Silk, you never saw this suicide note."

CHAPTER IV

WAYS AND MEANS

SERGEANT McGRATH came on the wings of a screaming siren. He was a chunky, beef-faced man with a determined slant to his chin. A policeman for twenty-odd years, Sergeant McGrath was as tenacious as a bulldog and as stubborn. Thoroughly honest and capable, there was not an iota of mercy in his makeup. He had sworn to uphold the law and if it meant his own skin, he would carry on. And Sergeant McGrath had sworn to get the Bat!

Tony Quinn, cane between his knees, sat in his accustomed chair in front of the fireplace. Sergeant McGrath made a swift examination of the dead man on the floor, listened to Silk's story and had fingerprint men dust the open window. They found marks made by the dead crook's gloved hands, characteristic marks predominated by a small scar on the surface of the glove's index finger.

McGrath strode into the living room, pulled up a chair and sat down facing Quinn.

"Hello, Sergeant." Quinn smiled a welcome. "Sorry to make more work for you."

"Work?" McGrath snorted. "This job is a pipe. It's okay—on the level, Quinn. Silk blasted that mug out all right and a good job too. He was a guy named Morey Grogan—one of them mugs who'll pull anything for a thin dime. Silk is lucky at that, because Grogan was a killer."

"I recall the name." Quinn stared straight into the fireplace with his blank eyes. "Silk was fortunate. I was too. I couldn't have defended myself, not being able to see."

Quinn's apparently sightless eyes watched the big officer. McGrath was getting set to pull a fast one. Quinn could sense it and he steeled himself.

"Uh-huh," McGrath said doubtfully and lit a cigarette.

McGrath took half a dozen deep drags on it and suddenly flipped the flaming cigarette straight at Quinn's nose. It missed Quinn's face by a fraction of an inch and landed in the fireplace. But Tony Quinn never moved a muscle. His staring blank eyes never flickered. And that had taken tremendous will power.

McGrath sighed deeply and relaxed. No man, possessed of his sight, could have avoided jerking his head back, or at least blinking as the cigarette came flying toward him. Quinn seemed to be blind all right.

"It's been a hell of a night," McGrath went on. "You're lucky you're not the D.A. any more, Quinn. Because the guy who is in your shoes now is going to have his hands full. First of all a jeweler named Graham cleaned out a few million bucks worth of his stock and put phonies in their place. Then he bumped himself off, right in front of his secretary and a clerk. He left a note explaining things.

"Next about twenty big shots come flocking to the station carrying jewels. They all had been tricked. They'd paid fancy prices for a lot of junk. Then another jeweler named Harriman disappears and we get complaints about him too, so we investigate and sure enough he's done the same thing. Maybe he bumped himself off too. We'll know pretty soon. To top it all off this guy Grogan gets blasted clean to hell."

Quinn's face was drawn and sad. "Did you say I'm lucky not to be the D.A., Sergeant? I'd sell my very soul to step back in that office and direct this jewel case you're talking about."

McGrath turned a beefy red. "Yeah—yeah, and you'd do a good job too. Say, I didn't mean it that way. I—I know how you feel, Quinn. I'm sorry."

Quinn laughed grimly. "Forget it, Sergeant."

McGRATH PUT a friendly hand on Quinn's shoulder and began to say something. Then his old doubts assailed him again. He kept quiet, but he walked over to the desk and used the phone. He spoke in monosyllables and once grunted in surprise.

He hung up and returned to Quinn's side.

"More trouble. They just located Harriman. He drove his car off a cliff at the Palisades Road. Burned up pretty bad. Oh well, when they save the state a lot of dough, you can't get sore at 'em. Just the same it's going to be one sweet mess to clean up."

"You're right," Quinn said slowly. "Perfectly right, Sergeant. A sweet mess."

When the house was finally cleared and the body of the thug taken away, Silk sat down weakly and mopped his forehead. Quinn still remained seated before the fireplace. Not until more than an hour had passed did he move.

Then, at his gesture, Silk pulled down the curtains. Quinn arose, walked briskly and with no pretense of blindness now, to the book-lined wall of the room. He manipulated a section of the book shelves and it opened to let him into a white-tiled laboratory equipped with almost every modern device for use in searching out the tricks and mistakes of criminals.

Quinn took the suicide note, supposedly written by Harriman, from his pocket. Carefully he smoothed the paper and deftly applied a spot of colorless chemical to several written words. The ink smeared and faded slightly. Quinn then placed a section of the letter beneath a microscope.

"Find anything?" Silk asked hopefully.

"This note," Tony Quinn replied thoughtfully, "was written more than seventy-two hours ago. It's a good stab at reproducing Harriman's handwriting, but Harriman never wrote this note. Why? Because Harriman only discovered today that his gems were phonies. There was no reason why he should have been planning suicide so far in advance."

"But how did that mug I killed get the note?" Silk asked.

"We'll never know, definitely," Quinn answered. "However, it's safe to assume that Harriman must have been murdered. This note was supposed to have been placed on his person, but somehow it wasn't. Perhaps the crook you killed forgot to take care of that detail in the excitement of murdering Harriman. It does indicate that we have a place in this investigation, Silk. We begin at once."

"Me too?" Silk perked up.

"You mostly. Silk, you know how to disguise yourself in two different makeups. Put one of them on at once. Then use the secret exit at the end of the estate. Go out and learn all you can about *Mynheer* Van den Killan. Everything, no matter how small, may be important. Find out about his habits, his friends, his finances. See if there is a possibility that he may have substituted that paste tiara for the real thing without his wife knowing it."

"I'm on my way." Silk grinned from ear to ear. "I wasn't a confidence man for nothing, Boss. I'll case this Van den Killan guy until I know which side he sleeps on."

Silk walked briskly to the door, hesitated a moment and turned around.

"What about you, Boss? Say, you don't think those mugs may come back and try to knock you off?"

Tony Quinn smiled tightly.

"If they do, I'll be quite ready for them. It may be reasonable to assume they'll come, because evidently they believe Harriman told me something. My silence must be important to their state of well being. Don't worry about me, Silk."

TONY QUINN spent another twenty minutes examining the suicide note. He was firmly convinced now that it was a forgery and a good one. If that note had been found it would plainly have indicated that Harriman had died a suicide. With his gems missing and paste replicas in their place, the police were bound to assume that he had appropriated them and when he was on the verge of exposure, had taken the easiest way out.

But what of Graham? The other jeweler had suffered a similar loss. According to the meagre information that Quinn possessed, two persons had been eye witnesses to Graham's suicide. Still he couldn't help wondering about it.

Quinn slipped out of the hidden laboratory. His eyes seemed to film over and he used his cane in making his way across the room. He sat down before the fireplace again, assimilating every phase of the case in his agile mind. He was lining up probabilities and theories. An investigation was in order and soon the Black Bat would prowl again while the underworld shuddered and crawled back into its filthy hole.

The phone rang. Tony Quinn got to his feet slowly and made his careful, methodical way to the instrument. Every movement was that of a blind man. Silk was on the wire, agitated and plainly worried.

"Boss, there's three or four guys casing the house. I slipped out the back like you said, but on a hunch I took a gander around the place. They're watching the place all right and they don't look like cops to me."

"Thank you, Silk," Quinn answered. "Don't return. Carry out the orders you already have and don't worry about me."

Quinn hung up and frowned. It was somewhat difficult to formulate a plan of action when he had to retain his pose of a blind man. If those thugs ever guessed that he could see, they might quickly associate him with the mysterious Black Bat, because of his known hatred of criminals and the criminal world when he had been district attorney. And should that news ever reach Sergeant McGrath, it would be all up.

Quinn turned around and for one of the few times in his pretended career of a blind man, he almost gave himself away. Standing in the doorway was a tall, wide-shouldered, sleek-looking man. He had a narrow waxed mustache and thick lips. His clothing was expensive-looking and showed reasonably good taste. His voice too, was well modulated when he finally announced his presence.

But the most significant thing about him was his right hand buried in the pocket of his coat. Quinn knew the fingers of that hand were curled about a gun.

With a supreme effort Tony Quinn forced himself to disregard this intruder. He was supposed to be blind and therefore he could not show that he realized someone was in the house.

CHAPTER V

PUSHOVER MURDER

QUINN USED his cane, tapping his way across the floor toward his favorite chair beside the fireplace. The man in the doorway spoke and Quinn swung around, almost tripping himself on a chair.

"Is there someone here?" he asked querulously. "I thought I heard a voice."

"You Quinn?" the intruder asked. "Sorry if I scared you. The front door was open so I just walked in."

"Yes—yes, I'm Tony Quinn. You'll have to excuse me. I—I'm blind. Your voice—it isn't familiar…"

"We never met before," the caller said. "My name is Topping. I'm a pal of Philip Harriman. You know him, don't you?"

"Harriman? Oh, yes. Yes, of course. He was here to see me only this afternoon. About some trouble at his store. I expected he might contact me again."

"He asked me to bring you to him," Topping said and grinned. It was a knowing grin that he believed Tony Quinn could not see. "Harriman's in a lot of trouble and he wants you right away."

Quinn hesitated. To walk out with this man might mean quick death—a bullet, or a knife in the back. Yet if he refused, the same treatment might be administered immediately. Quinn recognized his danger before him, but danger made his blood run quicker, his heart pound faster. And there was a chance, too, that he might learn something that would aid him in this puzzle that had unexpectedly confronted him.

"I'll come at once," he said. "My hat and coat are on that hat rack in a corner. Would you mind getting them? I'm a bit clumsy when I look for things."

"Sure, pal," the man who called himself Topping said blandly. "Glad to help you. Tough being blind. You can't see at all, can you?"

The chair crashed against Quinn's shoulder.

"Not a bit. Thank you for helping me with my coat. Now, if you'll take my arm and guide me down the porch steps. I know the rest of the way. Is Harriman far from here?"

"I've got a car," Topping informed. "A couple of my pals are with me, but you don't have to mind them. They're friends of Harriman's too. Say, did he give you all the details of his trouble?"

Tony Quinn's right foot moved off the path and hit a small shrub. He stumbled and only Topping's quick movement saved him from a bad fall.

"I'm sorry," Quinn apologized. "No, Harriman didn't tell me anything to speak of. Some trouble about his jewels being missing. He wanted advice as to his insurance."

"Yeah—yeah, but he's worse off now. He's got to see you. Okay, pal, up with your leg. You're getting into a car. That's it. Now just sit down. Fine! I'll get in beside you."

Tony Quinn's eyes stared straight ahead, but they saw Topping nudge one of the two men on the sidewalk. His lips moved in soundless words.

"Blind as a bat. This job is a pushover."

The car rolled away and Tony Quinn braced himself for trouble. They would hardly attempt murder on a lighted street or in traffic. Until they actually hit the outskirts, he was comparatively safe. He took a firm grip of his cane and waited for the inevitable moment when he would be forced into action.

The car headed north, turned more than a dozen corners and passed directly by Graham's jewelry store. At the next corner the driver turned again, applied the brakes and finally stopped at the curb.

TOPPING TOOK Quinn's arm.

"We're here, pal. Now all you got to do is follow me. I'll keep your arm. So will my friend. He'll take the other arm, see? That's so you won't trip and hurt yourself."

"Thank you," Quinn said. "Thank you very much. Where are we? Seems as though I smell the river."

"We're about three blocks from it," Topping answered. "Harriman's holed up—I mean he's waiting down the street."

They walked for a third of a block. Topping held Quinn's right arm and a pudgy, dark featured thug had his left. Another man trotted well ahead while the fourth, who had driven the car, brought up the rear.

Quinn saw Topping gesture and the man in front nodded. He veered off the sidewalk, looked up and down the deserted street and then hastily pulled up a sewer cover. He rolled it two or three feet away and then moved aside. Quinn felt the little hairs at the nape of his neck rise up. They were going to let him walk right into that sewer. That suited him perfectly. He'd vanish as a blind man, but, once in the darkness of the sewer, he could easily swim to safety.

"We cross the street here," Topping said. "Just hang onto my arm. Now this way."

Quinn's head was high, his blank eyes staring straight ahead. He moved toward the gaping sewer and felt like cracking the smirking thug who stood just out of his reach.

Suddenly Topping gave Quinn a shove. The apparently blind man stumbled forward. His foot went out, then down. His body followed and he plummeted through about eight feet of space before he thudded against the muck at the bottom of the sewer. To Quinn's amazement there was no water and an instant later Topping jumped down followed by two of the other men. The driver apparently had returned to the car.

Quinn was roughly seized. All pretense was gone now. Topping's voice was harsh.

"Okay, you wise D.A. Maybe Harriman didn't tell you much, but we don't take chances at this stage of the game. It's lights out for you, but you oughtn't to kick. Hell, it's a favor! I'd rather warm a morgue slab than be blind anyway."

"You—you're going to—to kill me?" Quinn asked incredulously and with just the right amount of fear in his voice. "But I don't understand. You're making a mistake."

"Maybe," Topping said, "but orders are orders. When Grogan didn't knock you off, it was put right up to me. I'll make it easy. Now don't try to fight or I'll bust your jaw. Get moving!"

A flashlight illuminated the sewer as they trudged along through the muck. Quinn stumbled and clutched at the rounded sides of the tube every few steps. Then Topping nodded to one of the other men and at the same time brought Quinn to a stop.

The thug seized a rusty handle set in one side of the pipe. He tugged and a section slid out. Quinn was forced through and he found himself in a narrow passageway carved out of rock and earth. Newly dug too, if the smell of the dirt meant anything. There wasn't room enough to walk erect. He had to crawl.

Gradually he sensed that he was climbing upward. Then he came upon a room, dug like a small cave. Inside were cots, food and tables with cards flung upon them. In one corner empty tin cans had been hurled with the carelessness of a bachelor camp.

"Sit down," Topping commanded and gave Quinn a hard shove.

QUINN REELED forward, tripped and fell heavily. He lay there, moaning gently. Topping sat down on a rude bench.

"Now this job has got to be done with class," he told his two aides. "We can't muff it or the cops will get wise. Also watch that blind guy. He can't see, but he used to be a pretty smooth article. Here's the dope and it's right from upstairs, see?"

"Hey Blackie," one of the thugs asked, "you never told us much about the guy who pays off. What's he look like? Where does he get all this mazuma he tosses around?"

"Blackie," alias Topping, ground out an oath.

"You were told to ask no questions. I'll tell you this though, so it'll settle the thing once and for all. Nobody knows what the chief looks like—not even me. When I meet him, it's in a dark room where I can't see no more'n this blind guy. He gives his orders in a whisper and he always leaves fifteen minutes before I do. But he pays off and this is the biggest deal anybody ever cooked up. So we didn't ask questions."

"Okay, Blackie," the thug muttered. "Only I don't like workin' for a mug I don't know."

"Well, stop being nosey," Blackie snapped. "I don't like it and neither does the chief. Now listen—this blind guy is important, see? He's a pal of the cops. They're bound to make a careful investigation. So here's what you do. Get one of them big buckets which we used to haul dirt in when we were digging. Fill it full of water—and get the water from the river, understand? Shove his head in the drink and hold him there until he's dead. Then take him to the real sewer, toss him in and he'll float to the river."

"I get it." One of the thugs grinned. "They'll find him floatin' around and think maybe he fell offa the pier. A blind guy might do that."

"Smart, ain't you?" Blackie snarled, "Well that's the way it's got to be. I'll take his hat and cane, beat it to the pier where the sewer comes out and plant them there. I'll make a mark with my shoe like he slipped. Nothing to it. But you guys watch him. Give me about fifteen minutes to get things set and then hand him the works. Stay right here in the cave after you finish the job. I'll be back."

Tony Quinn pulled himself up against a wall of the cave. It was illuminated by two lights that derived their juice from dry cell batteries. He spoke in the whining, pleading tones of a blind man at his wits' end.

"I—I haven't done anything. There's no reason to kill me. I—I'm blind. Let me go! I won't tell the police what happened. I couldn't anyway because I can't see you."

"Which makes it swell," Blackie leered. "Like I said before, this job is a pushover. Okay, boys. Fifteen minutes and then dunk him in some water."

Blackie took Quinn's cane and hat, stepped through the door into the dry sewer and vanished. Quinn lurched to his feet, reeled forward a few steps and one of the thugs hastily drew a gun. Then he grinned sheepishly and put the weapon back in his pocket. Quinn's hands were stretched out before him. He struck the wall, reeled back and his hands dropped on a chair. He fumbled around and sat down. There was a small table just in front of him. He found this, apparently by sense of touch.

ONE OF the thugs picked up a huge bucket, signaled his companion and went for the river water. The other killer pushed a chair up to the table and sat across from Quinn. Being alone with a man he intended soon to murder got on his nerves. Somehow he didn't like this. It was too easy.

He drew his gun again, placed it on the table and kept one hand curled around the butt.

Quinn was feeling over the table, as if trying to ascertain his position. Finally he sighed, as if in resignation of what was to come. The killer, gripping his gun, presented a problem. Quinn had intended to act swiftly, but now that did not look possible.

One hand dropped into his pocket and the thug's gun came up to cover him. Quinn kept right on fumbling, as though the gun didn't exist. He pulled a pack of cigarettes from his pocket, extracted one and put it in his mouth. The killer relaxed, but he kept the gun ready.

Quinn seemed to have some trouble with the cigarette. His hand shook badly. Some of the tobacco dropped out of the paper tube and then the whole cigarette came apart. Quinn fingered the slip of paper, rammed some of the tobacco back into it and rolled the cigarette again. He moistened it with his lips.

"Would you mind giving me a light?" he asked. "I don't know where you are, but I'm quite harmless. A cigarette builds you up a trifle. I—I wish I had a drink."

The thug lit a match and held it toward the end of the cigarette. Suddenly Quinn's lips pursed and he blew violently. The loosely packed tobacco, in the split paper, flew out and into the thug's eyes. He howled and clawed at his face. Quinn leaned across the table and belted him on the chin.

The man went catapulting backward, stumbled over a chair and fell heavily. But he was up again in a flash, and the fallen chair came with him. He hurled it and Tony Quinn had to raise one arm to shield himself.

The chair crashed against his protecting arm and shoulder. The thug reached under his coat and a spring holster threw a gun into his fist. He fired one shot and the bullet whined by Tony Quinn's ear.

Quinn made a dive toward the table and swept the battery-powered lamp it supported to the floor. The cavern was plunged into semi-darkness illuminated only by a weak light in a far corner. The killer fired two more shots, but he was nervous and jittery. This man who had been so blind could now see. Those dead eyes contained life and they glistened like the eyes of a cat in the gloom.

Quinn danced agilely to the left. The crook followed him and tried to center his gun. His finger grew white against the trigger but Quinn saw this and was ready when the fourth shot rang out. Before the crook could get his bearings again, Quinn was upon him. He seized the thug's gun hand, jerked the weapon free and hurled it into a corner. The gunman gave a bleat of fear and hastily retreated.

But he was by no means finished. His side coat pocket contained a single shot derringer and he swept this into view. He held his fire now, though, depending on that one small pellet of lead to finish off this strange being who moved so fast. The Bat whirled suddenly and did a nose dive along the floor. Not toward the crook but toward the corner where he had flung the gun. His fingers closed around it.

The thug fired and the sharp crack of his small weapon was echoed by the roar of the Bat's larger one. The thug dropped both arms suddenly. His eyes bulged, his chin dropped an inch. Then he plummeted to the ground. There was a hole squarely between his eyes.

IN TEN minutes the second thug returned. He backed into the cave, carrying the bucket half filled with water. As he turned, he saw Quinn in the dim light, saw his very much alive eyes and also the gun. He glanced toward his pal and saw him dead.

With an oath he whipped out a gun with amazing speed. It blasted once. Then there was another shot and the thug dropped to his knees. The vicious look on his face changed to one of bewilderment as death reached out with unerring aim. Between his eyes was a bluish hole. For this second time, the Bat's aim had been true.

Quinn searched the man he had killed first. In a vest pocket, folded over several times, he found a crude map. There was no time to examine it so he stowed the paper away. Then he went through the clothing of the other crook, but found nothing of interest.

Quinn hurried to the door leading into the sewer. He slammed it behind him and had the feeling that he was sealing up a tomb. He hastened down the sewer, and the extreme darkness meant little to him for his super-sensitive eyes penetrated the gloom as readily as though it had been illuminated. He had to go through the sewer to the river, just as Blackie had planned, for a blind man certainly would never find his way out of the sewer in any other fashion.

He made out another rusty handle, tugged at it and water rushed over his ankles. The real sewer had been built next to the abandoned one. He stepped into the waist deep water, waded his way along until he could see river lights. Then he let himself drop and the current caught him. He was swept out and hurled into the river. His body turned over and over.

He began to shout for help. His voice rang loudly and to his relief someone called back words of encouragement. He heard someone dive into the river and a moment later strong arms kept him afloat. If Blackie were watching now, he could only assume that Tony Quinn had been extremely lucky and that his own men had failed so badly they would flee for their lives.

CHAPTER VI

WAYS AND MEANS

IT WAS a patrolman who had rescued him. Quinn was wrapped in a blanket borrowed from a watchman's hut on the pier.

"I really don't know what happened," he mumbled while his teeth chattered. "Two men took me for an auto ride. Then something happened. I fell through a hole. Then someone put my head under water and held me there. I fought, got away and drifted through some kind of a tube. The next thing I was in the river."

The patrolman nodded sympathetically and touched his head for the benefit of the pier watchman.

"Sure, sure, friend. Of course you couldn't see nothing, huh?"

Tony Quinn's eyes were absolutely blank. "No. You're quite right. I'm blind. My name is Quinn. Tony Quinn."

The patrolman gasped and hustled Quinn into a radio car. Twenty minutes later he was safely home. Silk had returned and was there to minister to him. After the police left, Silk gave vent to his feelings.

"Plague them guys! Boss, you just got to start things rolling so we get a crack at 'em. Taking you out, thinking you were blind, and trying to bump you that way."

"It's a complication I couldn't foresee," Quinn admitted ruefully, "and I very nearly lost this bout with Fate. But the only two men who knew I wasn't blind are dead. This man called Blackie will believe some miraculous piece of luck saved me…. What did you find out about Van den Killan?"

Silk sat down. "Not so much, Boss. He's a Dutchman—you know that, of course. Lived the first thirty-five years of his life in Amsterdam. Then he went to South Africa where he got interested in a diamond mine. Say—is that guy crazy about jewelry! He buys up every important piece he can afford and he's got plenty of rocks in his safe. Credit is okay, bank account on the level. He's married, but has no children. He's supposed to be retired, I guess. Wife pals around with a bunch of society people, especially one guy named Clifford Carlyle who has plenty of dough too."

Outside a siren wailed and died. Silk sprang to the window.

"Boss, it's Police Commissioner Warner and Sergeant McGrath! What can you tell 'em? That cop who rescued you musta turned in a fast report."

"I'll tell them the truth," Quinn said, and smiled. "You were out on an errand when those thugs took me. Remember that!"

Silk let Commissioner Warner and Sergeant McGrath in. Warner rushed up to Quinn and shook his hand fervently.

"Just heard what happened, Tony. Great heavens, that must have been an awful experience!"

"It was," Quinn replied with a wan smile and pulled the blanket closer about him. "I really don't know yet how I survived. Three or four men came for me. They took me somewhere—don't ask me where, because I don't know. They ducked my head in water and held me there until they thought I was drowned. I held my breath as long as possible although I did swallow and breathe in some water. Then they threw me into some kind of a tube. Unless my sense of smell has gone as completely as my sight, it was a sewer. I felt cold air as I dropped off a regular falls. Then I began to yell for help."

"Yeah?" Sergeant McGrath stepped in front of Quinn. "What would them mugs want to bump you for? Unless"—he added this slyly—"you had pulled a fancy trick on them some time or other, or they thought maybe you were going to—some little trick like the Black Bat would pull, for instance."

COMMISSIONER WARNER whirled around. "Sergeant, you've said enough. Why in thunder you keep insinuating that Tony Quinn is the Black Bat is beyond me. He's blind—do you hear? Totally blind! Every doctor he's been to says the same thing. The Black Bat happens to be your pet hate. Well, perhaps he does deserve a good stiff prison sentence. He has broken about every law man ever created. Yet that doesn't make him Tony Quinn, you fool. Lord only knows how you ever got that wacky idea in the first place, McGrath, but it's about time you forgot it."

McGrath grumbled something under his breath and backed away. Warner apologized profusely.

"The Black Bat put one or two things over on McGrath and he can't get it out of his system," he said to Quinn. "Of course McGrath is perfectly right in trying to unmask the Bat. The fellow should be brought to justice, heaven knows. Some day he may turn into a real criminal himself and stop running down crooks and he'd be a tough one to catch…. Tony, what's your theory as to the reason for this attempt on your life?"

"Attempts," Quinn corrected with a wan smile. "I'm beginning to think that the man that Silk killed was also trying to murder me. The reason? There can be only one. Philip Harriman came to see me this afternoon. He told me that some kind of a stupendous robbery had occurred at his store. He asked my advice, as an attorney. Perhaps these crooks believe he told me more than he did. Still, I don't understand it. I can't imagine what they would think Harriman told me that could interest them. Anyhow—didn't you tell me Harriman had committed suicide?"

Warner pulled up a chair and sat down. He leaned close to Quinn.

"I'm beginning to wonder, Tony. It was Harriman's car all right, but—Well, it caught fire after it plunged off the cliff and there wasn't much left to identify. The body we found was charred from the flames, and all that was left to identify it as Harriman's was his signet ring.

"The fact remains, though, that Harriman's stock of gems has been thoroughly plundered and some damned good paste replicas put in their place. Graham's stock is similarly depleted, but Graham very definitely committed suicide. We have two witnesses who saw him put a bullet through his brain. I wonder—was it really Harriman who was destroyed in that car?"

"Then you think that Harriman may not be dead and that he not only robbed his own store, but Graham's as well?"

Sergeant McGrath strode forward.

"That's what I think," he growled flatly. "Look—those two jewelry stores were like banks. There were time locks on the vaults and no cracksman in the world could have busted in. Weren't any signs the vaults had been touched anyway. My idea is that Harriman looted his own stock and maybe Graham played along with him. Only Graham couldn't take it and bumped himself."

Quinn nodded slowly. "Perhaps you are right, Sergeant. Still, if Harriman is the man behind the robberies—and he isn't dead—then why should those thugs come here to kill me? Harriman couldn't have sent them. He knows very well that he told me nothing of importance."

Sergeant McGrath's face grew grim. "I think maybe he did. What's more, he also found out that you are the Black Bat. He told you too much and he wants to kill you before the Bat goes into action. He didn't try it that first time because he didn't find out the truth about you until later."

QUINN SHRUGGED and his blank eyes looked straight into the fireplace.

"It's a reasonable theory, Sergeant, if you really believe I am this rather spectacular creature who calls himself the Black Bat. I'm genuinely sorry you think that way because it makes a lot of trouble for you. You keep chasing clues frantically and your mind makes them point to me. But I assure you, I am quite blind. In fact I'd sell my very soul to be this Black Bat."

Commissioner Warner arose and gestured to McGrath.

"You're more of a fool than I thought, McGrath. Suspicions, suspicions. Why don't you get some that will clear up this damned case? Why don't you locate those stolen jewels? They can't just vanish. Go out and find the Black Bat too if you wish. Find him—throw him in a cell and I'll see that he's given the justice he deserves. Now get out of here. Wait for me in the car."

McGrath, his face flaming red, stalked to the door. Silk gave him a crooked grin and a low chuckle. Commissioner Warner put a friendly hand on Tony Quinn's shoulder.

"He's obsessed with the idea you're the Bat. But between you and me, Tony, this Black Bat has done the department a lot of favors. If I could help him in any way, at any time—Well, you know how it is. My duty is to put him behind bars. But my heart tells me to shake his hand."

Solemnly Warner picked up Tony Quinn's hand and wrung it. Then he nodded to Silk and vanished into the night.

Silk, his features aghast, hurried to Quinn's side.

"Say, did you hear what the commissioner said? Why, that guy, too, practically accused you of being the Bat!"

"But in a nice way." Quinn grinned broadly. "In a very nice way, Silk."

Silk shook his head. "They're up a tree, anyhow. That's plain enough. They're doing a lot of guessing and getting nowhere." He paused, and his forehead wrinkled thoughtfully. "And another thing," he cried. "What's happened to all the stuff already stolen? If Graham bumped himself off because he figured things were getting too hot, he must have hidden the rocks somewhere. The same goes for Harriman unless… Boss, do you think Harriman is really dead? Maybe he and Graham *were* in cahoots. Graham got scared, finished himself off and Harriman planted some stooge in his car and burned him up."

Tony Quinn rubbed his chin calculatingly.

"Those theories of yours, Silk, jibe with those of Commissioner Warner and Sergeant McGrath. The police are quite satisfied that Graham did commit suicide so I suppose we shouldn't question that fact. However, Silk, I make it a habit of questioning all facts, especially those which are most obvious. The stolen gems must be hidden somewhere, true. Yet to find them we must first locate our master crook.

"There are a few suspicions in my mind already. Harriman is, of course, one suspect. I hate to think that of him for he was—or is—my friend. Still he may have duped all of us cleverly. We'll try to find out. First of all I'm going to examine Graham's jewelry store—from the inside."

"How?" Silk asked incredulously. "McGrath said it's just like a bank."

"I don't know how, just yet," Quinn admitted. "But there are always ways and means."

CHAPTER VII

THE TRAP

NOISELESSLY QUINN slipped through the secret door and into his laboratory. There he divested himself of his lounging robe and other outer clothing. He donned a black suit, a black shirt. His shoes were black, with spongy rubber soles and heels. An automatic went into a spring shoulder holster, and a black hood was thrust into a side pocket. He drew on black gloves and donned a wide-brimmed hat pulled low over his face.

With a few swift changes that would be complete, once the black hood was slid over his head and scarred face, Tony Quinn had become the Black Bat. In darkness, which his own eyes could so readily penetrate, he would be nothing more than a deeper shadow in shadows.

Quinn nodded to Silk, opened a door and stepped down a ladder into a tunnel. But unlike the one inside the old sewer, only Quinn knew this tunnel, for he had painstakingly helped to dig it. He hurried along and came out through a secret door set in the floor of a garden house.

Slipping across the lawn he emerged on a side street along which there were no houses and little traffic. He turned a corner, looked carefully around and then bolted toward an old coupé that stood at the curb in front of a boarding house.

Butch, the Bat's giant assistant, lived in that boarding house and left this car at the curb for the Bat's use. Quinn climbed into it and drove away.

The Bat took a mighty risk in these expeditions, for should anything happen, he would be recognized upon close inspection. Those telltale scars were known to practically every policeman in town and there were eighteen thousand on the force.

So every movement the Bat made was cautious and planned ahead of time. That was why he was now somewhat worried. He had to invade a virgin territory of which he knew nothing and a dangerous territory at that. A crook, with his plans all laid out, would have a difficult time breaking into the Graham Jewelry Company—yet the Bat intended to do just that. He was far from satisfied with the story he had been told of Graham's suicide; even though two persons had witnessed the act and there had been a note in the dead man's handwriting. The Bat knew only too well how weak the human eye can be—and how unseeing under certain circumstances.

He left the car and merged with the shadows of the great buildings until he reached the store. Windows were covered by steel curtains and burglar alarms would guard every foot of the interior.

The Bat stepped into a doorway and eyed the building doubtfully. Despite the darkness, every detail was clear to his supersensitive eyes. Someone was moving around, just inside the door. A watchman, of course. Probably there would be one or two others and most certainly every window and door would be provided with an alarm system.

Then the Bat smiled a bit. He returned to his car, drove to a quiet section of the city and phoned his own home. Silk answered and the Bat gave precise instructions.

"I'll wait exactly five minutes after you reach the place," he said. "Be sure to impress Butch with the idea of caution. We can't slip now, Silk. It would be disastrous."

The Bat glanced at his watch, walked to the street and picked up a loose section of curbing that had fallen away. He put this into his car and drove back to the neighborhood of the Graham Company.

AN HOUR slipped by before he went into action. He made sure the street was deserted and that no patrolman was in sight. Then he drove slowly down the street, cut close to the curb and as he passed in front of the jewelry building, he hurled the piece of curbing.

It struck the large plate glass window in the center and smashed it. As the Bat stepped on the gas pedal, he heard the automatic alarm system banging away. He drove for blocks, parked and got out. He made his way back toward the building and saw the radio patrol cars, the protective agency's police and the firm's watchmen gathered in front of the building surveying the damage. No one had seen the Bat hurl that piece of curb; nothing was missing from the window. The radio cars began pulling away, but the protective agency's police guarded the shattered window.

Then a truck, once painted a dull gray and now covered with the white from plaster and with several other hues from paint, pulled to the curb. Two men climbed down. The larger one, a veritable giant, wore a painter's cap low over his face. He began fussing with ladders and lengths of board. The smaller man nodded affably to the police.

"Got here in quick time, huh, boys? Say, that's some hole in the window. Got to board her up tight until tomorrow. She'll need a whole new pane of glass then."

The two men measured the window, dragged lumber into the jewelry store and then the smaller man returned to the truck for a box of tools. As he crossed the sidewalk, he loosened his collar with a violent stretching of his neck.

In the darkness, the Black Bat's scarred features were transformed into a grin. It was working very well indeed. Butch, who was the huge, ungainly carpenter, and Silk, who was now in disguise, had secured admittance to the jewelry store. There were usually ways and means of accomplishing any purpose.

The radio police gradually left. The agency police stuck around until the window was boarded up effectively. Then, as the two carpenters went back into the jewelry store for their equipment, the watchmen took over.

Exactly five minutes later the Bat drew his hood over his features, transferred a heavy automatic to a side coat pocket and edged his way through the shadows toward the building. He slipped down an alley, vaulted a fence and came out in the rear of the jewelry house. A light winked twice and the delivery entrance door swung wide. Silk grinned broadly.

"If you were working against the law, Boss, every cop in town would have a big headache."

Butch stalked up, towering over the Bat and Silk. He nursed a fist tenderly.

"Them three watchmen are out, Boss. They won't do no squawkin'."

The Bat never doubted that, for when Butch hit a man, he stayed down. He moved into the store, closing the door behind him. Silk flipped a switch. All the burglar alarms were in working order again. The phone rang. The Bat answered and told the inquiring protective agency that everything was in order once more.

"Now," the Bat told Silk and Butch, "watch the doors. Silk, take the front, and you take the rear, Butch. If you see anybody—even the patrolman on the beat—give me warning. I'm going upstairs to the office where Graham met his death. Don't walk near the safes or the consultation rooms. There will be infra-red warning rays around them."

THE BAT hurried up the elaborate, modernistic staircase, found the office labeled with Graham's name and stepped inside. He passed by the secretary's desk, stopping only long enough to glance in the desk drawers and at the appointment book.

He closed the private office door behind him and went directly to Graham's desk. Using a flashlight with a taped lens, he made a rigid examination of the premises, especially the area directly around the high, solid-backed chair in which Graham had been seated when he died.

The rug was a light green and a spot of blood showed vividly plain. From its location the Bat estimated that it had come from Graham's temple through which the slug had smashed its way. He turned the light on the chair itself and suddenly his eyes contracted behind the slits of the mask. On the back of the chair, halfway from the bottom, was a jagged smear of dried blood. It clung to the deep red leather of the back and might have escaped less critical and observing eyes than the Bat's.

The Bat walked behind the chair and squatted. He noticed that he was completely hidden from the view of anyone standing in front of the desk or from the doorway to the outer office.

"Graham was murdered," the Bat told himself. "The killer knocked him unconscious, hid behind this chair and when McFayden and the secretary entered, it was the killer's hand they saw rising from beneath the desk. Graham's hands were hanging limply down. But the killer got some blood on the sleeve of his coat and unknowingly brushed it against the back of this chair. It's murder—not suicide."

He began examining the papers on top of the desk. There was nothing of interest but the Bat's keen eyes saw a pad. On the blank surface of the top piece of paper were slight indentations, as if someone had written on the pad and that writing had been torn off.

The Bat hurried into the secretary's office and opened the pencil sharpener so that he was able to spill some of the dust from the pencil lead onto a bit of paper. He carried this back into Graham's office and gently blew some of the finer particles of graphite dust onto the scrap pad.

The dust settled into the indentations to bring into relief what had been traced there.

Vaguely, the Bat made out a drawing of what seemed to be an immense diamond. It was crudely done but plain enough. Below it was one significant word. "Kill—"

It looked as though there had been other words written as well but not firmly enough to make an impression on the under sheet of paper. The Bat opened a drawer, found Graham's check book and compared the writing in it with the writing that formed the one word—"Kill." It matched!

"Graham wrote this," the Bat told himself grimly. "He was in the presence of his murderer, knew he was doomed to die and wanted to leave some clue that the killer wouldn't recognize. That clue is in the drawing of the diamond. It must be! But Graham didn't fool the killer for he must have recognized the danger of this drawing and the few words written below it. He removed that paper from the pad but in his excitement forgot that there might be an indentation from the point of Graham's pencil."

The Bat carefully stowed the slip of paper into a pocket. Then he searched the desk drawers thoroughly. There was nothing of interest, but in the bottom of the waste basket he found ashes of what seemed to have been a letter. Working swiftly, the Bat extracted a glass cutter from a small kit of instruments that he carried.

He sped down into the store proper and cut two six-inch sections of glass out of a counter.

RETURNING TO the office, he slid one piece of glass beneath the ashes until the charred bits of paper were upon it. The second piece of glass he used as a cover, pressing the ash firmly down with it. He held the two pieces of glass together with rubber bands that he took from Graham's desk. Then he replaced the waste paper in the basket and covered up all other signs of his work.

One thing the Bat knew now. Graham had been murdered cleverly but he had tried to leave a clue to the identity of the killer. He had failed—but only partially. That drawing of a diamond might mean something.

As he crossed the floor toward the door he heard a soft whistle from downstairs. Instantly he sped to the stairway landing and peered down. Shadowy figures were before the drawn curtain of the front door and a peremptory knocking indicated that the visitors sought to summon the watchman.

"Silk," the Bat whispered hoarsely, "you and Butch go out the rear exit! Get on to that all-night drugstore and wait. I'll call you soon as I can. Hurry!"

Silk didn't protest. When the Bat issued orders, they were to be followed explicitly, no matter what the consequence. Silk hated to leave the Bat in a trap, as this looked to be, but he went anyway. It wouldn't help any if all three of them were trapped.

The front door opened and two men came in. One held a gun in his fist.

"Odd," he grunted, "where those watchmen are. *Herr* Wohl, do you think—"

"*Ach*, I do not know," a gruff voice responded. "Perhaps we should the police call."

The two men stepped deeper into the store and reached the weak rays of light from the bulbs above the vaults. One was a thick-set stoop-shouldered man who wore nose glasses and had a pompous mien. The other man was slender and nervous. He held the gun.

CHAPTER VIII

ESCAPE IN THE DARK

M**OVING CAUTIOUSLY,** the two invaders reached the stairway and peered up into the darkness. Neither one took note of the slightly darker section of shadow that was the Bat.

"Something is wrong," the slender man said sharply. "I think we ought to phone the police. Maybe the man who broke the window came back."

"*Ja*," the heavier man retorted. "It iss, perhaps, better."

They turned to hurry toward the phone on a desk in one corner. Then a voice came down to them from the upper regions of the store. It was a soft, yet commanding voice.

"Both of you—don't move unless it is your wish to die! You—with the gun—place it on the floor and then kick it into a corner. If you doubt I'm in a position to enforce my orders, look up here."

They looked, faces pale, mouths agape. The Bat had turned the tiny ray of his flash upon the gun he held. The slender man bent down, put the gun on the floor and kicked it out of sight. Then the two men walked slowly up the staircase, hands shoulder high.

"You are showing remarkable judgment," the Bat told them. "Now—into Graham's office where we can have a little talk."

"Just a minute," the slender man said hoarsely. "If you're a crook and want us to open the vaults, we simply can't do it. They are equipped with time locks."

"I'm not interested in the safe," the Bat said pleasantly. "I want information."

"Where are the watchmen?" Wohl demanded.

"Sleeping," he was told. "Peacefully sleeping, gentlemen. Right this way. And please stop for a moment while I make certain you are not further armed."

They were not. A moment later all three were in the quiet security of a dead man's office. The Bat perched himself on a corner of the desk and waved the two men into chairs.

"Mr. Wohl," he said gently, "please take that scowl off your face. You're a dignified, capable-looking man when you don't scowl."

"Mein Gott!" Wohl exploded. "Who are you? How can you see that I scowl? All is darkness here. I cannot see any part of you."

"They call me—the Bat. Like my namesake, I am able to see in darkness, Mr. Wohl. Now if you'll introduce yourselves, we'll get down to business. I mean no harm."

"I'm McFayden," the slender man burst out. "And I trust you! I've heard of you often. You're no crook. You fight crooks. I'll tell you anything you want to know. This man with me is Wohl, the gem expert who works here. I'm chief clerk. We got word from the protective agency that the window had been smashed so we came down to see what had happened."

The Bat nodded. "Now just relax. McFayden, you were one of the witnesses to Graham's suicide. Give me all the details."

McFayden shuddered and the Bat saw his lanky frame tremble.

An arm encircled McGrath's throat.

"There aren't many. I—I knew something had gone wrong. He was so nervous and worried. Then when I came back to talk to him—he'd sent for me—I saw him sitting right there, behind the desk. Then, while I watched him, he raised his right hand, took a gun out of the drawer and before I could even move, he—he shot himself through the head! Miss Curtis, his secretary, saw him do it too. We ran for help. He—he was dead when I returned."

"I believe you," the Bat answered simply. Then he turned to Wohl who sat bolt upright in his chair. "And you, *mein Herr*, I have known of for a long time. You are one of the best jewel experts in the world. For years you worked in Amsterdam as a diamond cutting supervisor. Am I right?"

WOHL NODDED sadly. "*Ja*. And I wish I had never left Holland. Ach, this suicide, this robbery! It iss beyond me. Now I have also lost my chob, *ja*. Who would hire a man who permitted millions of dollars worth of false chems to be placed in here as real ones? Harriman's expert, he also is much worried. I talked to him but a few hours ago."

"Where?" the Bat queried.

Wohl looked a bit startled to the Bat's sensitive eyes.

"We had dinner in the hoffbrau—*Unter-den-Linden* it iss called, For two hours we talked—until we heard the news of *Herr* Harriman's death."

"And Harriman's expert is whom?"

"A great man, *ja!* Greater than I, for he spent many years in India where truly great chems are sold. Rajas and princes trusted him. He is himself an Egyptian. His name—Anghis Khan."

McFayden arose abruptly and the Bat's gun covered him. "D-don't shoot," the jewel clerk quavered. "I—I just want to get a cigarette from the desk. Haven't any of my own."

McFayden walked around the desk and it seemed to the Bat as though he took plenty of room. The chief clerk's right hand came up, brushed back his hair and then he walked toward the desk. He took a cigarette from the container, lit it and returned to his chair.

Somehow, the Bat didn't like that bit of action. McFayden's face seemed to have suddenly become crafty too.

"I'll be going now," the Bat said. "You men have been of great help to me. Please remain exactly where you are. After five minutes you may do anything you please."

Gun leveled, he backed toward the door. More and more the Bat sensed danger although nothing had happened outside the private office and the same eerie silence held sway over the store. He opened the door, clumped through the secretary's office, stepped into the hallway and closed the door with a thud. But a split second later the door was open a crack and the Bat stood outside listening. The inner door was still open.

McFayden's voice was low, hardly more than a whisper, but the Bat had the hearing of a blind man. Every word came plainly.

"The Bat, is he? Well I'll show him, with his damned mask. Graham used to keep a lot of valuable stuff in his wall safe. When I passed by it, I put my hand through the warning ray. By this time the protective police and the regular cops will be covering the place."

"You fool!" Wohl grated. "That was the Bat, *ja*. I am sure of it, and he is not one to fight. Also he iss honest—the friend of the police, though they will not openly admit it. He did not harm us and you—you have called the police to shoot him down. *Ach*, that was wrong. He was not a burglar."

"That's what you say," McFayden whispered triumphantly. "But I happen to know he's killed a lot of people. Crooks maybe, but just the same he's wanted for murder. And he broke in here, didn't he? That man isn't safe to be loose. Next thing he'll turn crooked as they're all saying he will, and then what'll happen?"

THE BAT waited to hear no more. He rushed down the steps, two at a time. But he stopped quickly. Cars were pulling to the curb and uniformed men were rushing toward the door. By now the whole building was surrounded!

But the Bat remained calm, as he thought swiftly. All exits on the lower floor were definitely out of the question. The windows on the second floor were heavily barred and also eliminated. There remained only the roof.

Then a harsh voice demanded entrance as the banging on the front door grew peremptory. Sergeant McGrath! The Bat's heart began pounding. Of all men, McGrath would be the most persistent, once he learned it was the Bat who had invaded the premises.

McFayden passed within five feet of the Bat as he rushed down the steps. Wohl stood in the doorway of the office. The Bat sidled away, merging with the darkness. At any moment the lights would be turned on.

He studied the layout of the second floor, seeing as clearly through the darkness as a normal man would if the whole place was brilliantly illuminated. There was an iron ladder leading to a trap door set in the ceiling. That meant a roof exit. It would be protected to keep intruders from coming down, but hardly fastened so that it couldn't be opened from within.

He also saw a door, half ajar, leading into a stock room. The Bat ran lightly toward the iron ladder. As he reached for the rungs, the lights were turned on and a score of police burst into the store. The Bat couldn't risk climbing the ladder now. Instead he bolted into the supply room and gently closed the door.

Sergeant McGrath was giving crisp orders.

"Keep your eyes peeled and your guns ready. It's the Bat! Take him alive, do you hear? Shoot if you have to, but aim low. McFayden, you and Wohl stay downstairs! This Bat can shoot faster than chained lightning. I'm going up. The rest of you search the first floor and watch me too. Come flying if you hear a shot. And I'll show myself every minute or two. If he knocks me cold, I won't show. That'll be a signal for you boys to start in."

The Bat, listening from the other side of the storeroom door, gulped and broke out in a cold sweat. McGrath was clever—clever and capable. He was coming up alone so that none of his men might suffer needless risk. He depended on the fact that if the Bat struck, the police downstairs would close in. Whatever else he might be, McGrath was no fool.

McGrath inspected Graham's offices first and then darted into the room where the jewels were weighed and examined, a miniature laboratory. Finally he stepped cautiously down the corridor, gun hand extended slightly and the weapon nosed up so it could instantly be snapped down in firing position. He saw the storeroom door and the ladder to the roof as well.

On the other side of the storeroom door the Bat waited with held breath. McGrath kicked the door wide and eyed the darkened room suspiciously. He saw the light switch about three feet from the door and stepped toward it.

Something came flashing out of the air. An arm encircled his throat and prevented any cry for help. At the same time he felt his gun hand gripped so hard that nerves and muscles felt paralyzed. He gave a wrench, trying to free himself, but only succeeded in getting more firmly in the grip of his unseen adversary.

THEN A voice breathed softly in his ear:

"Sorry, Sergeant. I don't like to do this." And a fist slugged McGrath across the back of the neck.

Stunned, the officer reeled away a step as the grip on his throat relaxed. He was straightening up to hurl himself forward when the Bat's fist exploded against his jaw. McGrath started for the floor, but the Bat seized him and laid him down gently. Hastily he stripped off the officer's coat and donned it. He placed the unconscious sergeant's gray fedora on his head and backed out of the storeroom.

Below, a dozen patrolmen were positive they saw Sergeant McGrath emerge from the room.

The Bat had his hood stowed away in a pocket, but the fedora hid his features well. He hurried to the ladder and swarmed up it. Pushing open the trap door at the top, he stepped out on the flat roof.

The next office building was across an alley about four feet wide. The Bat raced across the roof, jumped and landed lightly. He was up again in a flash and three minutes later he was opening an office door and racing to pick up a telephone.

Butch's rough voice greeted him with a bellow of relief.

"Gosh, boss, I figured the cops had you that time. We shouldn't oughta have left, but Silk says we gotta, so we did. You okay?"

"So far," the Bat said grimly. "All that worries me is Sergeant McGrath. He thinks Tony Quinn is the Black Bat and in about two minutes he'll wake up and be trying to find out again. I'll be coming by where I told you to meet me, Butch. Stand ready! There is no time to lose."

The Bat hurried down to the lower floor. Peering through the glass door in the lobby he saw more police hurry into the jeweler's building. McGrath had apparently awakened and put up a howl. The Bat opened the doors, slipped out and reached an alley on the far side of the building. He raced down it, cleared two low fences and finally came out near the spot where Butch had left his coupé parked. He got in, started away and turned on a radio concealed under the dash.

A general alarm was being sent out and the report made the Bat sweat profusely.

"All cars… All cars… Converge on Twenty-two thirty-eight Teneyke Boulevard. Close all streets and surround the house. Keep guard and allow no one to enter. Wait for Sergeant McGrath's orders."

The Bat wheeled around a corner and tramped on the brake. Before he could pull to the curb, a man came running toward the car. The Bat slid over in the seat and opened the door beside the wheel; Butch jumped aboard and took over.

"Faster, Butch," the Bat groaned. "They're closing in now. Hear the sirens?"

CHAPTER IX

MURDER AGAIN

GRIMLY BUTCH bent over the wheel and the powerful motor under that dilapidated hood did things for him. He reached the extreme end of Tony Quinn's estate and slowed a trifle. The Bat leaped, landed as confidently as a cat and vanished through a section of high stone wall. Hastily he doffed his hood, stripped off McGrath's gray coat and hat, hid these under his own black coat and moved across a path toward the garden house. Through the darkness he could see a score of police taking up positions all about the mansion. McGrath was certainly determined to satisfy himself this time. If Tony Quinn should not be at home….

The Bat sidled into the garden house and vanished through a whole section of wall. Two minutes later he was in his own laboratory. The rumble of voices from outside was harsh. The Bat stripped off his clothes in a flash, rolled them into a ball and tossed them, with McGrath's coat and hat, down the secret passageway.

Now it was Tony Quinn—blind Tony Quinn—who listened intently at the secret door leading into the living room. The police hadn't reached that room yet. Trust Silk to see they were delayed as long as possible.

"Never mind what I mean!" Quinn heard Sergeant McGrath bark at Silk. "I'm an officer of the law and I'm going to search this house! Where's Quinn?"

"He's about somewhere," Silk answered nervously. "I—I don't know exactly where, because I've been busy in the kitchen. Probably he's sleeping. He should be at this hour."

McGrath pushed Silk out of the way and strode into the living room. He stopped dead and stared, with his mouth hanging wide open. In the deep leather chair before the fireplace sat Tony Quinn. His cane was between his legs and his sightless eyes were staring in the general direction of the hallway.

"What's the matter, Silk?" he asked querulously. "What's wrong? Silk! Silk—where are you?"

"Coming, sir," Silk called back and the relief in his voice was plain to Tony Quinn, at least. "It's Sergeant McGrath and about a hundred cops, sir. They're all around the place. I think he's gone nuts, if you'll pardon me, sir."

"Tell him to come in."

Tony Quinn was looking straight at Sergeant McGrath. Once Quinn's lower lip quivered as though he might enjoy a lusty laugh. McGrath's hair was tousled. His jaw was swollen and somewhat out of kilter. He was in his shirt sleeves and the shoulder of his shirt was ripped. But more than anything else, Quinn enjoyed the stupefaction on the detective's face.

"Where is the sergeant?" Quinn went on impatiently. Ask him in, Silk. All policemen are friends of mine. I've told you that often enough."

McGrath walked up to Quinn and stood looking down at him. Certainly this man was blind.

"I—I guess I made a mistake," McGrath mumbled. "I figured this time I had you. But listen, Quinn—maybe I'm wrong, and maybe I'm just a sucker. If I'm wrong, I apologize. If I'm a sucker, get this! I'll run you in if it's the last thing I do."

Tony Quinn's forehead wrinkled into deep lines. "I'm afraid I don't understand, Sergeant. Have I done something to aggravate you? I'm terribly sorry. I'm afraid I was asleep when you arrived. Dozed off in my chair here. Bear with a blind man. Sometimes sleep comes with great difficulty and when I manage to drop off, I usually finish my nap wherever I happen to be."

"It ain't that!" McGrath howled. "It's this! Look at the damned thing—if you *can* see!"

HE POINTED dramatically to his forehead. Emblazoned in the center of it was the image of a bat, wings outspread. But Tony Quinn looked slightly to McGrath's left.

"I apologize again," he told the officer. "Sorry I can't look, Sergeant. You'll have to describe what it is you wish me to know about."

"Aw, forget it!" McGrath swung around. "I guess I'm nothing but a fool. A fool, and the laughing stock of the whole doggone police force."

He gave orders and the house was cleared of policemen. The quiet that fell with the slamming of the front door almost hurt. Silk was mopping his face and drinking a rye highball concocted of nine-tenths whiskey.

"Silk"—Tony Quinn still looked directly into the fireplace and his lips didn't seem to move—"Silk, make certain McGrath left no guard."

Silk returned after a few minutes.

"They're all gone, Boss. I'm sure of it. Butch is on the lookout too and he just passed me the high sign. Are we going out? You haven't had any sleep."

"Sleep can wait."

Tony Quinn arose and, tapping his cane before him, walked slowly toward the secret door. Then, like a ghost, he vanished from sight. Silk slipped through the door also. He found Quinn switching on a powerful lamp on the laboratory bench. Beneath it, Quinn put the charred paper he had taken from Graham's waste basket.

"This," he told Silk, "I found in Graham's office. If Graham wanted to destroy this letter, permanently, he'd have burned it elsewhere. I think someone other than Graham set fire to the paper because he wanted no one to see it and he, himself, didn't want to take a chance on having this letter found on his person."

Quinn carefully raised one of the glass slides. With a delicate brush dipped in a colorless shellac, he set the remnants of ashes so he might work with them freely. Next Quinn, slid a strong magnifying unit over the ashes and peered through.

"This letter," he said in an excited whisper, "was written on Philip Harriman's stationery and it was signed by Harriman. The few words that are left show some kind of a deal was in order. Unfortunately, not enough is left to give me a clear picture."

Quinn set this clue aside, took from his pocket the folded paper which he had removed from one of the thugs who had tried to murder him. This gave him much more satisfaction.

"It's a floor plan of some kind of a store," he told Silk. "Look—even the counters are blocked in and so is a safe. A big one if the map is drawn to scale."

"But what good is it," Silk queried, "if it doesn't say where this place is located?"

Quinn smiled grimly. "It does, Silk. A draftsman evidently drew this up. His first sketch was erased, but take a look at those block letters which didn't erase perfectly. They indicate the two streets that form a corner where this store is located. Get me a directory, Silk. Hurry!"

Silk procured one. Quinn riffled the pages, found the street section and then slowly leaned back in his chair.

"THIS," HE said, "is a map of the interior and exterior of a jewelry store owned and operated by a man named Robert Gill. I know the place. Its amount and quality of business is on a par with that of Harriman's and Graham's. Silk, we've got to get busy. Gill's is the next place slated to be robbed. Put on one of your disguises—and hurry. Then get Butch's coupé and wait for me near the gate." Within fifteen minutes the Bat was driving the coupé toward Gill's store. Silk looked puzzled.

"What good is a floor plan," he asked, "that doesn't show those crooks how to bust in a vault? And another thing—there must be somebody you suspect."

"I don't know exactly what those floor plans mean," the Bat admitted, "but I'm going to find out. About suspects—there are several in my mind. Harriman, of course, may not be dead and may be working under cover. I hate to think that. Then there is a man named Wohl, who was Graham's gem expert. He and McFayden, Graham's chief clerk, were the men who came into the store when I was there. McFayden acted suspiciously and I don't trust him. He tricked me, sent in an alarm after he'd practically promised not to interfere. Perhaps I was questioning him too closely. When I pretended to leave, he made definite statements that indicate he doesn't particularly like the Bat."

With the hood over his shoulders, the Bat sent his coupé across town, down an avenue and finally they saw the store owned by Gill, the jeweler. It was an imposing place. Steel curtains were drawn down inside the windows and undoubtedly every modern alarm device was in use.

As the Bat slowed and rolled to the curb half a block away, lights suddenly flashed on in the store. At the same instant the burglar gong on the wall outside began to clang. Sirens whined. Radio cars were coming in all directions.

"There was another alarm flashed through," the Bat whispered. "Someone must have tripped a ray and put in an automatic call to the police."

"Look!" Silk pointed to the main entrance of the store. "There's a guy coming out."

"Gill!" the Bat said explosively. "I've seen his picture in the papers often. Silk, we're trapped! The radio cars have sealed up all side streets and the main thoroughfare. If we try to get clear now, they'll stop us for investigation. They'll strip this hood from my head! Even if I take it off right now myself, somebody is bound to recognize these scars—and won't that make Sergeant McGrath happy!"

"What'll we do?" Silk cried anxiously.

"Duck! Make it seem this car is empty. They'll pay all their attention to Gill for a few minutes and... Gosh, Silk, we're sunk! Here comes McGrath in his squad car. Must have picked him up by radio."

Sergeant McGrath was coming hell-bent. Brakes and tires squealed in unified protest as he stopped the heavy squad car. He was out of it in a flash. Silk placed a hand lightly on the Bat's arm.

"Listen, Boss, it's the only way. I'll swipe McGrath's car and make a run for it. They'll chase me, but that bus of his looks like it could run rings around them radio cars. The side streets will open up and you can make a break for it."

"Good man, Silk." The Bat nodded. His hand dipped into his pocket and he handed Silk a sticker, fashioned after the likeness of a bat. "You'll make it all right. Plant that sticker on the windshield when you abandon the car. That will prevent McGrath from blowing anyone else for the theft. Keep your head down. They'll probably open fire."

SILK SLIPPED out of the coupé, made a wild dive toward the building shadows and then sidled half a block down the street. True to the Bat's theory all police were clustered around the excited jeweler. Silk darted across the road and leaped into the detective cruiser. The motor was still humming. He released the brake, slid low behind the wheel and tramped hard on the gas pedal.

McGrath was the first to notice the theft of his car. He shouted a warning. Radio cars started after the cruiser. McGrath clung to one and began emptying his gun at the fleeing squad car. But Silk knew how to handle a car. He raced around corners, doubled back down avenues and finally pointed the nose of the cruiser for the outskirts.

No one noticed the dilapidated coupé that slowly pulled away from the curb and vanished into the night.

CHAPTER X

TORTURE FOR SILK

COOLLY SILK glanced up in the rear view mirror and grinned. All signs of pursuit had gone. He was alone and streaking down a highway miles from the city.

But was he? As Silk swept around a hairpin turn, lights suddenly flashed for a second in the mirror. Silk tensed. He was being followed—and by a car being driven without lights. They had been turned on momentarily, as the driver rounded the curve.

Police wouldn't do that. They would have opened fire if they were as close to the stolen police car as this mystery car was.

Silk felt a hollow sensation in the pit of his stomach. Was it possible that the burglars who had been in Gill's store had watched Silk steal McGrath's car and were following it? Had they also noticed that the Bat had made good his escape—and thought now they were on his trail?

Silk estimated his chances for escape from the pursuers and realized they were few. The car behind him was as fast as Sergeant McGrath's cruiser and once the men in it opened fire chase would end abruptly. If that did happen Silk had to let the Bat know what had occurred. He fumbled in his pocket and found a piece of paper and a pencil.

Placing the paper on one knee he scrawled a brief message while he piloted the speeding car with the other hand. Then he jerked open the glove compartment in the dashboard. There were several envelopes inside, used by McGrath to file his reports. Silk addressed one—not to Tony Quinn, for that would have been too dangerous—but to Carol Baldwin.

This done he suddenly eased up on the gas pedal and the pursuing car gained on him so rapidly that Silk could almost make out the marker plates. Silk determined on a bold move. He stepped on the gas again and pulled away, for the pursuing car had slowed considerably to avoid crashing.

Suddenly Silk yanked the wheel and sent his car careening off the highway. The pursuers flashed by and brakes began to squeal. But Silk had seen the marker plate. He hastily made note of it on the letter.

Then he backed around and headed toward the city.

All hope of escape was gone now for those men who were following him would start shooting at any minute. Silk sealed the envelope, fastened a one-dollar bill to a small portion of the flap and kept his eyes on the highway until he saw a rural free delivery box ahead of him. Abruptly he slowed, stopped beside the box and thrust the envelope and dollar bill inside. He had already hastily written instructions to forward it, special delivery. All he could hope for now was that the letter would be picked up in time to give Carol an opportunity to warn Tony Quinn of his danger.

As he pulled away from the mailbox, the pursuing car was sweeping down on him. But he was certain they had not seen him mail that letter.

He eased up on the gas pedal, pulled well over and waited for the pursuing car to pass. It drew abreast and Silk saw the snout of a tommy-gun covering him.

"Stop!" a hoarse voice yelled. "Stop or you'll fill yourself full of steel jackets!"

Silk groaned and clamped his foot on the brake. The windows of the cruiser were shatter proof, but steel-jacketed machine-gun slugs would smack straight through. Trying to run for it would be suicidal and they would catch him sooner or later anyway. Silk stopped the car, got out and raised his hands shoulder high.

HE WAS thankful that he was in disguise. Two men covered him and one gestured with the muzzle of his gun for Silk to step into their sedan He obeyed. The police cruiser was left where he had parked it and the sedan headed back toward the city.

"You've made a mistake, gentlemen," Silk said uneasily. "If—if you're kidnapping me, I won't be a profitable undertaking."

"Maybe," one of the men grunted. "But you will be profitable for an undertaker if you don't talk. We saw you swipe that cop's car. What was the big idea? But don't bother to talk now. Just lift your mitts nice and high while I give you a frisk."

Silk was searched thoroughly, but not until his captor encountered the small Bat sticker did Silk really lose hope. As the thug brought this out his eyes flashed and for a moment a wave of fear came over him. Then remembering the gun he held, and that two other armed men were with him, his confidence came back.

"The Black Bat!" he snarled, and the gun jabbed Silk harder.

"The Bat?"

The man at Silk's left gaped. The driver swerved the car crazily for a second as he squirmed around in the seat for a quick look.

"It's him all right," the leader of the trio grunted. "Man, won't the boys be glad to see him!"

Silk remained silent. He knew that adopting Tony Quinn's identity was tantamount to swift death, but the Bat needed time to get organized. Silk was narrowly watched now, but he was alert also, taking in every detail of the route to his destination.

The sedan entered the outskirts of the city, rolled down a quiet avenue and as the first streaks of dawn broke over the towering buildings, the car nosed into an alley and stopped beside a loading platform. A gray hearse was parked beside the sedan. Silk shivered. This was getting just a little too close to the ultimate finish.

"Get out!" he was harshly ordered. "Keep your hands way up. The first phony move means a belly full of slugs."

They pushed him up the four steps of the loading platform. A sliding door opened and he was shoved inside. The hearse belonged here all right. Silk was a prisoner in an undertaker's place of business.

A tall, wide-shouldered man with a narrow, sleek mustache listened to the report of his underlings and jerked his head toward Silk as the Bat's name was mentioned. He took the seal of the Bat and waved it under Silk's nose.

"So *you're* The Bat! I expected a powerful man, an intelligent-looking man—not a rummy heel like you."

"That's good," Silk breathed in relief. "Because I don't know who this Bat guy is. Sure I swiped the bus, but I didn't know it was a cop's car. I was casing the Gill jewelry place—getting set to make a play for the stuff in the window, when the alarm system goes off. I figured if I was caught, they might say I was the one that had busted in, so I grabbed that police bus and beat it. I found that funny looking sticker on the seat and shoved it in my pocket. I'm a right guy and if you boys made a mistake, I ain't the kind to hold it in for you."

THE TALL man grinned crookedly. He had black eyes that looked sinister to Silk and his lips were thick. Otherwise his features were regular, almost handsome. Silk had seen him somewhere. He was certain of it, but recognition refused to come.

"Now listen," this man told Silk, "you're going to talk. If you want to save yourself time and a lot of unpleasantness, you can either admit you are the Bat now—or tell me just who he is."

"I'm dumber than a clam," Silk said. "Because I don't know what the devil you're talking about."

The tall man scowled. He lashed out and the back of his hand struck Silk across the mouth. Then the man walked over to a telephone and dialed a number. At a signal, one of Silk's captors stepped behind him and pressed his palms against Silk's ears. The man at the phone asked for someone and apparently didn't reach his party for he hung up at once.

Five minutes crept by and the phone rang. This time Silk was permitted to listen.

"Chief," the tall man said, "this is Blackie. We got a guy down here who we think is either the Bat or somebody who helps him. He's a thin guy, about five feet six or seven. His hands are skinny too, and he don't look like so much."

Blackie listened for a few moments and then said:

"Okay. We'll find out what he knows. Can we make him talk? Listen— I know ways that would make the mummy of Tut-ankh-Amen squeal. I'll let you know when he sings."

Blackie rose from the chair behind the desk and approached Silk. He put his hands on his hips and surveyed the prisoner contemptuously.

"I've an idea," he said slowly, "that you might be a stubborn fool, so just to save time I'll give you a sample of what's in store for you unless we hear all you know. Boys, put him on that slab and strap him down."

Silk managed to get in one husky punch against the eye of the thug nearest him before they pounced down, lifted him up and deposited him on a long table used in embalming work. Straps pinned him firmly to the table. Blackie picked up a scalpel and fingered it.

He pulled up Silk's trouser leg and made a deft incision. Silk bit his lower lip. Not that it hurt—so far. There was hardly any pain from that sharp blade. Then Blackie took a blunt object that looked like a piece of dark crayon. He suddenly rubbed the point of it against the open wound on Silk's leg.

Instantly a flash that felt like a bolt of lightning shot through Silk's body. Blackie kept on rubbing the object and Silk's senses spun crazily. He never believed anything could involve such excruciating agony. Sweat poured down his face, turned his face gray under the disguise, and made his mouth go dry from sudden fever induced by the pain.

"And that," Blackie grunted in high satisfaction, "is a sample of what's to come. That dark stuff is silver nitrate and if it hurts a little just chalk that up to modern medicine, because the stuff also sterilizes the wounds. You won't die of poisoning—but you might die of shock induced by pain. Maybe it would be wise if you told me who the Bat is?"

"Maybe," Silk said through clenched teeth. "But I can't tell you something I don't know."

AGAIN THE knife cut deeply into Silk's leg and once more the silver nitrate seared through the wound until Silk's senses reeled. His tense body relaxed, his head fell back and he surrendered to blissful unconsciousness.

"Wake up!" Blackie slapped him hard. "Wake up!"

Silk opened his eyes. "The beauty of this treatment," Blackie went on maliciously, "is that when one leg goes numb we still have the other. Then the arms. It will take many hours before you finally die. Let's have it, you dope. You're not the Bat because he's a bigger man than you. But you know who the Bat is—and I'm going to find out. Do you tell me? Or shall I cauterize another little incision?"

"Go—to—hell!" Silk mumbled through parched lips.

He braced himself for another gouging with the silver nitrate pencil. But as Blackie bent over Silk, the light struck him and something clicked in Silk's mind. He knew who this man was. What good that knowledge would do him had become problematical, but Silk had not given up hope yet.

Two minutes later he lapsed into unconsciousness once more and all Blackie's slapping could not bring him back to his senses. Blackie shrugged and turned away.

"We'll wait until he wakes up. Anyway I've got to get busy. You boys watch him. If he gets away, I'll give *you* a taste of that silver nitrate stuff."

CHAPTER XI

THE TIP-OFF

EASILY THE BAT made his escape from the police lines, for Silk had drawn practically every car away. He drove to the street where Butch lived, parked the car and gave Butch a covert signal. Ten minutes later the Bat was in his laboratory, peeling off his hood and clothing, to become blind Tony Quinn once more.

An hour passed and no word from Silk. Quinn grew nervous although none of it showed in his placid features as he sat before the fireplace. Quinn took no chances, even when he was home, and supposedly alone. There might be others besides Sergeant McGrath who were suspicious.

So if anyone peered through the windows of Tony Quinn's home, they saw only a blind man, idling time away by living in his thoughts.

At five-thirty there was still no sign of Silk, and Tony Quinn had to act. He arose, tapped his cane slowly and made his way into the reception hall. Here no one could see him from the windows. He picked up the phone and dialed a number. The voice that answered was wide-awake and crisp.

Carol Baldwin even put some of her personal beauty into her words. She was Tony Quinn's dream of feminine perfection come true. She, alone, had given him back his sight and restored his peace of mind. Her own father had been shot by a criminal. The bullet had lodged in his brain, blinding him by severing nerves. It was the healthy corneas from his eyes that had been transplanted in Tony Quinn's. And her father's dying wish had been that she in some way ally herself with forces that opposed crime. For this reason she had become Tony Quinn's capable and trusted assistant.

"Can you come over?" Quinn asked. "It's important. Drop by and pick up Butch. I'll wait for you—in the lab. Use the entrance and be careful you aren't seen."

"Has something happened, Tony?" she asked anxiously.

"Yes—it's Silk. I'll explain when you come. Hurry!"

During the thirty minutes that elapsed before the arrival of Carol and Butch, Tony Quinn grew more and more worried. If Silk had been caught by the police, Sergeant McGrath would have been on the job long before now. And Silk had got away to too good a start on the police cars to be caught. There was something else and it could mean but one thing. Some clever crooks—in all likelihood the same who had been attempting to rob the Gill jewelry store, had observed Silk steal McGrath's car and had followed him. They must have had good reason for that, also—had probably in some way identified him with the Bat. Just how, he could not guess, unless the crooks had caught a glimpse of the Bat's black costume, and then seeing Silk escaping had leaped to the conclusion that he was the Bat, and had discarded his black hood in order to escape. Even if they did not believe Silk was the Bat, once they had caught him, Silk had that Black Bat sticker and if it should be discovered, he would be subjected to all manner of ways and means to make him talk. Criminals, the entire underworld, would give a good deal to lay their hands on their enemy, the Bat.

CAROL ENTERED through the secret door. Butch closed it as he stepped into the room. Quinn took both Carol's extended hands.

"Silk has disappeared," he said swiftly. "I don't know what happened, but if he was making some kind of an investigation, he'd have called back by now. Somebody's got him—that's the only answer—and we must rescue him."

He turned his head and spoke to the hulking man.

"Butch, the only work for you at the moment is to prowl around the underworld. Visit the bars and other hangouts. Try to learn something about a crook named Blackie—a rather tall man whose most outstanding feature is his waxed mustache. Also listen and see if you hear any undue talk about the Black Bat."

"I'm on my way."

Butch nodded and vanished through the hidden door. Carol sat down while Tony Quinn paced the floor nervously.

"I'm worried, Carol," he said presently. "Silk is invaluable to our organization, besides being one of my best friends. If I only knew where to begin.... But I haven't the least idea how to start. His disappearance is of course mixed up with these jewel robberies, but just who has been getting away with those millions of dollars' worth of gems—"

"There are no suspects?" Carol asked him.

"Suspects! Oh yes—but nothing definite. Graham's store, as you know, was robbed of gems worth millions. Harriman's place was also looted, and something happened at Gill's place only a short time ago. Graham is dead. So is Harriman—as far as anybody knows. Yet there hasn't been any clue as to who actually got away with those gems—if those two men did or not—or where the gems are right now."

"Tony," Carol said tensely, "suppose I make the rounds of those three jewelry stores. I'll be a hard customer to please and stay at each one as long as possible. Perhaps I'll learn something. The chance is small, but unless you have something definite to work on, I think we should risk it."

Tony Quinn nodded. "The stores will open for business very soon now. If you learn anything, no matter how meager, let me know. And be very careful, Carol. The brains behind this business belong to an exceptional man. He'll be suspicious and wary. The slightest slip will mean death."

She pressed his hand, smiled at him and left.

The silence of early dawn settled on the house after Carol left. But sleep was out of the question for Tony Quinn, weary as he was, after the strenuous night just past. Silk was in jeopardy and there seemed to be no way of helping him. He might even be dead!

Tony Quinn's expression never changed, but deep within his breast a spark of hatred fanned itself into active flames—hatred for the men who might have harmed Silk Kirby.

Butch phoned in twice, with nothing to report. At ten-thirty Carol called.

"IT'S WORKED out wonderfully," she said. "I visited Graham's store first. I'm not sure what happened there, but someone else is taking over the business. I overheard clerks talking about Graham's secretary, the one who saw him commit suicide. They said that she had quit—refused to return because of the terrible thing she witnessed.

"I rushed home and changed my clothing and my appearance slightly. From a porter in the building, I learned the name of the ex-secretary. I went back to the store, told some smirking man named McFayden that I was a close friend of this girl and that I wanted the job she was throwing up. I had some references with me—you know the ones you fixed up for me to use whenever I needed them. And I got the job too! Almost instantly. Because they needed someone immediately. This McFayden seems to be in temporary charge and it wasn't difficult to convince him. Tony—I think he rather likes me."

"Which is one more reason why I'll punch him in the nose sooner or later." Quinn laughed tightly. "Good work, Carol, but watch yourself. That may be a nest of murder you're sticking your fair head into."

She laughed gaily and hung up. Quinn returned to his chair in front of the fireplace and sat down, cursing his helplessness. As a blind man he couldn't stalk the underworld—could not even show his face outside the door of his own home except to stumble along in his pretence of being blind. He couldn't visit such people as McGrath, or the police commissioner, or anyone actively connected with the jewelry firms. Tony Quinn was not supposed to be interested in such things. He was supposed to be a disillusioned, bitter young man whose affliction had made him practically a hermit.

"Police Commissioner Warner," Tony Quinn muttered. "I could bring him here. He might know something. Damn it, I can't just sit here like a fool doing nothing!"

He got up and walked to the telephone. The commissioner was instantly available to Tony Quinn. Half an hour later he arrived. Quinn let him in, apologizing for Silk's absence.

"I wanted to see you about last night's episode," he told Warner. "You understand, I hope, that I am not a coward, but being blind and unable to help myself much, I feel that perhaps those men might try to kill me again. Also I think I know why those two attempts were made."

Warner sat down, lit a cigar and applied his lighter to Quinn's unlighted cigarette.

"I'll post a twenty-four hour guard if you wish. But I suppose you wouldn't want that. I can see it in your face. Just tell me why you think they tried to murder you. Perhaps I will get some clue to start the ball rolling."

"Suppose the thieves trailed Harriman here—you remember he came to see me to discuss a legal question shortly before that auto accident—and believed he had told me much more than he really did," Quinn said. "They insured his silence with death and want to take the same means to keep my lips sealed."

WARNER SIGHED. "It sounds logical enough, but I'm not sure that Harriman really is dead, Quinn. It may be that he himself is the one who reasons you know too much; that he inadvertently told you more than he meant to, although perhaps you haven't realized that fact yet. Oh, damn it, Tony, I'd give my last dollar if you were back as D. A. Your brains turned the trick in cases as difficult as this one.

"And I've further news for you. I'm telling you all this, Tony, because it is my opinion that a fine legal mind is going to seed in your skull. You think that because you are blind you are unable to help at all. That's not true. Not so many weeks ago you helped tremendously in running down a mob of killers just by reasoning things out. I want that same kind of help in this case."

"I'll do what I can." Tony Quinn's tone did not show much enthusiasm. "Have there been any more developments?"

"Several very significant ones. First of all a jeweler named Gill—you probably recognize the name and know he is as prominent as the other two—is involved. When the news broke about Graham and Harriman, Gill got excited and examined all the stock in his store. He had his expert, some Italian named Professor DiNonno, go over the stuff too. They were convinced every bit of jewelry in the store was the real thing.

"Then, just before dawn this morning, Gill went to the store. He was still worried, and couldn't sleep. He opened the vault—and found that three-quarters of his stock had changed into paste over night! It was the McCoy when he put it in the vault at six o'clock and at four the next morning it was phony paste. This whole business smacks of the supernatural!"

"And the other complication?" Quinn asked quietly.

"Did you ever hear of a wealthy man named Van den Killan? He's Dutch and rich as Croesus. Anyway, Van den Killan has always been deeply interested in gems. Now he comes into the open and buys up

"The Bat!" Blackie yelled.

the three largest businesses in the country. Yesterday he purchased Graham's business, and Harriman's, and this morning he brought out Gill."

"But how on earth—" Quinn began.

Warner laid a firm hand on Quinn's knee.

"I know just what you're thinking. How could one man possibly have enough cash to buy three concerns like that? Frankly, it required little cash because the stocks were so badly depleted that the value of each firm lay mainly in its name. Gill had to sell out because he was on the verge of bankruptcy. The heirs of Graham and Harriman wanted to have the businesses liquidated—immediately—and pulled strings to get the probate court to agree because if they didn't, there just wouldn't be any estates."

Quinn mulled that over for a moment "Then Van den Killan, from all appearances, had the best motive of anyone for looting those stores. He has entered the jewelry business and at the same time has eliminated his stiffest competitors."

Warner sighed. "Just what I figured. But listen here, Tony, we can't be saying anything like that. Van den Killan is an important man. He's been decorated by several governments. His wealth is so great that it looks as if his going after more money is downright foolishness. What's more, now he'll be in the millionaire income group and have more taken away from him in taxes than this added burden warrants. I agree that some people can't seem to get enough money, but Van den Killan is different. He's given large sums to charity, he doesn't live like an emperor and his reputation for honesty is something to contend with."

TONY QUINN shook his head thoughtfully. "Those gems are somewhere. You're certain they haven't been marketed?"

"I'm not certain of anything except that Graham is dead. And certain of that only because I've seen his dead body. But those stones haven't been sold openly. The F.B.I. is helping us and they have covered the whole country. No, Tony, those gems are being held somewhere for the opportune moment when they can be turned into cash. That's a fairly simple deduction. What actually gets me is how on earth they vanish."

"Have you examined the vaults?" Quinn asked.

"Examined them? Humph! We practically tore Harriman's vault apart. Graham's was bigger, but we went over it carefully enough. Gill's vault hasn't been examined yet. What mystifies me most of all is that the substitute phony gems meet the specifications of the originals as to weight, cutting and color. Only an expert could tell the difference.

"What's more, everybody who has heard or read of these crazy cases, is having his own gems examined, which brings us to another new complication. So far well over a million dollars worth of stones, in the hands of people who bought them from either Graham, Harriman or Gill, have turned into paste. It's incredible."

"It is," Tony Quinn admitted. "The most amazing thing I've ever heard of. Sounds almost as though there might be some new scientific device for turning real gems into paste. There you would have your perfect solution. And Van den Killan would possess the only strong motive."

"I've even thought of that," Warner groaned. "But I can't feature any man destroying almost ten million dollars' worth of jewels just so he can take over three important jewelry stores. Unless"—Warner drew a sharp breath. "Do you suppose such a thing could exist and, perhaps, another device to turn the paste gems into the real ones?"

"That's much too wild a conclusion to grasp at, Commissioner. Give me a few hours to concentrate on the subject. I might think of something."

Warner arose. "Thanks, Tony. I need your help. In fact, if I knew who this Black Bat was or how to reach him I'd beg him to give us a hand. Outlaw he may be, but that man is clever."

Tony Quinn's lips parted in a wan smile as he shook hands with the commissioner. "Now you're talking like Sergeant McGrath, Commissioner."

"I know," Warner replied. "It's foolish of me, but I can't help expressing a hope, can I? If you weren't blind…. Oh, let's forget it! You aren't the Bat and he wouldn't be apt to help anyway. Phone me if you think of anything, Tony, and if you desire a guard, I'll post one when you say the word."

CHAPTER XII

THE BAT MOVES IN

FOR TEN minutes after Warner left, Tony Quinn sat before the fireplace. His fingers were curled into fists and he methodically beat the arms of his chair. Silk was still unheard from! No clues had developed as to his whereabouts and now the matter of the disappearing jewels had become more complex than ever.

"I've got to get out!" Tony Quinn told himself over and over again. "I've got to do something before I go mad. There must be some way that I can operate without being recognized. Silk can do it."

Suddenly he leaped to his feet. Silk was in disguise. Silk Kirby could always take on a new personality without undue trouble. Then why couldn't Tony Quinn?

He headed for Silk's room, but halfway across the hall he hesitated and sighed. Silk wasn't scarred from deep-burning acid. All he had to do was cover his face with makeup and saunter out.

"Just the same," Tony Quinn said savagely, "I'm going to give it a try."

He rushed to Silk's room, found the flat makeup kit and hurried back to his laboratory. There, under powerful lights, Tony Quinn began work. He knew a great deal about the art of disguise, for that subject came under his studies of crime and criminology.

He regarded his deeply scarred features in front of a mirror. Deftly he experimented with the creams and flesh tints. He filled in the scars on his face, burned deep by powerful acid, brushed over the waxy preparation that now concealed them and surveyed the result with considerable satisfaction. Next he used two aluminum cylinders that fitted snugly inside his nostrils. They broadened the shape of his nose, made him look entirely different.

EVEN HIS chestnut hair became jet-black under the influence of a chemical. Within twenty minutes Tony Quinn had vanished and an utter stranger looked back at him from the depths of the mirror. Now he could venture forth and work without fear of someone detecting the scarred face of blind Tony Quinn! His spirits soared, for now the Bat could work without a telltale hood.

The phone rang. Carol's voice was clipped and worried.

"Tony, I returned to my apartment during lunch hour and I found a letter from Silk there. I'll read it to you."

Hurriedly she did. It read:

> Car following. Looks like snatch or bump. Marker plates on car 3MA4975. Will stall as long as possible.

Quinn made a note of the numbers. "Good, Carol!" he said tightly. "If that car isn't stolen we'll have a clue. Return to work and watch yourself. If I find Silk and rescue him, someone at the store may think you tipped me off. You're new and they're bound to figure you as a plant if anything happens that they can't account for."

"Tony, do you really believe someone at the store is responsible for these crimes?" Carol asked breathlessly.

"I do," Quinn said. "So watch out."

"Tony—" Carol's voice grew soft and warm—"Tony, be careful. Don't take too many chances—please."

"Don't worry about me," he told her.

He hung up and hesitated a moment. He wanted to find out in whose name that car was registered, but dared not use the phones in his house.

Working swiftly, he changed his clothes and donned a light gray suit. He examined his disguise once more, made certain there was no danger of any part slipping or fading away. Then he stuffed his black silk hood into a pocket, stowed a gun in a shoulder clip and supplied himself with several Black Bat stickers.

He used the secret means of leaving his house, after first locking up securely. He drove far downtown, entered a crowded drugstore and took no pains to conceal his features. It was a rather novel thing, this openly flaunting those who looked for the Bat. Tony Quinn liked it.

"This," he told the Motor Vehicle Department clerk he got on the wire, "is Sergeant McGrath of Police Headquarters. I want the name and location of a marker numbered 'three-M-A-four-nine-seven-five.'"

"The owner, Sergeant," the man told him after a moment's wait, "is listed as Oliver Beam, an undertaker, at one-nine-O-nine Boulevard Drive."

Quinn hung up, returned to his car and drove it to within five blocks of the address just given him. There he got out, patted the comforting weight of his gun and was grateful that darkness had again set in. He walked directly past the undertaking parlors.

SILK KIRBY no longer possessed much feeling in his legs. Half a dozen incisions cauterized by the silver nitrate pencil had paralyzed the nerves. But now Blackie was ready to start work on Silk's arms.

"Don't be such a martyr," he told Silk. "Why not tell us who this Black Bat is? Why not save your own skin? We could use a guy like you in this outfit. You've got guts."

Silk managed a grin, but there was no mirth in it.

"Sure. You'd use me to fill up one of them caskets. Go ahead, Blackie, I'm a better man than you are. I'll never talk."

Silk had abandoned the idea of convincing these men that he knew nothing. They were positive that he did. Blackie shrugged and reached for the scalpel. Silk shut his eyes tightly and held his breath. He wouldn't be able to stand many more of these sessions, but hope was still high in his heart—and so was faith in the Bat. Sometimes the Bat could work wonders. If it was humanly possible, the Bat would be at work now, closing in gradually.

He felt the scalpel rest lightly against his forearm. Then one of the gang called out.

"Blackie—guy on the phone for you."

Blackie hurried into the next room, but Silk could hear his voice.

"No. I've given him the works but he's tongue-tied. Sure I can make him squawk, but it'll take time. Listen—this Black Bat is smarter than you think. If he's working on this case, we've got to find out who he is before he gets to us. I'm warning you. I'd rather have every cop and G-Man in the country on my heels than this Black Bat. He's not human."

There was a significant pause for a moment and then Blackie gave a sigh of resignation.

"Sure, I know you're in charge. Okay. I won't fool around any longer. We'll kill him and bury him somewhere. I still think it's a mistake, but what you say goes."

Blackie hung up, returned to stand beside Silk and picked up the scalpel once more.

"It's the finish, sucker. Orders are orders and you're slated for a nice quick burial. The only way to save yourself is by talking. What's the word?"

"You know I won't talk," Silk said calmly. "Get it over with."

Blackie fingered the scalpel and drew down the corners of his mouth. He poised the surgical instrument above Silk's throat and got himself set for the death thrust.

He heard a commotion behind him and turned. One of his men stood in the doorway—with a knife in his throat! He seemed to be supported by some invisible strings, for plainly he was dead. Strangled cries came from the throats of the two thugs watching Blackie. He turned deathly pale and dropped the scalpel.

For the dead member of his outfit wore a brand. The brand of the Bat! The silhouetted image of a bat was pasted squarely in the center of his forehead!

"The Bat!" Blackie yelled.

"Look out!" Silk screamed a warning. "There are three of 'em in here."

BLACKIE SCURRIED to the table and smashed a hard blow against Silk's jaw. Then he did one of the most foolish things in his life, though he had no idea of that. He swept the single lamp in the room off the table, smashing it. The room was plunged in a darkness that neither Blackie nor his two aides could penetrate.

But there was one present who could. The Bat saw the three men, poised with guns, ready to open fire. He smiled a little and picked up a folding chair, one of the kind commonly used by undertakers. Raising it above his head he hurled it straight at the trio.

One man went down. Another fired wildly at the door. Only Blackie retained any measure of calmness. He decided this was no place for him.

Quietly he edged back until he reached the rear door. Once he aimed his gun at the shadow that was Silk on the long table, but changed his mind about squeezing the trigger. The Bat might open fire too, shooting at the streak of flame Blackie's gun was bound to make.

Instead, Blackie turned the key in the door, quietly pulled it out and opened the door far enough to insert it in the outer side of the lock. Then he stepped out, closed and locked the door and ran for it. His two men inside would keep the Bat busy. If they were killed, that was their tough luck.

The two men trapped in the room realized that they had been tricked. One was on the floor, half conscious. The other backed into a corner. He saw something like a dark blob of shadow move into the room and he snapped a single shot. Before he could shoot again, the dark blob took rapid shape and came hurtling toward him. A hard fist exploded against his jaw and he went down.

The other thug reeled to his feet and the Bat felled him again with a single blow. He knelt beside the two men, pasted his insignia upon their foreheads and then took time to scribble a brief note with gloved hands. He thrust it under one thug's vest, leaving half of the note exposed. Then he hurried to the table, unstrapped Silk and carefully drew him over one shoulder.

The shooting was certain to bring police and he had to get away quickly. Moving like a ghost, the Bat approached the front door. Escape through the rear was impossible, for Blackie had locked that door.

Distantly the Bat heard a siren. He hurried into the deserted street and by using alleys and courtyards reached his parked car unobserved.

But the sirens were moaning nearer and in numbers now and he knew all cars would be stopped. The Bat opened the baggage compartment of the coupé, gently tucked Silk inside and then removed his hood. He stowed this in Silk's pocket, unstrapped his shoulder clip, and hid gun and clip behind the front seat of the coupé. He drew on a neat gray felt hat, got behind the wheel and drove sedately down the street past the house from which he had just escaped.

A patrolman held up his hand. Tony Quinn stopped and stuck his head out of the window. A detective cruiser howled up. Sergeant McGrath came striding toward the car.

"How long you been here?" he demanded.

Tony Quinn took a long shot. His usually well modulated voice took on a high-pitched, excited tone.

"Just driving through, Officer. I dunno what all this racket is about."

SERGEANT McGRATH turned a flashlight full on Tony Quinn's disguised features. He wasn't particularly impressed by the wide-faced stranger in the car, nor did he pay much attention to him.

"Beat it!" He waved Quinn on. "And fast. There's liable to be some shooting." He jerked around to one of the patrolmen. "You sure those mugs you found in that place had the Bat's signature pasted on their heads? Let's go."

Tony Quinn drove rapidly out of the danger zone, pulled up on a quiet street and fished Silk out of the baggage compartment. Silk was still dazed and extremely weak from the siege of pain inspired from Blackie's sadistic impulses.

"I knew you'd show up, Boss." Silk grinned weakly. "But man, you didn't come too soon. They were set to slit my throat.../ Hey, what the devil? Who are you?"

Silk had taken it for granted that this man beside him was Tony Quinn, but as his vision cleared, he saw an utter stranger at the wheel.

Tony Quinn laughed. "Like it, Silk? I used your disguise kit. For a first attempt it isn't bad."

Silk relaxed. "Oh boy, did you scare me! Good? It's perfect! You don't need any lessons, Boss."

"As you said," Quinn remarked, "I did come just in time. Things have developed, Silk. Developed to a point where there are a couple of very good suspects in our gem robbing with which your recent little playmates are tied up somehow. Up to now our murderous, thieving friends have had their own way, but from now on I'm taking the aggressive. They'll know just how much I mean business when they see that thug I had to kill. He saw me slip into the undertaking parlors and came at me with his knife. I was forced to get to him first."

"Boss!" Silk raised his head quickly. "I found something too. Listen—did you get a dark-haired guy with a big mouth and thick lips? Dressed like a dude?"

"He got away," Quinn answered. "A rat, if there ever was one. Left his pals to shift for themselves. Do you know him, Silk?"

"Do I know him?" Silk sighed. "That was Blackie Burns—the slickest jewel thief in the world! He works on only big stuff, Boss. That guy has swiped more rocks than any man alive. I can't figure him now though. Usually he works solo and takes all the profits for himself, but now he takes orders from some other guy. I heard him talking to the big boy over the phone."

"I know Blackie too. He is the man who took me for a ride that ended in a cavern. Perhaps"—Quinn's eyes narrowed—"Blackie is in on the deal only long enough to gain the confidence of the real leader. Then Blackie means to perform his little solo act. We can't be sure of that, but it's possible—and must be taken into consideration.... I'll drop you near the east gate, Silk. After I park the car near Butch's, I'll come back and help you inside."

Quinn looked at Silk's swollen, discolored legs and muttered an imprecation.

"I hope Blackie and I will meet again—soon. Don't try to walk, Silk. Just lay low until I come back."

CHAPTER XIII

THEFT

WHEN CAROL BALDWIN returned from lunch that afternoon she found a black-haired, wide-faced stranger seated in her office. McFayden was holding a spirited conversation with the man.

"I tell you, Mr. Gordon," McFayden was saying earnestly, "if you would permit me to examine your necklace, I'm certain I could tell you whether or not it is one of these astoundingly good copies."

"No," Gordon answered and smiled brazenly at Carol. "I insist on seeing Van den Killan. If his experts tell me it's genuine, I'll be satisfied. You are only a clerk. You have admitted as much to me."

McFayden spread his hands in a gesture of despair. "Very well." He glanced at Carol. "Miss Baldwin, will you ask Mr. Killan if he will see Mr. Gordon about a necklace? Priceless, he says. Personally, I wonder."

But Gordon ignored that stab. He only kept on grinning and hardly moved his eyes from Carol. She could almost feel his stare and she was worried. Comparatively unknown in this city and her association with the Bat never suspected, Carol had resorted to only a very slight disguise in obtaining her position. But she was suspicious about this stranger. He looked too fatuously guileless to be true.

She called Van den Killan and sent Gordon into the inner office. The big Hollander greeted him with outstretched hand.

"I am told you have valuable chems, *Mynheer*," he said affably.

"Sure." Gordon removed a plush box from an inner pocket, opened it and carelessly flung a necklace on the desk. "Tell me if I was stuck. I paid two hundred and ten thousand dollars for that baby and she don't look worth it, but the little woman has got to be pleased."

Killan held the glistening string of diamonds to the light and drew a sharp breath.

"To me it looks real. And a lovely piece of work. But my experts…. I have three of the best in the whole world. I let them look at it. Wait!"

Wohl came into the office first. He glanced at Gordon and then his eyes fastened on the necklace that Killan held.

"*Himmel!*" he cried. "Where did that come from?"

The drug took hold of him.

The expert who was introduced as Anghis Khan entered next. He wore a fez and sideburns that ran down half the length of his oval face. He was dark-featured and almost slant-eyed, showing traces of Oriental blood. Professor DiNonno proved to be a squat, swarthy Italian. They clustered around the necklace, fighting among themselves over its estimated value. Finally Gordon arose.

"If you men don't mind, I'd like to get this over with. The way you're acting, I think it's one of them phonies floating around town. Go ahead—tell me. I can take it."

ANGHIS KHAN turned and spoke in an Oxford accent.

"But of course it is real, my dear chap. It's worth every cent you paid for it. In fact, it might bring a great deal more. Because of the enormous thefts committed—those of which you have undoubtedly read—this necklace has increased in value about twenty to thirty thousand dollars. Articles like this are now extremely rare."

"I will pay," Van den Killan stated pompously, "two hundred und fifty thousand dollars—cash. You will sell, *Mynheer?*"

"I will not," Gordon retorted. "I bought that baby for my wife and it's hers. How much do I owe you for giving me the good news?" He drew out a massive handkerchief and wiped his forehead. "Gosh, it would have been a blow at that—paying two hundred and ten thousand for a lot of glass junk."

"Perhaps,"—Van den Killan moved toward Gordon and seized his arm—"I should tell my partner about this. Perhaps we can go yet higher. That necklace I must have."

"Partner?" Gordon frowned. "How many of you guys are in this business?"

Van den Killan disappeared for a moment and returned with a middle-aged man in tow. He was introduced to Gordon as Clifford Carlyle and looked much like the popular version of a college professor. He wore glasses suspended from a silken cord around his neck. His vest was white edged and every article of his clothing matched.

Gordon picked up the necklace, put it back in its box and backed up a little as if he were afraid of this congregation of gem experts.

"It is agreed," Van den Killan said, rubbing his hands. "Perhaps we can talk it over tonight, *ja?* At my house—or your hotel? I am prepared to go higher, *Mynheer.* That necklace I must have."

Gordon shrugged carelessly. "You can come see me at nine. I live at the Alexandria Hotel, but I think you're wasting time, gentlemen. I like this doodad myself."

Gordon closed the office door, walked by Carol Baldwin and then hesitated. He returned to her desk and took a card from his pocket.

"Did anybody ever tell you how beautiful you are?" he asked her and laughed when she turned pink. "No offense meant. Maybe one of those men in there would like my card. And say, you might look it over yourself, sister. It's got my name and address on it."

He turned away, whistled blithely and vanished out the door. Carol looked at the card contemptuously. Then her fingers felt something on the reverse side. She turned it over and her face really turned red.

Pasted in the center of the opposite side was—a black bat!

AT EIGHT o'clock Tony Quinn, in his disguise of Rex Gordon, had dinner in the grill room at the hotel. He noticed that two waiters served him. At nine, Hans Van den Killan was announced and sent up to the suite.

Killan sat down and rubbed his face.

"Business always goes better with a drink," he observed. "Permit me to order something, *Mynheer.*"

"Gordon" crossed his legs, dug himself deeper into the wide-armed chair he occupied and grinned like a contented kitten. A bottle of rye was sent up and Van den Killan prepared highballs. The man he knew as Gordon drank his slowly.

Then Van den Killan began to talk about what had brought him there. He spoke of the necklace at once, raising the ante, but got only slow shakes of Gordon's head as a reply.

"I don't think you can do any business," the man he called Gordon said finally. "The necklace is over there in my bag. I check out in the morning. Maybe, if the little wife don't like it, I'll ship it back and take your offer of twenty thousand more'n I paid for her."

Van den Killan looked sad, but recognized the finality in his host's voice. He arose, shook hands and departed. Tony Quinn, alias Gordon, stepped over to the window and watched the Hollander enter his car and drive away. He smiled thoughtfully and turned back.

The bait had been seized. News of the existence of this rare necklace had probably spread rapidly and without doubt had reached the ears of the man behind this series of bizarre thefts. Perhaps that man was Van den Killan, after all. Anyhow, whoever he was, a man as avaricious as the master thief would surely make an attempt to steal the necklace. But he would find a tornado when he tackled Rex Gordon.

Suddenly the lights flickered in an unaccountable manner. All at once Tony Quinn felt a wave of weariness creep over him. He hadn't taken time out for much sleep since Harriman had visited him many hours before, but he shouldn't feel this sleepy.

Abruptly, he stiffened with a sharp realization. He had been drugged!

Quinn half staggered toward the table on which Van den Killan's bottle of whiskey still rested. He picked it up, spilled some of it into a glass and tasted the stuff cautiously. There was no taste beyond that of good rye.

Reeling now, Quinn headed for the telephone. He had been tricked beautifully all right. If he could reach Silk or Butch... or Carol.... But Quinn's hand had only touched the telephone when the drug's influence took over his entire system. He dropped to his knees, then quietly fell to the floor where he lay breathing stertorously....

To his befuddled senses, it might have been hours later before Tony Quinn stirred. He was aware of a buzzing sound that was even louder than the ringing in his ears. The phone! Memory came back with a bitter rush. He lurched to the desk and hauled himself to his feet. An anvil chorus beat out its measures in his head.

Silk was on the wire, anxious and distraught. Quinn ordered him to remain at the house. Then he sat down on the bed and gently massaged his temples. A drink of water made him feel a little better. Finally he lifted his suitcase and put it on a chair. Its contents seemed intact when he opened it, and to his amazement the plush jewel case rested in exactly the same position in which he had placed it.

HE OPENED it and the necklace glistened under the light. Then Quinn applied a magnifying glass to his eye but he did not study the gems. Quinn was no expert in diamonds. But he did carefully examine the clip of the necklace. There should have been a faint scratch on the underside of the snap. It was not there. Not that he expected that it would be, for the necklace had been a lure for this master thief, and apparently he had taken the bait.

"The cleverest act of substitution I've ever heard of," he told himself grimly. "Worked quick, too. They must have made up this replica and stolen into this suite with it while I was under the influence of that sleeping drug. If I was just a man named Gordon who had bought his wife a necklace, I'd be completely fooled and leave the city thinking I still had the original."

Was the brain behind this jewel plot Hans Van den Killan's then? Had he slipped a drug into the whiskey, returned later and made the substitution? Quinn had told the Hollander where the necklace was so that he might properly bait the trap. No one else had heard—unless....

Quinn made a quick study of the suite, looking for wires and a microphone, though there seemed little possibility that anyone would have time or opportunity to install one. As he had rather expected he found no trace of one, but realized that if by any long chance there had been one the thief could have removed it easily.

He picked up the bottle of whiskey, corked it and slid it into his pocket. He transferred the contents of the glass, containing a few drops of rye, to a small vial and put this in his bag also. Then he checked out, took a cab to the railroad terminal and vanished in the crowd there. If he was trailed, Quinn knew that those who watched him would be satisfied that he had gone, wholly unaware that he had also been neatly tricked.

Once he felt sure he had outwitted anyone who might possibly be watching his movements, Quinn climbed into a taxi and had himself driven to a busy spot where his old coupé was waiting. He stopped long enough to buy the latest edition on the news-stands, stopped several blocks from his home and read the brief newspaper items that concerned this strange jewel robbery case. Most of the facts he already knew but there was one item indicating that a meeting of police and jewelers was being held at the home of Hans Van den Killan. Quinn's lips compressed in a thin line. There was more work for him.

CHAPTER XIV

THE SMELL OF BLOOD

HANS VAN DEN KILLAN greeted his guests warmly. He seated them in a spacious living room and his servants passed around drinks. Clifford Carlyle, the Hollander's new partner in the former Graham jewelry business was there, offering suggestions for the benefit of Police Commissioner Warner. McFayden lurked in a corner, apart from the others. Wohl, Anghis Khan and Professor DiNonno were arguing heatedly, paying no attention to other guests. The last to arrive was a man named Fawcett, a jeweler who had requested the privilege of attending.

Commissioner Warner finally arose and spoke quietly.

"Gentlemen, we are here to study this problem that confronts us. During the past few days astounding thefts have been committed and the direct results of them have been suicide, bankruptcy and the loss of faith in all jewelry dealers. Men and women who invested large parts of their savings in gems, have discovered that they have been tricked.

"Two such people attempted suicide not three hours ago. They were elderly men who dared not risk their superfluous cash in bonds. They bought diamonds and got—cut glass! Customers who have traded with the firms owned by Graham, Harriman and Gill have discovered that their purchases were frauds.

"On the surface it appears that the jewelers deliberately substituted the fakes and took the real gems for their own use. My opinion is that this theory is wrong. I believe that a super-criminal is responsible."

"And so do I." McFayden stepped into the center of the room. "Furthermore I know his identity—as much as anyone does, at least. It's the Black Bat. He was in our store. I saw him with my own eyes. So did Wohl."

Wohl waved his hands excitedly.

"*Ach*, gentlemen, this man called the Bat—he came one night and he talked good sense. For myself I do not believe he is a crook."

Warner sat down slowly.

"Yes," he said. "I know both of you met the Bat. Sergeant McGrath came close to landing him that night. I regret that he did not succeed, for the Bat is a dangerous man and you may be right. Mr. McFayden.... But to the business of the evening. We have with us Mr. Fawcett, who is also a jeweler. He insisted that he be allowed to attend. Now we shall hear from him."

Fawcett nodded curtly and walked to the center of the room.

"I own a jewelry shop two blocks from Maiden Lane, as most of you probably know," he said crisply. "I came here mainly to talk about protection and ask your advice as to how I can properly safeguard my goods. This afternoon, I purchased the Bourbon tiara, the crown jewels of Spain's royal family. If they are lost, I am utterly ruined, for every cent I could scrape together is invested in them."

"You put them in a bank, of course?" Warner asked.

Fawcett shook his head. "I didn't have time. They arrived much too late. They are in my office safe and I shall personally guard it until morning."

Warner's gaze centered on Van den Killan's fat face. The Hollander seemed hypnotized by Fawcett's statement. He kept muttering "Bourbon tiara," over and over again.

SUDDENLY VAN DEN KILLAN'S expression changed. His jaw hung slackly down, his eyes were wide and he was licking his thick lips. Clifford Carlyle jumped up and turned pale. McFayden gave a strangled cry. Off in one corner the three gem experts, Wohl, DiNonno and Anghis Khan stared in awe. Warner turned quickly, and drew a startled breath.

Standing before the heavy curtains shrouding the French windows was a broad-shouldered man dressed entirely in deep black. There was a hood over his shoulders and cold eyes flashed through the slits in the mask. He held a gun in each hand.

"Gentlemen"—the Bat bowed ironically—"I am here only to listen and observe. If you will carry on just as though I were not present—"

"That man's a thief and killer!" McFayden yelped.

He took a step in the direction of the Bat. One of the guns centered on his chest and he stopped, licking his lips and swallowing with difficulty.

"Sit down, McFayden," the Bat said pleasantly. "We're interested in facts tonight, not your stupid suspicions. Commissioner Warner—carry on."

Warner cleared his throat. "I suppose there is nothing else I can do. But I warn you, Bat—one of these days you'll be brought to justice."

"For heaven's sake get it over with," Carlyle shouted irritably. "Do you think I enjoy standing here, facing a masked man with two guns, while you make ineffectual threats, Commissioner?"

Warner shrugged. "Very well. Here are the facts as I know them. Millions of dollars worth of gems have disappeared and the cleverest replicas ever created have been put in their places. When or how these gems were stolen we don't know. Possibly two dead men might enlighten us, but unfortunately we do not have communication with the spirit world. The fact remains that because of these thefts the value of gems like diamonds, emeralds and rubies, has skyrocketed. It means that the thief will profit more than ever if he can sell his stolen goods."

"True!" Hans Van den Killan broke in excitedly. His fat face was flushed. "But we can do nothing. Of course the diamond mines are not operating full blast these days, but they will start again, if we do not recover the stolen chems. It would be fatal to the jewelry business should the diamonds be discovered *after* the diamond syndicate releases more stones. With rubies and emeralds the danger is not yet so great."

"What about insurance coverage?" the Bat asked calmly.

Warner waved his hand in exasperation. "We can't do anything with it. The companies naturally contest every attempt to collect, maintaining that the gems must have been fakes when they were insured. Can anyone prove they were genuine? How in the world could such substitutions be made? I don't blame the companies for holding up payment."

The Bat's eyes flashed around the room.

"I notice a man who is a stranger to me—"

FAWCETT, THE jeweler, arose slowly. He was by no means confident that this eerie masked figure wouldn't open fire at any moment.

"My name is—is Fawcett. I—I'll pay you a thousand dollars to help me. I'll—"

"I don't require fees for my work," the Bat answered. "I heard you tell about the Bourbon tiara. It was foolish of you to advertise your possession of it."

"He'll have protection—plenty of it," Warner snapped. "These depredations are at an end. From now on every jewelry store will be guarded, every suspicious person stopped and questioned. My mission is twofold—to round up the men or man responsible for this gigantic theft, and return to their owners the jewels that have been stolen from them."

Van den Killan caught the Bat's eye. The fat-faced gem fancier still seemed fascinated by Fawcett's tale.

"You—have the Bourbon chems?" he asked awedly. "The royal chewels? I would half my fortune give to own them."

"We can talk that over later," Fawcett snapped irritably. "Right now I'm afraid. Graham is dead. So is Harriman. Maybe they didn't commit suicide. Maybe they were both murdered! I don't want to be the third man to die. I—I—Oh, why did I ever buy that damned thing anyway?"

All eyes were upon Fawcett. He was pale and shaken. Van den Killan hastened to pour him a glass of brandy. In the commotion, Commissioner Warner was the first to glance at the further end of the room. He caught a sharp breath. The Black Bat was gone!

During the excitement the Bat had quietly slipped through the French window and vanished into the night. Thirty minutes later Tony Quinn, dressed in baggy tweeds and a smoking jacket, tapped his way across the living room of his own home. Silk, walking with some difficulty, entered with a tray of food.

"Nothing happened while you were away," he reported. "No sign of McGrath. Did you learn anything?"

"That the whole gem industry may be shaken by this series of theft," Tony Quinn replied. "It's worse than I realized, Silk. And your legs. How are they?"

"Just stiff," Silk replied. "Blackie cut pretty deep, but that silver nitrate he rubbed into the wounds cauterized and sealed them. They're healing fast. I'm ready for action, Boss. Any time you say."

"It may come quickly, Silk. Tonight a jeweler named Fawcett made a blunder. It may prove fatal to him. He admitted buying some particularly valuable gems. When he mentioned the fact before the select audience that heard him, I could almost smell blood."

"You mean—one of them guys that was at that meetin' is the killer?"

"There isn't much doubt about it," Quinn answered wryly. "They all have their reasons. Hans Van den Killan would sell his soul to own the jewels he craves. McFayden is a little rat without morals or conscience. Clifford Carlyle, Van den Killan's partner, is something of a blank space. I can't figure him out. Even Fawcett acted suspiciously, in revealing that he owns those gems. Then there is Wohl and Khan and DiNonno. Those men know jewels. They came into contact with most of those stolen. The only thing to be said in their favor is that they have long records for honesty and efficiency here and abroad. I have personally checked that myself."

"IT'S THAT little squirt McFayden," Silk reasoned. "But there's Blackie too—somewhere on the outside lookin' in. I don't like the set-up. Blackie ain't the kind to work for somebody else. He's a lone wolf and he goes in for big stakes. Never heard of him working with a gang before."

"True," Tony Quinn reasoned, "but Blackie's real identity may not be known to the backers of this crime. They may believe he is nothing but an ordinary gangster looking for easy money. Blackie, you see, might be planning far ahead, laying the groundwork for a coup that will result in his getting all the loot. Or Blackie may have changed his stripes and all this telephoning he does to some superior is faked to deceive his own men.

"We're no nearer the truth now, Silk, than we were at the moment when Harriman came to see me. I laid a trap myself tonight, baited it and had it sprung right in my face. Two years ago I purchased a necklace because I was able to obtain it at a bargain. It was stolen from me tonight and I don't know who took it. Van den Killan is the most logical suspect, but others also knew I had it. All that's left for my trouble is this little souvenir."

Tony Quinn tossed the replica of his diamond necklace on the table. He picked up the phone and called Butch.

"Work for you," he said. "Leave at once and cover the Fawcett Jewelry Store near Maiden Lane. Conceal yourself and watch everyone who even looks in the windows. Take down a description of each person who acts suspiciously. And be ready for action when the store opens in the morning. I may appear in a disguise, as a black haired, boy-faced man without these scars. I'll wear a gray suit and hat. Got that, Butch?"

"Got it," Butch replied. "Is it okay for me to tell Carol you're safe? She's been calling every few minutes, Boss."

"I'll tell her myself," Tony Quinn said. "Get busy, Butch, and no slipups."

Tony Quinn deflected the receiver a moment and then called Carol. It would be soothing to hear her calm voice; almost unusual to talk rationally with someone unexcited. Quinn's heart beat just a little faster when she answered the phone.

CHAPTER XV

MURDER

UNTIL THE early morning hours after dawn, Tony Quinn stayed in the privacy of his laboratory. There he first analyzed the contents of the whiskey bottle from which Van den Killan had poured a drink for the man he believed to be Rex Gordon. The liquor contained an appreciable quantity of chloral hydrate.

"Doped," Quinn muttered. "Just as I thought—and only Van den Killan had access to that bottle. It was delivered sealed."

He examined the contents he had taken from the glass from which he had imbibed the sleep-inducing potion. To Quinn's amazement it was pure rye and nothing else. It contained no trace of a narcotic. His case against the Hollander broke down rapidly.

Suddenly Quinn recalled the fact that two waiters had served him in the grill room of the hotel. Had he been drugged then? Possibly the action of the drug had been carefully studied by the person who ordered it administered and it had not taken effect until after Van den Killan left.

"The man who stole the necklace might have slipped some of the same drug in the whiskey bottle," Quinn reasoned aloud. "That would throw the blame on Van den Killan all right. Only he forgot to put more of the drug in the glass that I drank from."

"I got an idea," Silk put in. "Suppose Van den Killan knew damned well you'd suspect him. Maybe you were drugged in the grill room and this Dutchman shoved that Mickey Finn in the bottle because he figured you'd have it tested anyway. But he didn't put any of the stuff in the glass, so you'd figure he couldn't have done it and the guy who did was trying to put the blame on Van den Killan."

"We're getting nowhere," Quinn said irritably. "The fact remains that Van den Killan knew where the necklace was and he had every opportunity to grab it.... Breakfast, Silk, and in a hurry. While you're getting it ready, I'll put on my handsome face."

At ten minutes of nine, Tony Quinn, in his disguise of Rex Gordon, walked into the ornately furnished jewelry store owned by Fawcett.

"My business is with Mr. Fawcett personally," he told a clerk. "Most important. You might whisper it concerns the Bourbon gems."

The clerk nodded knowingly. "Yes, sir. Mr. Fawcett is waiting in his office. He's been there since before the store opened. Up those stairs, sir. The last door at the end of the corridor."

Quinn found the office and tapped on the panels. There was no reply and he grew tense. He tried the knob and found the door unlocked. As he opened the door his hand drifted toward a shoulder holster and froze there. Fawcett was in his office all right. But Fawcett lay sprawled across his desk in a pool of thickened blood. He had been dead for some time.

Quinn closed the door quickly. He stepped over to the body and made only a brief examination. Fawcett's throat had been slit from ear to ear. There was no sign of any struggle and Quinn reasoned that the murderer must have been in the office with Fawcett's knowledge and consent. Probably someone the murdered man trusted.

He saw a huge, modern vault in a corner and with gloved hands he tried the great door. It was securely locked. Quinn frowned. Would the killer have taken time to close and lock the safe if he had robbed it? Or hadn't the Bourbon jewels been placed in it at all?

SUDDENLY QUINN tensed. His abnormal hearing detected the sound of hoarse breathing outside the door. From below came the sound of a stifled groan. Quinn hastily backed into a washroom. Then he drew his mask over head and shoulders, removed his guns and snapped off the safety attachments.

"Mr. Fawcett!" It was the voice of the clerk to whom Quinn had talked. "Mr. Fawcett!"

The Bat took a long chance. He opened the washroom door slightly and called back a summons to enter.

The clerk came in first and behind him stalked Blackie Burns, with a gun in his fist. Two of Blackie's men trooped in also. They all stopped in amazement at the gory sight before them. Blackie gave a strangled scream of rage. He lifted his gun and crashed it against the clerk's skull. Then he gave crisp orders to his men.

"We been buncoed, but this ain't the finish, boys. Not by a long shot. I just got to make certain I'm right. Joe, beat it downstairs and make sure nobody gets in here. Snap it up."

"Shall we swipe some of the rocks downstairs?" Joe asked avidly. "There was a lot of 'em, Blackie."

"All trash probably," Blackie snapped. "Beat it—and never mind the stuff downstairs. It's five-and-ten junk compared to what I'm after."

Blackie walked directly over to the safe. He took a slip of paper from his pocket and began twirling the dial. He had the combination, for the door swung wide within a minute.

The Bat watched Blackie scoop out the contents of a drawer until he found a crimson, plush-covered box about ten inches high and two feet long. He opened the cover and sighed—a single, long-drawn-out breath of relief.

"It's okay," he said quickly. "Now we run for it. I don't get the meaning of that stiff, but let the cops worry. They'll figure the guy who bumped him swiped the jewels too. It's a cinch for us."

The Bat's guns came up and he raised his foot to kick open the door. Suddenly a siren whined and a dozen quick shots came from downstairs, in the store proper. Then Sergeant McGrath's voice yelled orders and there was more shooting.

"Stung!" Blackie gasped. "Stung proper! This was a plant! Stay by the door and hold 'em off while I see if there's an out. Pump them cops full of lead if they show."

"Yeah, but I don't wanta be caught in this room with a stiff, Blackie," the thug still with him whined. "They're liable to think I did it."

But Blackie was paying no attention to his aide. He ran to a window and peered out. A bullet smashed through the glass. Blackie pumped two quick shots into the courtyard and drew back. He spotted the washroom door and rushed toward it, barged into the small room, gun extended.

Something whizzed behind him. The gun flew from his grasp and a brawny arm wrapped itself around his throat. He struggled with all the strength of desperation, but that locking arm never relaxed until Blackie slumped, his face blue and his breathing difficult. Then the Bat slugged him under the chin, raised the limp form and draped it over one shoulder.

THE THUG in the office spun around as he heard footsteps. His gun blasted once and the bullet ripped past the Bat's head. The Bat's guns roared and the man went down with a bullet in each leg.

Footsteps and hoarse shouts announced the arrival of the police. The Bat looked about for an avenue of escape. There was none! Deftly he slipped Blackie off his shoulder and dumped him in a corner. Then he flattened himself behind the office door.

Sergeant McGrath burst into the room, gun drawn. Another detective was right behind him. They saw Fawcett's corpse, saw the unconscious wounded thug, and sped toward them.

Neither heard the door close gently. Then McGrath sensed the presence of danger. He straightened up from his examination of the dead Fawcett—to look into the decidedly dangerous end of a heavy automatic. His fellow detective already had his hands raised high.

"Reach, Sergeant!" the Bat said with a chuckle. "I'm sorry to do this, but necessity knows no such thing as friendship."

"Don't call me your friend," McGrath bellowed. "This time I've got you cold! You're a killer! A rotten, cowardly killer!"

"You have me cold, as you say," the Bat said, and laughed, "except for the fact that you are at the end of my guns. Fawcett was dead when I arrived. The wounded man is, unfortunately, my work. I had to shoot that thug or be killed myself. He is, of course, your prisoner, and you are welcome to get anything out of him you can, if he knows anything much—which I doubt."

"You can't get away with it!" McGrath snarled. "This store—is full of police. There isn't a chance for you! Not even if you shoot me down."

"But I wouldn't do that—unless it was positively necessary, Sergeant. Please don't make it so. Now put your gun in one of the desk drawers. Your pal will do the same. Turn your backs to me while I search you. Not that I think you carry two guns, Sergeant. A man of your prowess wouldn't find use for a second one—but—we can never be sure."

The Bat searched the two men deftly. Forcing them to face the wall and place their hands high up against it, palms level with the paper, the Bat stepped toward Blackie. The gem thief was groaning and trying to sit up. The Bat moved to cover him also.

"Blackie," he said. "Blackie—wake up! Get to your feet!"

Blackie obeyed that voice, for it possessed an almost hypnotic influence. His eyes opened wide when he saw the masked figure.

"Blackie," the Bat said, "we're going out of here, you and I. Escorted by none other than Sergeant McGrath and his worthy assistant. It's up to you now. I'm going to hand you a gun. Put it in your side coat pocket, understand? You'll keep McGrath's friend covered while he escorts you to a police car. Can I depend on you, Blackie?"

"If it'll get me out of here, I'll do anything," Blackie retorted.

His wits had snapped back to normal and he recognized the fact that the Bat was trying to effect an escape for both of them.

"How do you expect to get away with it?" McGrath growled at the wall.

"With that hood on your head the boys will know you."

THE BAT chuckled happily. "Ah! I shall remove the mask, Sergeant. Your long-felt desire to see my ugly face is to be gratified. Now follow these instructions or by thunder you'll never go home to your wife and family again. Blackie has a gun too. You will pretend we are your prisoners. You will take my arm. Your friend will take Blackie's. To all appearances you will be escorting us to your service car. But you will be our prisoners, we'll shoot if you disobey. Blackie, you carry that jewel box."

"Take off the mask!" McGrath raged. "Take it off and I'll do anything you say. I know the face under that hood. And you're right about it being ugly. Acid burns don't make a man look beautiful. Tony Quinn, you're at the end of your rope now."

"Turn around, Sergeant," the Bat said quietly. "I'll show you what I look like."

Both detectives turned. Blackie, wholeheartedly aligned with the Bat now, kept them covered. McGrath held his breath as the eerie figure in black began removing the hood. His jaw dropped as far as it would go when he saw the features of the man under the mask. Automatically he checked every detail of the face. The wide nose, the thin lips, the pleasant eyes and the straight black hair. Certainly this was not Tony Quinn. There wasn't the slightest resemblance.

"Like me?" the Bat asked with a wide grin. "I'm not exactly good-looking, but certainly not ugly. Ah, we go into action! Your men are coming up. Take my arm, Sergeant, and if you feel something prod your ribs occasionally, don't try to brush it away because the trigger of my gun is unusually sensitive. Ready, Blackie?"

"And how!" Blackie grimaced. "You're okay, Bat. I figured you were on the side of these heels, but I was wrong. You won't be sorry you helped."

"March!" the Bat ordered.

It was a strange procession that wended its way down the steps and through the store. Plainly it seemed that Sergeant McGrath had captured a prisoner and was hurrying him to one of the police cars. Detective Halloran also had his man firmly held by the arm. The only thing lacking was the smile of triumph that was usually on McGrath's features when he had effected an important capture. McGrath's face was strained and pale.

"You're doing splendidly," the Bat whispered out of the corner of his mouth. "Keep it up—and live, Sergeant."

THE FOUR of them piled into a detective cruiser. McGrath started the motor and drove away.

"I suppose it's the end for me now," he said tensely. "You won't dare let me live after I've seen your face."

"I promised," the Bat said, "that you would not suffer any bodily harm and I meant it. We'll drop you somewhere on the outskirts. The walk back will cool you off, Sergeant. You're steaming like a locomotive."

"Hey, wait a minute," Blackie growled from the rear seat. "You got me out of an awful mess, Bat, but these two cops don't live, get me? They take the works. Why damn it, my mug is on file! They'll identify me and then every cop in the world will be on my trail."

"They will not be harmed, Blackie," the Bat reiterated. "Sergeant McGrath is a friend of mine and even though I've just met this other detective for the first time he's a friend also. By all means they do not die."

"Yeah?" Blackie grated. "We'll see."

Halloran gave a shout of strangled horror as Blackie shoved his gun against his head. Blackie squeezed the trigger, but only empty click's resulted.

"Pull off the road and stop," the Bat ordered McGrath. He had swung around in the seat and his gun covered Blackie now. "Blackie, your heart is as dark as your name. You're a born killer and hardly fit to live, but I'll give you a break you don't deserve. Get out of this car and run for it! At the next corner is a dairy truck. Steal it—unless your conscience bothers you. Get going! Can't you see I won't be able to hold McGrath in check much longer?"

CHAPTER XVI

USELESS BAGGAGE

JUST FOR an instant Blackie gaped, but he obeyed. Once he glanced over his shoulder, as though he expected the Bat's gun to cut him down. He jumped into the dairy truck and sent it rolling away.

The Bat saw something else too. It escaped the eyes of the two detectives, for they could see nothing but the muzzle of the Bat's gun. A rickety old coupé whizzed by, but it slowed as it began to near on the dairy truck ahead.

"And now," the Bat told McGrath, "we'll part. I'm sorry to have inconvenienced you."

"Rats!" McGrath rasped. "Of all the low-down, mangy cusses I've ever run up against, you're at the bottom of the heap. Sometimes I used to call myself a fool for trying to run you down, but now—I'll get you if it takes my last breath!"

The Bat smiled contentedly, reached into his pocket and drew out two pair of handcuffs.

"These are yours, gentlemen. You will clasp one section around your wrist. Sergeant, hook yourself to the wheel. Your friend will use the blanket rack in front of him. Hurry now—or would you prefer to be slugged?"

The detectives obeyed; McGrath sullenly, Halloran with something of a wry smile.

"Okay, Bat," Halloran said. "I don't know what your game is or why you let that killer get away, but I'll say this—you kept your promise. Me, I'm glad to be alive after watching that lug try to blast my head open. So you unloaded the gun you gave him? All the time I been covered with an unloaded gat. I take my hat off to you, whoever you are."

"And you, Sergeant?" The Bat stepped out of the car and bowed slightly toward McGrath. "Aren't you the least bit appreciative?"

"The night they pull the switch on you, I'll laugh out loud!" McGrath thundered. "That's how much I appreciate you."

The Bat grinned. He saw a car coming down the road. Quickly he ran toward it, raised his hand and flashed Sergeant McGrath's badge.

"Car broke down," he told the gawking boy who stopped for him. "Step on it. I've left my buddy in the car with a killer. Got to get help."

In the car Sergeant McGrath tugged vainly at the handcuffs.

"He took our keys and the key to this car also," McGrath snapped. "But I admit I was wrong. Tony Quinn certainly wasn't under that mask. I've been a fool."

McGrath's free hand scooped up a piece of black silk. The Bat's hood. He flung it back on the seat angrily. A nice souvenir to be left with. Well, he'd get the man who wore it yet—even if he wasn't Tony Quinn....

As soon as he was well out of sight, the Bat got from his commandeered car and dashed for the nearest phone booth. He had to get all necessary work done before McGrath was released and put a description of the Bat over the radio. A few minutes after that happened, every patrolman in town would be on the watch.

The line was busy when the Bat called his home. He fretted impatiently and tried again. This time Silk answered.

"The address," Silk said smoothly, "is Two Thirty-five White Street. Butch just called."

"Stand by," the Bat ordered. "I may need you. How are the legs?"

"Aching—to get busy. Don't forget me if you need help, boss, especially should you meet up with a certain party. I'd like to be there."

NUMBER 235 White Street proved to be another funeral parlor. When the Bat reached the place he surveyed the neighborhood and spotted his coupé parked two blocks away. Butch was impatiently waiting back of the wheel.

"I saw them cops lead you outa that jewelry store downtown," he said excitedly. "Holy gee, Boss, I thought it was all up. And in that disguise I wasn't even sure it was you. But I followed, like you said, if things went wrong. I parked way up the road and when this guy beats it I tailed him, figuring that if you needed help, you'd give me the high sign as I went by."

"Good work, Butch. Now I'm going to need your muscle. I allowed the man you followed to go free just so that he could lead me to such a hideout as this. We're going in after him."

"Lead me to it!" Butch clenched his fists. "That must be the guy who started to make hamburger outa Silk. I'll make a stew outa him. Just lead the way."

The Bat smiled, but there was no mirth in that contortion of his lips. He surveyed the funeral parlors for a moment or two and then signaled Butch.

"It's up to you," he said, low-voiced. "If Blackie spots me—and he knows what I look like in this disguise—I wouldn't get any further than the front door. You walk in—and look sad, if a St. Bernard like you can do such a thing. Get as many of those men close to you as possible and then go to town. Got it?"

"Yeah—oh yeah." Butch's face lit up in enthusiasm. "Will I take 'em!"

Butch straightened his coat, slicked down his thinning hair and put a mournful expression on his huge face. He opened the door of the undertaking parlors and removed his hat subserviently. A squat, ape-like man came from a rear room to greet him.

"I wanta get prices on a nice job." Butch looked at the rug. "It's—it's for a pal o' mine, see? Nuthin' too good for him, y'understand."

"I'm sorry," the squat man said. "But we're full up, mister. Why don't you try somebody else?"

"Because I like this joint." Butch looked up slowly. "My pal liked this joint. You gonna let me see the boss, or do I pull the joint apart, huh?"

The squat man backed away hurriedly and disappeared. But he returned in a moment and there were three husky men at his side. They ranged themselves like a formidable army phalanx, on either side of Butch.

"Now what was it you were sayin', wise guy?" the little man demanded.

Butch's saddened features suddenly lighted up once more. His right hand moved at an astounding speed for a man his size. Giant fingers closed about the little man's throat, lifted him high into the air, a kicking, squealing creature. Two of the larger men reached for Butch and their smaller companion descended like a tomahawk. They went down under the impact. The fourth thug howled in rage and charged. He ran straight into a punch that seemed to explode something within his skull. He dropped heavily and didn't even quiver.

The other three were trying to get up, but Butch stood close by and rapped them hard on the top of their heads as they came up. He was enjoying himself immensely and secretly hoped the Bat would arrive by way of Bermuda. At least he did until a harsh voice snapped a command. Then Butch looked around to stare at a gun, and behind it a dark-featured man with murder glittering in his eyes.

"Reach, you big palooka!" he commanded. "Quick, or I'll chill you."

BUTCH BACKED up a few steps and elevated his arms. Every muscle and nerve was tensed. Butch couldn't think too fast, but he had the power of a pile-driver and the speed of a flashing piston. Blackie recognized that and took care not to get too close.

"What's the big idea?" he demanded of Butch. "This is a funeral home. Haven't you any respect for the dead?"

"Yeah," Butch growled. "Boy, I'd have a lot of respect for you—dead. But seein' you're alive, I'll hang a couple of lanterns on your eyes."

"Walk into the rear room," Blackie snapped. "Come on—no stalling. Somebody sent you here and I want to find out just who it was. Maybe a mutual friend, eh, gorilla?"

Butch marched into the rear room. The first thing he saw was a large, red plush box on a table. Pasted on the cover, now open, was a paper representation of a black bat!

Blackie saw it too and gave an alarmed shout.

"So that's the game? While you kept me busy, your pal busted in here, huh? Okay, you big lug. You work for the Bat! For a minute or two I figured him for a right guy, but all he did was get me free from the cops so he could trail me here. Well, he's gone—and he's got the swag I risked my hide for. But I've got *you*, Big Boy! When the Bat returns that bunch of rocks, he can have you back."

Blackie's four aides were clustered just inside the door, eyeing Butch malevolently. Blackie hurled the empty jewel box on the floor and swore.

"Sap, that's me! I fell for the Bat's line, but this ain't over yet. Not by a long shot."

"Quite right, Blackie," a voice said calmly.

Everyone in the room spun around, while a chorus of rasped breaths exploded. The Bat, hood over his head and shoulders, stood just inside the door. The guns in his hands menaced the quintette of crooks.

"Butch, come over here beside me. Draw your gun and watch these men. If one of them so much as sneezes, shoot him! They'd do the same if our positions were reversed."

"Next time," Blackie raged, "you'll get it, you wise guy! First you played me for a sucker and then you swiped that bunch of rocks. Well, try and sell 'em! It can't be done except through the right channels and I know 'em. You don't!"

The Bat moved into the room and flung a glistening diadem of jewels on the table.

"Those," he said calmly, "could be peddled in Woolworth's. Others played you for a sucker, too, Blackie. You swiped a nice mess of paste."

Blackie's face contorted into a mask of passionate rage. He seized the shimmering stones set in a golden crown.

He forgot that guns menaced him. Forgot everything but the fact that he had been buncoed. He ran over to a window and tried to scratch the glass with one of the diamonds. Failing, he gave a shout of rage and hurled the thing to the floor.

"Easy, Blackie," the Bat warned. "Now listen to me. You work for someone. That man has tricked you as neatly as he has tricked everyone else. Do you think the police descended on Fawcett's jewelry store by sheer accident? Do you believe Fawcett's murder wouldn't be pinned on you if the police managed to arrest you? It was a plant—meant to strap you in the chair. Who staged it, Blackie? Who is the man you work for—the man who has robbed people in this city of millions in gems?"

BLACKIE'S FACE turned crafty. "I don't know what you're talking about. I work for myself, see?"

"But you practically admitted, by your own words and actions that you were given a bad steer," the Bat went calmly on. "Someone baited that trap for you. Baited it with worthless paste. He'll do that again, Blackie. He'll do it because he's afraid of you. He's got what he wants from you, and now you've become useless baggage. Next time you may not be so lucky. What if I hadn't been there?"

"Hey Boss!" Butch stepped forward. "How about me taking him apart, huh? All he needs is a little of that persuasion stuff."

"No." The Bat rejected the idea. "We don't handle things that way—not at this stage of the game. Blackie will think over what I've told him. I'll contact you again—when I'm ready to hear you talk. Until then, Blackie, watch your step."

Butch caught a significant glance from the cold eyes behind the mask. He stuffed his gun into his pocket and fell to work with vigor. In three minutes Blackie lay sprawled on top of his own men, all piled into a heap. Butch wiped his hands and grunted in satisfaction as they went out of the door together.

He was silent for a long time as he drove the Bat in the general direction of his home. But Butch didn't like the way things progressed, and finally said so.

"Maybe you made a mistake lettin' that bird go," he offered.

The Bat had stripped his mask off and was folding it into a compact wad as he answered.

"No, Butch. Blackie is a peculiar type of crook. He's clever and he usually gets what he goes after. Silk knew him, years ago. Blackie is in this game to get everything for himself. He won't welch now—when his goal seems near at hand. Nothing would have made him talk. And of course, I couldn't very well notify the police to come and get him because I want Blackie loose. Sooner or later he'll lead me to the man we want. Your job is to try and pick up Blackie's trail. It may be impossible because he'll lay low, but do your best."

CHAPTER XVII

CAROL'S DESTINY

AS THE shadows lengthened Carol Baldwin glanced at the clock and made ready to call it a day. She was locking her desk when McFayden barged into her office in the jewelry store.

"You're to take this package to the Harriman branch store on your way home," he said with a wide smile intended to open the way for an extended conversation. "It's important, so don't fail to deliver it at once."

"Leave it on the desk," Carol replied. "I'll stop off with it. Don't worry."

McFayden walked toward the door, hesitated and turned back for another look at this blond vision of loveliness. Carol met his stare coolly and he flushed. She picked up the small package, slipped it into her purse and with a final adjustment of her hat, walked down the stairs, through the store and into the street.

"Cab, lady?"

A taxi pulled up at the curb. The driver was grinning at her. Carol felt a sudden premonition of danger. She turned to rush back into the store, but a man stood directly behind her.

"You better take a ride, lady," he said. "It would be healthier than yelling for the cops."

She glanced down and saw that his hand was deep in his side pocket. There was no question as to what that hand gripped. Carol retained her composure with an effort.

"Is this a threat?" she asked. "What are you after?"

"Get in the cab and find out." The man smiled thinly.

Carol didn't know him, for she had never seen Blackie Burns before. Yet she did recognize the menace he offered. Her eyes flashed to one side. A patrolman was casually making his way down the street. Carol took three steps toward the taxi and suddenly veered to the left. Instantly Blackie seized her by the arm and literally hurled her into the cab.

"Hey!" The patrolman broke into a run. "What's the idea?"

Blackie's concealed hand moved a trifle.

"This!" he snarled.

A gun exploded. The patrolman stumbled and fell heavily, skidding across the sidewalk. He raised his head, tugged at his holstered gun and then the agony from a wound in his shoulder overcame him. He fell back limply.

The taxi cut into the traffic, raced by two red lights and swerved around a corner. It stopped beside a sedan.

"Get into that other bus and make it snappy," Blackie rasped.

Carol obeyed. There wasn't anything else she could do. The cab pulled away and before it reached the next corner, two radio cars flashed by in swift pursuit. Blackie scowled, snapped an order to the driver and the sedan headed north along an avenue.

"Well, Beautiful,"—Blackie regarded his prisoner appreciatively—"you didn't get so far in trying to take a powder on me, did you?"

"You," Carol returned crisply, "are an insufferable, stupid moron. The type of a coward who doesn't give the other fellow a chance. Did you have to shoot that patrolman?"

"Sure," Blackie declared complacently. "He'd have bumped me if I hadn't stopped him…. Now listen. Baby, you keep that tongue of yours in check, see? If it didn't wag so much, you wouldn't be in this jam."

CAROL LEANED back against the cushions.

"I don't know what you mean," she said shortly.

"Aw, stop trying to kid me, will you?" Blackie grinned. "Not so very long ago a certain party phoned me. You tuned in on that call somehow. What's more you ain't no friend of Graham's old secretary. We checked up. You notified a guy who goes around masked, like it was Hallowe'en, about that phone call. So he came to see me and he made a lot of trouble. You tipped him off, so you must know who he is. Think that over."

"Are you certain," Carol asked blandly, "that you weren't recently behind the bars of an asylum? There's no necessity for lying. You know I carry a package meant for the Harriman Jewelry Company. That sly Mr. McFayden handed it to me. Just another idea on how to rob the store, I suppose. Everything else you mention is a complete puzzle to me. The package is what you want."

"Hand over that purse," Blackie ordered. "Oh, you'll get it back. I just want to see whether or not you travel heeled."

He dumped the contents of the purse on the seat, riffled through the myriad articles a woman carries, then tossed the wrapped package McFayden had given her into Carol's lap.

"Open it," he ordered, "and see if it's jewelry I'm after."

Carol broke the cord, peeled off the paper and revealed a small jewelry box. She pressed the spring and the lid flew open. There was nothing inside.

"McFayden," she breathed softly. "This is his work! He sent me on a fool's errand, thinking I'd take that taxi planted in front of the store. You're one of his men. He's the thief who has robbed the store, and you're in it just as bad as he is. I don't know why either of you should want to kidnap me, but—"

"Now ain't that nice," Blackie sighed. "You sure pick things up fast, Beautiful. Only you're a little wrong. I'm the boss of this outfit; not that sneaky guy McFayden. It depends on me just how you're treated. Now, if you'd whisper the real name of the Black Bat, I might get soft hearted and let you out."

Carol sniffed. "I don't know what you're talking about. The Black Bat!"

Blackie crossed his legs. "Okay, lady. All I know is that you work for the Bat and soon as you're missed, he'll come flying. He'll find you too, because that guy is smart. Twice he surprised me, but this time I'll do all the surprising. You can relax. Nobody's going to hurt you—yet."

Carol glanced out of the car window and saw that they had left the city and were heading toward Connecticut. Once or twice she had a glimpse of the Sound. They were silent as the car whizzed along, then at last it passed through a small town, turned to the right and headed straight toward the Sound waterfront.

Carol had a mental vision of being held prisoner aboard some boat. So far as she could reason, it would be impossible for the Bat to find her now. She had left no clue, wasn't expected to report for hours yet, and inwardly she was glad. For if Tony Quinn ever realized she was a prisoner, and guessed where she was, he would come quickly and run straight into a death trap.

SUDDENLY CAROL made a lunge for the car door. She had it half open when Blackie's big paw descended on her shoulder. He hauled her back and shoved her against the seat.

"Spunky, ain't you?" he said, and grinned at her. "You'll lose some of that. Okay—we're here. Like the scenery?"

Carol could hardly keep her tears in check. She peered out of the window and saw that the car had stopped inside a high concrete gate. The door was swinging shut now. A small gray stucco building occupied the center of the enclosed area and piled in several places were huge, concrete boxes.

"Nice, huh?" Blackie smiled. "Them things are burial vaults, lady. They put people in 'em and plant 'em in graveyards. You'll know just how it's done if your mouth freezes up. Now get out of this car, and no funny tricks. You can't get away from this place—not unless you got wings."

Carol stepped out of the car. Two men in overalls smirked at her. Blackie took her arm and she was forcibly led into the stucco building. There she saw various molds for casting these huge vaults. A furnace was roaring at one end of the building.

"Pleasant little place," Blackie said blandly. "We make metal vaults too, for ritzy people. The business is on the level and nobody suspects the place, so it won't do you much good to start hollering. Nobody ever comes here. Now let's go into the office and have a little talk, huh?"

Carol walked between the half finished vaults and shuddered. Anything could happen here. Why, she might be murdered and buried in one of those concrete boxes! Blackie, as she had heard him called by his men, was wholly capable of such a deed. Carol could tell that by the chilly glint in his black eyes and the malicious grin across his lips.

She sat down in a swivel chair. Blackie draped himself on a corner of an old desk.

"Now listen to reason, lady," he said. "You know we got the goods on you. Nobody else could have tipped the Bat as to where we had one of his pals. Know what happened to him? The Bat's pal, I mean?"

"How could I," Carol queried with just the right degree of innocence, "when all of this is just a mystery to me? I don't know what you're talking about. I didn't tip anyone off and I did not listen in on a single phone call. Where could I have listened from? You mean from the jewelry store?"

Blackie grimaced and walked toward a door at the farther end of the office. He gestured for Carol to follow him. She was led into a dark, damp room, shoved into a chair and Blackie deftly tied her. Then he stepped back.

"Rubbing out dames ain't my style, lady, but you got only a few hours to make up your mind. Just start praying that the Bat will get here before the big shot does. You see, the boss of this racket ain't as soft-hearted as me."

"Thank you," Carol said stiffly, "for such consideration. I'll remember it when you are brought to trial for kidnaping. Just who is this man you call your boss? I thought you were the head man around here?"

"You'd like to know, wouldn't you? Maybe you will, but keep on hoping you never know because once that happens, you'll die. I'll bring some food and water later on. If you feel like yelling, go to it. Nobody can hear you. The Bat will start looking for you at the store and he'll get the dope that will lead him right here."

BLACKIE WENT out, closed and locked the door and eerie darkness descended on Carol. With a supreme effort she retained control of her nerves. Once she laughed mirthlessly. Wasn't this what she had wanted? An active part in the Bat's campaign against crime? Hadn't her father's wish led her into these dark, dismal passages where danger lurked every inch of the way?

Thoughts of her father gave Carol back a large measure of composure and courage. He had suffered and died so that crime's vicious tentacles might not sweep out and encompass all that was decent and right. Could she do any less?

Grimly Carol tested the bonds that strapped her to the chair. Ten minutes of frantic pulling and tugging only tired her. Yet there was one thing she could do. Blackie expected the Bat to find this hideaway and put in an appearance. There would be a trap set—a death trap! She might be able to warn the Bat. To do this, she had to retain full control of her wits and never relax her vigilance for a single second. She banished all thoughts of fear and kept listening intently for the first sign of the Bat's coming.

Outside of the building, Blackie surrounded himself with the seven men who presumably worked in this vault manufacturing plant. He gave the men precise instructions.

"Leave the gate open so he'll walk right in. That guy is bound to find this place. I have a man planted at Graham's store who will slip him the location of this place. Let him inside and then go to work. No matter what happens, the Bat is not to leave this place alive. Don't kill him unless necessary, but if it looks like he's getting away, blast him down. That's all—except I might mention a reward of two grand for the guy who grabs the Bat."

Blackie stalked back to the office and sat down. He picked up the phone, dialed, and called the city.

"Blackie," he reported. "Things are shaping up swell. Our customer arrived okay and we're trying to make a sale right now. If the other party arrives we close the deal. Got it, Boss?"

"Good, Blackie," the voice at the other end said. "I was beginning to lose faith in you. And let me assure you once more that the affair at Fawcett's was not of my doing. It happened to be a trick of someone else. We're almost ready to close up and nothing must interfere."

Blackie replaced the receiver and leaned back, highly gratified at the way things were going. He grinned at the telephone and thumbed his nose at it once.

"Yeah," he soliloquized, "we're about ready to close up. Only when that happens, Mister Wise Guy, you'll be on the outside of the door."

CHAPTER XVIII

DEATH VAULT

VEERING TOWARD the sidewalk, Butch's coupé stopped along the curb of a street not far from the river. The man who emerged looked carefully around before he ventured far from the car. Tony Quinn was in his disguise of Rex Gordon. In it he could move about more or less freely so long as he kept a watchful eye out for the police.

He had attempted to change this disguise, but it had not worked out too well. Certain peculiarities of Tony Quinn's face made radical changes of appearance difficult and then, too, he had little time to experiment. Still it was better this way than appearing in the hood of the Bat!

He kept well to the shadows of the building line as he hurried up the street. Certain he was unobserved, Quinn ran lightly into the middle of the street, quickly propped up the sewer lid and dropped into the abandoned drain, letting the lid fall back into place.

He jerked his gun out and stood quietly listening. No sound reached him. He drew his hood from an inner pocket, donned it and hurried down the tube until he found the rusty iron grip of the secret door.

The first thing he saw when he stepped through the door was that the two dead men lay just as he had left them when he had escaped from the cave. The Bat shivered a little as he crossed the room carved out of the earth. At the far end he pulled away a packing case and discovered what he sought—a narrow round tunnel. He wriggled through the opening and crawled steadily upward along the slanting shaft.

Finally he reached a spot where a smaller cavern had been cut. The ceiling of this was propped up with heavy two by fours. And that ceiling was smooth and looked like concrete. He pulled away the timbers, stood erect and was able to place the palms of both hands against the cement square. He pushed with all his strength and the section of ceiling moved up.

By using the timber props as supports the Bat finally got this trap-door half open. He seized the edge of the floor above, hoisted himself up and lay panting from his exertion, on a cold cement floor.

His super-sensitive eyes made out his surroundings, despite the intense darkness. He was in the massive vault at Graham's jewelry store. This fact did not startle the Bat, for by careful reasoning he had already guessed that the tunnel would lead him here.

When, as blind Tony Quinn, he had been led to the sewer, he had observed that the underground tube lay only a block from where Graham's store was located. The cavern, dug just outside the sewer had showed plenty of evidence of fresh soil being carried through it. All that meant another tunnel, dug in the direction of Graham's store.

In this feat of engineering lay the answer to the mysterious burglary of Graham's gems. Harriman's store, and Gill's also, might be similarly tapped by underground passages.

The Bat drew out a map which Silk had obtained for him. It showed the routes of every sewer line in the city, both old and new. Gill's store, the Bat noted, was almost as close to the sewer as Graham's but Harriman's place of business could never be reached by any subterranean passages originating in a sewer. The Bat pursed his lips in a soundless whistle.

If there was no tunnel beneath Harriman's vault then suspicion fastened on Phil Harriman tenaciously, or on somebody in his store. Graham's and Gill's stores could be robbed from inside but Harriman's, without a tunnel, had to be burglarized by opening the vault door, an impossible act except by one who knew the combination and had free access to the premises.

THE BAT thought also of the tiara which had been shipped abroad. It showed that at least part of the loot had already been disposed of through foreign channels. The tiara, according to Mrs. Van den Killan, who had been in possession of the duplicate of faked gems, had been worn by a woman at an affair in Amsterdam. Van den Killan was a Hollander and bound to have good connection in the Netherlands. If he was engaged in criminal work his wife probably knew nothing about it, and the presence of the tiara at the ball might very well have been a sheer accident which Van den Killan could not have foreseen.

The Bat made a swift examination of the interior of the vault. Then he closed the trap-door, placed the uprights to support it and slipped back down the tunnel into the sewer. By consulting the map again he proceeded to a point from which Gill's store might be reached by the least amount of digging. He saw another of those rusty iron handles, pulled it and stepped from the abandoned sewer into another cavern. He found the tunnel and five minutes later pulled himself up into Gill's massive vault.

"It looks," the Bat surmised, "as though Harriman or somebody close to him is elected. Unless his store is also equipped with one of these tunnels I can only assume that he or one of his aides robbed his stock. And a tunnel under his safe—at least one made from a sewer is practically an impossibility."

Returning to the cavern dug alongside the old sewer, the Bat found evidences that it had also been used as a hideout. The tunneling operations must have taken a long time to accomplish and the crooks who performed the work had probably lived in the cavern. The Bat examined a heap of rubbish in one corner. He found several empty books of matches. One advertised a filling station in Eastown, a small Connecticut village. Another bore the ad of a grocery store in the same town. There were others, mostly all identified with that small village.

"The crooks must have lived there for an extended period," the Bat reasoned. "How else would they have obtained these match books from so many different sources in the same town?"

On the rickety table he discovered a worn pack of playing cards and a small pocket calendar. This made him draw in a quick breath. It was issued with the compliments of the Sherbrooke Burial Vault Company of Eastown, Connecticut.

In the Bat's mind facts clicked. Funeral parlors had been used by the crooks and there was a definite connection between such places of business and a burial vault concern. Where could the master thief find a better spot to work unmolested? A burial vault manufacturing plant would hardly fall under suspicion of any investigators and the necessary equipment used in preparing the copies of the stolen gems might well be housed there.

The Bat decided to examine this Connecticut burial vault concern without further delay. Another angle struck him. The real gems were shipped abroad—or part of them at least. No better method could be employed than by enclosing them either in a burial vault, a casket, or even the body of someone whose remains were to be shipped abroad.

He made his way out of the sewer and hurried to a phone booth. Hurriedly calling Silk he learned that there was still no word from Carol. The Bat's worries increased. Above all things he did not want to risk her safety. But without a clue he could only work as rapidly as possible in running down the mob and hope that he might find some trace of her whereabouts during this work.

IT WAS long after dark when the Bat reached the small Connecticut town and drove to the vault manufacturing plant, or near it, rather. He left his coupé and reconnoitered. He saw the high concrete wall that surrounded the plant and also saw that the door, set in that wall, had been left slightly ajar. There were no lights in the yard, but that wasn't unusual. It was long after working hours. The open door attracted him, but Quinn knew better than to expose himself so boldly.

Moving into the dark shadows cast by the high wall he stood there, listening intently. He was rather far from the town itself, and there were no houses nor other places of business within half a mile.

Then he stiffened. His extremely sensitive hearing detected the sound of someone moving about on the other side of the wall. The Bat glanced up. If the plant employed a watchman, which was unlikely, he would be using a flashlight or lantern. Some of the light would illuminate at least a small portion of the yard and reach to the top of the wall. But there was not the faintest trace of light.

He heard the man on the other side of the wall curse once as he stubbed his foot against something. The Bat smiled grimly.

He noticed that electric light poles were ranged about twenty feet from the wall. In the darkness they were almost invisible, but the Bat's eyes saw them as clearly as though they were flooded with a spotlight. He moved toward them. His clothes were black and when he pulled up his coat collar, the whiteness of his shirt was covered.

He drew on his black hood, wrapped his arms around a telephone pole and shinnied up it slowly and cautiously. From a point twenty feet away he knew he was invisible to ordinary eyes.

Halfway up he surveyed the vault manufacturing plant. He penetrated the darkness easily and picked out two forms standing just inside the gate. Both men carried clubs and wore guns strapped to their thighs. Two others were slowly pacing a beat around the plant itself.

The Bat slid down silently, made his way to the rear of the plant and finally clambered up a tree. He crawled out along one branch until he could drop directly on top of the cement wall. Landing like a cat, he clung to the rough surface for a moment, then went over the side. For a second more he hung by his hands, then let go and hit the ground with a soft thud. He was up instantly and running toward a far corner of the premises, where the darkness was intense.

A guard strolled by, glancing up at the wall every few steps as if to make sure no intruder scaled it. He heard a slight scuffling sound behind him, reached for his gun and then tried to yell a warning. An arm curled around his throat, muffling the cry. A fist struck hard at the back of his neck. It was a scientific blow that brought immediate results. The guard went limp.

Carefully the Bat carried the guard he had captured into the darkest corner, set him down gently and made a brief examination. He nodded, satisfied. The guard would be unconscious for many minutes.

As softly as the nocturnal creature for which he was named, the Bat crossed the yard and edged his way toward the factory building. One of the other two men on guard shivered and patted his holstered gun to reassure himself. He knew that the Bat was expected to pay this place a visit, and the reputation of the Bat had penetrated every inch of the underworld. This man was afraid. The Bat could strike swiftly and with terrible effect. Only the promise of rich reward kept the fellow who was watching for him going.

HE STARTED his patrol that stretched around the corner of the building. A shadow moved out and he started back in terror. Too late he tried to sing out a warning. The Bat's right fist cracked against the guard's jaw. His left followed with a second paralyzing blow. As the guard slumped toward the ground, the Bat caught him and eased the fall.

He straightened up and those exceptional eyes spotted danger. The other guard, assigned to the factory door, had heard the scuffling. He barged around the corner, gun ready. The Bat's right hand moved like the strike of a cobra. There were two shots, almost blended into one. The guard spun around, dropped heavily and lay moaning.

In a flash the Bat raced toward the factory door. From the wall gate two more men came sprinting toward him, shooting as they came. Slugs slammed into the stucco wall of the building, but the thugs were shooting in darkness and at a shadowy form that flitted like a ghost. The Bat fired from the hip and one man tumbled into a heap. The other turned tail and raced toward the gate. The Bat let him go.

He reached the factory door and pushed it open. Nothing happened. He stepped inside and someone moved. The Bat turned his head and through the darkness saw two advancing forms, clubs held high. He ducked under one swinging blow, drove a fist deep into the stomach of one man and sent him reeling back. The other killer brought his club down in a vicious arc.

It was impossible to duck it, but the Bat rolled back with it and avoided the full fury of the blow. Before the killer could raise his club again, or reach for his gun, a fist exploded against his jaw. He sat down, half dazed. The Bat stopped long enough to smash him again, wheeled and rushed the other man who was getting to his feet.

The impact of the two bodies sounded like a head-on collision of two heavyweights in the ring. The Bat took a blow over his heart, leaped back to avoid another lashing punch and then came in, fists swinging. He struck a mighty blow full against the killer's nose, rapped a second to the chin and finished up the fight with a one-two that connected squarely with the man's jaw.

Gun in hand now, the Bat turned slowly. His eyes penetrated the darkness and he saw a small door to his left. Alert, he moved toward it, wary of a trap. Suddenly a beam of light came from beneath the door. He raised his gun and his finger tightened on the trigger. The door swung open slowly and the Bat gave a low cry of horror.

Inside the room, tied to a heavy chair in the center of the floor, was Carol. She was gagged, but her eyes implored him to run. The Bat refused to obey that plea. He knew only that the girl he loved, the girl who willingly risked all manner of peril for him, was in danger.

"Carol!" he shouted and rushed through the door.

Too late he realized that he had been tricked, after all. With all his thoughts centered on Carol, he had relaxed his vigilance for a bare fraction of a second.

Something crashed down on the back of his neck. He hurtled forward under the force of the blow, fell to his knees and tried to lift the gun. Another blow caught him on top of the head. The room began spinning. Carol's face, a mask of horror, rocked and gyrated like some figment of a wild dream. Vaguely the Bat felt strong hands seize him. His mask was ripped off and he heard a grunt.

"YEAH, THAT'S him!" Blackie gloated. "What he runs around with a mask for, I don't understand. It's the Bat and we've got him now. Grab his legs and help me toss him into that vault. The big one!"

The Bat was lifted, carried across the room and hurled into a spacious burial vault. Blackie stepped back, manipulated a block and tackle device until the heavy lid of the vault swung directly over the concrete box. He kept pulling the chain and the lid dropped slowly. Blackie stepped back with a sigh of satisfaction.

"Let's see him get outa there. He walked right into it—just as I figured he would, once he spotted the dame. Now we know she's connected with the Bat, so it's curtains for her."

"What about him?" One of the men pointed toward the burial vault.

"He'll keep," Blackie said. "Nobody could raise that lid and he'll be there when the boss shows. This is the best night's work we've ever done."

"But he'll smother in there," Blackie's aide cried.

Blackie assumed an expression of mock sadness.

"Now won't that be just too bad. Listen, I'm going into town. You and Joe take this dame down to the Sound and find a small boat. Tie a lot of weights to her legs and when you get far enough out, toss her over. Better take this bottle of chloroform along. It'll make things a lot easier and she won't rock the boat. The Bat can stay here and rot."

CHAPTER XIX

SILK TAKES A HAND

ONLY SHORTLY before dark, not long after Carol had started her long car ride, though as yet nothing was guessed of that, Silk had received a phone call from the Bat.

"I'm heading out to the Sherbrooke Burial Vault Company out near Eastown, Connecticut," he told Silk. "That firm may have a tie-up with the Grady Funeral Parlors and with Blackie. It looks to me like some set-up to work in with this series of jewel robberies and worse crimes. If I don't come back, you'll know where to start looking, Silk."

"Can't I go along?" Silk implored. "My legs are okay now."

"Stay where you are!" the Bat ordered. "If anyone comes to see me, stall them. When you hear from Carol, tell her to lay low. She'd better not report for work again at the jewelry store. I'm afraid they may get to thinking it was she who tipped me off as to where you were being held, Silk."

Silk hung up glumly. Then, instead of waiting for Carol to phone, he called her apartment. There was no answer. Silk hung up thoughtfully, then made a sudden decision. Working fast, he disguised himself, locked the house and departed via the secret exit. He hurried to Carol's apartment and rang the bell.

When there was no response, Silk called the superintendent of the building. He hadn't seen Carol, although she was usually home by this time. Silk determined on a bold move. He taxied to the Graham Jewelry Company and rang the night bell. A watchman opened the door a crack.

"You mean Van den Killan's secretary? No, buddy, she ain't here. Say, maybe… But no, that can't be! Who'd want to snatch her?"

Silk's eyes grew wide with horror.

"What do you mean?" he asked. "She's my sister. What's this about a snatch?"

The watchman shoved his cap to the back of his head and frowned.

"She was leaving when I reported for work. A minute afterward a cop was plugged right outside. He said, later on, that a dame had been forced into a taxi and taken away. But it couldn't be your sister, buddy. She'll turn up. Maybe had a date with a boy friend."

The watchman turned away, then seemed to have another thought.

"Say buddy I did hear somebody tell the hack driver to head for some town in Connecticut—Eastown, I think it was."

Silk moved away, thanking the man. Cold perspiration formed little beads on his forehead. Carol had been kidnaped! The Bat's bunch was right. They figured Carol had tipped off the Bat.

What to do! The Bat couldn't be contacted for advice. If anything must be done, Silk was now on his own. He didn't know which way to turn. He needed the Bat. Perhaps in some manner the Bat had also discovered that Carol was gone. It might be that he was following her already. Silk hoped so, sincerely. Carol's brave act had saved his life and Silk was grateful.

"The Sherbrooke Company was what the Bat said—where he was goin'," Silk muttered. "In Connecticut. I could drive there in less than an hour."

HE BRIBED a taxi driver to skip traffic lights, dismissed the cab far uptown and hurried into a garage that specialized in renting cars. Silk showed credentials, made a substantial payment and drove a fast roadster in the direction the Bat has taken. By guarded inquiry, Silk located the Sherbrooke Company and as he drove down the dark lane leading to the place, he doused his lights.

Suddenly Silk tramped on the brake, turned the wheel sharply and left the road. He made a complete turn in a field, headed back in the direction from which he had come and made sure the car couldn't be seen from the road. He climbed out and made his way across a marshy field until he crouched behind the thick trunk of a tree about a hundred yards from the plant.

Two quick shots startled him. Silk drew his own gun and made ready to move into the battle. As he neared the gate set in the high wall, he saw headlights of a car turned on. Silk dropped flat, parted thick grass and watched. To his amazement, he saw someone carried out of the plant and hustled over to a big car. The headlights reflected against the wall and Silk made out the identity of the prisoner. It was Carol!

Her arms were tied and two men threw her bodily into the rear seat. One climbed in after her, while the other manned the wheel. Someone ran up to the car. It was Blackie, and Silk's eyes narrowed in hatred. But he bided his time and finally Blackie and one other man began carrying limp burdens across the yard. Silk grinned at that. The Bat had been here all right. And he had left copious evidence of his work.

Blackie drove out of the yard first. Silk let him go. He wondered about the Bat, where he was, but reasoned that if Blackie had captured him, the Bat would have been spirited away also. Silk was positive none of those limp forms had been that of his employer.

The car, with Carol in the tonneau, rolled out of the yard, stopped, and the driver returned to close the gate. Then the sedan rolled over the narrow road.

Silk began running toward his own roadster. He piled into it, smashed his way through underbrush and without turning on his lights, set out in pursuit.

As Blackie's car reached the main highway, it turned left. The second car took the right turn and Silk followed that one. Carol's safety was the paramount thing right now. Silk was torn between a desire to rescue her and to return to the plant in search of the Bat. It was a decision that worried him, but he depended upon the Bat's prowess. Carol was just a helpless girl, probably on her way to certain doom.

Silk trailed the car expertly. When it left the highway, five miles south, Silk turned also and in time to see the sedan roll through the gates of someone's estate. He could smell the Sound and as he reached the gates, he saw the water.

Jamming on the brakes, Silk leaped out of the car, drew his gun and raced through the gates. There was a marker with a name printed on it, suspended from the rustic fence. Silk skidded to a stop, long enough to read the name.

"Clifford Carlyle," he grunted. "That's the guy who is partners with Van den Killan. So these mugs are using his estate, huh? Maybe Carlyle can explain that."

SILK NOTICED the sedan parked alongside the big house. He made a circle of the place and came out on the opposite side, along a smooth, sandy beach. Silk wished now that he had the Bat's eyes. The eerie darkness presented a problem. Silk couldn't see more than four or five feet.

Then a muffled scream made his blood run cold. He snapped off the safety of his automatic and ran straight toward the sound. A dark figure loomed up. The man whirled as he heard Silk. A gun appeared in his hand and a jagged streak of flame cut the darkness. The bullet fanned Silk's ear. He squeezed the trigger of his own gun. The man spun around and dropped.

"Got him, Bat!" Silk yelled. "There's another mug! If he hurts the girl, we'll drown him. Let's go!"

"No!" the second thug shrieked. "No! I won't hurt the girl. D-don't shoot. I don't want to fight the Bat. Blackie made me do this!"

There was genuine terror in his voice. Only a matter of minutes before the Bat had been dumped into a burial vault with a heavy lid placed over it. The thug

The oxy-acetylene torch cut through the steel.

had witnessed that piece of drama with his own eyes. Yet the Bat was here! He had escaped, performed a superhuman feat which no ordinary man could possibly have accomplished. The Bat's reputation assumed a near supernatural phase in the frightened crook's mind.

Silk's trick of pretending that the Bat was here had worked splendidly. The thug began running madly toward the house. Behind him he left a rowboat that gradually slipped out to sea.

The thug racing away tripped on his own feet once and fell headlong. He arose and darted crazily along the beach. Then a bullet zipped by him and he stopped abruptly. Hands reaching for the stars, he stood trembling like a leaf in an autumnal wind. A gun prodded his spine.

"Where is the girl?"

"In—in the rowboat. She ain't hurt, honest. You can't blame me for this. Blackie made me do it. I—"

A gun butt crashed against his skull and silenced him. Silk was racing toward the water before the thug had completed his fall. He peered through the darkness and exclaimed in horror. The rowboat was drifting out on the Sound. Silk stripped off his coat, forced his shoes off without untying the laces and gave a running dive into the surf. He swam with the short, chopping strokes of an inexperienced swimmer, but managed to reach the boat.

A rope dangled off its prow. He seized this, pulled himself up a little and saw Carol lying in the bottom of the boat. Silk had to exert all his strength to swim and tow the craft behind him. Finally, however, he beached it. In a flash he raised Carol's head, saw the chloroform-soaked sponge and hurled it into the water.

With Carol in his arms, Silk waded ashore. He set her down gently, untied the ropes and chafed her wrists. At last she opened her eyes and gave a violent shudder.

"It's me," Silk told her soothingly. "It's Silk. You're okay, Carol."

SHE SAT up.

"Silk—you! Silk!! They got him! Tony is in a burial vault. He'll smother! I heard Blackie say no man could live more than half an hour in that vault. W-what time is it?"

Silk gulped. Far more than half an hour had passed since he had started trailing Carol. By now the Bat must be suffocated.

"Put your arms around my neck," Silk told Carol. "We're going back!"

Silk helped her into the roadster. He rolled out of the estate, stepped hard on the gas pedal and tore up the highway. Too late! The thought hammered at his brain. Carol was sobbing quietly, her head against Silk's shoulder. It looked like the end of the Bat.

He had probably died trying to save her, and she had been the bait in the trap that had spelled his doom.

"He'll be all right," Silk soothed her, but he couldn't get much assurance in his tone. "No bunch of punks like Blackie and his gang can get the Bat. And maybe we're in time at that. Look—there's the road leading to the plant. Hang on—it's going to be rough sailing."

CHAPTER XX
THE FINGER OF SUSPICION

D**AZEDLY CONSCIOUSNESS** returned to the Bat soon after the lid of the burial vault sealed him into the crypt. He opened his eyes and for a moment was gripped by a horror more grim than anything he had endured since the days of his blindness. Ordinary darkness meant little to the Bat, for his eyes could penetrate it. But now, not knowing where he was, he could see nothing but blackness just as intense as the utter stark inkiness of the blind.

He rubbed his eyes and sat up. His head bumped against something extremely substantial. Eagerly he felt around until he realized that he was confined in some kind of box. The Bat gave a sigh of relief. Anything was better than a return to blindness. His mind, attuned to accept such dire possibilities, had instantly grasped the idea that the blow on the head had returned him to the Stygian pits of his former affliction.

He was bathed in perspiration and his head ached like a sore tooth. He sat up as far as he could, and the sensitive tips of his fingers grimly related the whole story to him. The Bat knew where he was now—in one of the huge burial vaults of six- or eight-inch-thick concrete.

He wondered if Blackie had sealed him inside. Regardless of whether that was so or not, precious little air was coming into his tomb and if anything was to be done, action was necessary.

The Bat turned over clumsily, raised his back and set it firmly against the lid of the tomb. The muscles in his shoulders stood out like whipcords, his arms became massive pedestals that supported him and gradually raised the concrete lid.

A little fresh air entered and the Bat eagerly sucked his lungs full. Things cleared a bit after that, but when he relaxed, he knew only too well that three men wouldn't have the combined strength to raise this lid far enough for him to squirm through.

He remembered Carol, tied in that chair. The Bat wasted no more time. His agile mind sought a way out of this death trap—and found one. A slight, hazardous chance, but a chance nevertheless.

In his pocket he had a clip of steel-jacketed .45 bullets. Blackie had not taken time to search him. After all, a man entombed in a concrete burial vault that weighed more than a ton wouldn't be able to put any kind of a weapon to use.

The Bat slipped several of the cartridges into the palm of his hand, then he set his back against the lid once more and exerted all his strength to raise the lid about half an inch. He held his breath, supported the massive load on one arm and deftly inserted a cartridge into the crack between the casket and the lid. Now, at least, he would get fresh air.

Again he performed the same backbreaking stint until the second cartridge was inserted on the other side. There was some danger of the pressure exploding the bullets, but the Bat had made certain that the steel-jacket tips were pointed outside. Now he had two small but sturdy rollers beneath the lid. Gradually he eased the lid forward, rolling it by fractions of an inch, on the bullets. He inserted two more and now he could move the lid faster and easier.

AT LAST he had cleared almost two feet of space. Wriggling his body, be managed to raise his head out of the tomb. For a moment he rested, waiting for his strength to return and the ache in his bones and muscles to subside.

Further and further he shoved the lid out, then, until its own weight raised the end near the Bat. It teetered like a seesaw for a moment, then raised up and slid off the vault. One corner broke and the whole heavy affair smashed to the floor.

The Bat leaped out of the vault. In the darkness that no other eyes than his could have probed, he saw his own gun, kicked into a corner. He leaped for it, picked it up. The weight of it felt good in his hand. He made sure it was loaded and ready for action.

Rushing to the door, the Bat flung it wide, then ducked back. A car, driving without lights, had pulled into the yard. Two people were getting out and the Bat's gun came up. He stepped outside the door.

"Reach!" he snapped.

There was a grunt of dismay from one of the intruders and a short little cry from the other. They turned to face this menace and the Bat gave a shout of delight. In the darkness he recognized them. Silk, dripping wet, had driven the car. Carol was standing beside him.

"Boss!" Silk shouted.

Carol rushed toward the Bat and for a long minute was enfolded in his arms. Silk danced about, asking a dozen questions and getting no reply whatsoever.

"Boss, we figured you'd be dead! I was set to track down Blackie and strangle the rat. What happened? How'd you get loose?"

The Bat led them into the plant and pointed to the broken vault lid.

"There's the answer," he said cheerfully. "I raised the lid, shoved bullets under it and pushed the lid off."

"Let's get out of here," Carol suggested with a shudder.

"In a few moments," the Bat said. "The inventive mind behind this series of crimes isn't operating this plant because it's a good place to dispose of his enemies. He must have a laboratory somewhere in which he makes up his paste copies of the stolen gems. This is the likeliest spot for such work. I'm going to look around. Silk, watch the gate and if anyone comes, warn us."

The Bat opened various doors and found only supply rooms or small workshops. Then, leading off the west wall of the small office, he found a door that refused to open. He rapped the pane's smartly and his knuckles stung. He picked up a piece of metal and tapped it against the door. It rang metallically. The door was made of steel and probably as secure as a vault.

Prowling around, in one section of the plant the Bat found an oxyacetylene torch used to weld together the sides of the metal burial vaults. He rolled the heavy apparatus to the steel door, started the intensely hot flame and cut through the steel as if it were soft cheese.

He cut away the entire lock and the door swung open. The Bat switched on lights and Carol gasped in amazement. The interior of that room was lined with work benches on which was the equipment necessary to the manufacture of paste jewelry. There was a massive safe set in the concrete wall. The room itself was a veritable vault.

THE BAT used the torch again and this time he spent precious minutes before he had the vault door open. But his work gratified him a moment later for within the vault he found more than half of the stolen loot.

"This," the Bat said softly, "is the headquarters of the criminal chief of all this business. Here is where he studies the gems so he can make perfect duplicates of them. Still we don't know who he is and he will, of course, have no outward connection with this plant. But we've put an awful crimp in his plans now. Silk, get on the phone and call the State Police Barracks nearest this spot. Tell them to rush a detail up here, that over two million dollars' worth of stolen gems are in this vault. Later on Commissioner Warner will contact them. Hurry!"

"Wait!" Carol gripped the Bat's arm tightly. "There is something more I haven't told you. I was so glad to find you uninjured, Tony, that it slipped my mind. McFayden is the man to blame for all this danger you and I have barely escaped. It was McFayden who sent me on a trumped-up errand so that I might be kidnaped. This man you call Blackie is just an agent."

"McFayden?" the Bat frowned. "That complicates matters, but he'll have some explaining to do. All the more reason why we must hurry. Should Blackie or any of his men return before the troopers arrive, it will be up to us to hold them off."

Silk rushed into the office and got on the phone. The troopers would be sent immediately, he was assured.

"Outside," the Bat ordered, when Silk returned. "We'll wait in the darkness until the police arrive and then run for it."

"Boss," Silk said, "the mugs who snatched Carol were on that fellow Carlyle's estate. You know, he bought into the Graham jewelry store with that Dutchman Van den Killan. Maybe Carlyle and McFayden are in cahoots."

"We'll soon know," the Bat replied.

Twenty minutes later three state police cruisers rolled into the yard. A captain was the first to enter the burial vault plant. He saw the yawning safe door, saw the gems gleaming brilliantly and also he saw—the insignia of the Bat pasted upon the vault.

"It must have been the Bat who phoned," he shouted. "And me thinking he was just a myth. Spread out, boys! Maybe some of those mugs will come back and I'd like to surprise 'em. Keep your guns ready."

"Say, Captain," a trooper asked, "what if this Black Bat should show up? Do we take him? Do we open fire on him?"

"You do not," the State Police captain ground out. "If he shows, I'll personally shake his hand. Maybe I'll even kiss him, I dunno. He put us on the trail of the biggest haul in stolen stuff that's happened in a century. Look at them rocks sparkle!"

"What's next on the program?" Silk asked as a few moments later he was driving the Bat and Carol toward the city.

They were all squeezed into the seat. The Bat's arm rested around Carol's shoulder.

"Back to the house," he told Silk. "We all need a rest. But not a long one. Blackie happens to require some attention and he'll get it—soon. Then the brains behind him will pay the piper. Those murderers have pulled their final trick."

"Promise you'll be careful," Carol begged. "I never realized before just how much you meant to me."

SILK SIGHED and glanced the other way. The Bat looked into Carol's shining eyes.

"And I've never fully realized just all that you have done for me. In that vault I thought for a moment that blindness had come once more. The veil which you tore away from my eyes, Carol. I thought you were gone forever. It's odd how clearly you can think under such circumstances. I'll never place you in peril again."

"Oh yes you will," Carol countered. "This case isn't finished yet, and if I can help in any way I'll do all you ask and more, if possible. Don't forget, this fight against crime is as much my battle as yours."

They were silent after that, and shortly had reached the rest of Tony Quinn's estate. By using the secret entrance, the Bat and Carol reached the house while Silk parked the coupé near Butch's rooming house.

The Bat stood before a mirror and slowly removed all traces of his disguise. The scars returned, making a mockery of his face. He grimaced at them. Carol touched his arm.

"Don't, Tony. Those scars are the brand of the Black Bat. Unless you had suffered so, the Bat would never have been born. They don't matter to me, for I know the man behind them."

Tony Quinn's eyes gradually became fixed and glassy. The old expression of lassitude returned. He donned his tweeds and a smoking jacket, picked up his cane, and slowly tapped his way toward the door leading into the library.

"Just practice," he assured Carol. "It's been hours since I was blind Tony Quinn."

He tapped his way across the room and sat down in his accustomed chair before the fireplace. Silk returned and prepared a light meal. They ate it, in that same room, for Carol had to be ready to flee if anyone came. Her connection with Tony Quinn was unknown to any but Silk and Butch.

"When do we get McFayden?" Silk asked impatiently. "He's been breathing free air too long to suit me."

"Silk—Carol," the Bat said slowly, "I don't like to contradict you, but I'm afraid you are wrong. Perhaps McFayden did send you on a fool's errand, Carol, one by which you were exposed to danger. Yet McFayden is not the man I want. I believe he was duped himself into sending you into Blackie's hands."

"Do you mean he isn't the brains?" Carol asked, surprised. "But he must be, Tony! McFayden could have called that number and ordered Silk's death. He was able to gain access to Graham's vaults and rob them. He tricked you—almost threw you into Sergeant McGrath's arms."

"I reiterate"—Tony Quinn looked blankly into the fireplace—"McFayden is not our man. You see, I know the identity of the brains behind Blackie and all this murder and robbery. I've been sure of it for hours."

Silk started to object, but Quinn suddenly raised his hand in a gesture for silence.

"Someone is using the secret entrance," he said in a low voice.

Silk whipped out a gun and covered the hidden door. It opened and Butch came in, panting and excited.

"Boss!" he cried. "Boss, it's McFayden that's back of all the hellishness! I spotted that dirty little rat trying to get rid of a chunk of rock. A big diamond he couldn't afford to buy. The mug he tried to hock it with turned him down and McFayden beat it so fast I lost his trail. But it's him all right."

CHAPTER XXI

NOCTURNAL VISITOR

POLICE COMMISSIONER WARNER tossed nervously in his sleep. Perhaps the shadow of a man who entered his bedroom by way of the window was responsible for that. The lamp beside Warner's bed was turned on. He sat up quickly and one hand darted beneath his pillow for the gun he invariably secreted there.

"It isn't necessary to go for a gun, Commissioner," a voice said calmly. "Or if you believe a weapon so necessary, please accept mine."

A .45 automatic hurtled through the air and dropped on Warner's bed. His eyes, now accustomed to the light, made out a weird form standing three feet away. It was a man, dressed entirely in black. A broad-shouldered, yet agile type of person. There was a black hood drawn over his head and throat.

"The Bat!" Warner exclaimed. Involuntarily his hand darted for the gun, then paused. "Excuse me, sir," he said a little sheepishly. "I did that purely from instinct. Take your gun, Bat."

The Bat sat down on the edge of the bed. The cold eyes that gleamed through the slits in the mask made Warner chill. Yet he knew those eyes were those of an honest man, of an individual who fought on the side of the law. Without the law's red tape, possibly, and without much mercy for desperadoes who shot and killed their way to riches.

"Thank you," the Bat said calmly. "I haven't misjudged you, Commissioner, and right now I particularly need your confidence. I'm on the verge of unveiling the mind behind this weird business of the jewel robbers and subsequent murders. I know his lieutenant; I know how the whole sordid business was done, but as yet I have no proof that will hold in a court of law. That proof I must allow you to furnish, for I doubt any judge or jury would be swayed very far by the words of a masked man sitting in the witness stand."

WARNER GRINNED. "And I doubt very much that Sergeant McGrath would estimate your true value to our side, sir. But you say you know who is behind this. Great heavens, tell me! Give me one clue and I'll do the rest."

"That clue will come later," the Bat answered. "For the moment it is necessary for you to call a conference of every man interested in this case. That means McFayden, Clifford Carlyle, Van den Killan, Wohl, Anghis Khan and Professor DiNonno. Request that all of them come to your home at three o'clock—this morning of course. Have your men awaken them with that message. Do not allow any detectives to be planted outside the house. Sergeant McGrath may be with you, though, and two or three other trusted men. It's possible you may need them."

Warner glanced at the clock on his night table.

"That gives me three hours. I'll do it, Bat."

"And I can give you some cheerful news," the Bat went on. "At least a part of the loot is recovered. It is now in the hands of the State Police in Connecticut. You might send several men to the Sherbrooke Burial Vault Company near Eastown, Connecticut. The killer, you see, owns that burial vault concern. He also owns four funeral parlors in this city. The object of that is to provide a safe hiding place for the jewels. He has encased them in the cement of burial vaults. Possibly some are even already interred."

Warner reached for the telephone and gave orders to the inspector in charge of Headquarters. He hung up slowly.

"I've tried to figure out the man behind it all, but damn it, Bat, I can't," he said mournfully. "The whole trouble is that almost everyone connected with the case has such a sound, honest reputation. Take Van den Killan—he has the most logical motive; because he has acquired ownership of three important business houses for a song. But Van den Killan is immensely rich and honest enough. Carlyle, his partner, is more or less unexplained and my suspicions have fastened on him strongly. He bought into the business with Van den Killan. He is wealthy, but there has been considerable talk of certain deals—strictly business and within the law, of course—that he has pulled in his day.

"Gill is bankrupt, and anyhow a man wouldn't put himself out of business in order to rob others. McFayden, in my opinion, is a sneaking little rat, but he doesn't seem to have the brains necessary for a job of this sort.

"Anghis Khan and Professor DiNonno I've investigated thoroughly. They have handled millions of dollars worth of gems here and abroad. If they had crooked tendencies, they would probably have shown them long before now. The same goes for Dr. Wohl. He worked in Amsterdam supervising the cutting of extremely valuable gems. Why, he even cut the great Mogul Diamond with his own hands!"

"And Harriman?" the Bat asked softly.

COMMISSIONER WARNER jerked erect.

"There you have touched upon the most logical suspect. The condition of the corpse we found in his car indicates that it was purposely disfigured and burned so it could not be positively identified. What I believe is that Harriman substituted the body of another man so we'd think he is dead. Graham is, of course, out of the question as a suspect."

"Graham," the Bat said quietly, "was murdered. And I might suggest that you investigate the floors of Graham's and Gill's vaults. I've already located the tunnel that leads directly into their safes, but I don't think you'll find one beneath Harriman's."

"So that was how it was done!" Warner ejaculated, his jaws closing with a snap. "But I can't agree with you, Bat, that Graham was murdered. Two witnesses saw him shoot himself!"

"Nevertheless he was murdered," the Bat said. "And then too, there is another murder you haven't mentioned. The murder of Fawcett!"

The commissioner smiled a little. "That one is on the records as being either your work or that of Blackie Burns. We discovered Blackie's identity when McGrath had to go through about ten thousand rogue's gallery pictures to place Burns, but he did all right. McGrath also sent in the two men you left in that funeral parlor. We questioned them for hours, because of that note you so kindly left on one of them. Those men were just paid mobsters who haven't the vaguest idea as to what it's all about. They don't even know Blackie's real identity."

The Bat laughed. "Nor does the man who hired Blackie. That precious scoundrel, Blackie Burns, is working both ends against the middle. He intends to make away with the loot—and soon too. I had hoped either he or the man who employs him would fall into the hands of the troopers in control of the burial vault plant. But if they did come back there, they probably saw the police cars and lights and fled. Perhaps it is best because men would have died in that encounter, and there has been enough of murder in this case."

The Bat touched the switch on the night lamp and plunged the room into darkness. For a moment he hovered above Warner.

"And I thank you for another clue you just gave me. A clue I found impossible to locate myself. It merely clinches the case, but it is essential."

There was a rustling sound at the window and then complete silence. Commissioner Warner leaned weakly back against the head of the bed.

"I gave him a clue?" he mumbled. *"I* just gave him a clue! I don't remember saying anything to give him a lead."

THINGS WERE getting a little too hot for Blackie Burns. First of all, he was pretty certain now that the police had identified him as one of the top-notch jewel thieves in the racket. Then there was the episode at the burial vault plant. Blackie had narrowly missed capture there. Only the fact that he had spotted the state police cars parked along the road saved him. As it was, more than half of the looted gems were now in possession of the police. It was time for a showdown and Blackie's avaricious nature asserted itself.

Ten minutes before, Blackie had entered a room that was plunged in complete darkness. There, by prearrangement, he had found the unknown for whom he worked. He had listened to suave promises, boasts that the finding of more than half of the gems meant little, for there would be other jobs soon.

But Blackie was not satisfied. The Bat was closing in too fast. Blackie wanted to get out with a whole skin—and as much of the loot as possible.

Therefore, instead of obeying the orders of the man whose orders he had been docilely taking, Blackie had slipped out of the darkened room instead of waiting ten minutes as he had been requested to do. He was out of the secret meeting place as fast as the mysterious man who guided his criminal activities, and when he saw a man hurrying down the street, Blackie went in swift pursuit.

The man he trailed shortly entered a house. Blackie's eyes narrowed. It was time for the showdown. He hefted the weight of a gun in his side coat pocket and went on.

He paused abruptly and looked up and down the street. Somehow Blackie was afraid. He cursed the Bat, but chilled at thought of him too. Then he climbed the steps of the brownstone front house he had seen his quarry enter, rang the bell and when the door was opened, Blackie grinned and shoved his gun against the man's stomach.

"Sorry," Blackie grated. "Keep your hands up, Boss. I don't like to do this, but I got a hunch you're going to pull out."

"You fool!" the man in the shadows snapped. "When the time is ripe, you'll get your share of the stuff. Didn't I order you not to attempt to prove my identity? Coming here, like this, is dangerous. And it was your fault that the Bat escaped from the burial vault plant. It was your stupidity that caused him to find those gems and my laboratory. You must have mentioned something about that room in his hearing. I've been on the verge of ordering your death several times, but when you entered this little game, I promised you'd be provided for and I meant it. You and the boys already have a split from the proceeds of the gems I peddled in Europe and you must admit it was ingenuity that smuggled them out of the country."

"I admit I should have killed the Bat," Blackie said ruefully. "But he must have had help. No man could have lifted the lid off that vault. It takes a crane to move one of those around. Just the same I want to see what's left of the swag right now! Just to prove you haven't been holding out. Show me the stuff and I'll do anything you say."

THE MAN in the shadows approved.

"Good! The Bat did, of course, take about half the loot away from us, damn him. I left it at the burial vault plant so you would know I was not trying to cheat you. You know also that a quarter of the loot has already been sold in Europe. Fortunately I kept another quarter in a place where the Bat could never locate it. That part is checked at the railroad terminal.

"Here are the checks. You may get the stuff and keep it in your room. Examine it to your heart's content, Blackie. I'm not holding out on you. I may have insisted on saying where the loot was to be kept, but except for this last quarter of it, you knew every moment just where I had it.

"I turn this final portion over to you now so you will have no further suspicions of me, and know that I trust you, too. When you get it, just wait in your room until you hear from me. Is that clear? By the way you still occupy that room at eleven thirty-nine Riverview Avenue, don't you?"

"Right," Blackie said. "I'll get the stuff and go there to wait. I'll sit on the stuff and nobody gets in. When you come we'll split. But say, Boss, why don't you handle this end of it?"

"You'd suspect me of running out," the man in the shadows answered. "Besides I haven't time to get it. That fool of a police commissioner has called everyone connected with the case to his home. At three o'clock in the morning, less than an hour and a half from now. I must go there to avoid being suspected."

"Maybe he's wise," Blackie said, but he gulped.

"He knows nothing," came the contemptuous reply, "How could he? Every track is covered. The Bat found those other gems through sheer luck. Before dawn I shall be at your room to discuss the final sharing of what we have taken. That is all—except, be very careful. A slip now will mean your death. You understand that should we be captured, you are as guilty as I."

"But I didn't kill nobody," Blackie protested. "I—"

"Wait! Listen!" The mysterious leader held up one hand. "Blackie! There is someone upstairs. Follow closely and if you so much as see a shadow move—open fire."

"Got it, Chief." Blackie raised his gun.

Softly they crept up the staircase. They inspected each room until they reached the last one, the master bedroom. Blackie pointed his gun at a closet door while his killer chief prepared to jerk it open.

"He must be in here," the killer-thief growled. "Be ready to shoot."

But when the door was flung back, nothing happened. The spacious closet was filled with clothing, but by the light filtering from the bedroom it seemed plain that there was no sign of an intruder.

"I am getting nervous," the killer said, mopping his face. "This has lasted too long and I am glad it is now over with. Follow my orders, Blackie. Before dawn we shall feast our eyes on the greatest collection of gems in existence."

THEY HURRIED downstairs and Blackie departed. Three minutes after the closet door was closed, a portion of shadow in the farthest corner moved slightly. The door opened a crack. The shadow took on a more substantial form, became a man dressed entirely in black.

The Bat! His dark clothing and the fact that every inch of his face and hands, had been covered had made him practically invisible. His eyes could see every move made by the killer and Blackie, but they had not been able to distinguish him from the clothing in the closet. It had been a close call for the Bat.

With a coat draped over one arm, and moving with no more noise than a ghost the Bat retreated to another room, clambered out a window and vanished into the night. In spite of the darkness and shadows which made the killer chief a blur to Blackie, the Bat had seen the face of the man he sought, had listened to his preparations for flight. The Bat's testimony would have convicted the man in a split second. Yet that testimony could never be told before a judge and jury. The Bat worked without thoughts of reward or glory. To him went only the dangerous preparation of a case and the police finished it.

CHAPTER XXII

MURDER'S GUN

REACHING THE sidewalk, the Bat got into a car that slid up to the curb and stopped.

"Butch," he said, "we're nearing the finish of this business. Silk is holding down our end at the house. Carol has done her share—and well. You have only one more thing to do. At the next corner you will get out. From behind a hedge of that house, which happens to be unoccupied, watch the brownstone house from which I just emerged. A man will leave it shortly.

"Give him fifteen minutes. Then enter through a rear window which I have left open. In the library, there is a large portrait of Cecil Rhodes, the South African diamond king. That portrait is part of a false door. Open it and a wall safe of good dimensions will be revealed. On this slip of paper I'm giving you is the combination of that safe."

Butch took the paper and stuffed it into his vest pocket. "You sure don't miss up on anything, do you, Boss?"

"At this stage of the game there can be no misses," the Bat said firmly. "I watched our killer gloat over his loot. When he put it back in the safe, I used these super-sensitive eyes of mine to good effect to get that combination that will open the safe. As soon as you open it, examine the contents of the valise inside. You will find, among other gems, a diamond necklace with a slight scratch on the underside of the clasp. That necklace is my own and I don't want the police to identify it.

"When you have done that, take the valise of gems to Police Commissioner Warner's home. Sergeant McGrath's car will be in front of the house. Put the valise on the front seat of the car and then run for it. You understand everything?"

"A cinch," Butch said, grinning widely. "Boy, wouldn't I like to see McGrath's pan when he finds that bunch of rocks in his own car!"

BUTCH GOT out and took up his position behind the hedge. The Bat drove away, parked along a side street on the other side of town and made his stealthy way to the door of a rooming house. With a skeleton key, he opened the door quietly, walked up the stairs and entered one of the rooms. He turned on no lights.

Twenty minutes later the door opened and Blackie entered. He was carrying two suitcases that appeared to be very heavy. Blackie switched on the lights, pulled down the cracked, worn window shade.

"So I'm to sit here and wait for his nibs, am I?" he gloated. "That's what he thinks. There's enough rocks in these suitcases to keep me for life, and am I going to live."

Blackie picked up one suitcase, set it on a table and reached for the lock.

"I wouldn't do that, Blackie," a quiet voice said.

Blackie spun around, and his face drained white. Both hands shot upward. He made no attempt to reach the gun under his arm. Something about the Black Bat warned him that might prove disastrous. Perhaps the .45 automatic trained on his chest had something to do with it.

"Listen"—Blackie licked his lips—"I'll made a deal. You take one of these bags and I'll take the other. I'll scram for good."

"I wouldn't take one of those bags for any kind of a gift, Blackie. You'd be a fool to do it, too. Why? Because all the time you have believed this man for whom you work. You've had faith in him. Tonight you seek to doublecross him but he is more intelligent than you. You are the one who has been tricked."

"You—you're crazy," Blackie managed, but without much assurance now.

The Bat's left hand threw a penknife on the table. "Take that and slit open the side of each of those suitcases. Be most careful how you do it, Blackie. The little gems contained inside won't sparkle. They'll just give one mighty roar and hurl you into little pieces. If you opened those bags in the regular way, the contents would be set off."

Blackie's eyes were popping and a slow fury began to fill his soul. Carefully he made an incision in the side of the bag, worried the hole larger and finally he had the whole side open. Within he saw layers of small bits of metal topped by a black tin box which had one set of wires leading to three dry cell batteries and a second set attached to the mechanism that would open the bag.

Blackie sat down weakly.

"You win," he gulped. "He was set to frame me all right. You saved my life and if I can help in running down that heel, I'll do it. I'll talk in return for a light rap. Anyway, didn't that wise guy try to bump me? All you gotta do is grab—"

"I know his name," the Bat smiled behind the mask. "We're going to see him—now. You'll have your chance to prove there is some spark of manhood in you. And Blackie, remove the gun from your shoulder clip. Throw it on the bed and be careful just how you perform that operation. My automatic is equipped with a hair trigger."

POLICE COMMISSIONER Warner occupied the center of the floor. He spoke quietly, but from time to time he glanced anxiously at a mantel clock. It was fifteen minutes past three and his guests were getting more than a little impatient. Every man who had in any slightest way come into this jewel robbing and murder case sat before him.

Van den Killan arose.

"This is enough for me," he growled. "Out of my bed you took me and for what? To listen to you talk about things I know already."

"He's right," Clifford Carlyle, Van den Killan's partner, grumbled in acquiescence. "I don't understand your attitude, Commissioner. All of us have been through some particularly trying circumstances these past few days. We need rest—not this tableau you've arranged for us. If there are any vital questions, ask them and let us go."

McFayden arose, drew down the corners of his mouth and headed for the door. Sergeant McGrath intercepted him, put a hand against the jewelry store clerk's chest and shoved him into a chair.

"Next time," he growled, "I'll use my fist on your jaw. What's your hurry? Don't you like the atmosphere?"

McFayden's eyes flashed around the room angrily. "I'm not afraid of anything," he snarled. "I'm innocent."

"Are you quite certain of that, Mr. McFayden?"

The voice came from somewhere among the darker shadows of the room. Velvet drapes moved with a slight swish and the Bat stood before them. Both hands held guns and they covered everyone in the room. McGrath gave a yelp of rage and his hand darted toward a hip pocket. It froze halfway there. Those guns in the hooded man's hands were held steadily. "Sergeant," the Bat called out, "why be so hasty?"

McFayden was on his feet, trembling like a leaf.

"You—you can't accuse me!" he yelled. "I haven't done anything."

"You haven't done anything much," the Bat put in mildly. "You are a thief, McFayden. You helped yourself to several baubles from the stock of Graham's store. You figured that possibly they'd be listed as the loot of the brainy character behind all this murder and thievery. You tried to pawn one of those gems a few hours ago."

McFAYDEN GROANED and sat down. His chin drooped against his chest. "But I swear I didn't kill anybody!" he quavered. "There were just three diamonds I took."

The Bat nodded. "Quite right. Now we come to the real meaning of our little gathering. Among you, gentlemen, is a man whose brains concocted one of the most heinous crimes in modern history. Because of that warped intellect, men have died. Others have been robbed. The faith in every jewelry house in the nation has been shattered. Gems to the value of millions have been stolen. Men have been murdered ruthlessly."

Commissioner Warner jumped up, waved for silence.

"Wait—I have it! Harriman is the killer. He isn't dead! There are tunnels beneath the vaults of the Graham and Gill stores. There is none beneath the Harriman place. He must have robbed his own stock and used the tunnels to steal the gems from the other two stores."

"Harriman," the Bat said quietly, "is dead. It was his body you found in that burned car. Graham also was murdered. The killer was well known to Graham and came into his office. He forced Graham to phone for McFayden to come after several minutes had passed. That was because the murderer wanted a witness to Graham's apparent 'suicide.' Graham was knocked unconscious. Perhaps you recall now that there was a bump on his head which the coroner said had probably been made when his head hit the desk after he collapsed. But the murderer did that. Then he hid behind the chair in which Graham was seated. When McFayden and the secretary entered the murderer shot Graham, but to them it appeared to be Graham's arm that appeared above the desk, his hand that fired that shot."

McFAYDEN PROTESTED shrilly. "It couldn't have been! If anybody was hidden behind that chair, where did he go? I wasn't gone but a minute or two."

"You and the secretary ran out," the Bat said. "During that moment, the killer got away. He went into the vault, through the tunnel beneath the floor and vanished. He wanted both Graham and Harriman to 'commit suicide' so that it would seem as if they had looted their own stores. But things broke a little too fast when Mrs. Van den Killan discovered her tiara was a fake. You will recall that she saw the original of her tiara in Europe. Part of the loot was shipped there, hidden in either the caskets or the cadavers of people who had died here and whose bodies were shipped abroad."

"You informed me, during your visit to my room," Commissioner Warner broke in excitedly, "that I had given you a necessary clue. What was it? How did I give you a lead?"

The Bat chuckled. "Graham, as he talked to his murderer and knew he was going to die, tried to leave a clue. He drew a certain design on a pad and added a few words to it. The killer recognized the danger and ripped the paper off the pad. But there were indentations on the paper below the one Graham wrote on. I brought out the design and the word 'kill.' I knew Graham had written it.

"The design is that of a famous diamond, cut by a great expert many years ago—when that expert was honest. In assuming that Harriman was the killer because his store had no tunnel, you wrong his memory, Commissioner. Graham and Harriman intended to merge their businesses. They had even drawn up an agreement to that effect.

"The murderer knew this and did his best to destroy that paper. I found the ashes and tonight I entered Harriman's store, looked through his files and came upon the duplicate of that agreement. It gave Graham legal right to send a man over to estimate the value of Harriman's stock. That man is the killer!"

Warner whirled about. "Dr. Wohl!" he cried.

Wohl, his face pale, eyes bulging and lips drawn back into a snarl, retreated a few steps. He blubbered alibis.

"Stop it!" the Bat thundered. "You're the killer."

The Bat flung a coat into the middle of the room.

"When you killed Graham some blood got on your sleeve and you brushed it against the back of the chair. You didn't even know that blood was there. That is your coat, Dr. Wohl. I removed it from your house tonight. You came close to discovering me—remember?"

"Madness!" Wohl raged. "Madness and nonsense. I do not know what this masked crook is talking about."

"You cut the great Mogul Diamond," the Bat said evenly. "That was the design which Graham traced on that pad. You are famous for that piece of work and Graham hoped someone might put two and two together and realize that tracing was a clue. Unfortunately for Graham, he also tried to write a message which you spotted and destroyed. Wohl, you went to Harriman's store to estimate the value of his gems. You went there several times and with each visit you switched paste gems for the real thing. That was why no tunnel was necessary for the robbery at Harriman's."

"You can't prove anything!" Wohl yelled. "There is nothing against me."

THE BAT gestured with one arm and Blackie emerged from behind the curtains. Wohl's white face grew ruddy with rage. Despite the guns in the Bat's hands, Wohl took a desperate chance. He reached into his coat pocket and fired without removing the gun he had concealed there. Blackie's shirt front turned crimson. He staggered back a step and clapped a hand to the wound. Then he sank slowly into a chair.

Wohl had no time to shoot again. Like a streak of black lightning, the Bat was across the room. He shoved Wohl back with the flat of his hand, measured him and as Wohl's hidden gun came up to fire again, the Bat hit him on the point of the jaw. Wohl staggered back, banged into a chair and tripped over it. He landed in a heap, shrieking curses at the Black Bat.

"It's Wohl," Blackie was saying weakly. "He hired me to help him. I'll tell everything. He took photographs of jewels that were in for repairs. He made up duplicates and switched them. He did everything—the murder of Graham and Harriman, anything else. He robbed their stores. Gill's too! He even tried to doublecross me, the dirty rat. Oh, I'll talk all right! Somebody get me a doctor."

Sergeant McGrath leaped upon Wohl and handcuffs clicked. Warner gave terse orders. "An ambulance for Blackie. McGrath, watch Dr. Wohl."

Warner turned slowly, talking to the Bat as he did so.

"You have my thanks, whoever you are—" he began, then suddenly realized he was talking to thin air.

The Bat was gone!

Sergeant McGrath gave a shout of rage. "He got away! He took the stuff that Wohl swiped with him."

"You're wrong, Sergeant." The Bat's voice came from behind the velvet curtains at the window. "You'll find the swag in the front seat of your car. It's been there for some time."

The curtains moved outwardly as an early morning breeze caught them. For a full minute only an eerie silence held sway. Then Blackie groaned.

"I'll put my finger on that killer," he moaned. "I'll tell you everybody else who helped too. Doublecross me, will he…!"

Warner turned to McGrath. "Well, Sergeant, what have you to say about the Black Bat now? Pretty helpful agent, eh?"

"He's against the law," the sergeant growled. "That's all I know. And I'll get him, one of these days!"

"Well, at any rate," Warner said, hiding a grin, "I understand you were convinced the Black Bat is not our old friend, Tony Quinn. At least, you won't go around accusing poor blind Tony."

"Oh, yeah?" Sergeant McGrath said, his face reddening. "When I examined that hood that was left in the car, I found some grease stains! That means the Black Bat was in disguise—and it could be Tony Quinn! One of these days…."

Commissioner Warner chuckled silently as he left Sergeant McGrath looking grim and with a faraway look in his eyes.

III
THE BLACK BAT STRIKES AGAIN

CHAPTER I

GRAVEYARD MURDER

A CAR PULLED up to the cemetery gates at ten minutes of one in the morning. Three men clambered out. All wore high boots and they proceeded to drag out several shovels and picks.

One of them stepped up to the cemetery gates, took a key from his pocket and opened them. Another rolled the car through. Then the gates were closed and locked. Slowly the car wended its way around the many turns of the cemetery road until the driver threw a spotlight on a serried rank of tombstones. But only briefly, for the moment he saw what he wanted, the light was doused.

Assistant District Attorney Lew Scott, one of the trio on some odd nocturnal mission, picked up a shovel and a pick.

He was an eager young man, ambitious, honest and well liked. He faced one of his companions, a man smaller and thinner than himself and much more nervous.

"For the last time," he said softly, for the cemetery seemed to demand whispers, "you are sure? We'd be the laughing stock of the city if you happen to be wrong—and there might also be a nice little lawsuit in connection with this."

Jim Fisher, the man addressed, licked his lips and loosened the collar around his throat. The third man joined them before Fisher could speak—Dawson, an assistant coroner, as young and alert as Scott.

Apparently, therefore, this grave-digging party was highly legal, even if stealthy.

"I've a signed exhumation order in my pocket so we can go right ahead," Dawson said. "I'll perform a rough autopsy on the spot, the moment the coffin is opened. The body has been interred only two days so that will be easy to do. All I need are samples of the hair, nails and the stomach lining. It won't take more than fifteen minutes for my share of the job."

Jim Fisher walked over to the car and sat down on the running board before he answered Scott's question.

"I'm positive," he stated with grim finality. "Ralph Galvin is dead—in that grave. The doctor claims he died of a chronic stomach ailment. I've been away, as I told you. As soon as I got back and found out what happened, I sensed that something was not right. Galvin never suffered from any stomach trouble. Why he used to boast of how strong his digestive organs were."

LEW SCOTT nodded. "Yes, yes. You've told us that a dozen times. What I want to be certain of is that letter you got from Ralph Galvin. You destroyed it, remember. You have no written evidence."

Fisher shrugged. "Ralph mentioned that he'd discovered there was an insurance policy on his life that he didn't even know about. A policy to the tune of two hundred and fifty thousand dollars. In the first place Ralph couldn't afford a policy as large as that.

"And he certainly would have had to undergo an examination to take out a sum of insurance so huge. I thought nothing of it until I returned and learned that Ralph had died—suddenly. I think that whoever insured him without his knowledge must have provided a substitute for the medical examination and then killed Ralph to collect."

Assistant District Attorney Scott peeled off his cost and vest.

"Very well. It seems to me a clear-cut case and we have the right to go ahead. Perhaps I should have consulted the deceased's family first, but if things are as you indicate, Fisher, we'd only be throwing in our hand face down. Apparently someone in the family stands to collect and before we act against that person, we must be absolutely certain that Ralph Galvin did not die a natural death. Man the shovels, boys. We'll exhume the body, give Dr. Dawson a chance to make an examination, then we'll bury it again until his routine is finished. If you are right, Fisher, we'll officially exhume it tomorrow for the second time.... Let's get it over with."

All three attacked the newly filled grave with vigor. It took them almost two hours of back-breaking work to expose the surface of the metal lid of the outer casket. District Attorney Scott hauled himself out of the grave, hurried over to where the car was parked and took a gasoline torch from the trunk. He lowered himself into the grave again, pumped air into the torch and lit a match to it.

Applying the flame to the sealed lid, he melted away the lead that made the outer casket air-tight. With chisels, the other two men carefully opened the copper box until finally they raised the lid out of the grave. Ropes went down next and Fisher passed them beneath the casket.

Carefully they hauled it up until it was swung out and placed on solid ground.

Scott used a screw-driver to open the casket, lifted up the lid and exposed the body within. Fisher shuddered and turned away hurriedly.

Only Coroner Dawson was used to this kind of grisly work. He handled it as a matter of course. From a doctor's kit he produced the necessary instruments. Snipping a lock of the dead man's hair, he carefully placed it in an envelope and sealed it. Then he cut portions of the finger-nails and stored them in another envelope for examination later.

A wind had sprung up as they worked. Dr. Dawson put the envelope containing the lock of hair on the ground. It was lifted by the wind and carried off a dozen feet. Scott scampered after it. He caught it as it fluttered down on another grave. He pulled a broken flower pot out of the ground and thrust the envelope inside it. To further insure its safety, he turned the clay flower pot upside down.

"That will hold it until we're ready to go," he said. "Now Doctor, while you perform the actual surgery, I think I'd like to talk to Fisher again."

DAWSON NODDED and selected his instruments. He began working deftly. Near the car Jim Fisher was trembling despite himself.

"I'm not a coward," he defended himself, "but this business is nerve-racking. Wouldn't be so bad if I didn't know the man, but Ralph and I—Well, we'd been pals since we were in the first grade. I tell you he didn't die a natural death! If it had been an accident—or pneumonia—or an infectious disease, I wouldn't have questioned it. But chronic stomach trouble! Good heavens, that's impossible!"

Assistant District Attorney Scott drew the collar of his suit coat around his throat. It lacked only about two hours of dawn and the night had become chilly and raw.

"I know," he told Fisher softly. "That's why I fixed up this secret exhumation. If we're wrong, no harm has been done. If you are guessing right—we've got a nice murder case right in our laps. I haven't told anyone what we intended to do. Neither has Dawson, and I know you have not. From a study of the symptoms that Ralph Galvin betrayed, Dawson has already judged that he may have died of arsenical poisoning. Victims of that drug act as if suffering from chronic stomach ailments, especially if the poison is administered over a period of time—as is usually the case in insurance murders. Those samples the doc is taking will tell the story one way or another. I… Fisher, listen! Did you hear something?"

Fisher nodded. "Yes. Sounded like someone prowling around those bushes north of here."

"Doc!" Scott called softly. "Hey, Doc—come over here."

Dr. Dawson ambled over and grinned broadly when Scott voiced the belief that they were being observed.

"Nonsense. Your nerves are jittery. It's the atmosphere that's got you. Who in the world would be prowling around a cemetery this hour of the morning except a trio of ghouls—like us?"

Carol Baldwin

He laughed at their discomfiture and headed back toward the open grave. Suddenly he clapped a hand to his chest. A low, strangled groan came from his lips. He reeled a step or two, carried more by his momentum than his muscles. He half turned around, as if to beg aid. Then he crumpled and fell heavily.

Assistant District Attorney Scott leaped from the running board of the car where he had been seated and sprang toward the fallen doctor. Fisher, eyes bulging in horror, saw Scott stop dead and slowly, like the work of a slow motion camera, fold up and topple to the ground ten feet from where Dr. Dawson lay.

Fisher gave voice to a wild, shrieking yell. There had been no sound, yet both these men had dropped as though a silent spectre had snatched away their lives. Fisher raced over graves, vaulted a tombstone and tripped over a projecting pot of flowers. He scrambled up with a choked sob and raced on.

Something smacked into the ground near his feet and lent impetus to his flight. Then he felt something else hit him between the shoulder blades. A searing, agonizing pain gripped his whole body. He staggered another dozen steps before he collapsed. Vainly he tried to pull himself erect, clawing at the edge of a stone for support. He turned his head to look back.

A FIGURE—ONLY a dark blob of shadow—was standing fifty feet behind him. A rifle was at the man's shoulder. It made no sound, but a bullet from it found a target in Fisher's body. It smashed through his left lung, penetrated his heart, killing him instantly. He fell, draped over the tombstone, a hideous nightmare of horror.

The murderer walked calmly over to where Dr. Dawson lay, moved him with his foot and saw the blood oozing from a wound directly over the heart. His lips curled in contempt. He proceeded to where Assistant District Attorney Scott was sprawled on the ground. Scott's body twitched. Life was not quite extinct.

As calmly as though this were an everyday occurrence, the murderer raised the rifle slightly and sent a slug smashing through Scott's head.

Pulling off the gray gloves on his hands, the killer grasped the silencer on the end of his rifle and unscrewed it. He thrust this into his pocket, shoved the rifle under his arm and went over to the exhumed body. He picked up the envelope Dr. Dawson had left there, examined it and put this into his pocket also.

He spent twenty minutes going over the ground carefully, searching for the slightest clue that might give him away. Then he walked swiftly back to the row of small trees forming a hedge beside the cemetery road. The night swallowed him up with no sign that he had been there except the four bodies he had left behind—one cold in long death, the other three still warm and bleeding.

There had been no witnesses. Only the dead could testify against this living monster. It was close to the absolute perfect crime. Only one slight detail remained, and the killer knew nothing of that.

CHAPTER II

PHANTOMS OF THE NIGHT

IN A spacious house located in one of the better sections of the vast city, a man sat before a fireplace. He wore a smoking jacket and held a cane between his knees. His eyes were blank—like those of a blind man—and around his eyes were deep, horrible scars etched by corrosive acid. The man was about thirty and except for the scars, good-looking. He had a well molded chin, and lips that could smile warmly or grow thin and bitter.

Tony Quinn spent many hours in just this position, for to all intents and purposes Tony Quinn was blind. A dozen prominent doctors had testified to that and gave him no hope of recovery. Once a promising young district attorney, Tony Quinn had fought a physical battle in a courtroom to protect vital evidence against a grasping gangster. Acid, meant to destroy that evidence, had been splashed into Tony Quinn's eyes, blinding him—for life, according to all the doctors he had visited.

But Tony Quinn was not blind. Those blank, staring eyes could see perhaps better than any pair of eyes in the world. By the cooperation of a dying man who had also fought crime and been made a cripple by criminals, Tony Quinn had been given new eyes. The operation had been performed in secret and except for the doctor who had accomplished what other surgeons refused to attempt, and three other persons, no one realized that Quinn could see.

One of those who knew was seated in a straight-backed chair at Quinn's side now. A mass of newspapers lay at his feet. Norton Kirby, known as "Silk," was an ex-confidence man who had come to rob Tony Quinn and remained to become his staunch friend and ally. Silk wore the quiet livery of a servant.

"Something, isn't it, sir?" Silk mused. "Imagine—Assistant District Attorney Scott, Assistant Coroner Dawson and this Jim Fisher, all murdered in a graveyard beside a recently exhumed corpse. Sounds like a ghost story. You knew young Scott, didn't you?"

Tony Quinn nodded sadly.

"He began his career in my office when I was the district attorney. A nice boy, Silk. And clever, too. There were great things in store for him. Now he's been murdered. Why? The police don't know—no one seems to. It can't be just an act of revenge, else why was Dr. Dawson also murdered, and this man Jim Fisher?

"Silk, they were up to something. They exhumed the body of Ralph Galvin for a purpose. Someone murdered them so they might never voice their suspicions. For a man to shoot down three people ruthlessly means that what they were suspicious about must have been a vast thing. Read me that part—about what the police think."

Silk cleared his throat and began where he had left off. That part of the news story read:

> Commissioner Warner has taken personal charge of the investigation into the gruesome cemetery deaths that have stirred the city. There are no clues as yet, according to the police, but they are making a thorough and intensive investigation.
>
> The body of Ralph Galvin, apparently exhumed by the three murdered

men, has been taken to the Stanley morgue for further examination. The only theory offered thus far indicates that Jim Fisher, a friend of the dead Ralph Galvin, must have suspected that all was not right with Galvin's death.

In the pocket of the assistant coroner was an exhumation order. Assistant District Attorney Scott apparently had accompanied the other two men so that he might also test some story which Jim Fisher may have told.

An autopsy has been performed on the body of Ralph Galvin. Coroner Williams states that death was natural, that there is no indication of violence and none of poison. It is his expressed opinion that if Scott and Dr. Dawson were hoping to find some incriminating evidence in the body of Galvin, their hopes would have been blasted.

"THAT'S ENOUGH." Tony Quinn held up his hand. "Silk, there's far more to this than appears on the surface. I knew Lew Scott, remember. He wouldn't have gone off half cocked on some crazy story told him by a stranger. Exhuming a body is serious business and Scott knew that. I think"—he paused for an expressive moment—"we ought to have a look at that body in the morgue, Silk. Then a trip to the cemetery would be in order. The police are pretty routine sometimes. They may have missed something out there."

Silk didn't answer. He arose, walked over to the windows and pulled down the curtains. Then he made sure the doors were locked. Finally he doused the lights in the room.

"Ready, sir," he said simply.

Tony Quinn arose, thrust his cane beneath one arm and walked rapidly toward the west wall of the room. Though everything was steeped in darkness and Silk had to maneuver his way slowly, Tony Quinn moved as rapidly as though the room were brilliantly illuminated.

There was a reason for this. Tony Quinn could see as well in darkness as he could in light; perhaps even better. That operation on his eyes had rendered them more acute and given them a penetrating power over darkness.

A section of the wall slid back. Quinn and Silk vanished into a white-tiled room lined with shelves and racks containing chemicals, apparatus and books on every conceivable phase of fighting crime. For Tony Quinn's adopted mission in life was a battle with all the elements of the underworld and those crooked men and women who occupied high stations in life.

Quinn opened a small cupboard and took from it a black suit, a pair of black gloves, black crepe-soled shoes and a peculiar hood. He donned the clothing swiftly and then placed the hood over his head. It came well down over his shoulders and was attached to his arms so that when he raised them, the cape arrangement seemed webbed and winglike. He cast a weird shadow against the white-tiled wall—the shadow of a giant bat.

Tony Quinn, in fact, was the Black Bat. He had adopted the name and insignia of this nocturnal creature because a bat is supposed to be blind and operates only in darkness.

"You had better stay here," he said to Silk. "Police Commissioner Warner usually drops in when he gets a headache over such crimes as this one. If he calls, tell him I'm asleep and that you don't wish to awaken me. Tell him I've been despondent over my blindness and haven't slept in days. That will stall him until I get back."

"Yes, sir," Silk answered with a tinge of sorrow in his voice. "But I thought, sir, considering the fact that we haven't had much excitement lately, that you might—"

Tony Quinn pulled the hood from his head, shoved it in his pocket, and grinned.

"Silk, old boy," he placated, "unless I'm very wrong, there will be a great deal of work for you before we close this case. I don't play hunches, but there's a strong supposition in my mind that the man or men who killed those three haven't finished their work yet. Hold the fort. I'll be back in a few hours."

QUINN DONNED a floppy-brimmed hat, drew it well down over his scarred features, then pulled a lever set in the wall. A part of the floor slid back to reveal a ladder leading into a passage hewn out of the earth. He waved to Silk, slid down the ladder and crawled along the passage until he came out in an enclosed garden summer house, far to the rear of his estate. This formed a perfect way for him to come and go as the Black Bat.

He slipped through the garden gate, looked up and down the silent street and saw no one. As he moved through the gate he kept close to the high wall and his black clothing blended so well with the darkness that he was practically invisible.

When he turned a corner he saw a coupé parked at the curb in front of a rooming house. That coupé was always left there for just such emergencies. It was registered in the name of one Jack O'Leary, better known to the Black Bat as "Butch." O'Leary was one of the three persons who knew Tony Quinn's nocturnal identity.

Quinn took a key from his pocket, unlocked the car door and slid behind the wheel. He rolled down the cross street, pulled his hat low and turned into a well lighted avenue. Now his nerves began to jingle. If he were stopped for any reason and spotted in these black clothes, there would be suspicions. Almost every patrolman in the city knew Tony Quinn and firmly believed he was blind for life. If they saw him driving a car—well, Tony Quinn hated to think of the results.

Therefore he was most careful about how he drove, meticulously obeying traffic signals and keeping well within the speed limit. He drove far uptown and parked the coupé along a dark side street. After a careful look around he stepped out, swept off his hat, threw it into the coupé, and donned the mask of the Black Bat.

The private morgue to which the exhumed body recovered from the cemetery had been taken was just around the corner. He cut through a neighboring yard, stepping over obstacles that would have tripped any man with normal eyesight. Even the slender wires of a croquet set were as plain as telegraph poles to Tony Quinn's eyes.

He came out behind the one-story building which housed the morgue. No one was on duty, for who would ever be expected to enter a morgue? True, the exhumed body had been of great importance in a triple murder case, but now the autopsy was completed, the findings reported and the corpse only waiting for reburial.

The Black Bat crept silently to the front of the building. He made a swift examination of the door lock and had it open in three minutes. The manipulation of locks was one of the many fascinating branches of criminology that Tony Quinn had studied so intently.

He closed the door behind him softly. He carried no flashlight, for such an article would have been superfluous. The Bat saw everything plainly.

The corpse was covered and rested on a slab in one of the small autopsy rooms. He drew back the sheet, exposing the body. For ten minutes he examined it and finally gave up. There were no clues here. If this once had been Ralph Galvin—and certainly it had been so identified—then Lew Scott must have erred in exhuming it.

The Black Bat slipped out of the morgue, reached his car and drove straight to the cemetery. He climbed over the high fence, dropped lightly on the ground and proceeded to search for the scene of the triple murder. It wasn't hard to find for the grave still yawned open.

FOOTPRINTS WERE useless, for police and cemetery employees had trampled the ground into a mire. The Black Bat stood beside the grave and slowly turned around. His eyes swept over the ground, missing nothing. He saw a broken flower pot standing upside down on a grave about twenty feet away. Otherwise this grave was neat.

Flowers near the headstone had withered and died days before, but they indicated that the grave was cared for and that visits were fairly frequent. Therefore, why the broken flower pot spoiling the otherwise tidy grave?

The Black Bat strode toward the plot. He saw where the broken pot had been taken from the ground, literally ripped out, for soil had also been raised with it. He turned the pot over and, half buried in the dirt, he saw the soiled white edge of an envelope. Eagerly he picked this up, ripped open the sealed flap and saw a lock of hair.

Thrusting this into his pocket, the Black Bat felt a quiver of excitement course through his system. Someone had cut that hair from the head of the corpse and Dr. Dawson was the most logical person to have done so. In making tests for certain poisons, the hair is frequently used. And the Black Bat knew that the body of the supposed Ralph Galvin, now at the private morgue, did not have a lock of hair snipped off!

He had examined that body well enough to be certain. Anyhow, when a thorough autopsy was performed in a morgue, with all facilities at hand, examination of the hair would not be necessary. Therefore a substitution had been made! The corpse in the morgue was not the one exhumed by Dr. Dawson! Why? Galvin's family was considered one of the best. They were honest in all their dealings and were definitely not the type to insure a close relative, kill him for the insurance and then commit a triple murder so that their crime might not be discovered. Nevertheless, the Black Bat was sure that for some grim reason Galvin's body had been stolen.

He walked back to the open grave and looked into it. Something stirred at his feet and he glanced down. There was a puff of dust arising from the dry top soil, and the report of a gun. Instantly the Black Bat gave a leap that carried him over a high tombstone.

NOTHING HAPPENED, but the Black Bat wasn't one to wait for attack. He believed in the element of surprise to overcome his enemies. Ducking from behind the tombstone, he ran very lightly over the grass in a crouch.

He knew the exact direction from which the slug had come and made a half circle of the area.

Then the Black Bat saw them. Two men, crouched at the side of a vault, were trying to penetrate the darkness and spot their masked victim. One of them spoke in a hoarse whisper, every word audible to the Black Bat's sensitive ears.

"I tell you I had a look at that guy. He's got a hood on. I know he has or I woulda seen his face, wouldn't I? Dorkey, I got a hunch that was the Black Bat! If you ask me, we oughta lam outa here as quick as we can."

The other man snarled an oath.

"The Black Bat ain't no better than any ordinary guy. What can he do that we can't? I hope it is the Black Bat because he's gotta show himself sooner or later and then—*blam*—he goes down with a couple of nice silent bullets in his back."

CHAPTER III

DOUBLED IN DEATH

THE BLACK BAT smiled tightly and crept forward again. He was within a dozen yards of the two men when the frightened one discovered he had to do something to relieve the tension. He snapped on a flashlight and sprayed the beam toward the open grave. The other man snarled a warning and reached for the flash. It dropped to the ground and its ray struck the Bat squarely.

He fired from the hip. His bullet crashed through the lens of the flash and a curtain of darkness, deeper than ever, closed down over the graveyard. But the brief moment of light had been enough. Two slugs screeched past the Black Bat's ear. His own guns blasted twice, the reports so close together as to seem almost one.

The heavier of the two assassins folded up. All his joints and muscles seemed to have turned into soft wax. With a yelp of terror, the other man fled. Instantly the Black Bat was after him. The man leaped for the cemetery fence, clawing at the top wire. He pulled himself up frantically, a steel-like hand gripped his ankles and hauled him down.

He put up a short fight, trying to administer a jabbing uppercut, but it sailed through air. A fist buried itself in his stomach and he doubled up with a grunt of pain. He felt both his arms seized, then he was pinned against the fence. His worst fears were realized as he looked up and saw the somber hood covering his captor's head, saw the winglike cape that cast an eerie shadow—the shadow of a bat!

"Don't hit me no more!" he quavered. "I—I can't stand it. Don't hit me."

A steel-like hand hauled him down.

"Your name and where do you come from?" the Black Bat demanded. "Speak fast. All this shooting may draw the police. I haven't time to waste with you."

"Joe Hudson," the thug gasped. "I come from Frisco, honest. Me and Dorkey was to blast anybody that came to the grave at night. We was paid a grand to keep watch. I dunno who paid us. There was a guy named Bishop who runs a hock shop on Carmody Avenue. We were told he was a right guy and we went there to buy us a couple of heaters. He offered us this job. That's the truth, so help me! I wouldn't lie to you."

"I don't believe you would," the Black Bat said quietly. "Anyway if you have, you'll be sorry. I'll leave you here, tied up. But if I find no such man exists as this Bishop, you'll talk when I come back—plenty! Stand against that fence, spread your arms and legs as far apart as possible. Now—hold it."

With a coil of fine silk cord he took from his pocket, the Black Bat tied Hudson's wrists to the wire fence, then fastened his ankles. He didn't bother with a gag.

"You'll keep for a while," he said. "I'm going to see if your pal is beyond any help."

Only a cursory examination was necessary. The thug called Dorkey was dead, a bullet drilled squarely through his heart. The Black Bat returned to Hudson and tested the fellow's bonds to make sure he could not escape. Then he pasted a black sticker on the man's forehead—the cut-out image of a black bat with wings outspread.

"THAT'S JUST to remind the man who hired you that he has some competition," he said grimly. "It will also help you to explain to the police just how your pal came to be killed. And—mark this—when you get out of jail, make tracks for the Coast. If I see you again, I won't tie you with rope—I'll weight you down with lead."

The Bat scaled the fence easily and raced to his parked car. He knew one pertinent fact anyway. Dr. Dawson had examined the body of Ralph Galvin all right. He had snipped a lock of hair from the corpse—and that clue rested in the Black Bat's pocket.

Now he had to investigate this pawnbroker named Bishop. And find out why the Galvin family had identified a double as their kin.

When he was safely behind the wheel of his car the Black Bat stripped off his hood. So far he saw no signs that the shooting affray in the cemetery had been heard. The place was far from any habitation and no police guards had been posted anywhere nearby.

The pawnshop of Monty Bishop was a frowsy-looking place, surrounded by cheap restaurants and antique shops. A night light burned above the safe and the place was closed for the night. The Bat parked his coupé in a convenient spot, made sure he was unobserved, and crossed the street to plunge into an alley beside the pawnshop. At the rear he discovered that Bishop lived behind his store. Lights were burning in two windows.

Drawing his hood well down over his head, the Black Bat edged toward one of the windows and peered through the dirty curtains. What he saw made him spring into action. A man was lying across a bed. His face was pallid, his outstretched arms twitched and his entire body apparently was racked by pain.

The Black Bat didn't take time to force a door. Instead he smashed a pane of glass with the butt of his gun, reached in and opened the latch. He swung over the sill and rushed to the man's side, lifted him onto the bed and made a swift examination. The man was dying fast, obviously poisoned. His face was purpled from congested blood, his lips were blue and his eyes bulging.

He tried to talk but no sound came from his gaping mouth. Vocal muscles were already paralyzed. The Black Bat could do nothing. It was too late for antidotes and he couldn't give one anyway, for he had no idea whether the lethal dose had been an alkaloid or a metallic poison.

Bishop died three minutes after the Black Bat reached his side. The murderer had acted with amazing speed to silence the man before the Black Bat arrived.

With a sigh the Bat turned away. His best clue obliterated. Whatever lay behind all this murder, it was supervised by an efficient, far-planning mind. One who killed at will.

A frugal supper was on the table, stone cold now. The Black Bat examined a dish of gruel from which Bishop had apparently eaten his last meal. He scooped some of it into a small bottle and stowed this away. Then he began a careful examination of the premises. He expected to find nothing, so was not disappointed when his search was completed. Bishop's food might have been poisoned hours before—and by some casual so-called "friend" who possibly had a logical reason for calling.

THE BLACK BAT moved toward the door—and suddenly stopped. A man's shadow had passed across the window. For only one fleeting second, yet the Black Bat saw it. Drawing his gun quickly, he spun around when he heard the front door of the store being battered down, and heavy, running footsteps. Men were closing in from the front and someone was on guard outside the only other exit. From the bold manner in which they operated, they obviously were police.

The Bat waited no longer. His gun lanced flame and the overhead light crashed out. The room was plunged in deep darkness. Then someone smashed down the back door. As the man came through, the Black Bat scrutinized him and groaned inwardly. It was Detective-sergeant McGrath of the police—McGrath who had taken an oath that he would bring in the Black Bat dead or alive. Someone had tipped him off. Someone who knew the Black Bat would visit Bishop, find him murdered, and be placed in a precarious position.

McGrath had sailed through the door with gun ready.

"Got you, Bat!" he gloated. "There's no getting away this time. Reach high or I'll drill you."

He saw a shadowy form flit across the room, then take more formidable shape as it was etched in silhouette against a window. McGrath did not shoot. He wanted the Black Bat alive. He wanted to rip that damned hood from his face and expose Tony Quinn. For McGrath would have bet his last dime that Tony Quinn was the Black Bat.

Even McGrath's commissioner laughed at that one. Tony Quinn was blind. How could a sightless man perform the escapades attributed to the Black Bat? But all the arguments had not swayed McGrath's stubborn conviction that he was right.

Raising his gun high, he charged. He brought the weapon down hard and his heart jumped in elation as the butt found a vulnerable spot. His victim dropped heavily and lay still.

"Lights!" McGrath yelled. "It's okay to come in, boys. Somebody get a bulb. The Black Bat put a bullet through the one in here. But I've got him! I've got the Black Bat this time! Step on it, will you? Get some lights in here and gather around. This is the night of nights!"

Someone supplied a bulb and the room was flooded with light. McGrath, gun still held ready, for he knew how tricky the Black Bat could be, knelt beside the hooded figure. He turned the limp form over, grasped the edge of the hood and took a long breath. The supreme moment was at hand. The Black Bat would be revealed and Sergeant McGrath could now turn his own brand of scorn on those who had scoffed at his theories. He ripped the hood up and over the man's head.

McGrath's jaw dropped wide. He blinked, then deliberately closed his eyes for half a minute. When he opened them again, he saw that he had not been wrong in what he had thought he had seen. The face beneath that hood was the face of Bishop. The pawnbroker! McGrath gulped and swore. Bishop couldn't be the Black Bat! That was out of the question. Yet here he was, hood and all. There had been only one man in the room so far as McGrath knew. He drew back his hand to slap Bishop to consciousness, but paused sharply and bent closer. He blurted an oath.

"This guy is dead! He can't be the Black Bat anyway!"

A YOUNG probationary patrolman elbowed his way forward, eager to be of help.

"You're right, Sergeant! Know what I think? The Black Bat was in here and he put that hood over Bishop's head and let you slug him—let you wrestle with a dead man while he escaped through the back door. Say, that guy certainly is clever—" he said, excitedly.

"Ya-a-ah!" McGrath yelled. "Who's asking for your advice? Why are you pack of damn fools standing around like a bunch of morons? Somebody call the coroner! Somebody get the fingerprint boys and the Homo Squad. I didn't kill this guy. He was dead when I slugged him. But I'll get the Black Bat if it takes me the rest of my life. He can't get away forever—not with tricks like this he can't. And I'll find out who tipped me that the Bat would be here tonight. I'm just getting warmed up."

"Steamed up, you mean," one patrolman muttered as he turned away. But he was careful that McGrath did not hear him.

CHAPTER IV

THE BAT MOVES IN

McGRATH HAD another shock half an hour later. When he returned to his squad car, he found a Black Bat sticker pasted to the rear view mirror. Gears clashed as McGrath started away from the curb. It was bad enough to be tricked—but in front of a whole detail of cops! Nothing could be worse. He vowed that next time he even had a glimpse of the Black Bat, he would shoot—and shoot to kill.

He cooled off considerably on his way back to Headquarters. It was best if he passed this off lightly, without betraying the rage that surged in his heart. The desk lieutenant seemed to have heard the news. He snickered when McGrath came in.

"Sergeant," he said with a wide grin, "Commissioner Warner wants to talk to you."

"Yeah!" McGrath ground out. "That's all anybody does is talk—talk, talk, about the Black Bat. I'm the only man who even tries to go out and get him. What's my reward, I ask you? Like a bunch of sapheads, you all laugh at me. Well, one of these days you'll laugh in the other direction because I'll drag the Black Bat in here and line him up in front of the desk. What's more, when you book him, the name will be Tony Quinn!"

McGrath swung down the corridor to his office. He composed his features before he reached for the doorknob. McGrath didn't feel any too good. Commissioner Warner was something of a marvel at handing out subtle cracks about efficiency. McGrath was in for a tongue lashing and he knew it.

Commissioner Warner was seated behind his desk, chewing on a cold cigar. His face was lined with worry and thought. He looked up, almost wearily.

"Come in, Sergeant. Sit down. What happened at Bishop's?"

McGrath gulped. "Well, the Black Bat was there all right. No question about that. He—he shot out the lights and then he threw a dead man into my arms—Bishop. He'd put his damned hood on Bishop's head and how was I to know it wasn't the real Black Bat? Anyhow—he got away. But he's going to have a hard time explaining Bishop, Commissioner. Somebody fed that crooked hock shop dealer enough poison to kill a mule. Maybe you got other ideas, but I think the Black Bat's gone in for murder—just like I always said he would. Sooner or later them playboys who think they're Robin Hoods get too gay, and what happens? A bump-off—and not in self defense either. You don't poison a guy when he starts to haul off and paste you one on the nose."

Commissioner Warner nodded somberly. "I'm afraid you're right, Sergeant. We've another example of this. About thirty minutes ago someone discovered a man lashed to a cemetery fence—yes, the same burial grounds where the triple murder was committed. This man has been identified as a cheap little crook from the Coast. He wore a Black Bat sticker on his forehead—and a knife through his throat.

"There was another dead man on the premises—shot by a forty-four caliber gun. The kind the Black Bat carries. It looks as though he's reverted to type. I never thought he'd come to the point of lashing a man to a fence and then murdering him in cold blood."

ABOUT THE same time that Commissioner Warner was admitting that perhaps Detective-sergeant McGrath's prophecies had turned out to be true, the Black Bat had once more become Tony Quinn. But not blind Tony Quinn, for he was at work in his white-tiled laboratory, preparing an apparatus for use in doing a Marsh test for arsenic. He talked to Silk as he worked.

"I can't puzzle it out, Silk. Those men at the cemetery were not to watch for anyone who might come looking for clues. That means the killer who placed them there knew that the police, with all their searching, had missed something. I think I have that right here—in this envelope."

Silk looked into the envelope and grunted in surprise.

"Hair?" he asked.

Tony Quinn nodded. "Exactly. My theory is this. Dawson, the assistant coroner, clipped a tuft of hair from the body of Ralph Galvin which he had helped to exhume. For some reason we'll never know, he put this envelope containing that bit of hair into a clay flower pot and turned it upside down. Now the murderer would naturally examine the corpse of Galvin, after he had disposed of the three living men. He'd notice that a tuft of hair had been removed and he'd look for it because this would be a vital clue for the police to find. When he didn't find it he must have worked fast to obtain a substitute body and then hide Galvin's corpse."

"But hair," Silk protested feebly. "What good is that, sir? I thought you had to test parts of the stomach."

Tony Quinn smiled and shook his head. "Not with an arsenical poison. Once it goes through the system, portions are taken up by the hair roots and passed right into the hair itself. We'll soon know."

Silk crossed his legs and leaned back, looking up at the ceiling. "I'd have given a year's pay to be able to see McGrath's face after you tossed him that dead man."

Tony Quinn chuckled. "I didn't see his face. When I realized he had me trapped, I removed my hood, drew it over Bishop's head and held him upright until McGrath came with his gun swinging. Then I simply ducked out the door before McGrath had a glimpse of me. He was too busy gloating over his capture."

Quinn lighted a Bunsen burner beneath the small glass retort. He dropped half of the hair clippings into a solution and attached a long glass tube to the retort. In a few moments gas was evolved. Then he touched a match to the end of the glass tubing which had been drawn out into a fine nozzle. Light blue flame sputtered and as the supply of gas was intensified, it became steady, burning with an almost colorless light. Carefully cleaning off a piece of porcelain, Quinn held this in the tiny flame and watched it grow dark with smudge. He shut off the apparatus.

"And there you are," he told Silk. "Arsenic without the slightest doubt—and plenty of it. Ralph Galvin's body was filled with the stuff. His stomach ailment may have been chronic, but only because somebody had been feeding him poison over a period of time."

"But I thought they'd tested Galvin's body." Silk began.

QUINN SHOOK his head. "Galvin's body was spirited away and another corpse put in its place. No—don't tell me that Galvin's family identified him. I'm aware of that, but—either they deliberately lied because they wanted to protect themselves, or they were forced into it. That shall be your job, Silk—to discover what made them lie."

Silk arose eagerly. "I'll begin at once, sir. A little disguise I used before will do the trick."

Quinn frowned. "It will have to be done cleverly, because if the Galvin family is menaced we can't afford to risk their lives. So you do this, Silk. Find out what company carried the insurance on Ralph Galvin. Go to his father and take the part of an insurance company's investigator. Act as though this was just a matter of course. If he asks questions, tell him you work independently, that the company insists on getting two reports. That will account for any other investigator having beat you to it."

Silk headed for the secret door leading into the study. He tensed suddenly, for a crimson light began flashing. Instantly Quinn drew on his smoking jacket, picked up his cane and darted for the door. He slipped over to the fireplace and dropped into the big chair which was his accustomed seat.

Silk straightened his coat and walked sedately to the front door. He opened it and was brushed aside by Police Commissioner Warner. The commissioner was alone, but there was an unholy purpose written on his face.

As soon as he strode into the room he stood before Tony Quinn, looking down at him in sudden embarrassment.

"You're excited, Commissioner," Quinn said softly. "What's wrong? Why don't you sit down?"

Warner crossed over to a chair and dropped into it. He put both hands on his knees and leaned forward, eyeing Quinn's blank eyes sharply and telling himself he was an intolerable fool. Certainly this man was blind. Hadn't a dozen doctors testified that his sight would never be recovered?

"I suppose I'm an idiot, Tony," Warner said. "I came here, all hot about you. Sergeant McGrath, as you know, insists that you are the Black Bat. Sometimes I've been inclined to think so too, but I've never permitted myself to dwell strongly on that point, for up to now the Black Bat has been of great help to me and my department. But tonight—tonight, Tony, the Black Bat has ruthlessly murdered three men. Two anyway. I'm not so sure about the last one. We found one of his victims lashed to a cemetery fence. There was a Black Bat sticker pasted on his forehead and a knife in his throat."

Warner's eyes narrowed as he snapped the last few words. If Tony Quinn were the Black Bat, he would show excitement over this. Muscles would twitch, his fingers would become nervous and tap the arms of his chair. Then Warner relaxed with a sigh. Quinn's facial muscles had not moved a hair's breadth. His fingers rested lightly on the arms of the chair and his vacant, staring eyes looked just over Warner's right shoulder.

He spoke gently.

"I'm sorry to hear that. Because Sergeant McGrath has insisted on maintaining that I am the Black Bat, I've naturally become interested in the doings of this man. However, don't you think it would be a difficult task for a blind man to tie someone to a fence and then stab him to death? Can't you see how impossible it would be for someone who had no eyes to commit murder or prowl around during the night as this Black Bat does?"

Warner made a wry face. "Of course I'm wrong. I *know* you can't see. I don't mind admitting that in the past I have had a sneaking regard for the Black Bat and I even hoped it might be you, Tony. Now I'm glad this is quite impossible. Murder is a one-sided game—the police hold all the cards. From now on the Black Bat will be fired upon at sight—fired upon by men who will have instructions to kill him."

Still Tony Quinn's expression did not change.

"Too bad," he murmured. "But, as you say, murder is murder. No man has the right to commit it—except in pure self defense. You're all wrought up, Commissioner. Those cemetery murders are getting you down. I can tell it."

"And why shouldn't they?" Warner demanded. "An assistant D.A., an assistant coroner and a young man of mighty good reputation are all slaughtered in a cemetery, with the only witness a corpse that they had dug up. What does it mean? Why did they exhume the body? Why were they murdered?

"The corpse showed nothing suspicious. There was no more reason for those three men to exhume the body than there was reason for their being murdered. I tell you, Tony, this has me guessing. I can't tie it up with anything. There are no loose threads, no pointing fingers, not even an anonymous phone call from a crank. We're stymied, myself and every one of my highly trained policemen."

Warner jammed on his hat.

"I'm sorry I bothered you, Tony. When I'm wrong, I'm the first to admit it. If that fool McGrath comes around pestering you, throw him out."

Silk held the door open and after Warner reached his car, Silk gave a long-drawn-out whistle.

"Say, it looks like something!"

Quinn did not move. Curtains were raised and there was no telling who might be watching. Above all things, Tony Quinn knew he must not give the slightest indication that he could see.

"It does, Silk," he said. "That little crook Joe Hudson was alive when I left him lashed to the fence. I did paste the sticker between his eyes, to let the world know that the Black Bat was taking a hand. But I didn't kill him. The man who hired Hudson and his killer pal must have reached the cemetery after I left, found Joe Hudson helpless and murdered him, knowing the blame would be placed on the Black Bat. He learned from Hudson that I was headed for Bishop's and he beat me to it. This means we've got to get the wheels going, Silk. We must work fast. And very, very carefully—for our friend Sergeant McGrath will be watching us."

"Hadn't I better warn Butch and Carol?" Silk queried. "Just to put 'em on guard."

Quinn nodded. "And to prepare them for action. Slip out the tunnel and see Butch personally. His phone may be tapped. Have him tell Carol, and be sure you aren't observed. When you come back, I'll have a plan formulated."

Silk disappeared through the secret door. Tony Quinn sat back, letting his head rest against the back of the chair. His eyes were wide open and starkly blank, but his mind was pounding home facts, registering little details and storing them up for the future.

CHAPTER V

SILK MEETS DANGER

OF ONE thing Tony was sure. What Warner and his police department thought to be only a series of baffling murders was in reality but the beginning of more trouble. There would be ramifications to reach into the depths of the underworld represented by such characters as the murdered Joe Hudson, his pal Dorkey, and Bishop, the pawnbroker.

The tentacles of this crime series would lift upward into another world where men and women like Ralph Galvin and his highly respected family moved. And over it all would lord a cunning, vicious beast to whom human life was as nothing. A clever being, quick to turn the misfortunes of others to his own benefit. When his hireling had been overpowered by the Black Bat, he had thought fast enough to pin murder on the shoulders of the night marauder. Quinn was beginning to acquire a certain reluctant respect for this man.

His agile mind began planning, lining up what he already knew with probabilities. It would be necessary to use all his forces in this game of life and death. Silk would be a natural to investigate the Galvin family. He had the poise and smoothness to deal with people of that kind.

Quinn thought then of Butch O'Leary, a man mountain of strength and weight. A slow thinker perhaps, but a vast menace when he got rolling.

Then there was Carol, in all her loveliness; Carol who had entered his life so mysteriously and given him back his sight. Quinn's mind went over the past, slipping easily into it. At Carol's request he had gone secretly to a small Mid-western town where a country doctor had performed an operation that the greatest surgeons in the world had refused to try. Carol's father had been a police officer. He had been shot in the back and in the head and was a blind paralytic, slowly wasting away.

It had been Carol's father who had donated portions of his blind, but healthy, eyes so that Tony Quinn might see again. The bullet that had smashed into his brain had severed optic nerves, but though the eyes could no longer see, they were intact. By some strange freak of Nature those eyes, parts of which were grafted to Quinn's eyes, gave Quinn the power to see in darkness as readily as in daylight. There was no accounting for this phenomenon except that it might have been Nature's method of repaying Quinn for the months of blindness that he had endured.

Then Carol's father had died and she had come to demand that Quinn allow her to take part in his campaign against crime. Her quick wit made her a valuable ally and between the two a warm friendship was ripening into love.

Those three knew that Tony Quinn was not blind and that he had become the Black Bat. They would carry that secret to their graves.

WHEN SILK climbed out of a rented car about mid-morning the next day, those who knew him would never have recognized him. The quiet, thin servant of Tony Quinn had become a red-cheeked, loudly dressed individual. He strode up the sidewalk to the big mansion of the Galvin family and kept his finger on the door buzzer until a pretty girl admitted him.

"From the insurance company," he told her. "I'd like to see the whole family. It's very important."

A man with white hair and worried, tired eyes came out of a room. Silk recognized him instantly. This was Peter Galvin, retired banker and the father of Ralph. Peter Galvin motioned the girl away.

"You are from the insurance company?" he said to Silk incredulously. "But I thought everything was already agreed upon. Your man, who saw me yesterday afternoon, assured me that there would be no more delay in paying the policy."

"Double check, Mister," Silk said with the air of a man who didn't like to be contradicted. "I've got to see every member of your family—all of them."

Peter Galvin nodded somberly, motioned Silk into a huge living room, then summoned the other members of the family. They arrived one by one and Silk, apparently engrossed in studying a file of papers, eyed them individually. There were four—Galvin's wife, her mother, Galvin's youngest son and a daughter still in her teens, the pretty girl who had opened the door.

"Is this all of you?" Silk asked suddenly. "I thought—"

Galvin sat down fearily.

"I can't see why all this fuss is necessary," he complained. "My daughter Elaine isn't here. She—she couldn't stand all the publicity and went to her aunt's for a rest. Now what is it you wish?"

"Wait a minute," a man's voice bellowed.

Silk looked around. In the doorway stood a beetle-browed, narrow-eyed man. He was well dressed, but it took more than clothes to distinguish him from the underworld to which he obviously belonged. He had one hand deep in his coat pocket and Silk sensed that a gun was trained on him.

"Just who is this guy?" the man in the doorway demanded. "Before we tell him anything, I'm calling the insurance company. I think we got a crook on our hands. Galvin, phone the company and be damned quick about it."

Galvin sprang to obey and the way he acted made Silk think that he and his family were utterly dominated by this black-browed thug. Tony Quinn's reasoning seemed to be working out.

Galvin returned in a few moments, white and shaken.

"Th-the insurance company tells me that they have no representative of this man's description and that they are prepared to mail me a check for two hundred and fifty thousand dollars today. He—he must be a fraud."

"Yeah, that's what I figured," the burly man snarled. "Listen, you—I'm Galvin's secretary, see? My name is Collins and what's yours? The right one, I mean."

Silk only crossed his legs and leaned back in his chair. Because he could think of nothing to say, he wisely kept his mouth shut. If Collins hadn't gripped a gun, Silk might have made a dash for the door. That was hopeless. He would be cut down with a bullet before he took a dozen steps.

HE HAD failed the Black Bat. The only thing to do now was remain quiet, refuse to disclose his purpose in coming to this house, and pray that his disguise would not be penetrated.

"So you're dumb, huh?" Collins snarled. "Well maybe you'll open up to the cops. Stand up, wise guy, and elevate your mitts. Hold 'em just like that while I give you a frisk."

Collins found no gun. He sifted through the blank pieces of paper in the brief case that Silk carried and hurled them on the floor. Then he jabbed Silk with his gun, marched him into the hallway and picked up the phone. He dialed a number.

"This is the Galvin residence," he said. "There's a phony here who says he's from the insurance company, which is a lie. Send a couple of boys down to pick him up, and make it snappy."

Peter Galvin moved nervously to Collins' side.

"Don't you think we might handle this without the police?" he asked, and his voice trembled slightly.

Collins showed his teeth in a wolfish grin.

"I'm taking charge of this rat. You keep out of it. He's a fake and the cops can take care of him. What are you trying to do—protect him? Is he a pal of yours?"

"I—I never saw him before in my life," Peter Galvin quavered. "I swear it!"

"Then shut up," Collins barked.

Silk leaned indolently against the wall and smiled slowly.

"For a secretary. Collins," he drawled, "you show doggone little respect for your employer. If I were Mr. Galvin, I'd push your teeth right down into your mouth and fire you without pay."

Collins stepped close, which was exactly what Silk had hoped for. A man of his ilk would try to gun whip his victim as the worst possible kind of punishment his warped brain could conceive. Collins had just that idea in mind. But as he raised his gun, Silk suddenly lost the indolent attitude he had assumed. He went into a crouch and smashed home a savage punch to the midriff.

Collins howled in pain, brought the gun down, but only succeeded in crashing it against Silk's shoulder. Silk grinned slightly, brought over a short right hook and drove Collins' nose awry. Blood spurted from it and Collins reeled back. He tried to raise the gun, but Silk was much too fast for that. He seized the gun hand and gave the wrist a hard twist. The gun landed on the floor.

From the living room came the screams of the three women. Peter Galvin was backing up, hope shining in his eyes. Then Collins, sensing that this human tornado was getting the best of him, clipped off orders.

"Galvin, conk him with something! Bean him with a chair. Do it, or you know what'll—"

He did not get much further for Silk brought his jaws together in a teeth-grinding blow. Collins roared and lunged for Silk, who sidestepped easily. He was not paying much attention to Galvin. The older man was just as much menaced by Collins as Silk. He should welcome this battle and the overpowering of the thug.

But Collins' words had had a strange effect on Galvin. He had turned pale and wild-eyed. Suddenly he picked up a chair, raised it and brought it down on Silk's skull. Silk collapsed to his knees. Collins, though half groggy, was quick to take advantage. His cowardly kick clipped Silk just under the jaw. Silk keeled over and lay still.

He awoke in a moving car, but when he opened his eyes, only darkness met his stare. He almost screamed, thinking he had gone blind. Then he realized that he was enveloped in some kind of heavy canvas sack. Barely enough air was seeping through to keep life in him.

HE REALIZED that to struggle now would only bring about quick retaliation from his captor—or captors. So Silk wisely decided to play possum. Sooner or later something would happen to give him a break and then, too, he doubted that Tony Quinn would have let him follow out this scheme without some kind of protection.

Silk estimated that the car was driven along for about thirty minutes after he regained consciousness, but that meant nothing for he had no idea how long he had been out nor in what direction he was being taken. He could hear mumbling voices, but the enveloping sack prevented him from discerning any words.

Finally the car stopped and he was hauled out, sack and all. Two men, apparently, dragged him over the ground and bumped him up three or four steps. A door slammed and there were more voices. Then the sack was opened and draped down over Silk's shoulders in such a way that he was as much a prisoner as if steel cables bound him.

He blinked in the light and glanced around. He was in some kind of big house that was well furnished. Four men stood before him, gazing down and grinning broadly, but not in mirth. Their harsh faces showed only a sadistic gloating.

One of them was a scrawny, ungainly type with loose fitting clothes and a hatchet-like face. He seemed to be in command.

"I guess," he decided, "we'd better turn this baby over to Gringo Joe, eh, boys? Gringo can make anything talk from a tree to a mummy. Cart him down cellar."

CHAPTER VI

A TRAP FOR THE BAT

SILK WAS yanked to his feet and dragged across the room to a small, narrow door. One of the men opened it and a steep flight of steel stairs was revealed. Silk was propped up at the head of the steps and given a violent shove. He rolled down the stairs, bruising himself badly with every turn. He heard the door above slam shut and mocking laughter from behind it.

Silk sat up slowly and started to peel off the strangling sack. He looked around the room and saw a long white table against one wall. Then his gaze traveled to the left and his muscles suddenly froze. A man was seated in a straight-backed chair that was tipped until it slanted against the wall. A man? To Silk he seemed more like some monstrosity out of the past.

He was huge and had primitive features. His eyes were piggish and definitely pink. His lips were fat and ugly. He had arms that were covered with as much hair as an ape's. His waist was narrow, his chest barrel-like. Here was a man possessed of an unbelievable brute strength and a tiny brain that probably would function in a bestial manner to match his appearance.

Silk struggled out of the sack and stood up weakly. He was still reeling from the effects of that fall and his head felt as though a ton weight had dropped upon it.

The brute rocked his chair forward until it creaked under his weight. He raised one hand and crooked his finger.

"So I have a nice fresh customer, eh? Come here, my little one. Come closer so that I may see just how tough you are."

Silk doubled his fists, puny things against a monster such as he now faced.

But Silk had rare courage. There was no element of fear in his makeup. Yet he knew that little beads of sweat were standing out on his forehead. This man reeked of a horrible menace.

The brute sniffed in contempt.

"Thin and scrawny," he decided. "Now turn around and look at that table. Look, I say, or shall I take out your eyes and bring them over there?"

He arose as his voice became a bullish roar. Silk turned his head. On the table were various wooden forms and some tools. They meant nothing to him.

The brute drew closer and suddenly one huge paw flicked out. It closed around Silk's throat and lifted him as if he were nothing but a small rag doll. Like an automaton, the beast carried Silk over to the table and set him down.

"That long box"—he pointed to the object—"is my own little invention. You put the arm in it, full length. Then I pull the box apart maybe three or four inches. Next I take the steel hammer and bring it down. The bone breaks like a matchstick, you understand? The longer box is for the leg. I can break it in five places so you will never walk again.

"Now look at that steel box at the end of the table. It is large enough for you, no? If you are put into it, with the metal door closed and then little hammers banged on the outside, just above your ears, you will go mad within three hours. You will be a nervous wreck, fit only for a hospital. Now do you begin to understand why you should tell me everything?"

Silk tensed and prepared to spring on this giant. He knew how futile his strength was, but anything was better than submitting to these medieval forms of torture.

SUDDENLY HE crouched and drove the most powerful blow he was capable of into the pit of the big man's stomach. His fist hit what seemed to Silk like a panel of steel. It drew only a loud howl of derision from the monster. Silk felt himself seized in a viselike grip. He was lifted off his feet and swung up on that bench. One arm was forced into the long, boxlike affair and strapped there. The giant held him down with one hand and picked up a hammer.

"I shall break it just above the wrist first," he announced gleefully. "It hurts the most there. Then if you do not talk, I shall break it again—and again until there is no arm left. But perhaps the tongue—now it wags a little bit, eh?"

Silk gritted his teeth and closed his eyes. It was too late now for the Black Bat to intervene. And even if he came, what could he do against this monstrosity? It was better, Silk decided, that he should die than have the Bat appear.

The hammer came down in a testing blow, but it brought a spasm of agony to Silk. He bit his lower lip until the blood ran. Over and over again in his mind pounded the thought that he must not talk. No matter what happened, he must not give way!

IN PETER GALVIN'S big house, Collins slammed the front door shut with a grunt of satisfaction. Silk had been carried out and thrown into the back seat of a sedan that was now pulling away from the curb.

Peter Galvin touched Collins' arm.

"I—I don't like this. Those men didn't look like detectives and that wasn't a police car. What are you up to?"

Collins sneered and struck the older man across the face with the flat of his hand. Then he snorted in contempt and walked up the stairs. At the top he turned around.

"You mind your own business and stay healthy," he snarled. "Then somebody else will stay healthy too, get me? And stop that blubbering or I'll knock you stiff."

He set his jaw aggressively and swaggered down the hallway to his room. This was the life Collins enjoyed—bossing around a millionaire and his whole family. Telling them where to get off. And they would behave. Collins knew that.

He opened the door of his room, muttering about fools who stuck their heads into a trap. As he turned around, his mutterings ceased and were replaced by a long-drawn-out gasp. A man was seated in a chair near the bed. He was tall, well built and completely encased in black. The hood over his head flared out below the shoulders until it looked like the ribbed wings of a bird.

"The Black Bat!"

Collins managed to get out those two words. Then his hand started toward his pocket.

"I wouldn't do that, Collins," the Bat said quietly. "Not unless you believe suicide would be preferable to a long term in prison—or possibly the electric chair."

Collins gulped and stared at the automatic resting lightly against the Black Bat's thigh. He raised one hand and nervously massaged his throat.

"YOU—YOU'RE IN the wrong house. This is Peter Galvin's house. I—I'm his secretary. I—I—"

"Be quiet," the Black Bat said. "And don't make me laugh. Secretary, did you say? Why man, you couldn't compete with a two-year-old child in a spelling bee. But you can talk a little. Supposing you tell me just where your two good friends took that insurance investigator."

"They weren't pals of mine," Collins mumbled. "They—they were cops. That insurance guy was a fake. I—I—"

"Where did they take him?" the Black Bat went on relentlessly. "And while you're at it you might also tell me on whose payroll you happen to be. Don't say Peter Galvin's. You're here only to see that he and his family stay in line. I want the truth."

Collins sat down weakly and rubbed his hands. The weight of the gun in his pocket gave him no confidence at all. This was the Black Bat who faced him; the Black Bat who could shoot faster than any man and outthink any clever brain.

Collins' eyes flashed around, looking for an avenue of escape. He saw the window open behind the bed. That was how the Bat had gained entrance. Collins estimated his chances of taking a long jump and a header out the window. It was only eight feet to the ground; the rear of the estate rose up high.

"I asked you a question," the Black Bat reminded him.

"I don't know what you're talking about. Honest, I—I just work here. Listen, I ain't no crook. I'm on the level, I tell you. Ask Galvin. He'll say the same thing."

"Galvin would say any words you put into his mouth," the Black Bat countered stonily. "You hold some cudgel over his head. I'll ask you about that later. Right now—where is that insurance investigator?"

The Black Bat's gun came up and centered on Collins' chest. The crook shivered, for those glittering eyes from behind the mask spelled sudden death.

"I can't tell you just where they took him." He licked his lips as he spoke. "But I—I got a road map marked out in case I wanted to go there too. It's in the pocket of my other suit, in the clothes closet."

Collins could not see the twist of the Black Bat's lips. All he was concerned about was that the Black Bat was falling for what he was saying. Falling hard. Collins suddenly acquired a new regard for his own quick wits.

The Black Bat walked up to Collins, took the gun from his pocket and searched him for sleeve or leg weapons. Then he walked over to the closet, opened the door and stepped inside.

Like a flash Collins was out of the chair. He slammed the closet door shut, heard the spring lock snap, and went out the window as though a ghost was on his tail. He landed in a clump of bushes, tore his clothing and his flesh, but got up instantly, raced to the garage at the rear of the house and climbed into a fast roadster. He shot out of the driveway, turned right and gave her the gun.

Collins didn't see another car start away from the curb, a block north of Galvin's house. He only felt a sense of relief he had never experienced before.

"If I had had a roscoe, I'd a gunned the Black Bat out," he told himself. "That guy ain't so clever—falling for an old gag like that."

THE PURSUING car kept a good distance back, but right on the trail. The man behind the wheel was a huge individual with a bent nose and a decidedly cauliflower ear. His hands were miniature hams, with fingers abnormally thick. Butch O'Leary was just as powerful as he looked. Slow-witted perhaps, but tenacious. Nothing short of a serious accident would stop him from following Collins.

But Collins suddenly sensed the presence of a trailer. By glancing in the rear view mirror he saw the coupé turn when he did, speed up as he stepped on the gas, and slow when he decided to take things easy. Collins gulped and a wave of fear crept up over him.

Maybe this was the Black Bat! But no—how could that be? The Black Bat was still locked in that closet, unless he had smashed down the door and that would have attracted Galvin and his family.

Collins decided to make absolutely certain that he was being followed. At the next corner he swung right, made a similar turn at the following street intersection and did a complete loop around the block. The pursuing car was right behind him.

Collins headed out on the highway again and brought his foot down to the floorboard. He left the pursuing car far behind and with a flourish he leaned on the horn and shot by another car—a sedan—doing about fifty-five. As he whizzed by, he had a glimpse of the driver—a decidedly pretty girl.

CHAPTER VII

SWING TO ACTION

AFTER A couple of miles Collins eased up. He did not want a run-in with a motorcycle cop, for then that coupé might catch up with him. He noticed that the sedan with the girl driver hung in the distance, but Collins paid no attention to her.

He would have if it had been possible for him to watch that girl. She held the trail easily, having taken over when Butch was discovered. The Black Bat left few things to chance. He wanted Collins to rush to the hideout and he wanted him trailed. Therefore, if Collins suspected he was being trailed he might not go to his original destination, so Carol Baldwin had been following well behind Butch. When Collins made his several turns around a block, she knew what he was up to and stepped on the gas to race well ahead of him.

Butch dropped back and let Carol take over then.

Collins suddenly slowed and turned into the driveway leading to a large house that was the main part of a big country estate. He stopped beneath a portico, shut off the motor and got out. He saw the girl's sedan whizz by, but thought nothing more of her.

Inside, he gave a brief version of what had happened to the gaunt leader of this wolf pack.

"What could I do?" Collins spread his hands in a gesture of resignation. "He had the drop on me. Then he took my roscoe. I shoved him in the closet, locked the door and jumped out of the window. What's he able to do anyway? Not a thing. If he puts the pressure on Galvin, the old fool won't talk. Not so long as we got the kid safe. Say, that fake insurance investigator showed up okay, didn't he?"

The gaunt man nodded.

"He's down in the cellar—keeping Gringo company. In a few minutes he'll start talking. I think he's a police spy."

"Sure he is," Collins agreed. "Only the Black Bat was worried about him. But that's nothing. The Black Bat works right in with the cops, don't he? We'll know soon as Gringo does his stuff."

"Yeah," the gaunt man said, "but just to be sure, I'll put a couple of boys outside to watch. I hope the Black Bat does find this place. Gringo would make a dead birdie out of him in about five minutes. Now I got to make a report. You take over."

"Okay, Antal." Collins used the gaunt man's name for the first time. "Nobody will be snooping around when I get through."

Antal walked upstairs, entered a room and locked the door. He went over to a dictaphone machine, sat down and adjusted a record. Then he picked up the mouthpiece and spoke in a monotone. This is what was recorded:

> Everything is going just as we planned. There has been a slight interruption from the Black Bat, but he has been thrown off the trail. Galvin gets the check in the morning. He will cash it and turn the sum over to us. Then we shall dispose of his daughter and tell him she is still being held so he won't talk to the police. A false insurance investigator appeared at Galvin's and Collins captured him. He is now in the hands of Gringo and when he talks, I shall report his story by the usual means. May I

compliment you on that scheme for throwing the blame on the Black Bat? It has worked out so well that the police have issued orders that the Black Bat is to be shot on sight. We must hope that he will be, for he is the only man I fear. I shall await your further orders by the usual methods and there is certainly nothing to worry about at the moment. Within three months, at the most, we shall clean up to the tune of several millions of dollars.

Antal shut off the machine, slipped the record off the rotator and carried it into another and smaller room. He remained in there for about twenty minutes. Then he came out with a neatly wrapped package, addressed and properly stamped.

He summoned one of the men, handed him the package and issued brief orders.

"Take the car Collins drove here in. Drive to the city and mail this from the Central Post Office. Return the moment you have finished."

The messenger took the package without comment. He had done this same thing many times before. Each time he examined the wrapper and noticed that it was carefully sealed, so he stemmed his curiosity and never tried to find out what was inside....

THE BLACK BAT, locked in the closet, remained there for about three minutes after Collins made his escape. Then he merely reached down and turned the latch. Collins had not remembered that most clothes closets equipped with spring locks can be secured from the outside, but opened from within without the use of a key.

Gun in hand the Black Bat went out of the room and down the stairs to the first floor. He heard women sobbing and the steady beat of a man's feet as he nervously paced the floor. The Black Bat stepped into the room, gun lowered, and his other hand gesturing for silence.

"There is nothing to be afraid of," he said in a soothing voice. "Sit down, Mr. Galvin. There are a few details I must know."

"But Collins?" Galvin gasped. "He—he... That mask. I don't know—"

"Collins is gone and he won't be back." The Black Bat laughed softly. "Furthermore I'm betting that he is burning up the highway between here and the place where they have your daughter held prisoner."

"How did you know she was a prisoner?" Galvin cried and arose half angrily. "If this is some kind of a joke, if you're a member of this damned outfit that's been bleeding me, torturing my wife and family, I—I'll stand for no more of it, I tell you. I refuse to—"

"Hush, Peter," Mrs. Galvin said. "This man may wear a mask, but I think he means to help us." She turned to face the Bat. "There is no use in holding anything back. Yes, they have my daughter Elaine a prisoner somewhere. They threaten to murder her unless we obey them. Ralph died, a week ago. He died suddenly, but for several weeks before he had suffered from stomach pains. The doctor signed the death certificate that death resulted from a chronic stomach condition—gastric ulcers."

The Black Bat pulled out a chair and straddled it. He placed his gun on a small table and motioned toward it.

"I am trying to help you—all of you. I know the trouble you are in, but I'm certain we can remedy these conditions. My gun is at your service if you wish to turn me over to the police."

Peter Galvin waved thoughts of the gun aside.

"No—I'm ready to talk. I couldn't stand much more of this suspense anyway. I think that my son Ralph was murdered. After his death, we discovered that he had taken out an insurance policy five months ago and named me the beneficiary. It was for two hundred and fifty thousand dollars—and incontestable. Then this man Collins came and told us that my daughter Elaine had not reached her aunt's and that she was a prisoner. Unless I obeyed orders, he said, she would be murdered. The first order was for me to hire this scoundrel Collins as my secretary."

"And Collins then forced you to go to the morgue and identify the body of the man found in the cemetery, as your son. Yet it wasn't. That man was a stranger to you, wasn't he?"

Galvin lowered his gaze to the rug.

"Yes. It was the most despicable thing I've ever done. But what choice did I have? There is Elaine—in danger every moment. I had to do it."

THE BLACK BAT nodded his masked head. The phone rang and Galvin started for it, but the Bat signaled that the call was for him. He answered and a girl's voice talked briefly.

"Butch dropped back and is returning for you. They have a place on Route Eleven. Watch for telephone pole numbered eight-nine-seven-two-one-three. Check your speedometer and the house is just three-tenths of a mile further on. It's pretty well hidden from the road. No signs of Silk."

"Thank you," the Black Bat said quietly and hung up.

He could not talk to Carol with the Galvin family within earshot. He returned to the living room and offered them no explanations.

"Be assured," he told Mrs. Galvin, "that your daughter is still alive. Until that insurance check is paid over to Collins, they wouldn't dare murder her. And if you wish to aid me in effecting her rescue, please do not consult the police nor anyone else. Not even your attorney. At the moment I'm rather badly wanted through something that is no fault of my own. I'm the Black Bat."

He heard the chorus of gasps and smiled behind his mask. These people, living a quiet decent life, would not have heard of the Black Bat frequently. The police were far from being enthused about publicity of that sort.

The Black Bat picked up his gun, stuffed it into a holster and made his way to the rear door of the house. He stepped out into the semi-darkness of late afternoon and within half a minute a car shot into the driveway. The door opened and the Black Bat got in beside Butch.

Butch backed out of the drive again and pointed in the direction toward which Collins had fled.

"He was a smart guy," Butch said. "He spotted me and I'm good at tailin'. But Carol was behind me and she shot ahead. Collins zipped right by her and never tumbled. She called, huh?"

"She called," the Black Bat said. "There is no time to be lost, but don't exceed the speed laws. If we were stopped, the delay would be much greater than that involved by taking our time. Silk is in that place, Butch. I'm afraid they may be working over him, trying to make him talk."

"They won't," Butch declared confidently. "Not Silk. Y'know I like him. He's a little guy and he can't fight nohow, but just the same there's somethin' under his skull. And he's right—every way. If they hurt him, I'll bust a few heads, I will, and no foolin'. Say, boss, what's it all about? You know yet?"

The Black Bat had donned his floppy-brimmed hat which concealed the mask over his head. The advancing darkness aided him also and he felt reasonably safe.

"I'm not sure," he told Butch. "So far it's a plot to cheat an insurance company. Anyway I'm only interested in saving Silk now. Silk and a girl who will probably be held a prisoner in the same place. Slow up—drive closer to the telephone poles so I can see the numbers."

Half a mile further down the highway, the Black Bat ordered Butch to head into a lane lined with overhanging branches, where the car would be well hidden. He got out, removed the wide-brimmed hat and motioned Butch to follow. The darkness was intense now, but that only aided the Black Bat, for there was no darkness to his eyes.

HE SAW the big house, nestled in the middle of a grove of high pines. Then the Black Bat signaled Butch to drop flat. A man with a rifle across one arm was slowly pacing the outer edge of the spacious lawn. The Black Bat's hand rested on Butch's arm for a moment and his lips barely moved as he whispered:

"Stay right here! I'll draw him this way and leave the rest to you. Don't let him make a squawk."

Butch nodded eagerly and massaged his big hands. The Black Bat slipped away into the darkness until he crouched just behind a bush along the beat which the guard paced. As the man sauntered by, the Black Bat made a sibilant sound through his teeth. The guard spun around.

"Yeah?" he asked hoarsely. "Is that you, Trip? What's up?"

He received no answer. Gun under his arm, finger tight against the trigger, the guard began reconnoitering. He did not want to give an alarm—just in case he was wrong. Antal had not been too good-natured of late.

The guard thought he heard a rustling in the brush to his left. He turned toward the sound. Something huge and ghostly rose up behind him. An arm curled around his neck, throttling him, while another hand gripped his gun hand, with such force that he was unable to pull the trigger.

Gradually the guard's struggles ceased and he lapsed into unconsciousness. Butch grunted, laid him down gently and proceeded to tie and gag him. This done, he looked for the Black Bat, but there was no sign of the man he worked for.

Butch knew his orders in a case of this kind. He squatted and waited.

CHAPTER VIII

RUSE AGAINST RUSE

CIRCLING THE house, the Black Bat spotted the second guard. This man was wary and not to be drawn into any trap. Nervous, too, for he had not seen his fellow guard at the front of the house.

The Black Bat suddenly stood erect and started to leap toward the man. But a bit of dry wood crackled under foot. The guard spun, gun spitting a hail of death. The Black Bat dropped instantly and the bullets snarled over his head.

Then another shadowy form loomed out of the darkness. It was Butch, drawn to the spot by the gunfire. He landed on top of the guard, knocking him flat, and wrenched the rifle from his grasp. He measured him with a short right and sent him reeling into the brush.

But now men were streaming out of the house, all well armed with guns and flashlights. The guard yelled to indicate his direction and then did a stupid thing. He charged Butch. The guard figured on getting in one savage kick to the belly. Fair tactics were no part of his career. His left foot shot upward. Butch swayed aside, reached down and seized the leg. He lifted the man, spun him in a grotesque adagio dance and then let his head smash against a tree trunk.

Someone fired and Butch ducked out of sight. He made tracks for the denser undergrowth of the forest behind the house, but pursuit was close at his heels. He lost his pursuers, after a few moments, and paused to glance back. He saw a barely distinguishable form climbing a porch pillar. It was the Black Bat. While the occupants of the house were busy trying to locate the prowler, he had taken advantage of their excitement and found a way into the house.

When he reached the porch roof, he flattened himself against the side of the building and sidestepped to a window. It was partially ajar and a moment later he had slipped into a bedroom.

The estate outside was agleam with lights as the searchers tried to track down Butch. They had discovered one guard at the foot of a tree, possibly with a fractured skull. They spread out, intent on making a wide search. Two men were sent to the highway to watch for the culprit.

The Black Bat grinned behind his mask. If one of these men found Butch, it would be to his own sorrow. Butch was a past master at the art of lying in wait and leaping with a suddenness that brooked no defense.

The Black Bat opened a door slowly. A muffled, harsh voice reached his ears and he headed toward the source of it. He listened at one door and a few words were distinguishable.

"—and you will administer the lethal dose tomorrow. Two days later have one of your women present herself to the insurance company as the beneficiary. There will be no delay in paying the benefits of the policy. Then that woman—disposed of in—usual manner. No—"

The Black Bat flicked down the safety of his gun, turned the knob slowly and hurled the door wide. He leaped through it, gun ready. But there was no one in the room and that mechanical voice had ceased. But a steady buzzing sound reached his ears. He saw a compact playback machine with its record still spinning. The Bat moved toward it.

Then the lights went out and a second later a door opened a crack. A jagged streak of orange flame followed in the wake of a bullet meant for the Black Bat's heart.

BUT BY plunging the house in darkness, the intended killer had practically done the Black Bat a favor. For the killer was now himself handicapped by lack of light, while the Black Bat could see just as well.

The Black Bat's gun blasted twice. He heard a groan, then the sound of some one falling heavily. An ordinary man might have rushed toward that door, opened it and observed the results of his accurate shooting. The Black Bat was not an ordinary man. He merely tiptoed to the further aide of the room, crouched and kept his gun trained on the half-open door. His sensitive ears detected the sound of steady, hoarse breathing; not the labored breath of a wounded man.

Finally the gunman could stand the suspense no longer. His intended victim had not responded to the ruse and he figured that possibly he had slipped away, satisfied that his bullet had ended the life of an enemy. The door opened and the gunman was starkly revealed. It was Antal, the gaunt leader of this mob.

Antal tried to peer through the gloom, but it was impossible for him to see anything. He moved toward the door, slowly and cautiously, gun extended and ready for action.

Antal had not the slightest warning of what happened to him. He only heard a swish that ended in an exploding crash against his head. He slumped to the floor. Before unconsciousness took him, he managed to scream one word:

"Gringo!"

The Bat had no time to examine the man he had downed, for there was still Silk to worry about. He crept down the stairway. No one was around and he guessed that the sound of the shooting had not reached the outside where the other members of the gang searched for Butch.

The Black Bat tried various doors and saw no trace of Silk. Then he heard a stifled scream and loud, raucous laughter. He moved toward a small steel door that gleamed almost brilliantly through the darkness— to his eyes alone. It was locked, but the key was there and he opened the door, closed it softly and listened. Someone was at the bottom of the steps. Someone who looked like a gigantic gorilla.

SILK, HELD down on the table by the superhuman strength of this huge man, had realized that his life hung in the balance. He must stall in some way and Silk knew only one method. He was glib of tongue and his persuasive ways had turned more than one trick.

As the hammer came down in that painful, although only testing blow on his forearm, he groaned. Gringo leered down at him.

"I—I can't stand this!" Silk moaned. "I'll talk. Let me up. I'll tell you everything."

Gringo's repulsive features looked almost disappointed. Silk knew then that even if he talked, even went the limit by telling the whole truth, he would still die at the hands of this savage monster. Gringo seized him by the necktie and yanked him into an upright position. He stepped back a pace, fondling the steel hammer suggestively.

Silk talked fast.

"It's like this, see? Me—I'm a right guy. But I work alone and I didn't know I was cutting in on anybody else's racket. So I read about this business with Ralph Galvin and I says to myself, here's a chance to make some soft dough. I was going to spill a fancy line to the old guy—tell him his kid was alive and all that stuff. Then, for a nice juicy fee, I'd get him back. Understand? Once I had my hands on the dough, he'd never see me again."

GRINGO TURNED his head expectantly toward the further wall. Silk followed his gaze and saw a small amplifier hooked to the wall. It buzzed for a moment and then Antal's harsh voice came from it.

"He's lying, Gringo. That's the poorest story I've heard in years. Give him one more chance. If he doesn't talk, break his arm and then break every bone in his body until he opens up. I'll be listening."

Silk realized that the whole cellar was wired, that Antal could listen to every word spoken in this torture chamber. He repressed a shiver and his agile mind worked swiftly. Bluff was the only possible way out now. Sheer bluff!

"All right," he said. "I know when I'm licked, but you can't blame a man for trying. I'm a private detective, hired by the insurance company to make a thorough investigation of Ralph Galvin's death. And I might add that if you mugs plan to lay your paws on that money, you've got another think coming. No report from me—no dough from the company. We're stalemate, brother.

"Also, if I'm not heard from by ten o'clock tonight, the police will come looking. They'll go to Galvin's and force the truth out of the old man. You haven't pulled any wool over my eyes, my unseen friend. Not by a long shot. Galvin is being bamboozled into paying that money over to you. That's why he obeyed Collins and slugged me with a chair—me, who was trying to help the poor old guy."

The amplifier clicked and buzzed. Antal's voice reached them with more orders.

"Give him pen and paper," he said crisply. "Make him write a report that everything on the Galvin case is on the level and that the payment should be made on schedule. The message is to be placed into an envelope, left unsealed and addressed to the proper authority at the insurance company offices. I'll see that it reaches there within the hour."

Gringo leered at Silk. "You hear? Walk over to that little table and use the pen and paper in the drawer. Write as he says and do it quick, less'n I lose my temper and break your arm."

Silk sighed. He wrote two drafts of his supposed report, making them as long and detailed with fake news as possible, and when he finished each one, he swore and ripped it to shreds. He started the last one, writing slowly, praying for time so that the Black Bat might swing into action if that was possible.

Then, he couldn't stall any longer. Gringo was getting impatient and that raucous voice over the loud-speaker would open up at any moment. Silk scrawled a fake name at the bottom of the report, folded it and then addressed an envelope to a mythical person. Gringo took it with a snarl. He faced the microphone.

"It is done, Antal. You will send for it?"

"At once." The loud-speaker broke into life. "And if it does not meet my expectations, you may dispose of your friend as slowly and painfully as you wish. It is my opinion that he is a fraud anyway, for I am sure the policy is to be paid at once. Still, we must take no chances."

Silk sat tensed in his chair, awaiting the slightest break in his favor. Though he knew that physical battle with this monster would have the same results as tackling a bull elephant gone mad. Gringo climbed the steps, paying absolutely no attention to Silk. There were no means of escaping from the sound-proofed cellar. The only exit was the door at the head of the steps.

GRINGO HANDED over the envelope, but for a brief instant he was busy, grinning at the messenger. During that instant, Silk ran lightly across the room, scooped up one of the small steel hammers and held it behind him. He was back near his chair when Gringo turned around to eye him suspiciously. Three or four minutes went by; then the amplifier carried the terse message of Antal.

"The message is satisfactory. I think this man has finally told the truth. Guided by the report I now have, the insurance company will promptly pay its debt. You may kill him, Gringo. He is no longer of any use whatsoever to us."

Gringo's big mouth opened and he drew a long breath of satisfaction. He extended his great hands and moved toward Silk. Suddenly he dived. Silk dodged the rush, but landed against the torture table and instantly Gringo was upon him.

The big man moved with amazing ease for all his hulk. One of his hands rested on the table for a second and Silk took advantage of that.

He brought down the small steel hammer with all the strength he could muster.

Gringo gave a long-drawn-out howl of agony. Tears rolled down his cheeks and he was convulsed by the pain that shot up his arm. Then he growled with rage.

The injured hand dangled limply at his aide, but with the other extended, he grabbed at Silk's arm and caught it in a viselike grip. He hurled Silk against the wall, knocking him half senseless by the force of the tremendous heave.

Before Silk could gather his spinning wits and get up, Gringo had the fingers of his sound hand curled around Silk's throat. He lifted him like a rag doll and hurled him on top of the table. He picked up one of the hammers and raised it.

Then the amplifier blasted the sound of a shot.

There was silence for an instant, then Antal's voice screeched.

"Gringo!"

Gringo banged Silk's head against the table and left him there, unconscious. He moved toward the stairway, extinguishing all the lights in the cellar. He heard the door open above him and stealthy steps begin the descent.

Gringo snarled in the darkness and prepared to finish off this latest victim with one gigantic sweep of his mighty arm.

CHAPTER IX

BRUTE STRENGTH— AND NO BRAINS

G**RINGO SAW** a black-clad trouser leg emerge out of the gloom, and reached for it. But that leg was suddenly jerked out of range. Something hurtled above his head and landed lightly on the cellar floor. He whirled, and ran into a straight-arm jab that smacked him squarely on the chin.

An ordinary man would have been knocked cold by it, but the massive muscles of Gringo's frame resisted the blow effectively. He reached in the darkness and his good right hand landed on a substantial shoulder. He drew his victim closer.

The Black Bat felt those mighty fingers close on his shoulder and from the pain realized instantly that they were powerful enough to break every bone in his arm. He had his gun, but was too close to use it now. Anyway, most of the feeling in his right arm was gone. The gun dropped to the floor.

Gringo growled with pleasure, forced the Black Bat back through the darkness until he had him pinned against the wall. But strength was already flowing back into the Black Bat's arm. He raised it suddenly and struck a mighty blow squarely against the giant's throat.

Gringo felt that one. It turned his string of lurid curses into a choked gibber of pain. He let the Black Bat go momentarily and backed up. Instantly the Black Bat moved in. If he could land another of these blows, he might dispose of the man. The Bat realized that he was up against an opponent who was nearly a superman in strength and weight.

But Gringo was ready. He thrust out his arm stiffly and caught the Black Bat under the chin. The blow that hurled him backward made him lose his balance. He fell heavily. In a flash Gringo was kneeling over him, one hand raised to smash the Black Bat's skull like an eggshell.

"His hands!" The voice that came from the table was barely recognizable as Silk's. "He can't stand hurting his hands!"

The Black Bat squirmed free as Gringo's dull-witted mind slowly took in the meaning of Silk's words. Gringo started to arise too, as the Bat sprung up, but he had to support himself with his good hand against the floor to do so. Instantly the Black Bat raised one foot and ground the heel of his shoe onto that huge paw.

His heels were crepe, but he exerted plenty of weight and Gringo screeched in agony.

Silk was down off the table, staggering drunkenly forward to do what he could to aid the Black Bat. Gringo scrambled up, but in the darkness he could not see the Black Bat swiftly drawing an automatic from a shoulder holster. He did, however, see Silk's form loom up in the darkness. Quickly he gripped Silk about the throat and raised him off his feet.

"This man—your friend," he growled to the Black Bat. "Lie down on the floor—quick—or I break this man's neck with my fingers!"

The Black Bat had his gun raised. Silk was being held up as a shield, but what Gringo did not know was that the Black Bat could see. The automatic jolted once. It was one of the few times in the Black Bat's career that he sent a prayer speeding with the bullet. He knew how quickly this giant might carry out his threat. One convulsive grip of those fingers and Silk would be dead.

The bullet struck Gringo in the temple. He drew his massive frame erect, opened his mouth to screech, but no sound came. Slowly his fingers relaxed their grip and Silk tumbled to the floor. Gringo followed him later, landing with a crash that shook the house.

THE BLACK BAT sped to Silk and helped him up. Silk glanced at the dark bulk of the giant and shivered.

"Another two minutes and he'd have broken me in little pieces. That was a close one."

The Black Bat nodded, walked over to the table and examined the paraphernalia on it.

"Silk, turn on the lights so you can see this too. Does it mean anything to you?"

Silk turned on the lights and hurried back to the table. He looked once at the instruments of torture, then closed his eyes. "I know what they mean, sir. That gorilla was getting ready to use them on me."

"Yes, I realize that," the Black Bat said. "But look at this layout. It's the type of thing that insurance gyppers use. They get their suckers insured, then break their arm or leg with these instruments. Probably use an anesthetic. The policy holder collects and the gang takes a cut.

Silk, I'm beginning to understand many things. This mob is well organized. There is a keen mind to direct every move they make.

"It's an insurance swindle racket on a huge scale. Insuring young Galvin for a quarter of a million proves this also. They are handling his case differently, though—and cleverly. Plain extortion or ransom might not get them anywhere. So they make sure Galvin is provided with money—and there they are. This Jim Fisher, who was found shot to death with Scott and Dawson must have suspected, or known something. Scott exhumed the body secretly. He probably figured that in that way he would arouse no suspicions so that the gang might spread out and get away. There will be others involved—scores of them. Such a gang as this couldn't be organized so well unless the boodle ran into millions."

"You're covered!" a girl's voice cried. "Drop that gun!"

"You're right," Silk agreed. "This gang is equipped with every modern thing all right. There's even a microphone rigged up down here and an amplifier to transmit the messages of the skinny guy who bosses this job. He yelled to Gringo, and that saved my life."

The Black Bat hurried up the stairs.

"There is a girl held here also," he said as he went along. "Peter Galvin's daughter. She is to be held hostage until Galvin comes through with the benefits of his son's insurance policy."

One of the thugs dropped his gun and clawed at his shoulder.

The Black Bat opened the door, found the house still steeped in darkness and stepped into the hallway. A man moved silently across his range of vision. The Black Bat could even tell the color of his hair and his clothing. The Black Bat raised his gun quickly, but it was too late. Lights flashed on. Two men were standing before him, guns pointed at his heart.

"Hold it!" one of them snapped. "You busted up this outfit nice and neat, but you're all done now, Bat. This is where the payoff comes—and to your pal as well."

Silk had his hands raised shoulder high, but was tensing to leap straight into the fire of those weapons before the Black Bat could move. Silk owed his life to the Black Bat and he meant to repay the debt if he died for it.

Fingers grew white against the triggers of the leveled guns. Cold-blooded murder was starkly vivid in the eyes of the two killers.

AN EXPLOSION suddenly roared out, but it was not from the two murder guns. One of the thugs dropped his weapon and clawed at his shoulder. The other shot a swift, fearful glance around, pale and shaken at this death that had come from an invisible hand.

"You're cornered!" a girl's voice cried. "I can see you but you can't see me. Drop that gun!"

The thug's gun thudded to the floor and Silk pounced upon it. The Black Bat moved forward.

"Take them into the other room," he ordered Silk. "Tie them—tight—so they'll keep until the police get here."

Silk gestured with his gun and both men marched ahead of him. As soon as the door closed, the Black Bat extinguished the lights in the hall. Quick, eager footsteps clicked through the house. A girl's soft, warm arms went about the Black Bat's neck. He held her close.

"Carol, you didn't obey my orders and get away from this spot after you phoned me," he said admonishingly.

She looked up at him, able to see only his dark outline.

"How could I leave when I knew what you were up against? Butch has been keeping all the others busy somewhere in the forest. There hasn't been any more shooting so I suppose he's put them to flight. But I saw these two slip back and enter the house. I watched them through a window, then when the trouble started I slipped through it and shot. They knew you were in the cellar and they hid, waiting for you to come up. I—I never shot anyone before. It isn't so—nice."

The Black Bat patted her shoulders, then held her at arm's length.

"You only nicked him," he said. "Jail doctors can fix him up quickly enough. And I'm grateful, Carol. You returned my sight once. Now you've saved my life. I used to think you had no place in my work. I've certainly changed my mind on that score."

Carol laughed happily.

"You'll more than think so when you find out what I've got," she said. "After I phoned you, I came back. The car that I followed here came out with a new man at the wheel. He had some kind of package and I was curious. I followed him, slipped ahead and parked my car off the road. Then I—I hitch-hiked. He picked me up. I—I'm afraid I rather encouraged him. Then in a nice quiet spot I stuck my gun into his ribs, took the package and made him get out. I imagine his feet are terribly sore by now. We were miles from anywhere."

She brought the package from a hiding place outside the front door. The Black Bat took it, examined the seals and glanced at the address. The written words loomed up as though they were spotlighted:

To Ronald Tunick—
2397 Belmont Drive

"Carol," the Black Bat said quickly, "he is the president of the Security Insurance Company."

He ripped away the seals ruthlessly and hauled out a cotton wrapped object. It was a dictaphone record. His eyes lighted up.

"Got it, Carol! The boss of this infernal scheme transmits his orders by a recording. The records are played off by that skinny lieutenant I knocked cold. He's still upstairs. Let's get him."

THE BLACK BAT raced up the steps, gun in hand. He stepped into the room where he had left Antal. The gaunt man was gone!

"Slipped through our fingers!" the Black Bat groaned.

"I know him," Carol said excitedly. "They call him Antal. I watched him before you came. He was outside for a few minutes. He—he's a horrible looking man."

"And as bad as he looks." The Black Bat nodded. Then he drew a sharp breath. "There's a girl here. Must be! Perhaps that crook abducted her again. Help me search. We've got to find her!"

But they were stopped before the search even began. Butch strode into the house with one man slung across his left shoulder and another tucked beneath his right arm. Butch was grinning from ear to ear. The Black Bat turned on the lights.

"We played tag long enough," Butch said gleefully. "I kept 'em away from the house long as I could. One of them birds jumped outa the window and lammed. He had a car hidden and he picked up three more of them bozos. But I nailed these two—and did they talk. Say, boss, one of 'em says there's a girl locked up in a secret room. It's off one of the bedrooms upstairs."

"Great!" the Black Bat cried. "Take those two in where Silk is busy with a couple of more of the same breed. Help him tie them up. Carol, upstairs with you. I'll find the girl."

They searched all the rooms. The Black Bat tapped on walls, examined mouldings and floors, but there was no sign of the hidden room. Then he turned out all the lights.

"Carol," he directed softly, "follow each wall and tap it with your fingers. Not too loudly. I think we may have a reaction."

Carol obeyed and then the Black Bat gave a low cry of relief. To his sensitive ears had come a faint call and tapping in answer to Carol.

Hurrying to the wall the Black Bat went over it carefully in the darkness. It was a papered wall, but he found that one edge of paper overlapped another. He ran his sensitive fingers over the edge and found a slight projection. He pressed it and a section of wall sprang inward to offer about two feet of space for admittance.

Carol slipped through before the Black Bat could prevent her.

"She's here—and safe!" she called back. "But they've abused her terribly. She's been struck across the face—many times. She needs a doctor!"

CHAPTER X

TONY QUINN—AT HOME

QUICKLY, CAROL helped a trembling girl of about nineteen into the room. She saw the Black Bat's image cast a grim shadow of a wing like ghost against the wall—and screamed. The Black Bat moved toward her.

"You mustn't be afraid," he said soothingly. "We came here to rescue you. Within the next hour you'll be home…. Carol, is your car handy? Then take her back. Just help her to the door and then get away."

The Bat watched Carol help the half-starved, nearly prostrated girl out of the house. Then he turned into the room where he had battled Antal. Butch and Silk joined him a moment later and the Black Bat showed them the recording that Carol had lifted from the messenger.

"This lieutenant, in command of this place, sent a message to his leader. In a moment we'll know what that message was."

He slipped it on the play-back machine and turned it on. The record scratched for a moment and then the strains of "Silver Bell," an old recording, filled the house with music. The Bat gaped and sat down slowly.

"That's the oddest thing—unless that recorded music has a message contained between the notes."

He played it as slowly as possible and then as fast as the machine would go. Only the ancient tune rankled in his brain. He removed the record and examined it closely. No message was scratched on its sides or in the hollow of the cylinder.

Carefully rewrapping the record, he searched the room. He found several other records, all of them smashed, but there was a good sized chunk of one left. He slipped this on the machine. It scratched out:

   …Singleton is ready. Seventy-five thousand-dollar policy. Get to work… according to plan… kill Collins. The fool… snooping… knows too much….

The rest was spoiled by great cracks in the surface of the record. The Black Bat reached for a telephone on the desk. He got a rural operator and was quickly connected with the Police Department. He asked for Detective-sergeant McGrath.

"This is the Black Bat," he announced calmly. "Now don't have hysterics. I know you want me for murder, but I didn't kill that man. He was alive when I left him. Listen to me, will you? A mile past the junction of White River Road on Highway Eleven, you'll find a dead man and four prisoners. They won't talk if you rubber hose them because they don't know anything, but I imagine you'll find they have records sufficient to put them away for a time. The dead man in the cellar tried to murder me. I was forced to kill him. Yes—I said forced! Also, this outfit is part of a gigantic insurance ring swindle. They insure people, kill them and collect on the policies by devious ways. Commissioner Warner should be—"

But the Black Bat suddenly realized he was talking to someone else. He heard the slight click as the connection was switched over. By now Sergeant McGrath was calling every law agency in the vicinity and throwing out a dragnet for the Black Bat. He hung up, gestured to Silk and Butch and they sped out of the house. A car was parked at the rear of the house and in a moment they were racing away from the city—not toward it.

The Black Bat knew that McGrath would put barriers across the highway and stop every vehicle. He realized also that McGrath was apt to speed personally to the home of Tony Quinn.

DETECTIVE-SERGEANT McGRATH was a peculiar personality. He was as honest as a man could be and whole-heartedly devoted to his duty. But he was possessed of one obsession—to run down the Black Bat and expose him as blind ex-District Attorney Tony Quinn.

The car, driven by Butch, swept down a cross road and came out on an alternate highway leading into the city. They saw no patrols, but when they neared Quinn's home, the Black Bat touched Butch on the shoulder.

"Stop two blocks from the house. Silk, you get out. If McGrath is prowling around, stall him until I slip in through the tunnel passage. And remove your disguise, now."

Silk nodded. He removed all traces of his make-up and smoothened his clothing. Then he tilted his chin at just the right angle as befitted a gentleman's gentleman, and strolled nonchalantly down the street.

McGrath, with four patrolmen, was seated on the front porch. As Silk approached, McGrath jumped up and grabbed him.

"Okay, there's no use lying. Quinn isn't in that house. I've been banging on the door for five minutes. The Black Bat's loose, too, and you'd better know where Quinn happens to be or I'll know he's the Black Bat."

"But Sergeant"—Silk pulled himself free—"I'm afraid you're quite wrong. The master is in the house. He rarely answers the door when I'm not there. You know how sensitive he is about his affliction."

"Affliction, my foot!" McGrath bellowed. "He can see just as good as you or me. Better, if the stories I hear are correct. I know he's the Black Bat. I know he was twenty miles from here less than twenty-five minutes ago and I've got the roads covered so he can't get back. I'm going in that house and stay there until he shows up. Then maybe we'll see what kind of an excuse he can offer for a blind man taking a walk all by himself at night."

Silk shrugged, walked up on the porch and had some difficulty in finding his key. McGrath scowled at him.

"No use stalling. I've got men thrown around this whole house. Quinn isn't inside because he's out, being busy as the Black Bat."

Silk opened the door, turned on lights and McGrath pushed his way past him. He strode into the living room and directly up to the chair which Tony Quinn habitually occupied. There McGrath stopped short and his face began to grow crimson, in a wave of color that mounted from his neck up and over his whole face. Tony Quinn was seated in the chair. His head was resting against soft cushions and he was fast asleep.

Silk elbowed McGrath out of the way with a disdainful glance.

"I could have informed you the master was here, but I knew you wouldn't believe me. He didn't hear you because he is wearing ear stoppers, to cut out all sound. Watch!"

Silk gently pulled a plug of especially prepared substance from Quinn's ear. Quinn stirred and his head jerked erect. He didn't try to face those in the room, but there was a look of alarm on his scarred face.

"Who is it?" he demanded. "Who is in this room?"

"Sorry to have startled you, sir," Silk said smoothly. "But Sergeant McGrath was outside when I returned from my usual constitutional. He insisted that you were out somewhere flying around in the guise of a bat."

QUINN'S LIPS parted in a smile.

"So sorry, Sergeant," he said. "I hate to disappoint you, but some day you'll learn I am not the Black Bat. I've been at home all evening. It is evening, isn't it? But of course—Silk served my dinner hours ago. A blind man, with a horribly scarred face like mine, doesn't enjoy himself outside very much. Sometimes I wish I was this Black Bat person you speak of. Now you want my alibi, I suppose. I haven't any. I spent the afternoon writing at my desk over there. Some law work—the only thing that keeps my mind off myself and keeps me from cracking up."

McGrath walked over to the desk. He noticed that Silk had his back turned. Deftly McGrath folded one sheet of paper on which Quinn had been writing. He stuck this into his pocket and returned to face Quinn.

"I'm wrong, this time," he acknowledged grudgingly. "But I still think... Oh, what's the use! If I bothered you, I'm sorry. Good night."

He strode out of the house, whistled for his men to break up their cordon around the place and was off. Silk rubbed his chin thoughtfully.

"I was watching him in a mirror, sir. I wonder what he swiped that bit of paper for?"

Quinn kept on staring blankly at the fireplace.

"He isn't missing a trick, Silk. He hopes, one of these days, to force the Black Bat to write. He'll have a sample of my handwriting and then—handcuffs."

Tony Quinn yawned and went to bed....

With the morning, Quinn resumed his accustomed spot in the living room and while he acted the part of a blind man, his mind went over each minute detail of the bizarre events that had transpired during the past two days.

He was lost in thought when the doorbell buzzed. Silk admitted Police Commissioner Warner. Though Warner did not know it, Quinn appraised him swiftly. Warner looked harried and worn. He showed lack of sleep and the nervousness that comes with fatigue. Warner sat down and rubbed a hand over his eyes.

"Something is wrong, Commissioner," Quinn said. "Can I help?"

Warner sighed. "You have no eyes, Tony, but you certainly know what's going on. Help me? If you only could! Listen to this. Last night the Black Bat fought a tremendous battle against odds that startled everyone who knows. We rounded up several wanted men, found a dead gorilla in the cellar and evidence that the house was used as a sort of laboratory by a gang of insurance swindlers. The Bat put us on the trail and we've done some investigating. There were crews working in cemeteries all night. We've uncovered twenty-two cases of murder for profit and in every case the beneficiary, who received a substantial sum, has vanished."

Tony Quinn sat erect. His cane beat a steady tattoo on the polished floor.

"THERE'S A connection then, between those deaths and the murders in the cemetery—the night that Scott was murdered," he mused. "Have you investigated that angle?"

"We've run a fine comb through it and found murder. Murder without clues. Last night Peter Galvin came to my office and confessed that the body he identified as his son was that of a total stranger. He told me that his daughter had been kidnapped and held as a hostage, that a thug was placed in his house to watch over him. Until he turned over the two hundred and fifty thousand dollars that was due on the policy covering his son's death, the girl would be held.

"Then—well, it seems the Black Bat took a hand last night. I think Galvin knows something about the Black Bat's activities, but he won't be tricked into admitting this. His daughter actually saw the Black Bat and some kind, beautiful girl took her home after the Black Bat rescued her."

Tony Quinn chuckled softly and Warner growled something under his breath.

"I realize now, Commissioner, why Sergeant McGrath came blundering in here last night," he said. "He still thinks I'm the Black Bat and I suppose he hoped to find me out. I wasn't."

Warner sighed. "Oh, I know. He came to me this morning with the whole story. Said he wanted to get the jump on you in case of a formal complaint. You know, Tony, the last time I was here I condemned the Black Bat, said he was a murderer. I'm sure I was wrong. I know I was wrong! If only you *were* the Black Bat! I need help—desperately. I need someone who can operate without all the red tape of the law. If I've ever hoped before, I hope now that the Black Bat can hear me."

Tony Quinn's face didn't move a muscle.

"You know, Commissioner," he said quietly, "that a bat has abnormally large ears. He might hear around corners."

Warner arose and put a friendly hand on Quinn's shoulder.

"I also know that bats are—blind. If you think of any way to help, just call on me, Tony. I—"

The doorbell buzzed again. Silk announced the visitors with a voice that almost reached a falsetto in his excitement.

"Mr. Hugh Morgan and Mr.—Ronald Tunick!"

CHAPTER XI

A COLLECTOR OF RECORDINGS

RONALD TUNICK! The man to whom that musical recording had been addressed by Antal. Tony Quinn had to restrain the impulse to turn and look at this man.

He satisfied the desire when Tunick was shaking hands with Warner. He was a portly man with graying hair and keen, darting eyes. His companion was slender, animated and eager—the go-getter type. He was carefully dressed and carried a briefcase under one arm.

"You are aware, Commissioner," Tunick said, "that I am the president of the Security Insurance Company. This man is Morgan, my ace agent. He's one of the best insurance solicitors in the business. Headquarters told me you were coming here and I took the liberty of dropping in. Ah—this is Mr. Quinn."

Tunick held out his hand. Tony Quinn didn't move. Warner whispered something and Quinn smiled.

"No need to whisper the news, Commissioner. I know rather keenly that I'm blind. Glad to know you, Mr. Tunick—and you, Mr. Morgan."

Tunick mumbled something about being sorry and Quinn waved his hand.

"I suppose," Quinn said, "that you are here about these insurance murders. The commissioner was just telling me about them. Very interesting."

"And costly," Tunick grunted. "Every few minutes we learn that we've paid a claim on a man murdered for the value of the policy. Three-fourths of the cases so far happen to be our clients. Morgan wrote several of them—the largest ones unfortunately."

"But I only deal in large amounts," Morgan put in smoothly. "I was hoodwinked somehow, but I'll be double damned if I know how. I've prided myself on being most careful in this game."

"Something has to be done!" Tunick shouted hotly. "The public won't stand for mass murder like this without an arrest. Put your best men on the case, Commissioner! Stop at no expense. This is murder—mass murder!"

"Every man on my force is working on the case, from the newest rookie to the most seasoned detective," the commissioner assured. "We're doing all we can, Mr. Tunick. Have patience."

While they talked, Quinn's cane tapped continuously, as if he were deep in thought. But those taps carried a message that only Silk understood. From his post at the door, he decoded the message, waited three or four minutes, then stepped into the room.

"Sorry to interrupt, gentlemen, but the master asked me to tell him when a certain radio program went on." And he added in an undertone that almost made Quinn break out in a grin: "It's his only solace."

Silk snapped the switch and a dance orchestra blared a hot number. Quinn seemed to relax.

"Wonderful band," he said. "I love music—good, modern music—and the peppier it is, the better it suits me."

Tunick growled something and then spoke louder.

"I hate that brand of so-called music. It's Tin Pan Alley. I like the old ones. In fact, I make a hobby of collecting old recordings. I pay fancy prices for them, too, and get my money's worth. There's an advertisement in several newspapers asking that old time records be sent to me."

"I'm sorry," Quinn said. "Turn the radio off, Kirby."

SILK SNAPPED the switch again and discretely withdrew. In the hallway he mopped his forehead. Things were getting hotter than that music. So Tunick collected old records. Like the recording of "Silver Bell," sent him by a murderer named Antal.

Tunick talked for twenty minutes, recounting the cases that had been so far uncovered. Several of the deaths were attributed to chronic illnesses and found, upon autopsy, to have been poisoning. Others involved drownings and still others automobile accidents with fatal results that now began to look like staged "accidents."

Quinn absorbed all this information and realized with a cold chill, that he was probably fighting the most vicious gang of killers this country had ever known. When the trio departed, he called in Silk.

"We can't lose any more time," he said firmly. "I can't operate very well in daylight so it's up to you, Butch, and Carol. Phone them from outside. All three of you search every hospital in town for a patient named Singleton—probably dying or dead last night. Find out all you can about him and notify me at once. Snap it up, Silk."

For the rest of the day Quinn fretted at his enforced idleness, but he did not dare swing into action. It was too dangerous, especially with

McGrath on the warpath. Silk returned in time to prepare dinner, but with no results.

At nine o'clock there was a tap on the other side of the secret door. Silk quietly moved about, drawing the curtains. Tony Quinn rested his head against cushions that Silk arranged. It looked as if a blind man were going to rest for the evening.

But when the curtains were finally drawn, Quinn jumped up and entered his laboratory. Carol was there, seated on one of the high stools, with a pleased expression in her eyes.

"Carol!" Quinn cried. "You've found him!"

"His full name is Montgomery Singleton and he used to be a broker," she said promptly. "He has wads of money and he's been free with it. A week ago he was in a mild sort of an accident and got a metal sliver in his arm. Dr. Lawrence Luddy treated him, but he developed an infection and—he's on his way out. They gave him forty-eight hours more to live and one of the internes even went so far as to put his arms around me in sympathy. I'm Montgomery Singleton's woman of mystery. He's in love with me and he doesn't even know it."

Quinn peeled off his smoking jacket and grinned.

"Out with the light, Carol. I'm changing into costume. Dr. Lawrence Luddy is about to have an after office hours' visitor whose only ailment is an unholy desire to ask a lot of questions."

When the lights came back on, Tony Quinn had disappeared and a resolute man with flaming eyes drew on black silken gloves. He thrust his hood into a pocket, examined two automatics and stuffed them into holsters.

Carol stepped up to him.

"Tony—please be careful. These men are no ordinary killers. They're fiends! I've read all about what the police have discovered so far."

Quinn laughed lightly.

"The Black Bat usually returns to his nest in the cave, Carol. Thanks, anyway, for worrying about me. You go back to your apartment and stand by for orders. A smart, beautiful girl like you isn't to be left out of this game."

He waved to Silk, opened the passageway and vanished.

DR. LAWRENCE LUDDY maintained luxurious offices on the second floor of the medical building. He was a middle-aged, well fed person inclined to be cantankerous and fussy. It was ten o'clock. His nurse had gone and his last patient had been treated and sent home.

Dr. Luddy yawned and removed his white jacket. Then he heard the door of his outer office close. He swore softly, damning patients who thought they could make an office call at any time of the night. He opened the door, intent on administering an opinion along these lines. But instead he blinked and slowly raised his hands.

The man in his outer office was dressed in black and wore a hood with a cape that made him look like a fantastic bird. There was an automatic in his hand.

"I'm sorry for both the gun and my costume," the intruder apologized, "but the weapon is to prevent you from creating a scene. The mask for my own protection. I am known as the Black Bat."

Dr. Luddy backed away a few steps.

"You're wanted for murder! Why are you here? What do you wish of me?"

"Sit down!" The Black Bat draped himself on the edge of the doctor's desk. "All I want is information. You performed a minor job of surgery on a man named Singleton, didn't you?"

Luddy nodded mutely and then, with an effort, found his voice.

"Yes—yes I did. A piece of metal entered his arm and I removed it. He developed tetanus despite the fact that I gave him a shot of antitoxin. It happens in such cases sometimes."

"Only this time," the Black Bat said softly, "it happened too conveniently. Singleton took out an accident insurance policy three weeks ago. It pays a quarter of a million dollars in the event of accidental death. Singleton is now dying. You know the family. Who will collect?"

"Why—why I suppose it will be his sister. He isn't married and she would be his heir."

"Doctor,"—the Black Bat's eyes regarded the medical man critically—"would you mind showing me the instruments you used in removing that sliver of metal from Singleton's arm?"

Luddy shrugged, arose and walked over to a cabinet. The Bat watched him intently. He didn't trust this man.

Luddy removed an oiled silk kit, opened it and spread out scalpels, ranging from minute ones to the large knives used in major amputations.

"I keep them sterilized with an antiseptic solution," Luddy explained. "The removal of a splinter of metal involves no chance of infection if done properly."

"Then you didn't sterilize any instrument before operating on Singleton?" The Black Bat nodded. "I thought not—without offense to your ability, Doctor. I agree that instruments, properly kept and handled, do not require sterilization for such minor work. Have you a microscope?"

Luddy nodded, opened a cabinet drawer and took out a high powered instrument.

"Suppose you take a culture from these scalpels," the Black Bat said. "Stain them and see what you get. Believe me, sir, this is not just a hobby of mine. I think that Singleton was deliberately infected and the only way that could have been done was through your instruments."

LUDDY TURNED pale. He jumped up, arranged slides and staining solutions. In five minutes he had his eye glued to the microscope. The hand control in the mechanism shook slightly.

"You—you're right," he said tensely. "Every one of these scalpels contains an invisible layer of some soluble substance infected with streptococci. Good heavens! If I'd used these instruments on anyone else, the same thing would have resulted. Thank God, I had no occasion to use them. Now what's to be done? I—I don't know—"

He opened a drawer in his desk, as he spoke. It was a wholly innocent motion, but the hand that deposited the microscope slides in the drawer also seized a small pearl-handled pistol. He brought it up, in line with the Black Bat's chest.

"Drop your gun!" he snapped. "Drop it or I'll kill you."

The Black Bat's automatic fell to the floor. Dr. Luddy let it remain there as he arose and herded the Bat toward a davenport. He motioned that he was to sit down and keep his hands high. Then Luddy backed up toward his desk and the telephone on it.

"I understand quite a few things, Mr. Black Bat. You're a crook. This happens to be blackmail. I suppose for a certain sum you'd have held your tongue. Oh, I know you could have ruined me professionally. Singleton will die—there isn't a chance for him. But I see through your smug little scheme. You couldn't possibly have guessed that my scalpels would be infected unless you had done it yourself. I'm going to turn you over to the police!"

"Doctor,"—the Black Bat's voice was very calm—"you are making a grave mistake. How do you suppose your reputation would resist the idea that you have known Singleton a long time and that you've been courting his sister for several years? If she inherits, then you, too, inherit—provided you marry her. I'm only trying to protect you, to find out if you can give me a lead as to who infected those scalpels. It must have been done before Singleton had his accident, because I'm sure that was staged."

"As though I'd fall for that line!" Dr. Luddy sneered. "You're going to be handed over to the police—immediately."

Luddy raised the phone and dialed the number. He gave the police operator a cryptic idea of what was wanted, then hung up. The Black Bat's hands were high. He had arisen and now stood with his back against the wall, near the office door. Against one shoulder he could feel the light switch. He made a motion, as if shrugging in despair.

His shoulder blade raised the switch and the lights went out.

Dr. Luddy pulled the trigger and hurled a slug through the glass panel of his office door. That was the only shot he fired. The Black Bat was upon him, wrenching the gun free, forcing the doctor toward the davenport. He pushed him into it.

"That was foolish," he said. "Now stay where you are. Don't move. When the police arrive, I'll let them know just where you stand. Not a sound out of you."

Dr. Luddy, wide-eyed in terror, sat primly erect, hands extended. He heard someone bang on the outer office door and realized that the Black Bat had locked it. Then the door was crashed in. Heavy feet stamped across the waiting room and pushed open the door of the consultation room where Luddy sat.

"D-don't turn on the lights!" Luddy half screamed. "It's the Black Bat! He's got me covered. He'll shoot!"

CHAPTER XII

BUSY BUS BOY

F**LASHLIGHTS BROKE** the darkness, swept the whole office and then the lights were turned on. A uniformed man eyed Luddy with a critical eye. There was no one in the office. A window was open about an inch, but no human being could have crawled through that space.

"W-what happened to him?" Luddy gasped. "He—he was right over there. The lights were out. He put them out. I had him covered, but he got the best of me."

"Sure, sure," the sergeant said soothingly. "Now just what did the Black Bat want of you?"

Luddy looked up eagerly. "He said that I had—"

There he stopped. His face was bathed in perspiration. He dry-washed his hands until they hurt. If he ever tried to explain, they'd lock him up, probably charge him with murder, involve him in this huge ring that was killing off victims to collect on their insurance.

Something, whipping swiftly, like a snake leaping out of a coil, struck the window. The police rushed over to it. They saw nothing and turned back.

"Well?" the police officer demanded.

Dr. Luddy looked at the rug. "I—I guess I must have been wrong. My nerves, they're ready to break. Please leave me alone. I—I'll be all right. I'm a doctor. I know about these things."

The blue coat jerked his head toward the door.

"Plain nuts," he whispered to the other men. "If he wasn't such a big shot, I'd drag him in. But he doesn't look violent. We'll take a chance and let him go."

They descended to the lobby, walked back to where the police car was parked at the curb. The driver got behind the wheel. Then his eyes grew round. He pointed with a finger that trembled slightly. There was the miniature image of a black bat pasted in the middle of the windshield.

"Back to Headquarters," the police officer snapped. "This job belongs to Sergeant McGrath. He's the baby who likes to get on the Black Bat's trail. Me, I'd rather monkey around with a buzz saw on my left and a man-eating lion on my right. Let's go!"

From the nearby doorway, the Black Bat watched the police car rush off. He was still panting slightly from the exertion of his escape. In the darkness he had used a coil of light, but strong, silk rope to effect his escape. By passing it around a radiator pipe, he had quickly lowered himself to the alley, then whisked the rope out of the window, leaving no trace as to how it had been done.

A bitter rankling in his heart for Dr. Luddy's deliberate doublecross made him plaster that sticker on the windshield. It would start things going, announced the fact that the Black Bat was still working against Dr. Luddy.

The Black Bat entertained something far stronger than a hunch that Luddy could have told more than he did. His actions made him a definite suspect. Who could plan such murder any more smoothly and easily than a doctor? Luddy would bear some further investigating on the Black Bat's part.

One thing he did know—that Singleton had been deliberately murdered. Cleverly, and with all the efficiency that the murder ring displayed in every one of its cases. The Black Bat continued to keep

Luddy's building under observation. If Luddy came out in a hurry, he wanted to know where he went.

A SLEEK three-thousand-dollar limousine slid to the curb. A man got out, carefully adjusted his tie, drew his coat neatly together and buttoned it. Then he bent down and ran two fingers along the already immaculate crease in his trousers. This done, he walked importantly toward the office building lobby and vanished inside.

The Black Bat's eyes gleamed. The visitor was undoubtedly heading for Dr. Luddy's office. All the other physicians and surgeons who maintained offices in the building had gone for the night. And the newcomer was Alexander Paradon, Attorney-at-Law. A shyster, but smooth as satin, with a brain that could outthink almost any other attorney he ran up against.

He did not dabble in various forms of law. He specialized—in handling insurance claims. Paradon had become the deepest and most vicious thorn in the side of all insurance companies that they had encountered in their extended histories.

Now Paradon was visiting Luddy; unquestionably called there in a hurry. The Black Bat whistled softly and decided that things were beginning to take shape. It was too dangerous to eavesdrop. Luddy would be suspicious and then too, Lieutenant McGrath might come flying to the scene at any moment.

The Black Bat slipped through the night, reached his car and drove away. He removed his mask, donned his wide-brimmed hat and left the car in front of Butch's boarding house. Then he made his way along the quiet street, beside the wall of his own estate. Making sure he was unobserved, he slipped through the gate, proceeded along the secret passageway that led from the garden house and into the laboratory.

Silk was waiting when blind Tony Quinn tapped his way to the chair in front of the fireplace.

"Nobody called, sir," Silk reported. "Is everything quite all right?"

Quinn sighed. "It's all wrong. I haven't the least idea who is behind this murder ring. Suspects—oh, yes. There's this Dr. Luddy I just visited. He either unknowingly infected Singleton or he's as cool a killer as I've ever seen. His sending for Paradon is another thing I don't like. What's Paradon mixed up in this for? Except for a massive fee. And so far as I can figure out the only people who profit are the leaders of the ring and they get one hundred percent."

"Pardon me, sir," Silk said, "but when Tunick, the president of that insurance company was here, I watched him closely. He seemed a trifle nervous and that special agent with him—Morgan, wasn't it?—kept running his fingers through his hair and watching the door to see if anyone spied."

"I noticed that too," Quinn said thoughtfully. "From newspaper accounts and from what Commissioner Warner said, most of the policies were with Tunick's company. And Morgan had written up three-fourths of those."

"I don't like it," Silk said. "To make matters worse they've had the jump on us every time. There's no telling how many more murders they will commit."

TO AN observer who might be peeking through a window, Tony Quinn seemed to be casually talking about everyday affairs. His face showed none of the turmoil within him.

"We won a single round, Silk," he said. "We broke up part of his gang at any rate. And we have that dictaphone record. I don't know what it means or how it can possibly carry a message, but I do know that this Antal, second in command of the gang, sent his messages that way and received them in the same manner. I heard one of his records playing when I slipped into the house. Those records give us our only lead so far.

"They are addressed to Tunick, which is highly significant, and he has admitted collecting old recordings. We have the address to which they are mailed, but the thug from whom Carol hijacked our recording, has probably admitted what happened to his superiors. Now they'll use a new address or method of sending them."

Silk leaned forward. "Let's suppose that recording went through, sir. In the usual manner—to that post-office box of Tunick's. We could watch, see who came for it and trail the man. Maybe that mug Carol outwitted decided it would be healthier if he took a trip to China."

Quinn let a slow smile come over his face.

"We think along the same lines, Silk. Prepare the package. Forge the seals and mail it in the original wrapper. Tomorrow morning you disguise yourself—the banker type this time, because they already know your other method of concealing your identity. Trail the man who comes for the package and have Butch follow you. Carol will be somewhere in the background just so there will be no slips. Now I think we ought to eat. A two-inch steak would be just about the thing."

Silk grinned. "It's on the fire, sir. I anticipated this...."

The next morning Silk's closest friend would not have recognized the man who seemed to have difficulty in writing out an application for a foreign money order in the Central Post-office. Silk had turned into a pompous, overbearing man in a white-edged vest, white spats and glasses that dangled from a black silk cord around his neck. He wore a derby, a tailored coat and striped gray trousers.

For an hour Silk had been there, watching the post-office box where the recording had been placed. At ten-thirty a familiar figure ambled into the post office and Silk's eyes narrowed. It was Morgan, ace agent for the Security Insurance Company. He looked around, eyeing each individual. His gaze passed right over Silk, but it registered the appearance of the white-haired banker.

Morgan took a key from his pocket, opened the lock-box and pulled out a sheaf of mail. He carefully sorted it, tied a piece of cord around the stack of envelopes and then picked out the package which Silk had mailed.

Though he watched narrowly, Silk could not see that Morgan betrayed any undue surprise. He simply thrust the package into his coat pocket, heedless of the bulge it made, and ambled out.

Silk gave him about two minutes, then followed. He picked up Morgan's trail easily. The man walked rapidly along the busy street and Silk, far in the background, felt reasonably secure. Morgan turned into a cafeteria, tipped his hat to the blond cashier and selected a table in a far corner. He placed his stack of mail on the table, took the package from his pocket and put that on the top. Then he picked up a tray and started serving himself at the food bars.

SILK WAS outside the restaurant, but he could watch every movement the insurance agent made. He kept his eyes on the package. A white-coated bus boy, tray full of dirty dishes, approached the table while Morgan was busy at the counter. He swabbed the table and Silk saw one of the cleverest sleight of hand tricks it had been his privilege to observe in years.

A package, the exact counterpart of the one that Silk himself had mailed, deftly replaced the original. The bus boy slipped the one he had stolen into a hip pocket that seemed to have been especially created to receive the bundle.

When Morgan returned to his table, he saw nothing amiss. Butch sidled up to Silk without showing any recognition. Silk's lips barely moved.

"Bus boy, now cleaning table in west corner. Watch service entrance of restaurant. Trail him. Send Carol over."

Butch leaned against a hydrant, inserted a wooden match between his lips, chewed on it thoughtfully for a moment, then ambled off. It was done with a neatness and dispatch only rivaled by the way that bus boy had switched packages.

Carol came along two minutes later. To her Silk gave other orders. "That smooth little guy just getting up with the mail in his hand. Watch out—he's slippery. Carry on."

Carol paused to look in the window of a hat store. When Morgan emerged, she turned away and followed him. Silk waited another minute, then went into the restaurant.

He walked up to the blond cashier and didn't blame Morgan for giving her the eye.

"Mr. Morgan of the Security Insurance Company promised to meet me here," he murmured. "I don't know him. Will you point him out?"

The girl said, "Sorry, Mister. He just went out this minute. Say, didn't I see you in front of the window a minute or two ago. Why just think, he was in here—right over in that corner—and you were out there."

Silk clucked his tongue. "Think of it. Now that you mention it. I do remember seeing a handsome man at that table in the corner. He left his mail on the table when he went for his food. I thought it most careless of him."

The cashier flashed Silk a knowing look.

"Well, he does that every day, just the same. I sort of keep my eye on his mail, but there ain't no crooks around this rest'runt, Mister. We run a decent place. His mail is just as safe on the table as if a mailman had it."

Silk gave her a big smile and tipped his hat.

"I can readily see that, or you wouldn't be working here. Well, I'll catch up with Morgan later on. Thank you very much."

So Morgan made a habit of leaving his mail on the table. It was too damned careless a gesture to be on the level. He was getting rid of that recording, without actually contacting the agent who came for it.

Silk began walking rapidly in the direction which Carol had taken.

CHAPTER XIII

A NICE OLD LADY

WHEN SILK met Carol she was coming back in a rush. She stopped him deliberately.

"Silk, we've got to chance an open contact like this," she said hurriedly. "I don't know what to do. That awful man, Antal, is in the lobby of the insurance building. When Morgan went in, I saw Antal watch ever so carefully. I think he's up to something."

"I think they are in cahoots if you should ask me, Miss Carol," Silk said. "Morgan just passed that recording to a pal. Did it mighty neat too."

Carol's hand gripped Silk's forearm.

"That isn't the worst of it. Sergeant McGrath is also watching the building. And Antal has several men parked outside. It looks to me like a kidnaping and if McGrath tries to stop them, he'll be killed!"

Silk said "O-o-o-h!" very slowly, then went on: "McGrath is a nuisance, but I know the master wouldn't want him hurt. Here's the angle. You tell the master. Don't use a phone. Go to the house personally. I'll watch out here. If anything happens, I'll phone. Have to take the chance. Run along now."

Silk ambled toward the insurance company's massive structure. He saw McGrath across the street, eyeing the place suspiciously. Silk knew what McGrath was after. He had become just as suspicious of Morgan and Tunick as he was of the Black Bat. The policies of the murdered men had not been distributed to enough companies. Practically all of them were insured by Tunick's firm. Either someone was making a sucker out of Tunick or the president of the firm was milking his own business to the tune of millions.

Silk had seen morning papers. The list of murders increased almost hourly, with the police working with frantic speed to uncover something—anything—so the newspapers would be satisfied.

Five minutes after Silk took up a concealed post where he could watch proceedings, a woman of about sixty came out of the building. Tightly clutched between her wrinkled fingers were several documents that looked like insurance policies. She was dressed in mourning and the lines of her wrinkled face showed that she had suffered severely in the immediate past. She was such a simple soul, even trying to smile through her tears, that Silk, who knew every angle of the sob sister business, realized that she couldn't be a fraud. She was much too genuine.

Then he saw Antal emerge and give a covert signal. The car full of his gunmen began moving slowing down the street. Silk burst out into a sweat of horror. They were after the old woman. They were going to snatch her.

Suddenly another complication arose. McGrath had straightened up. He knew Antal, had recognized him as a wanted man, and was swinging into action. Silk saw him reach for his service pistol. There was going to be a gun battle and that old lady would be in the middle of it. Silk caught a hard breath and began running.

At that moment Sergeant McGrath let out a lusty yell for Antal to stop. The gaunt killer turned with a snarling curse. McGrath rushed toward him, but in his concentration on the killer, McGrath missed the slowly moving car filled with gunmen.

Antal's lips parted in a sardonic scowl and he raised his hands. McGrath drew out handcuffs and approached Antal warily. Two men jumped out of the car. Both held clubbed guns. A pedestrian screamed. McGrath, caught between two fires, started to bring his gun down to stop the advancing killers.

ANTAL SWUNG into action then. His big fist struck McGrath at the nape of the neck. The doughty detective-sergeant swayed like a drunken man and hit the sidewalk. Instantly the two gunmen picked him up, dragged him to the car and hurled him into it. A police whistle shrilled somewhere and Antal began racing toward the old woman who had drawn back against a store window to get out of harm's way.

Silk met Antal with a terrific thump. It seemed like an accidental collision to any observer, but Silk's two fists smashed a pair of healthy blows to Antal's belly. The gaunt killer let out a roar of pain, swayed around, gripping his middle and emitting a string of curses.

A patrolman swung around a corner and Antal hesitated, torn between the desire to snatch the old lady or run for it. He decided on the latter. So far as he could see, no one had suspected his intentions and the old lady could wait until a more opportune time. Antal jumped into the moving car and it roared away, taking the next corner on squealing tires.

Silk moved to the old lady's side and tipped his hat.

"A nasty rumpus, madam," he said. "I can see how it has affected you. May I offer you a lift?"

The old lady clutched at Silk's arm. "Oh yes—you're so kind. Why, I—thought for a moment that I was really going to be hurt. That awful-looking man seemed to be coming for me. Of course it's just my imagination, but I'm so upset—"

Silk piloted her to a taxi. He did not ask where she lived. That could come later. Silk's mind was reeling under the swift turn of events. While he hated to let McGrath be kidnaped, he would have hated himself more if anything happened to this kindly old lady. McGrath was a police officer, paid and trained to face danger. This woman would be as helpless as a two-weeks-old babe in the hands of men like Antal.

Silk changed cabs twice, watching carefully to see that he was not followed.

"Just a habit of mine," he explained away his actions. "I like to ride and I like taxi drivers. By changing I'm able to give them all a little business."

Silk gulped and called himself a fool. If she swallowed that line, she was as naive as any person he'd ever met. She swallowed it all right.

"That's very kind of you. But you don't even know where I live, but it really isn't much further. I can walk."

Silk shook his head. "I wouldn't think of it. I'll see you right to your door, madam. If I'm not too inquisitive—you've lost someone dear, haven't you?"

She smiled wanly. "My grandson—Charlie's boy. He was hit by a car only day before yesterday. The funeral is tomorrow—from the undertaker's chapel. Now I'm all alone except for another grandson. My daughter's boy. But let me tell you who I am. You've heard of Arnold Bannister? I'm Beulah, his widow."

Silk almost jumped off the taxi seat. Beulah Bannister was a comparatively wealthy woman. Her late husband, a tire manufacturer, had left her comfortably well off. No wonder Antal had laid crafty plans to snatch her.

Then Silk thought of those papers the old lady held tightly in her hand. Silk knew how to handle people of her kind. All the old polish and suaveness of his confidence man career oozed out of every pore.

"I'M SO sorry," he said gently. "My name is Smith. I lost my dear ones years ago. If I could only be of some help to you. Oh, I know you have attorneys and men who would fight to get a part of your money, Mrs. Bannister. That's not my way. I like people for themselves. By the way—those papers in your hand. They look valuable. Hadn't you better place them in your purse? Here—let me do it."

She surrendered both her purse and the papers. Silk folded them once, but his keen eyes ran over the details on the title page of the first documents. He closed his eyes and shook his head. This old lady's grandson had been insured against accidental death to the tune of two hundred thousand dollars—and that was only one of the insurance policies she held!

A servant ran out to open the taxi door. The woman shook hands with Silk and bestowed a friendly smile on him.

"I won't ask you in now, Mr. Smith. Things are so off balance, with the boy's death and all. I would appreciate your coming to tea some afternoon—in about a week. I won't mind, you see. We are old people, you and I. We've grown to expect death, even if it comes to our dearest ones and not ourselves. I won't be impairing the boy's memory if you come for a friendly chat some afternoon. Goodbye—and thank you ever so much."

After she left, Silk found that his eyes were moist. Then, to the amazement of the taxi driver, he snapped a searing oath.

"If they've got plans to harm that old lady, I'll wring their filthy necks," he told himself. Then aloud: "Driver, take me to Union Station...."

At home, waiting for Silk, Tony Quinn paced the narrow confines of his laboratory nervously. Delay irritated him and he should have heard from Silk hours ago. It wasn't like Silk to permit so much time to pass unless something had happened to him. Something he could not get out of.

Then there was McGrath. Despite the bulldog tenacity he used in trying to connect Tony Quinn with the Black Bat, Quinn liked him for it. McGrath lent a certain spice of excitement to life. And he was honest, fair and as good a policeman as existed.

Carol had arrived with her information and departed to hurry back to the insurance company building and watch for further developments. Suddenly the signal light, wired to the front porch, winked to indicate someone was approaching the door. Quinn picked up his cane, assumed the staring gaze of a blind man and hurried back to the living room. But it was only Silk who arrived. Silk, as alarmed as Quinn had ever seen him.

"Have things happened!" He doffed his hat and slipped out of the disguise. "No need to worry about McGrath watching, sir. He's been snatched—taken by Antal and his gunmen. Where? I don't know, sir. There was an old lady—charming person. Antal was ready to snatch her when McGrath butted in. I hustled the old lady off and who do you think she was?"

"Stop asking riddles," Quinn said tartly. "I've got to find McGrath. Oh, I'm sorry, Silk. I know you did the right thing in protecting the woman. Out with it. Who was she?"

"Mrs. Beulah Bannister—and her grandson died yesterday, hit by a car—" Silk paused and a horrified expression came over his face. "I—I just thought of something, sir. The grandson was killed by a car. He was insured for over two hundred thousand dollars. She was cashing in on his policies. Oh, what a sap I've been! She must be part and parcel of the gang."

QUINN WHISTLED thoughtfully. "Maybe Silk. But it doesn't sound quite right to me. We'll have to look into it."

Silk looked puzzled. "The death of her grandson does smack of these devils who operate the insurance racket. Only I—I can't see how they'd have any hold on her, sir. She's such a nice old lady. She did mention another grandson, her daughter's boy. He's all she has left."

Quinn rubbed his chin. "We'll have to watch her, Silk. Maybe for her own protection. But first I must find McGrath before they kill him. They'll take their time about it and try to find out what McGrath has up his sleeve. He won't talk, so he won't be murdered at once. But we've lost the trail. Carol told me about the package and the bus boy. I haven't heard from Butch yet, but he'll report as soon as he knows anything. But we must find McGrath, then investigate the death of Mrs. Bannister's grandson. Silk, I believe we're beginning to close in. If I have my way, the rest of the innings will be ours."

Silk went to his rooms to completely eradicate the disguise.

It was an hour later when the phone rang. Silk answered it and stiffened to attention. Butch was calling, so excited that he could hardly talk and complicating things by pretending he was the manager of a laundry calling.

"The bundle you reported—Mr. Quinn's—well, it—it's gone. It must have been delivered to some other address, see? Maybe the party at two-three-five-six Boulevard Drive got it by mistake, see? I'm gonna find out if that's what happened, see? And I'm busy—gotta be traveling, see?"

Silk hung up quickly. He raced into the living room, but Tony Quinn, in his pose of a blind man, did not turn a hair.

"It was Butch—he disguised the call. He mentioned the address at two-three-five-six Boulevard Drive, see? I mean—sir." Silk blushed at the slip of the tongue.

Quinn grinned broadly.

"Butch evidently imparted some of his excitement to you, Silk. Anyway it's what I've been waiting for. And, damn it, I must keep on waiting. It will be dark within an hour. I must restrain myself until then. It won't be safe for me to prowl around until I'm in my own element—darkness. Get some coffee, Silk. And see to my guns. I've a feeling they'll go into action tonight."

CHAPTER XIV

TO SAVE A POLICEMAN

JUST AS soon as it was dark enough to venture out, Tony Quinn's personality slipped from him. Gone were the stark, staring eyes of a blind man. His resigned, almost morose look vanished. As the Black Bat he became alive and alert. His nerves were tingling, his eyes shining brilliantly.

He gave Silk instructions to contact Carol at once and have her call on old Mrs. Bannister. She was to ingratiate herself in the old lady's favor by some pretext or other. Carol could decide the circumstances, for she was clever enough to know where to draw the line. She was to be armed and ready for trouble. At the first sign of developing danger she was to call the police and stand by Mrs. Bannister.

"And you, Silk, will have to chance a caller here at this house. If anyone comes, we went for a drive and I'm walking alone in the park. Remind me to make a habit of that when we're not busy on some case. It's a good alibi and we need 'em. Conceal yourself and watch both Mrs. Bannister and Carol. If that skinny Antal shows up and tries to strike, shoot him. It's the only way to handle cornered rats. I'm depending on you, Silk, old man."

Quinn drew on the floppy hat, slid down the ladder to the tunnel and in five minutes was behind the wheel of the car that Butch kept parked for his convenience.

He headed west and turned up Boulevard Drive. The name was more or less facetious for it was nothing like a boulevard. There were no trees at all—only dirty factory smokestacks rearing their heads above the squalid tenement houses, most of them empty because of government housing projects being carried out in the vicinity.

The number Butch had given proved to be a boarded-up old place that looked as though a good windstorm might blow it down. The Black Bat drove right by the place, slowly, for he knew that Butch was somewhere in the vicinity and would recognize the car.

Antal pointed his gun down towards the man on the bed.

Ten blocks away the Black Bat turned around and came back. Before he neared the house, Butch jumped from a place of concealment and waved his hand. The Black Bat stopped and picked him up.

"There's five of 'em," Butch reported excitedly. "I tailed the bus boy from the restaurant to this joint, and I been watchin' the dump ever since they dragged McGrath inside. Boy, they sure didn't handle him gentle! That big punk, Antal, took an awful swipe at the poor guy—damn near knocked McGrath's head off—and all for nuthin'."

"We'll give them a taste of their own brand of medicine," the Black Bat decided. "You have my permission to knock as many of their heads together as you can. With one stipulation. Antal belongs to me."

Butch made a wry face.

"I knew they was a catch to it, Chief. I been wantin' to bust that guy ever since I first laid eyes on him. But how do we start? They got a couple of hoods parked at windows upstairs and they got tommy-guns. I know, because even if the windows are all boarded up, they got 'em on hinges so they swing out. They loosened one for quick shootin' and the wind banged it wide open. I saw the stutter gun, see?"

"I think that we'll steal a police car," the Black Bat said judiciously. "Under the circumstances—rescuing a police officer and all—we should feel free to use department equipment. What do you think, Butch?"

BUTCH'S JAW hung slackly down. "Sure, Chief. Sure—anythin' you say. But a police car—what are we gonna do with it? Drive it through the front door?"

The Black Bat grinned. "No, but we'll use it to drive those mugs to the front door. Keep your eyes peeled for a radio car. And Butch, be gentle with the patrolmen that we'll have to put out of commission temporarily."

Butch's grin spread all over his face.

They picked up a radio car in an outlying section, trailed it to a call box where one patrolman got out and phoned in. As he walked back to the car, he heard a shout from behind one of the houses that lined the street. It was distinctly a call for help.

"Let's go, Bill!" he snapped. "Sounds like trouble."

They left the car at the curb and raced down the street. A man was standing in a driveway waving his hands excitedly. They rushed up to him.

"There's a dead guy in my garage," Butch gulped. "I just went in and there he was, all—"

"Where?" both patrolmen chorused.

Butch pointed and they headed for the place. They took, perhaps, three steps before two massive hands gripped each man by the nape of the neck. Butch raised both of them off their feet and before either could gather his wits, he banged their heads together. Then Butch put them down carefully, found their handcuffs and used both pair to cuff wrists and ankles.

He tied efficient gags between their lips and carried them to the garage which the Bat had discovered to be as vacant as the house it belonged to. Butch put both men down, arose, and then bent down again to loosen their collars. They seemed a little blue in the face. Butch made a sympathetic sound with his tongue.

"Too bad. Imagine how them babies are gonna feel."

Then he closed the garage door, snapped a rusty padlock in place and ran to the street. The radio car pulled up with the Black Bat at the wheel. He sent it roaring back to Boulevard Drive and parked at an intersection. There the Black Bat fell to work with a screw driver, a wrench and a pair of pliers. Butch watched him mutely, unable to understand what all this fuss had to do with rescuing McGrath.

At last the Black Bat was finished. He set the dashboard clock carefully, tested a few wires and then drove the car to within twenty feet of the apparently abandoned tenement, traveling the last couple of blocks without lights. He shut off the motor, signaled Butch to work quietly and both slipped out of the car, darted between two of the old tenements and reached the squalid courtyard in the rear. The Black Bat spoke low-voiced warnings from time to time and saved Butch several nasty falls over sagging clothes lines and tin cans.

"We've got two minutes," the Black Bat announced in a whisper. "Butch, you can't see him, but there's a man in the second floor window. That's where they'll be—on that floor. Now, here is the idea. They'll all rush to the front of the house. When that happens, I'll climb the porch and get in that window from which a gunner is now peeking. Those boards will be on a hinge, as you indicated. I'll get in easily. As soon as I vanish, you count up to fifty—slowly. Can you count that high?"

"Huh!" Butch said. "I can go as high as a hundred. Okay. Then what?"

THE BLACK BAT smiled and drew his hood over his shoulders.

"Then you see what can be done about that locked door. Take it apart and go to town, Butch. No shooting unless absolutely necessary. There will be plenty of excitement without that. Ready?"

Butch had no time to reply. From the street came the sudden wail of a siren. It grew and grew in intensity until the eerie screech seemed to enter their blood. The Black Bat, watching the window above carefully, saw the gunman vanish. Although there was no more than a two-inch crack in the boards, the Black Bat was able to spot the guard's movements.

"Now start counting!" he ordered Butch in a whisper.

The Black Bat rushed across the yard, gave a leap and wound both arms around a porch pillar. He shinnied himself up expertly, reached the porch roof and darted for the window. He pulled back the boards that were nailed to what was practically a storm window, and stepped inside. Whipping out his gun he looked through the darkness. There was no one in the room.

Hurrying on, he reached a long hallway off which several empty apartments led. From the front of the house he could hear harsh orders being given in Antal's raucous tone.

"Each man take a window and use them tommy-guns," the gaunt man was saying. "Blast as many of the police as you can. I'll take care of this wise guy Headquarters man in the back. Remember, make your slugs count. Drive 'em back and then we'll smash out of the cellar where the car is hidden. It's a damn lucky thing we were set for this but I'd give my shirt to know how the police spotted this joint."

The siren was wailing away at a great clip. It sounded as though a hundred radio cars were converging on the scene. Echoes of empty buildings can give deceptive sounds.

The Black Bat merged with the darkness and waited. In a second or two Butch would come barging in. That would be the give-away. The Black Bat saw Antal, his gaunt, skinny frame plainly visible in the darkness as he hurtled toward one of the tenements. A heavy pistol was in his hand and murder was in his eyes.

Antal pushed open the door, hurried into a bedroom and stood over McGrath. The detective-sergeant's face was the color of raw beef from the slugging he had taken. Somebody had taken off his clothes which were draped over a nearby chair and he was in bloody pajamas too small for him. Blood caked his lips and matted his hair. But his eyes were defiant.

"So they caught up with you, Antal," he said coolly. "And you're about to gun me. That won't do you much good. You're slated for the chair and it's little matter if it's for my murder or someone else's. You've killed enough men in your day."

"So," Antal snarled. "Still wise, huh? Okay—I'll give it to you right in the belly so you'll be in misery for days and then you'll croak anyway. Maybe they'll get me, but you'll die, wise guy."

Antal pointed his gun down towards the man on the bed. His finger tightened against the trigger. Suddenly he became aware that one of the hinged windows had opened. A gray sort of light had drifted into the room. Antal raised his eyes—and felt the first wave of pure terror he had ever experienced.

Silhouetted against the further wall was the shadowy image of a giant bat, with wings outspread like great talons ready to close about its prey. In all his mad career Antal had never seen anything more sinister.

HIS HAND holding the gun trembled. His whole body broke out in a cold sweat. Palsied fingers let go of the gun and it clanged to the floor. He felt a cold breeze—like the wings of death—fan the back of his neck. Antal opened his mouth for a convulsive scream of terror. But a black-clad arm circled his neck, snapped his head back, and a fist crashed against the point of his jaw.

As Antal lapsed into unconsciousness he vaguely heard a terrific crashing sound. Butch had broken in the door.

Thugs, torn between the desire to protect themselves from the front or to see what was going on in the rear, gave way to panic. They fled for the cellar, but their paths crossed with that of Butch.

A tommy-gun spat once, a brief round. The thugs were slammed mercilessly against walls, or picked up and swung like clubs to crash against the heads of their own mates.

Butch was in action and he loved every minute of it. Big, brutal as only Butch could be when aroused, he moved about with amazing speed.

Upstairs the Black Bat knelt beside McGrath.

"They didn't handle you any too gently, Sergeant," he said. "Please bear with me if I have to be quick. That devil's din outside is bound to draw a lot of police and I don't care to meet any more than you, many thanks just the same."

McGrath's face was a study in contrasts. One moment he looked as though he would like to tackle the Black Bat, weak and hurt as he was. The next he looked as though he would like to hang a medal on his chest and shake his hand.

From below came Butch's hoarse bellow.

"All clean, Chief!"

"Beat it!" the Black Bat called back. "Travel fast."

Butch did not pause to question the Black Bat's methods. He scurried out into the back yard and leaped over a fence. In half a second he was gone from sight.

The Black Bat stripped off the tight wires that bound McGrath. The detective-sergeant tried to arise, but his arms and legs were temporarily paralyzed. He groaned and sank back on the floor. The Black Bat hastily stripped off the pajamas and somehow managed to get him in his clothes, then lifted him, like a child. He headed for the door. Antal, on the floor, groaned and clawed at the wall near him.

"That guy," McGrath said. "He's wanted. Wisconsin wants him on a charge of murder and I want him to resist arrest so I can paste his nose around to the back of his rotten head."

"Sorry." The Black Bat scampered down the stairs with McGrath slung over his shoulder. "Antal is the only man who will lead us to the real brains of this murder gang. I'm coming back for him."

CHAPTER XV

THE TRUCE

HELPLESS, McGRATH lapsed into silence. There were sounds of activity in front of the house now. Other police cars, drawn by the howling siren, had arrived. The Black Bat dashed down the cellar steps and discovered a sedan down there, headed straight toward one section of brick wall. He put McGrath into the front seat of the car, ran over to the wall and made a quick examination.

"Looks like the real thing," he said as he slid behind the wheel, "but it's only lightly put together for just such an emergency. Hang onto your hat, Mac. Here we go! I haven't time for Antal now, because he won't do me any good if those police arrest me."

The sedan shot forward just as Antal stumbled into the cellar. He saw the car crash through the wall as though it had been made of flimsy paper. Bricks toppled from masonry purposely put together with weak cement. The car ripped a vast hole through the wall, turned in the rear yard and headed down the driveway.

There were several shots, and shouts for the car to stop. Antal began running. He, too, went through that hole and vanished into the darkness before police could surround the place.

"Fine thing," McGrath grumbled as the sedan shot between the thin line of patrolmen. Bullets smacked against the bullet-proofed glass window. "Me, running from my own men. But you're head man, Bat. I'm in your hands and I don't qualify that statement at all."

"Thanks for having faith," the Black Bat answered.

"Hell!" McGrath snapped. "It's not that. My arms and legs won't move. Those wires cut off all circulation. Say, what siren was that anyhow? The boys didn't show for ten minutes after it started to wail."

The Black Bat chuckled. "I swiped a radio car, arranged the wiring to the dash clock and set it so that the siren would go off after I had time to slip into the house. It drew the guards away from the rear."

McGrath could not conceal his feelings.

"Nice work," he complimented. "And believe me I never thought I'd be handing out any compliments to the Black Bat."

The Black Bat lost any chance of pursuit, for this sedan had plenty of power under her bullet-dented hood. Finally he turned off the road and up a quiet lane. He stopped the car and doused the lights.

"Like a couple of sweethearts on Lover's Lane, Sergeant," he said gleefully. "But we'll talk instead of neck. You've got to be reasonable for the time being. We're in this together or I'd never have bothered to save you from Antal and his precious mob."

"It's a truce," McGrath agreed. "But it only lasts until we finish this talk, get me? After we part this time, I'll hunt you down, Bat. I'll track you down if I'm old and feeble when I finally land you. Go ahead—what do you want to know?"

The Black Bat rolled down a window. He regarded McGrath intently a moment. Then he said:

"We know an insurance murder ring is in operation. We know that a great number of people have been killed so their insurance could be collected. We know that Antal is first lieutenant for some warped-brained monster who wants to roll in wealth at the expense of as many human lives as becomes necessary. That's all—so far. Have you any ideas?"

McGRATH SHOOK his head.

"Nothing but a lot of suspicions that peter out every time we try to get something concrete."

"What about Dr. Luddy and Paradon, that shyster attorney?" the Black Bat asked.

McGrath emitted a whistle of surprise.

"So you did pay Dr. Luddy a visit! We thought he was off his track. I don't know about him. We once suspected he might be back of a big drug syndicate, but the Federal boys cleaned up the mess and there were no ties to Luddy. Paradon—I didn't even know he was interested, but that's something to work on. That guy would gyp his grandmother out of her admittance card to a home for the aged."

"What of Peter Galvin?" the Black Bat asked. "Has he been approached again? He was paid that policy and Antal certainly wanted to lay his hands on the check."

"He's staying under cover," McGrath said. "We've got four men posted around his house. If Antal shows there, he'll get his head blasted off. And is Galvin sore? Says we're interfering with his happy home life. Say, that guy hasn't had a happy home since he found out there were such things as blondes. And say, we found a torpedo named Collins in that house where you battled yesterday. He was shoved in a closet.

Somebody put a gun right against the back of his head and let him have it. Know anything about that?"

"Antal, Sergeant. He received his orders to kill him." The Black Bat sighed. "Our little conference has come to naught, Sergeant. I leave in your hands the guarding of Galvin and his family. We'll go back to town now and I'll drop off at a convenient spot."

McGrath was massaging his hands slowly. Without looking up, he spoke.

"Okay. But don't get any funny ideas that I'll stop trying to run you down. I'm grateful for the way you risked your neck to save mine. I—I guess I've never said that to anybody before. Just the same I mean it. And—I don't think you killed that hoodlum we found lashed to the cemetery fence. I don't think I ever believed it, but sometimes it helps a guy's ego along if he thinks the worst of his—er—enemies."

"I didn't kill him," the Black Bat said sincerely. "I left him there, tied, and with one of my calling cards pasted on his forehead. The man who murdered him also murdered Lew Scott, Assistant Coroner Crawford and Jim Fisher. He killed them so they wouldn't expose the operations of the insurance ring. Ralph Galvin's body was spirited away and a stranger put in his place. However, I know that young Galvin was poisoned—with arsenic. You slipped up there, Sergeant. One of the three men who were killed concealed an envelope with a tuft of hair snipped from Galvin's head. It showed that there was plenty of arsenic in his system."

"Hmmm," McGrath muttered. "So you're a chemist along with other things. Very well. We part when you say so and then the truce is over. I won't meet you under circumstances like these again because, after all, I am a law officer with an oath of office to uphold. You're a criminal—an outlaw."

The Black Bat laughed and nosed in to the curb.

"This is a nice desolate spot and not so far from civilization that you'll get flat feet in walking back. Also it will prevent you from contacting Headquarters and throwing out a dragnet for this car."

McGRATH GOT out.

"Thanks again," he said. "I'm grateful. Two minutes—two minutes hell—two seconds more and I'd have been dead. I still think you made a mistake in letting Antal go. He's bound to keep under cover from now on."

"Antal"—the Black Bat leaned out of the car a trifle—"will watch himself, but I happen to know that he will also show his fine hand soon.

He's got to, and I also know where he'll strike. Good night, Sergeant. And happy hunting for—the Black Bat."

In the rear view mirror the Black Bat saw McGrath start hiking, shaking his head from side to side like a sorely puzzled man. But the Black Bat had no notions about McGrath relaxing his vigilance. If anything, he would stick closer than ever to the Black Bat's trail....

Butch was impatiently waiting in the secret laboratory when the Black Bat reached his own home. He slipped out of his encompassing black clothing and donned his usual gray tweed trousers, his white shirt with a gay bow tie and the smoking jacket. He tamped a pipe full of tobacco, lit it and leaned back comfortably.

"What happened to McGrath?" Butch asked. "Didn't he put up an argument?"

"With the man who saved him from death?" The Black Bat laughed. "No, Butch, we had a truce, but it's ended now. He may even call here to see if Tony Quinn is home, but the signal will warn me if he or anyone else approaches."

Butch scowled. "I know McGrath's got a right to live, see? But he's out to get you. All we did was save him so he could keep on lookin'. But"—Butch's face lighted up—"did I have fun! Say, one of them bozos figured he could knock me cold with a right to the jaw. I just stuck out my chin and let him paste me. I didn't blink. But he did—when I banged his noggin against one of them fancy stairway posts. Busted it, I did—the post, I mean. What's next, chief?"

"Sleep for you, Butch. And don't get me wrong. Rescuing McGrath was the only decent thing we could have done. And it did provide me with something to chew on. Without knowing it, he gave me a tip. A meager one, but enough. We'll see if it grows to man-size before we sail in. Good night, Butch. Stand by for orders in the morning."

Butch ambled over to the hidden door like some well pleased Great Dane. He did not bother to use the ladder leading into the tunnel. He just jumped. After all, it was not more than two feet deeper than Butch's own hulk.

When he was gone, Quinn picked up his cane and went into the living room. He sat down and permitted that staring look to come over his eyes like a film. He was blind Tony Quinn again, the ex-district attorney who had been rendered wholly useless to the world by the cowardly actions of a gangster.

He was still seated there, intent on the problems circling through his mind when he heard a tapped signal on the other side of the secret door. He arose and walked over to a window. Suddenly he raised it and although any watcher would have believed a blind man was just trying to get a breath of fresh air, the Bat was listening intently.

The slightest movement in the brush, the faintest breathing of an excited person hidden in the darkness, would have warned him. Satisfied that no one lurked outside, he closed the window, locked it and drew the shade. Casually he repeated the performance with all the other curtains. Then he went to the laboratory door, opened it and took both of Carol's hands.

"I DON'T know what I'd do without you, Carol," he said simply. "When there is brain work to be done, I depend on you."

Carol smiled and pressed his hands warmly.

"You underestimate Silk, darling. He's doing a rather good job too. And Butch—why he's as faithful as any man can be. But listen to what I've discovered. I went to Mrs. Bannister's—and Tony, she's the nicest old lady I've ever met. That boy who is to be buried in the morning—she lived for him. It was an awful blow, but she is transferring her affections to another grandson—Newman Recor, his name is. Her daughter's boy. Not that she didn't love him before. That woman loves everyone."

"Listen, Carol," Quinn said quietly. "Have this in mind as you tell me what happened. Mrs. Bannister will inherit a large sum of money by reason of her grandson's death. Granted that she is well off already, some people don't know when to stop. Is she capable of planning murder for money?"

Carol's laugh warmed Quinn's heart. Laughter had gone out of his life before she entered it. He had lived in somber darkness until she came. Carol was like a tonic to him. His eyes, no longer filmed with the stare of the blind, told her this. She flushed just a little.

"Mrs. Bannister wouldn't kill a canary bird for a million dollars if she was starving to death. No, Tony, I give you my word that she is just as nice as she looks. But the grandson—Newman Recor. He is an undiluted heel."

Tony smiled. "I gather you don't like him. Who does he hang out with?"

"The only people who will have anything to do with him are those who want to profit by the spending money his grandmother gives him. Tony, I went to Mrs. Bannister and lied myself blue in the face. I hated to do it, but there was no other way and, after all, we are trying to help the poor old soul. I told her that her grandson, the one who is being buried in the morning, was in love with me and that we planned to be married. Do you know what she said?"

Quinn shook his head.

"That I could come and live with her, just as though we had been married."—Quinn lit Carol's cigarette.

"What I'm getting at is this, Carol," he said. "If Mrs. Bannister profited by her grandson's death and he was murdered—of which I'm reasonably certain—then someone else wants to cut in on her money. That can be done only through an intermediary. Now if this other grandson you've described inherits her estate and he is under the domination of the man behind this murder ring—well, we've got something to work on."

CAROL'S EYES grew wide in horror. "You mean they'll deliberately kill that nice old lady? They'll murder her just so that nit-wit of a grandson can get her money? Tony! No warm-blooded human being would do such a thing."

Quinn smiled crookedly.

"I'm not talking about warm-blooded, human beings, Carol. It's cold-blooded, merciless killers we're dealing with. Think! They've already killed thirty people that we know of so far. Would one more life make any difference? Not to them, and our aim is to stop them from carrying out their plans. Mrs. Bannister's fortune, increased largely by the insurance policies, would put them all on Easy Street, wind up their operations. She's a last resort, a final blow.

"But when they strike, we'll be waiting to take up some of the slack so Mrs. Bannister won't have to suffer. Phone Butch when you get back to your apartment. Tell him to join Silk and say they are to keep their eyes open. I'm making a little call about four A.M. when the going is clear. In the morning I'll prepare to outwit those killers and land them where they belong. In the electric chair."

CHAPTER XVI

SECRET OF THE RECORDINGS

DUMBLY QUINN helped Carol down the ladder. When she was gone, he called himself all kinds of a fool. He should have taken her in his arms and told her of the love that filled his heart. Yet—he couldn't. The Black Bat's career was too hazardous, and if he slipped back into the old routine of Tony Quinn, blind man, he would cheat her out of the best part of life. Out of youth and romance and love.

He looked in a mirror at the hideous scars burned deep in his face. Carol was used to them, or even she would flinch. He had seen men do it; men who did not know he could see. No, until the Black Bat's work was done Carol would be—just Carol. There was no solution to this problem.

Quinn stumbled back into the living room and rested until it was time for him to act again. Then he donned the black clothing of the Black Bat, slipped out of the house and made his way by devious routes to the spot where he had parked Butch's car when they had hijacked the police radio cruiser.

He drove through the business center of the city, now quiet and deserted, for it lacked only about two hours of dawn. Making sure that no patrolmen were in the vicinity, the Black Bat turned sharply and rolled down a delivery driveway to the rear of the Security Insurance Company's huge home office building.

Donning his hood he crept softly toward the service entrance. He got in easily, crouched in the darkness until he saw watchmen pass by on their rounds. Then he reached the stairway and went up it, making no more sound than a ghost.

He stopped in front of Ronald Tunick's private office, quietly forced an entrance and moved toward the big desk occupying one corner of the room. The fact that he needed no light in connection with his work helped greatly. Twice watchmen paced by the door without pausing. The Black Bat went to work swiftly. In one drawer which he skillfully unlocked, he discovered a sealed package, similar in size and with the same brand of wrapping paper that had been used for the bundle sent by Antal. He shook it, heard the muffled thump of a record cylinder and proceeded to open the package carefully.

Removing a record, he thrust it into his pocket, then made his way to the office of Tunick's private secretary. There he found a dictaphone machine. He appropriated a record which he placed in the package instead of the one he had found there, then retied the package deftly until only close examination would show that it had been tampered with.

He went through the papers in Tunick's desk, found a personal checkbook and discovered that Tunick was overdrawn almost five hundred dollars. A curt notice from the bank indicated that no more checks would be honored without a deposit.

Then, between the back pages of the checkbook, the Black Bat saw something that really made his eyes widen in surprise. It was a check, made out to Peter Galvin for two hundred and fifty thousand dollars covering payment of his son's insurance policy.

The Black Bat turned it over. The check had been endorsed in favor of Tunick—for value received. He drew a sharp breath. What was this check doing here? Had Galvin after all paid over the check as demanded by the insurance ring? If so—

The Black Bat replaced the check and arose. He walked softly to the door, listened a moment, and when he was certain that the way was clear he slipped out.

HE REACHED his car without incident and got behind the wheel. As he felt for the starter button, he suddenly froze. High up on the aide of the insurance company's building, a man was slowly being lowered from a window. He sat in what seemed to be a painter's chair. The descent was checked just outside what the Black Bat knew to be Tunick's private office. The man raised the window without any trouble and eased himself inside.

Ordinary sight would never have been able to follow the events of the next two or three minutes, but the penetrating power of the Black Bat's eyes enabled him to watch the intruder return to the window, stuffing a package into his shirt. Unquestionably it was the package containing the record that the Black Bat had left in place of the real one—which was now in the Bat's own pocket.

The man climbed into his precarious seat, waved a hand and was rapidly raised to another window two stories above Tunick's office. The Black Bat did not wait to see any more. There was no question in his mind but that underlings of the murder ring had maneuvered this stealthy bit of burglary.

The Black Bat did not want underlings, and he had an idea that the record which he had appropriated might provide a lead to the man behind this grim business. Also there was no time in which to attempt a roundup of the men in that building. The moment it was discovered that the record was a fake, the whole gang might swing into action.

Driving back home, the Black Bat parked the car in the usual place and in the security of his laboratory, he went to work. First of all he made a careful examination of the record, checking it especially for fingerprints. But he knew that Antal and the man who paid him were both clever enough not to leave such significant clues. He found nothing on the record.

Then he went into another room, carried a play-back machine into the sound-proof laboratory and inserted the record. He turned on the machine and groaned aloud as the melody of an old air greeted him. The music was as ancient as the tune. Just another one of Tunick's collections.

But the Black Bat's methods were amazing in detail. He was certain that this recording was a message of some sort. He placed it on the laboratory bench and lined up several standard dictaphone cylinders beside it. First of all, he compared the records. There seemed to be no appreciable difference until he weighed them. The one he had taken from Tunick's office was almost fifty grams heavier than the others.

He used a pair of fine calipers to measure the thickness of the records. Tunick's was thicker; only a matter of fractions, but bulkier nevertheless.

He took down text books and studied the composition of dictaphone records until he knew every process involved in their manufacture. Then he lit a Bunsen burner, held one of his own records in the flame for a second and nothing happened beyond a little smoke. He dared not risk their destruction by fire so he started an electric furnace and thrust the same record inside.

After five minutes he removed it with a pair of tongs. It was intact. Then he shoved Tunick's record into the furnace and through the glass window he saw an amazing transformation take place. The whole outside of the record seemed to melt and slide away like an orange peel. Quinn's breathing was fast as he fished the record out and wiped off the melted substance.

HE LET it cool and saw the tiny grooves inscribed on it by a recording machine. He knew now how Antal sent his messages without fear of detection. The real message was inscribed and overlaid with this substance similar to the record itself. Then the transcription of a genuine old record was put on it.

The man to whom the message was being sent had only to melt off the surface and play the recording underneath!

Quinn slipped the record on the machine, snapped the switch and Antal's raucous voice greeted him.

> I advertised, so directed, in the personal columns of the *Star-Chronicle* so you'd know I couldn't send these records through the usual source. One messenger, and his record, disappeared. I haven't been able to find out what happened, but I think the Black Bat had a hand in it. The record showed up today, mailed to the regular post-office box just as I'd sent it. Morgan picked it up on schedule and it was lifted in the usual manner, but the bus boy brought it to me because he figured it was a set-up. The

Black Bat is working hard and he's busted up plenty of my boys. However I have five new gorillas coming in from Philly tonight and we're set to play the trump card. Things are ready at the old lady's. The kid is ready to play and fell for our line like the sucker he is. We get him an alibi, snatch the old lady and dump her in the bay. We'll make it look as though she either knocked herself off or fell in the drink by accident. The kid inherits and we take him for all he gets. Then his lights go out. I'm having one of my boys put this record in Tunick's office, as you instructed. It'll be done after hours, but if Tunick should happen to blow in, he'll just think it came in the regular mail. At dawn we take the old lady and clean up. I took care of Collins all right, but I think it was a mistake. He wasn't a snitch and I can't figure what he knew to make him so dangerous.

The record ended and Quinn shut off the instrument. There were no windows in this laboratory and he hurried into the living room. Gray dawn was just filtering through the windows. Dawn! The zero hour when Mrs. Bannister was to be kidnaped and murdered!

Silk and Butch were on guard, true. But would they be able to stop the crime? Quinn had no time to lose. It would be highly dangerous for the Black Bat to operate by day, but this time he had no choice. The murder ring was depending on cleaning up after this job. The millions in it would put them all in the financial high brackets.

He left his hood off, but drew the soft hat well down over his face to hide the scars, grateful that it was still too early in the morning for the city to have awakened.

He drove straight to Mrs. Bannister's mansion home. As he rode by it, he saw no sign of Silk, nor of Butch. The Black Bat's heart almost ceased to beat. Either of them should have recognized the car and given a signal of their presence.

It meant but one thing to the Black Bat. Mrs. Bannister had been already snatched and Silk and Butch were either on the trail, or had been kidnaped too!

SILK, HIDDEN in the darkness outside Mrs. Bannister's home, had welcomed dawn with sheer relief. Butch was parked on the other side of the house and he, too, would be grateful for the gray light. Now it would be much easier to watch.

Silk stretched, yawned, and tried to work off the chill that had settled in his bones. Then he paused. A car had stopped half a block up the street and he saw indistinguishable forms slip through the gray dawn toward Mrs. Bannister's house. Silk drew a gun and snapped off the safety. But when he saw that there were four men, he held his fire.

Butch also saw the approaching men but, like Silk, he kept under cover. Not that either man bothered to think of his own danger. It was Mrs. Bannister of whom they thought. This mob would strike fast if things happened. Silk groaned and wished the Black Bat were at his side.

Two of the men, with guns in their hands, took up a position on the front porch, concealing themselves from the street by standing behind high shrubs. The other two, with the gaunt Antal in the lead, stepped up to the front door, used a key and entered.

They were gone about three or four minutes and when they emerged Antal held old Mrs. Bannister cradled in his arms. By the way her arms and legs sagged limply, Silk knew that she was unconscious.

A wave of hatred such as Silk had never before known surged up within him. He drew a bead on one of the gunmen, but wisdom overcame pure impulse. Shooting would only endanger Mrs. Bannister's life now. The best thing was to follow and watch for the slightest opening.

One of the crooks gave a low whistle. The car, parked up the street, rolled to the curb in front of the house. Half a minute later it pulled away. The kidnaping had been done quietly and expertly.

Silk did not hesitate for a second. Racing toward the rear of the house, he signaled Butch to hurry, and tried to open the garage doors. Huge staples, held with padlocks, prevented him.

Butch grunted, pushed Silk out of the way and seized one of the locks. He heaved, his mighty shoulders bringing every muscle into play. Gradually he pulled the big staples out of the wood. He opened the door. Silk nodded his thanks.

"Find the Bat," he told Butch in a whisper. "Tell him what's happened, and act fast. I'll follow the car. When I find out where they are taking Mrs. Bannister, I'll phone. Beat it!"

Butch moved away. Silk climbed into Newman Recor's flashy roadster and prayed that he would not awaken anyone in the house when he tramped on the starter. The motor responded smoothly. Silk shot out of the garage, turned right, and saw the kidnap car vanish around a corner five or six blocks up the street. Silk took the next turn, came out on an avenue and picked up the trail.

It took him well out of the city and gradually he realized they were heading for the harbor. Silk gulped and broke out into a cold sweat. It was easy enough to steal a car, but if they went aboard some seagoing craft, he would be in a tough spot. Silk did not know much about sailing and stealing a boat was a little beyond his depth.

When the sedan slowed, turned and entered a garage at the rear of a once exclusive yacht club, Silk stopped his own car and got out. He began running, veered to the left, and reached the end of a pier. From there he could see that a trim yacht was tied up to the dock in front of the yacht club.

"Steam up?" Antal emerged, calling. "Good! We sail in two minutes."

CHAPTER XVII

SILK IS TRAPPED

UNEASILY SILK realized that he would have no opportunity to warn the Black Bat. There were no phones around, and he had only two minutes anyway.

Stripping off his coat, he kicked off his shoes and lashed his gun around his neck with his tie. Extra cartridges were in his trouser pocket and he did not believe he would be in the water long enough to spoil them. Climbing down a ladder, he slipped into the water. Never a strong swimmer, Silk kept close to the docks.

As he neared the yacht, he dived and swam under water until he thought his lungs would burst. Then he bobbed up again and discovered that he was under the stern of the yacht. He seized a rope dangling overside and went up it like a monkey. There was no one on deck when he shoved his head over the rail. The crew was below, getting ready to sail.

Silk patted on bare feet across the deck, listened for a second at the companionway and when he heard nothing, he slipped down it, selected a cabin and hid in its narrow clothes closet.

Two or three minutes went by. He felt the ship tremble as engines throbbed. He heard voices and the sound of someone in the cabin. Silk pushed open the door a crack. Antal was placing Mrs. Bannister on the bed. Her wrists and ankles were taped with adhesive, but her eyes were open and shining in terror.

Antal strode toward the door.

"She'll keep," he growled. "One of you mugs stay outside this cabin and see that nobody gets in. We're heading out to sea until we're sure nobody is on our trail. I sort of have a feeling that house was being watched, and I'm taking no chances."

SILK SPENT the next five minutes in loading his cartridge clip with comparatively dry bullets. Then he crept into the cabin and tiptoed over to where Mrs. Bannister lay. Silk was in the same disguise he had assumed the day he had first encountered the old lady. She recognized him instantly and mild reproach shone in her eyes. Silk smiled at her reassuringly, bent down and put his lips against her ear.

"I'm not one of these crooks," he whispered. "I saw them take you and I followed. Don't be afraid! I'll get you out of this mess."

She moved her head up and down in a token of understanding. Silk snapped a bullet into the magazine of his gun and went back to his hiding place. After a few moments he heard the cabin door open and his heart pounded with excitement. A man was slowly advancing toward Mrs. Bannister, a glittering knife held high. On his face was a scowl and his eyes shone with the light of murder.

Silk slipped out of the closet, gun ready.

"Slow up!" he said softly. "Drop that knife or I'll drop you."

Then, to Silk's horror, the would-be killer, turned around with a broad grin. Silk sensed his danger, turned his head and groaned. Antal and two of his men were crowded in the doorway, guns covering Silk. He had walked into a well planned trap!

Antal strode forward. He wrenched the gun out of Silk's grasp and whipped him across the face with it.

"Of all the saps!" he exulted. "You swim out here, crawl on deck, and forget all about the nice trail of water you left behind. I figured you'd be hiding in here and you'd maybe be armed, so I framed this phony bump-off with a knife, because I knew it would draw you out. Now you'll go into the drink with the old lady. Only they'll find her floating around, and they won't find you because I'll put enough weights on your legs so you'll stand on the bottom of the ocean until you rot."

Silk said nothing. A little blood oozed out of the corner of his mouth from a badly cracked lip. The left side of his face was swelling rapidly as a result of the cowardly blow Antal had administered.

All he prayed for was one chance to take Antal by surprise. If he only could, Silk promised himself he would dispose of the gaunt, evil-faced killer for good.

Two of the crooks bound Silk hand and foot. He was flung on the floor and left there.

"Mr. Smith," a feeble voice called. "Mr. Smith."

Silk turned his head. He recalled that he had given Mrs. Bannister that name. She was looking at him sadly, but without a trace of fear.

"They are going to kill us, aren't they? You shouldn't have tried to protect me. I'm an old woman. Dying isn't so hard for me."

"We're not dead yet," Silk said savagely. "Something will happen. It's bound to."

But in his own mind Silk felt sure that they were both doomed. How could help reach them? No one knew where they were headed except Antal and possibly the captain of this yacht.

MRS. BANNISTER sighed in despair.

"I—I don't know what to think, Mr. Smith," she said tremulously. "My grandson's funeral is this morning. I can't understand why they took me away. If it's ransom they want, why don't they say so? I haven't much cash—my holdings are tied up in bonds—but I'll pay all I can."

Silk turned his head away. He did not want her to see his face for Silk realized what it all meant. There would be no ransom; not when they could murder her as easily as they could a two-day-old kitten. With her death proved, after her body was discovered, Newman Recor, her precious grandson, would come into the insurance money and the rest of her estate, and from him it would swiftly pass into the hands of whoever had directed this mad scheme.

Time dragged past. Then the cabin door opened. Two men stepped in. Both of them held rusty chains. They let them fall to the floor with a crash. Antal ambled into the cabin and eyed Silk with a fishy stare.

"I don't know what your angle in this business happens to be," he snarled, "and I don't care. Maybe you're a private detective set to guard the old woman; maybe you're from the police, or are a stooge for the Black Bat. I know you ain't the Black Bat because he's a bigger guy than you. Anyway, what's the difference? You're going overboard.... Boys, drape them chains on his ankles and let's get started. There's a thick fog that will hide anything we do. Damned lucky we sailed into it."

Silk was turned over on his stomach. The chains were passed around the rope that lashed his ankles tight. He did not dare glance over to the bed on which Mrs. Bannister lay. It was tough enough dying, without seeing the agonized expression that was bound to flood her wrinkled features.

Silk was dragged up on deck. Distantly he heard a ship's whistle hoot dismally as it sounded its way through the dense fog. The yacht was stopped and was drifting, her motors silent. Then a piercing shriek cut the fog—the high-pitched whirr of a siren aboard a police launch.

Antal turned pale.

"Dump this guy over! Hurry! Then heave the old lady into the drink. Me and the boys will take the launch back to shore. You members of the crew stick. Say Mrs. Bannister jumped overboard. Say she took a dive in the drink before you could stop her. Got all that?"

The man in the uniform of the captain nodded curtly.

"They'll never get wise," he mumbled. "And don't use the motor of the launch. Put those huskies of yours at the oars and muffle them with your coats. If the police hear you paddling, they may try to spot you. And you better hope this fog don't lift. I'll take care of all the rest of it."

Antal gave Silk a painful kick in the ribs. He motioned toward his men.

"Heave him over, then get the old lady. Snap it up!"

NEWMAN RECOR was about twenty-two, pasty-faced, underweight and plenty worried. He tossed uneasily in his sleep and finally opened his eyes. At that moment a hand dropped on his shoulder and the business end of a gun was centered over his heart. But it was not the gun that made Recor's heart crawl in terror. It was the man behind the gun.

"The—the Black Bat!" he gasped hoarsely. "Wh-what do you want?"

"Talk in a low voice," the Black Bat ordered. "No one knows I am here. Neither is anyone aware that your grandmother has been kidnaped. She was chloroformed. I found evidence of that in her room. You are the one person who will profit by her death. You know who kidnaped her and where she is to be taken. Speak—you weak-kneed little toad! Where is she?"

"I—I don't know what you're talking about!" Recor gulped. "Did—did you say she was kidnaped?"

"Listen!" the Black Bat said with a trace of a snarl in his voice. "You know what's happened. Well, I also know one way to prevent men like Antal from cashing in on your grandmother's death. They intend to collect from you. If you're dead, your grandmother's estate will be disposed of to various distant relatives. In that way Antal and his mob will get nothing. So I could outwit him by killing you."

"No!" Recor cried. "No—don't kill me. I'll tell you what I know. They aren't going to kill her. Just take her to an island where she'll be safe until after I can get some of the estate. Everything is fixed for me to clean up quickly. Paradon—"

Recor's features went bleak at that slip of the tongue.

Paradon, was it? The Black Bat grimly decided that Paradon was going to have an opportunity to use his gift of gab in convincing the Black Bat of his integrity.

"Where is that island?" the Black Bat snapped. "What pier do they sail from and in what craft?"

"Roscoe Bleecher's yacht," Recor gulped. "He's away and the crew has been bribed. My grandmother has Mr. Bleecher's permission to use his yacht, and they're going to say she went for a sail and fell overboard. But she won't be harmed. They promised me that."

"They're going to murder her," the Black Bat said stonily, "and make you the sucker. Can't you see, you stupid fool? By having knowledge of this mess you'll be guilty of murder as much as they are. They'll have you more under their thumbs than ever before. They'll bleed you of the entire estate. Now get up—walk over to that desk and draw me a map of the location of this island. Also write a description of that yacht. Hurry! We haven't much time."

A significant nudge of the gun and Recor jumped out of bed. Hastily he drew a crude map showing the location of the island, and scribbled a short description of the yacht.

The Black Bat swept up the piece of paper, stood before Recor a moment and delivered an unvarnished opinion of cowards. Then he stepped out the door, ran through the house and out into the rear of the estate. He cut through several other yards and reached his coupé.

There was someone inside. The Black Bat whipped out a gun. He moved closer, finger tight against the trigger. There was no time to be lost now. He would brook no interference from anyone, including Detective-sergeant McGrath.

BUT IT was Butch who waited in the car. Butch, clasping and unclasping his hands, heedless of the perspiration that dropped down his face.

"Boss!" he choked. "I thought you was never gonna show up! We musta crossed. I went to the house lookin' for you. Listen—Silk is tailin' Antal. He snatched the old lady. Silk said he'd call, but there ain't nobody to get his call now. I dunno what to do."

The Black Bat hauled out the map which Recor had drawn. It was crude enough to be almost undecipherable. He took a pencil from Butch's pocket and hastily wrote clearer directions.

"Take this," he instructed Butch. "Get it into Sergeant McGrath's hands as soon as possible, and without showing yourself. I've asked his help for the first time, but it's necessary now, for we must, to save Mrs. Bannister's life. He'll mobilize the harbor police and the coast-guard cutters. We'll need every boat available to shove off and find the yacht before those devils murder her. Get going!"

CHAPTER XVIII

MURDER ON THE HIGH SEAS

NODDING, BUTCH jumped out of the car and lumbered up the street. He hailed a taxi when he hit a main thoroughfare and was driven to the vicinity of Detective-sergeant McGrath's home.

Butch realized that if he showed himself, and McGrath got a good look at him that he would be of little use to the Black Bat from then on. For McGrath would center all his attentions on running down Butch. Therefore he resorted to the only means he could devise to warn McGrath and at the same time remain anonymous.

Creeping around to the side of the suburban bungalow, he found the window to McGrath's bedroom, and hastily tied the message to a huge stone. He backed up, flung the rock accurately and sped away as it smashed through the window.

The Black Bat, meanwhile drove to the dock where the yacht of Roscoe Bleacher, the wealthy sportsman, was usually tied up. He expected to see no trace of it and was not surprised to find it gone.

Looking around for some means of taking to the sea himself, he noted a private yacht club up the river a short distance. The Black Bat parked his car near the club, raced down the pier and quickly selected the fastest craft he could find—a sleek, high-powered racing boat, as swift a craft as rode any sea.

A watchman saw him, yelled an order for him to stop, but the Black Bat had the motor sputtering before the guard could open fire on him. He gave her the gun and the prow of the little craft rose up out of the water while her motor hummed smoothly.

He let the craft out, heading down the river. A dense fog was closing in and the Black Bat swore softly. Fog would protect the murderers and hamper him and the police. That is, if McGrath acted in accordance with that written message—which he hoped the sergeant would.

GRADUALLY THE fog closed in, deeper, more clinging. Then the shore was only a vague line. The Black Bat was far out now, and if the sea became rough, he would have a difficult time of it with this small craft.

Then he saw a vessel ahead—a trim white and brown yacht which he identified instantly as Bleecher's. He had only a glimpse of it before the fog closed down, hiding it from his sight. He heard a distant, dismal wail and then a high-pitched siren.

The Black Bat's jaws snapped shut with a click. McGrath had certainly lost no time. The police were closing in, too. This was going to be the riskiest assignment the Black Bat had ever encountered, for he would be caught between two fires—the police and the crooks.

The Black Bat cut off his motors suddenly. The momentum of his speed kept the small boat racing along until the bulk of the yacht loomed up. Dimly he made out several forms on deck. They were swinging an object, preparatory to hurling it overside. In a flash the Bat was on his feet, stripping off his hood, kicking off his shoes. Then he was diving into the sea, swimming with long, muscle-wrenching strokes.

There was a sinister splash about a dozen yards away. The Black Bat took a long breath and dived after it. He saw a murky object heading for the bottom. The Black Bat went after it like a fish, reached out and gripped the object firmly. Then he saw that the object was a man, and that heavy chains held him in a death embrace.

While his lungs clamored for air, the Black Bat went to work. Even as he and the man were heading fast for bottom he had a knife out, slashing at the ankle ropes. The chains came loose. The Black Bat and the man he had gripped began rising swiftly. As their heads cut the water, the Black Bat saw whom he had saved.

"Silk!" he sputtered. "Are you all right?"

Silk spat a mouthful of water.

"Ye—Yes!" Then he screeched: "Mrs. Bannister! They're throwing her over too! She can't swim."

"You can," the Black Bat panted. "There's a little speedboat somewhere in this fog. Find it and have her set to run for it."

The Black Bat clapped Silk on the shoulder, veered and began swimming back toward the yacht. Those aboard had no knowledge that Silk had been rescued. The thickness of the pea soup fog had kept that fact from them.

The Black Bat heard a scream that was suddenly muffled as though a giant hand had slapped across the victim's mouth. There was a splash. Something white hit the water and began to sink. The Black Bat dived again. In half a minute he had reached the side of the old lady. She was unconscious, probably from a brutal knockout punch. The Black Bat carried her to the surface, pillowed her head in the crook of an arm and floated, waiting for Silk to appear.

The yacht was getting under way again. He heard muttered oaths, then the sound of clumsily handled oars. The Black Bat had a vague glimpse of a speed launch. Antal and his band of cutthroats were deserting the yacht, leaving it to the crew to explain what had happened.

A hoarse voice bellowed an order for the yacht to heave to. Then a machine-gun spattered the fog in a grim warning that the order was to be obeyed.

DRIFTING WITH the racing boat, Silk saw the Black Bat, with his burden, through the fog and came alongside. He helped take Mrs. Bannister aboard. The Black Bat clambered over the gunwale and quickly drew on his wet mask. He placed the old lady in a comfortable position and felt her pulse. It was none too strong.

"Full speed!" he called to Silk. "We've got to get this poor woman to a warm place. That will be up to you when we get ashore. I'll pilot this craft back to the pier where I stole it. My car is parked nearby and I'll try to reach it or lay low until darkness."

"But where will I take her?" Silk asked.

"To Carol's apartment. She's unconscious and she'll remain so for some time. Freshen your disguise, tell her it's your home, but don't tell her the address, and keep her in one of the back rooms where she won't be able to see the street. I'll be along as quickly as I can."

Silk swept the craft toward shore.

"But won't her people worry about her?" he asked.

The Black Bat's fists clenched.

"That's exactly what I want them to do. One person in particular...."

Almost two hours later the Black Bat entered his home through the secret tunnel. He found Silk smiling and happy.

"Mrs. Bannister is coming along fine," he reported. "I gave her a hot drink and Carol put her to bed. She thinks Carol is my sister, sir. She doesn't know where she is."

"Find me dry clothes."

Tony Quinn had stripped off the mask and hood. The last hour had been a precarious one for he had been forced to drive through traffic and take his chances on being stopped.

Silk got the clothing quickly—duplicates of the black outfit which Quinn stripped off. Quinn accepted a drink of brandy gratefully, downed it in easy stages and studied his problem from every angle.

"We're nearing the end of someone's rope," he told Silk. "The only trouble is direct evidence. There isn't any, and no chance to uncover any, it begins to look like. I've one ace in the hole, but it may turn into a deuce. We've got to consider several people. Take Tunick, for instance. Those recordings are mailed to him. He collects old phonograph records, which are similar to the modern dictaphone records. He even advertises for them.

"He may be doing all this just to be able to get the messages that Antal sends to his employer. Then Morgan picks up the records at the post-office. Makes a practice of it. They are taken from him by stealth, but perhaps he knows this. Perhaps he sets the stage so they can be taken easily."

"I understand that." Silk frowned. "But what's the idea of them in the first place?"

"The leader of this insurance ring doesn't even admit his identity to his own men," Quinn explained. "I'm betting that Antal has no idea for whom he works. The loot is probably held in some safe place or shipped to the leader of the mob by some method as roundabout as they use for their messages. The head man can conceal his true voice and make no actual contact with his men. He's playing safe, Silk."

"What about this Dr. Luddy? He tried to band you a doublecross and anybody on the level would have worked with you."

TONY QUINN rubbed his chin thoughtfully.

"It's puzzled me, that angle. And his calling in Paradon looks funny too. We also have to consider everyone else connected with the case. Mrs. Bannister, her grandson Recor, and even Peter Galvin. There is so much at stake in this game that the most innocent person may prove to be the blackest."

Silk was facing a mirror and peeling off his disguise.

"What about grilling young Recor, sir? He must know something."

Quinn tapped his fingertips together thoughtfully.

"There is something else, Silk. Do this as soon as you are out of disguise. Take a cab, got to the offices of the *Star-Chronicle* and get me copies of each issue for the past two weeks. On your way back, tell Carol to leave Mrs. Bannister alone at eight o'clock. I'm going to call on her. She'll be able to stand the shock of seeing a masked man, won't she?"

Silk nodded. "That lady is tough—real pioneer stuff, sir. All she feels bad about is missing her grandson's funeral. I'll go directly, sir."

After Silk returned with a sheaf of newspapers, Quinn spent an hour reading the "Personal" columns and carefully checked the items. His lips parted in a slow smile as he inserted a fresh dictaphone record on his machine. He picked up the mouthpiece and began talking in a mechanical, disguised voice. This done, he carefully wrapped the recording, addressed it and called in Silk.

"There is still time to make the late editions of the *Star-Chronicle*," he told Silk. "Insert this ad for immediate publication. Then deliver this package. Meanwhile I'll pay Mrs. Bannister a visit."

An hour later Mrs. Bannister started up in amazement when she saw the somber black-hooded man silently move before her range of vision.

"Please"—he held his hand toward her—"I'm not here to harm you, Mrs. Bannister. People call me the Black Bat. I assure you I mean only to help."

She relaxed and heaved a great sigh.

"I—I've been through so much today, without really understanding what it was all about, that you did frighten me. But I'm not afraid of you. I can see your eyes through that mask. They are honest eyes and your voice has a ring of quality. How can you help me?"

The Black Bat sat down on the edge of the bed.

"AN ATTEMPT was made to murder you today. Your grandson was killed in an accident only a short time ago. He was heavily insured. I have reason to believe that you were to be murdered so that the insurance on your grandson's life would go to your other grandson, Newman Recor."

"All very true so far," she agreed. "What's next?"

"Your living grandson has not had the best of companions. I believe he is under the domination of someone who has forced him to abet this kidnaping of you."

"Then you think my own grandson wanted to have me murdered?" she asked incredulously. "Nonsense! It's not true!"

The Black Bat bowed his head slightly.

"He might have believed you were only to be held temporarily, Mrs. Bannister. I'll tell you this much—he certainly aided me in finding you. Tell me, how much insurance was involved? What assets have you that are easily convertible?"

Mrs. Bannister leaned back and smiled.

"You'll be as surprised as the next man. I'm supposed to be fairly well off. I am—on paper. In actual cash I have only enough to live on—very well of course—but I can't throw my money away. My grandson was insured for almost half a million dollars."

Galvin lowered his hands a trifle and Antal snarled a warning.

"And all of it with the Securities Insurance Company?" the Black Bat persisted.

Mrs. Bannister smiled. "Why not? I own half that company. My husband bought into it years ago. I've watched it grow from a small concern into one of the finest in the world. I don't publicize the fact that my only assets lie right in that company."

The Black Bat's eyes glittered. He arose.

"Thank you, Mrs. Bannister. You are in quite safe hands now and I suggest that you remain here until we have captured the man or men responsible for your narrow escape with death. Until we do that, your life will be endangered."

"I'll stay," she said. "I like it here. Most comfortable house I've ever been in, except for my own. And that Mr. Smith is so kind to me. Then the charming girl who says he is his sister, and isn't. They think they're fooling me. Well they're not. Neither are you, crawling in through a window when you could have used the door as well as not."

The Black Bat's lips twisted into a grin. No wonder Silk had been smitten with this old lady. She was astute, keen-eyed and wholly lovable.

"You're guessing badly, Mrs. Bannister," he told her softly. "But I'm glad you'll stay. Perhaps in a few hours it will be quite safe for you to go home."

She sat up, very erect.

"Young man, that mask doesn't deceive me for one minute. Oh, I don't know who you are, I'll admit, but you are honest and I trust you. There is one favor—please?"

He nodded. "Anything."

She leaned forward and spoke in a confidential whisper to the Black Bat.

"When you meet that awful skinny man they call Antal, slug him for me. He almost broke my jaw."

She sank back and watched the Black Bat step to the window and vanish as completely as a summer breeze. Her eyes sparkled.

"Remarkable young man. He'll teach that worthless grandson of mine a few manners too." Then she closed her eyes slowly and added fervently, "I hope."

CHAPTER XIX

THE CHASE CLOSES IN

EATING HIS hasty meal, Tony Quinn glanced through the other late evening newspapers that Silk had brought him. Silk took care that all curtains were drawn so that no one might observe a blind man avidly perusing the newspapers.

The evening editions told of Detective-sergeant McGrath's quick work in sending out harbor police launches and coast guard cutters to stop the yacht. The crew maintained that Mrs. Bannister had either fallen or jumped overboard before the yacht hove to after being signaled by a police boat. But Mrs. Bannister's body had not been found yet, though a thorough search had been in progress all day.

Commissioner Warner indicated that five new cases of murder for profit had been uncovered, all of the insured covered by Tunick's Security Insurance Company. There was a boxed item indicating that a meeting of the board of directors of the company was scheduled for this evening and the outlook was for a complete reorganization of the firm. Quinn scanned the list of directors and he gave a short gasp.

Dr. Lawrence Luddy was one of the more prominent members!

At ten o'clock, Silk, well disguised, ambled into the lobby of the insurance company building, took the elevator to the tenth floor and walked down six flights. He had a good look at the office two stories above Tunick's private office. He hurried back to the tenth floor, rang for the elevator and descended. The Bat was waiting in a car parked along a quiet, dark street.

"I got it, sir," Silk reported breathlessly. "And what a lead it's turned out to be. The office you said that guy on a bos'n's chair swung out of, to go down and get into Tunick's office, is rented to Attorney Paradon. His name is on the door in nice, new letters."

"Paradon," the Black Bat reflected. "Then he is in on it. Luddy must be too. But he has a reason, being a director of the company. What on earth are they after?"

"That's easy, sir," Silk broke in. "They're behind it all. They engineer these killings and they get the profits."

The Black Bat shook his head slowly.

"Wrong that time, Silk. They are mixed up somehow, but they didn't hire Antal or direct these murders. I know who did that."

"You—know?" Silk gulped. "But who? How do you know? How did you find out?"

"There is no time for explanations now. Silk, here is your detail. You are in the same disguise as when you met Mrs. Bannister. She is certain to have told Recor, her grandson, what you looked like when you first met her. He'll readily believe you are just one of the mob if you hand out a line with your customary skill.

"Go to the Bannister home. See Recor and tell him he's got to start getting things ready for the big pay-off. Tell him his grandmother is dead and they'll find the body when Antal gets good and ready to have them discover it. Rub it in—be as tough as you can. Say that unless he delivers on the line and within twenty-four hours he'll take the rap. And remind him he is just as guilty of his grandmother's murder as any other member of the gang."

"But he couldn't lay his hands on that estate so quick," Silk protested. "She can't be declared legally dead until they find the body, or a number of years pass by."

QUINN SHOOK his head.

"Recor won't think of that. Not if I have him properly catalogued. He'll go into a rage. Better have a gun ready, but don't hurt him. I want that boy aroused until he's prepared for anything. It's important."

"Yes, sir," Silk answered. "Shall I walk, or will I drop you off somewhere and go on with the car?"

"Drop me off near Galvin's home," the Black Bat ordered. "That's where the show-down will take place."

Silk started the car.

"I'm beginning to get it, sir. Galvin has had two hundred and fifty thousand dollars paid him on his son's insurance policy. Antal and his boss want it. They'll grab some other member of the family and force him to pay. But how are you so sure it will happen tonight?"

"Because," the Black Bat said, with a slow smile, "I've planned it that way."

Silk dropped him close to Galvin's home. Then he sped away to fulfill his part of the game.

The Black Bat, hood in place, guns ready, made his way across yards until he was at the rear of Galvin's home. He prowled around until he was certain no one else had the house under observation. Then he vanished in the darkness to await developments.

They came within thirty minutes. The Black Bat's supersensitive eyes caught a glimpse of a shadowy form slinking toward the rear door. As the intruder approached, the Black Bat recognized Antal. The gaunt killer had a heavy revolver in his fist and the look on his face spelled murder. Antal was coming to collect his cut, or else.

Antal moved along beneath a window, raised his head a few inches and peered inside. The Black Bat heard the hammer of the killer's revolver draw back with a click. Then Antal drew the brim of his hat way down, squared his bony shoulders and advanced toward the back door.

The Black Bat crept forward, slipping one of his automatics out of its holster. If Antal meant business, so did the Black Bat. At this stage of the game mistakes would be forever unalterable.

Then a car door banged on the street. Antal ducked hastily, ran several yards from the house and made his way forward to see if the callers were headed for Galvin's home. The Black Bat went too, but only to a point where his eyes could penetrate the darkness and make out the features of the three men who walked up the path to the front door.

Ronald Tunick, president of the Security Insurance Company was in the lead. His shoulders drooped, his face bore the resigned look of a defeated man. Behind him, aggressive and cocksure, were Dr. Lawrence Luddy and Paradon, the shyster attorney.

Paradon rang the bell with his cane. The door opened and Galvin appeared. Apparently he had been preparing to go out or had just come in, for he wore hat and coat.

"Come in, gentlemen," he said politely. "We'll have a drink and then discuss our business. My family is out of town. We'll be quite alone. I sent for you so we might have a final showdown on this ghastly business."

Suddenly Antal burst from his hiding place behind the hedge. His gun covered the quartette and his voice was a snarl of hatred.

"Yeah," he ground out bitterly, "let's go in and talk it over! I'm cutting myself in on this deal, too. I'm a smart guy, understand? I know what's going on and if one of you squawks, I'll drill him. Move!"

THEY WENT into the house too fast for the Black Bat to swing into action. The door slammed and he heard a burglar chain slip into place. He had a glimpse of the men as they passed by a window with a drawn shade. Antal still held all the cards and he was playing his hand cunningly.

The Black Bat ran lightly to the rear of the house and approached the back door. It was locked and he reasoned that if the front door was supplied with a burglar chain, the back door would be similarly equipped. And the Black Bat had no tools to overcome that difficulty.

He tested windows, found them all locked. He could not simply break into one of them for Antal, forewarned, would open fire without even caring who might be on the way to interrupt the party.

There was one other method, barring the risky idea of climbing a tree and trying to jump through mid-air and grasp one of the second-story windows. For there were no convenient porch roofs to this house.

The Black Bat ran swiftly to the cellar hatchway, raised the cover and dropped it in place after him. The intense gloom that shrouded the tiny cellarway only served to make things clearer for the Black Bat. He saw the cheap lock on the cellar door. From his kit of miniature tools, he took a tiny pair of pliers, inserted them into the keyhole and grasped the key on the other side of the door. By applying pressure and firmly turning the key the bolt slid back. He swung the door wide, stepped into the cellar proper and heard angry, muffled voices above him.

The stairway to the first floor loomed up and he climbed it, blessing the silence that his crepe soled shoes lent him. Noiselessly opening the door at the top of the steps, he slipped into the hallway and edging his way along the wall until he reached the heavy portieres decorating the door to the room where the men were assembled.

He drew one curtain away until he could peer into the room. Paradon and Tunick sat on a leather davenport, their hands resting on their thighs. Dr. Luddy occupied an overstuffed chair that all but swallowed him. Galvin, white and so obviously shaken that he had forgotten to remove his hat or coat, was seated behind a desk, his back toward the Black Bat. Antal menaced all of them, but most of his attention was on Galvin.

"This time," Antal was thundering, "I'm going outa here with plenty of dough. Galvin, you got paid off. Two hundred and fifty grand. We damned near got it, and if the Black Bat hadn't stuck his nose into my affairs, you'da paid it over without a squawk. Well, pay it over now!"

"But I haven't got a quarter of a million dollars in cash," Galvin quavered. "I—I can't possibly pay you."

"No?" Antal shouted. "Well I got some private dope, understand? I know you got that dough here—in cold cash too. You wanta get a slug in your kneecap—just for a starter? Come on! Get that money out and hand it over."

Galvin's hands shook violently. He lowered them a trifle and Antal snarled a warning. Galvin made a despairing gesture.

"But—but the money—it's in my desk. How can I get it if you won't let me?"

"Okay," Antal snapped. "Get it, and remember I'm watching you every second. One phony play and I'll drill you through the head. Get busy!"

TOSSING ASIDE his hat and coat, Galvin crossed the room and slowly pulled out the desk drawer. From his position near the door, the Black Bat caught the gleam of a gun just under Galvin's outstretched hand. Galvin was going to shoot it out. The Black Bat's own weapon came up and he drew a precise bead on Antal's head.

Suddenly Galvin thrust his hand into the drawer. It moved as fast as the tongue of a serpent. There was an explosion. Antal's weapon went off, but as he fired Galvin had slipped out of the chair and sought protection behind the desk.

Antal, his tall, gaunt frame erect as a ramrod, pivoted very deliberately, like a soldier going through his drill in slow motion. Then he uttered a long-drawn-out sigh and toppled over like a tall chimney with its base blasted out with dynamite.

Galvin arose, gun still smoking in his fist. He mopped his forehead with a handkerchief and sank back into his chair. Dr. Luddy hurried over to where Antal had fallen. When he straightened up, his face was grave.

"Dead. You got him right between the eyes, Galvin. That was a good piece of work. Anybody know who this gunman was?"

Galvin nodded. "Yes—yes. I know him. My daughter Elaine described him, and he matches the description perfectly. He is the man who kidnaped her, held her while I was being bled out of the money Tunick paid me for my son's insurance coverage. I—I don't feel very well, gentlemen. This has been an exhausting experience. I—I'm glad he's dead. He mistreated Elaine—starved her. I'm sure he meant to murder her after I paid him the money."

"And you know what I think?" Paradon broke in. "He also killed your son. He had him insured first, then he murdered him so you'd collect the insurance and he could get it from you with more murder."

Dr. Luddy swung on Tunick.

"Now I'll tell you what I think. You're behind it all, Tunick. You, the president of the Security Insurance Company, hired this killer. Retained him to commit murder so your company would pay off. Your pet agent, Morgan, wrote the policies, faked them too, I'm wagering. He used doubles for the medical examinations. Then, after a short time, your hired assassins did their bit. You knew to whom and when those policies would be paid. You knew when to strike."

Tunick heaved a vast sigh and leaned back against the cushions of the davenport.

"Gentlemen," he said, "tonight I'm a ruined man. The insurance company I helped to build is no longer mine. I signed my resignation as president and withdrew from the board of directors. However, I'll be damned if I'll admit engineering these murders. You have to call in the police to account for the death of this crook. Call them in—make your accusations before them. If they believe you, I'll surrender. I can't fight or argue tonight. I tell you I'm on the verge of a breakdown!"

Paradon picked up the telephone. He eyed Galvin.

"Keep Tunick covered," he said. "I'll get the police here and let them learn what we've discovered. That's why we brought you here, Tunick—to show you up, make you confess. If there was any way we could have kept the facts from the public, we would have done so. This will completely ruin the Security Insurance Company. We'll have canceled contracts, lapsed policies and no new business at all. Tonight I became a director of the firm. I wanted to maintain the reputation of the company—but I see now how wrong I've been. You can't circumvent murder."

He dialed the police and gave them a terse message. Then he hung up with a bang. Galvin, the gun shaking slightly, kept it trained on Tunick.

Suddenly every light in the house winked out.

CHAPTER XX

ALL THE CARDS— FACE DOWN

BREAKING INTO the sudden silence there was a sound of a scuffle in the middle of the room. Then the shadowy form of a man began running madly. Running as if death was at his heels.

There was an explosion. The shadowy figure uttered a shrill screech of pain, but went on. He reached the front door, tried to open it, but the burglar chain blocked him. He whirled and, despite his wounds, ran up the staircase to the second floor.

"Galvin!" Dr. Luddy's voice was hoarse with excitement. "Shoot him! Get him!"

The indistinct form reached the top of the steps and for a second was silhouetted against the two windows at the landing. A gun blasted. The shadowy form stopped dead, sagged against the window, then slowly sank to the floor.

A siren howled outside. Heavy footsteps announced the arrival of the police.

Sergeant McGrath was the first through the door. At his heels came Commissioner Warner. Someone went down cellar and replaced a blown out fuse. The lights came on. Galvin, still clutching the gun, surrendered it eagerly to McGrath's outstretched hand. Paradon ran up the stairs and looked at the man lying there; looked, without touching him. He saw blood on the man's face and that was enough. He descended the steps slowly.

"He's dead all right. No question about it. You got him through the head, Galvin—just as you got that other one."

"Other one?" McGrath yelled. "What's going on here? Mass murder?"

Galvin sighed. "Not murder, Officer. I shot in self defense and there are two witnesses—Attorney Paradon and Dr. Luddy. The man in the other room is named Antal. He kidnaped my daughter and came back here tonight trying to get money out of me at the point of a gun."

"If it's Antal," McGrath said, "nobody will blame you much, Galvin. Who is the guy at the top of the steps?"

"Tunick—Ronald Tunick, president of the Security Insurance Company. Paradon, Dr. Luddy and I had evidence enough to send him to the chair. Somehow the lights went out and he broke for it. I—I shot him down. After all, he was responsible for the death of my son."

Commissioner Warner took charge. He herded everyone into the spacious living room and took the center of the floor himself.

"Now I'd like an explanation," he said. "You three men indicate that Tunick was the leader of the murder-for-insurance ring. Can you prove it?"

Paradon jumped to his feet.

"We have absolute evidence, Commissioner! We suspected this for a long time. I rented an office above Tunick's. Tunick claimed to be a collector of old phonograph records. He received many of them through the mail. We suspected that some of those were more than they seemed. Last night I took my life in my hands and Dr. Luddy lowered me two floors from my own office, so I might invade Tunick's. I selected that method so there would be no clues to show I had been there. If I was wrong, I wanted to be sure before I called in the police.

"Well, I found a record on Tunick's desk. It was neatly packaged, but I knew what to look for. That record is now in my office safe. It was from this man, Antal, who lies dead at your feet. It gave Tunick instructions that he was to prepare the loot for a cut. Isn't that evidence enough? With Tunick's final move in trying to escape? That was the act of a guilty man."

COMMISSIONER WARNER signaled McGrath. The detective-sergeant gave soft orders to the men in the hallway. Two of them entered the room and took up positions near the front window.

"If Tunick was the guilty man, as you indicate," Warner said softly, "how is it that a young man named Newman Recor came to my office a few moments ago and told me a weird story about the murder of his grandmother? She was Mrs. Bannister, if that enlightens you. Recor states that he was forced to help in this murder, and that he doesn't believe Tunick was behind the killers. He told me that he—"

Warner ceased speaking abruptly. His eyes were wide, his mouth slightly open. Against the further wall was the huge image of a bat! It seemed to have poised in flight and become an unflickering design on the wall. Warner turned around slowly. The others, aware of a new presence, turned too.

The Black Bat stood just inside a window. Two guns were in his hands and the eyes behind the mask glittered brilliantly.

"If each of you will remain exactly as he is now, no one will be hurt. Sergeant McGrath, you might pass the word to your men in the hallway that if they try to open fire, I shall be forced to shoot, much as I dislike doing so."

Galvin stepped forward.

"This man is the Black Bat," he said. "He may be wanted by the police, but I classify him as a friend. He saved my daughter's life."

Commissioner Warner stepped forward a pace.

"It's all right, Bat. You have my word that there will be no shooting. My men will govern themselves according to those orders."

The Black Bat relaxed a trifle.

"Thank you, Commissioner. First of all, I might state that Ronald Tunick is not dead. Galvin's bullet hit the wall, not him. I pulled Tunick down and slugged him. If he looks dead, it's because of a superficial wound he received as he fled to the front door."

McGrath started for the hallway.

"I'd better put cuffs on him," he said.

"Wait!" the Black Bat called out. "Keep your handcuffs for someone else. Tunick is not the killer. I've been here for some time. I saw Galvin kill Antal and it was in self defense. However, I also saw Galvin kick a wire over there near his desk. That shorted the lights. Then he stepped up to Tunick and whispered to him to run for it, that he was giving him a break." He turned his head slightly. "Why then, Galvin, did you try to kill him?"

Galvin grew ruddy. "I did no such thing! Tunick simply ran for it when the lights went out. How can you stand there and testify to such events that transpired in darkness?"

"Because I can see in the dark," the Black Bat said. "I can also hear exceptionally well. The game is up, Galvin. You're guilty of murder—mass murder. Commissioner, if you'll bring in young Recor, he may have an interesting story to tell,"

McGrath moved toward Galvin, ready to pounce on him if he tried a getaway. McGrath could not figure out how in the world Galvin was the killer, but the Black Bat had not gone wrong yet. McGrath was taking no chances.

YOUNG RECOR came in slowly. He saw the Black Bat and shivered. Then, so fast that his words tumbled over one another, he blurted the truth.

"I was framed into this! A man I met in a night club got me into a card game and the others were in league with him. They cheated—took every cent I had. Then one of the players made an accusation. I had a gun. I took it out. Someone grabbed me, but the gun went off. The card sharp was on the floor—dead. They told me I'd go to the chair for it unless I obeyed their orders. I tell you I couldn't help myself! They threatened to tell the police about the killing. I don't believe now that man was dead at all. I believe it was all a frame-up! I saw Galvin at the night club when it happened. I think he engineered the whole thing."

Galvin clasped both hands in front of him and assumed the expression of an undertaker.

"This young man is somewhat mad," he said. "Did it ever occur to you gentlemen that my son, my own flesh and blood, was murdered by this ring? Have you thought of my daughter being kidnaped and held under cruel conditions so I would pay over the money my son's insurance policy provided? This is sheer drivel and I warn you it won't end here."

"You're right there, Galvin," the Black Bat said in a voice tinged with sarcasm. "It will only end when they march you from a death cell. You are not Ralph Galvin's father—nor Elaine's. Their father died years ago. So many years ago and so far from here that the fact was never known in these parts. You married his widow and her children took your name. There is a group photograph in Mrs. Galvin's room that shows her, the children and her first husband. I've checked further, through some old diaries I found in a chest. They'll convict you, Galvin, if your only defense is your relationship with Ralph and Elaine."

Galvin's eyes grew wide and terror-ridden. He walked slowly over to his desk and sat down; picked up a round paper weight and began to toy with it. McGrath watched him narrowly.

"You hired Antal through some intermediary, now dead probably," the Black Bat went on. "Antal didn't know who you were. You insured Ralph, then killed him. You had Elaine kidnaped and had Collins put in your home as a guard, to watch you. That was to throw all suspicion away from you for both the benefit of the police and the gunman who worked for you. But you sent Antal a phonograph record ordering him to murder Collins because he snooped and knew too much. That was a bad mistake, Collins could only snoop in your house, Galvin. He found out you were the mystery man and held it over your head. There could have been no other reason for eliminating him.

"You wanted to frame Tunick and you had Antal send those records to him. Morgan, picking up Tunick's mail, was unknowingly subjected to theft. The record containing the message was lifted and another one, really an old record of the type that Tunick collected, was substituted. Morgan carried the messages without knowing it."

Galvin said nothing but there was a look akin to madness in his eyes. Commissioner Warner seemed stunned.

"BUT WHY?" he asked. "Why should Galvin do all this?"

"At first Galvin only wanted to profit by murdering for insurance," the Black Bat answered quickly. "Then he rigged up a scheme to take over the whole insurance company. You see, he couldn't buy the necessary control with the money he had made from his other insurance-murder frauds, because that might have cast suspicion on him. He wasn't supposed to have so much money. But with the insurance from his stepson's policy he could do so. Not in straightforward fashion, of course. That would be too obvious. Therefore, he had the cover-up of his stepdaughter's kidnaping and the pretended extortion demands. He never intended to pay that ransom money. He'd have conveniently arranged for the girl's escape, I'm sure, if I hadn't rescued her. But it would look good, and he'd have been able openly to keep the money from the policy without any suspicion. As he did.

"Tunick paid him a quarter of a million dollars in full on the claim of his son's death. Galvin paid that money back to Tunick, who was on the verge of bankruptcy, for certain investments that gave Galvin firm hold on the Security Insurance Company. Not, as I first thought when I saw the check, for extortion demands. I wondered about that later, because I realized that Galvin hadn't been forced to pay the ransom, after all. Then if the check were for something else, he must have made previous negotiations with all intentions of paying—before he even had the money!

"To get the controlling interest, Galvin had Mrs. Bannister kidnaped and apparently murdered. Recor would inherit and among the assets of the estate were more bonds which would give Galvin complete control of the insurance company. Dr. Luddy was a director in the firm and he also believed that Tunick was guilty—inspired by Galvin's secret accusations. Paradon was in on it. He wanted a cut. Young Recor, in desperation, went to him for advice and, keen-minded as he is, Paradon saw just what this was all about."

"I committed no crime," Paradon yelped. "There is nothing on me. I'll talk. From what Recor told me and my own knowledge that Galvin was trying to corner a controlling interest in Security Insurance, I suspected it was Galvin. Then when Galvin actually bought Tunick's bonds, I knew. So did Dr. Luddy. There wasn't much we could do, without any tangible proof, so we decided to cut ourselves in, that's all. Galvin was a man of modest means. He needed money so he insured and murdered his stepson."

"That's enough," the Black Bat snapped. "It ought to provide disbarment proceedings against you, Paradon. And you, Dr. Luddy—did it ever occur that Galvin was framing you into a neat little trap by infecting those instruments and faking that accident with Singleton? You operated on Singleton. He is dead. Galvin could hold that over your head, tie you up with the murder ring if necessary and in that manner keep you down. You'd have felt his wrath before long."

"It—it's unbelievable!" Commissioner Warner mopped his face. "Of course things tie up and we'll develop evidence enough to convict, but Galvin—"

THE BLACK BAT spoke again. "Galvin is a peculiar person. He has a dual personality. One part of him exists for pleasure. Sergeant McGrath tipped me off about that angle not many hours ago and it sent me thinking. I had Galvin checked and found that he has two existences—one connected with gambling, women and wine; the other, a home-loving family man. When Jim Fisher returned and suspected something wrong about Ralph Galvin's sudden death, Galvin found it out and murdered those three men in the cemetery. He substituted another body for his stepson's and disposed of the real corpse in some other grave, I presume."

Galvin arose unsteadily.

"I want to confess," he said. "I—I—"

Then he raised both hands. He still held the paper weight with which he had been toying. The Black Bat saw that Galvin's right forefinger was thrust through a ring fastened to the weight.

Galvin's voice arose to a shriek. "All right—I killed them! I fooled all of you stupid morons. I'd have taken over the insurance company in a few months and then I'd have operated on the level. What if I did want money? Lots of it?"

McGrath advanced grimly. Galvin backed away a step.

"Don't come any closer," he shrilled. "This is a grenade I'm holding. I've kept it for just this purpose. You can't shoot me fast enough so I won't be able to pull this ring. We'll all go to hell together—the Black Bat along with us! I'm willing to die if he goes out too."

Suddenly young Recor went into a tackling dive. At the same moment the Black Bat's gun spat. Galvin's left hand, clutching the bomb, fell to his side with blood dripping from it. The bomb started to slip away from the pin. Recor made a grab for it with both hands. He twisted Galvin's wrist until it went numb and with the other hand he kept that bomb from being separated from the pin.

McGrath swung a blackjack. Galvin slumped to the floor and Recor cautiously removed the deadly bomb.

"That was a brave bit of work, Recor," the Black Bat said without tremor in his voice. "You've rather redeemed yourself. As a partial reward I'll tell you that your grandmother is alive, well, and by this time safely in her own home. Go to her, tell her what a fool you've been and make amends. Govern yourself like a man and if there is any punishment coming for your part in this, take it with your chin out."

Recor's eyes were shining happily. He could not talk. He could just nod his head violently.

The Black Bat faced McGrath.

"At your feet, Sergeant," he said, "is the wire that Galvin shorted. Pick it up and see what I mean."

McGrath stooped and seized the wire. Instantly the lights went out. When McGrath got them back on, there was no sign of the Black Bat.

CHAPTER XXI

McGRATH NAMES HIMSELF

P**LACID AND** patient, Tony Quinn, in his smoking jacket and tweed trousers, sat before his fireplace. His eyes were filmed over like those of a blind man. Silk sat beside him, apparently reading a newspaper.

"But Antal," Silk asked, "how come he went there? You said he didn't know that Galvin was the big boy behind the murders."

Tony Quinn chuckled softly.

"Galvin used to contact Antal by a recording. He'd advertise in the newspaper giving an address to which the recording had been sent. It was always one of these professional mailing addresses. Antal simply went there and got the recording. I had you insert an ad in tonight's paper. It indicated that Antal might find a new record at a certain address. He did—one that I prepared myself in the laboratory.

"I faked Galvin's voice well enough and gave Antal the news that Galvin had cashed the insurance check and had the cash at his home. Antal was to get it, keep it all for his share in the proceedings. I indicated that things were so hot the whole affair had to be dropped temporarily. That brought Antal to Galvin's in a big hurry. I hoped to overhear Galvin admit to Antal that he was the mystery man, but Tunick and the others showed up too soon.

"Therefore Galvin, figuring that Antal knew who he was and was trying to hijack him, used a gun. Antal got what was coming to him. That day Collins had you snatched—remember how Galvin slugged you with a chair? I couldn't imagine anyone in Galvin's position doing that. It made me suspicious. The rest of it I've told you."

Silk nodded and grinned. He started to say something when the phone rang. He answered it, spoke briefly and returned to Quinn's side with a puzzled expression on his face.

"That was McGrath," he said. "He wanted to know if you were in. Said he was on his way here."

Tony Quinn's face grew stark with horror.

"Silk, I slipped! It just occurred to me McGrath has a sample of my handwriting, stolen from this room. I sent him a message—an urgent one to help me save Mrs. Bannister. I was in a hurry and I didn't think. He also has a sample of the Black Bat's handwriting. If he has compared them—"

Silk broke out in a cold sweat. Someone tapped on the secret door. It was Butch. Silk told him what had happened and Quinn ordered Butch away in a hurry.

"McGrath will have nothing on you, Butch," Silk hastily assured. "Tell Carol to lay low, too."

Butch vanished and two minutes later McGrath arrived. He walked into the living room and sat down beside Quinn. He put a cigar between his teeth, bit off the end and threw it into the fireplace. Then he fumbled around in his pockets for a match.

Quinn stared straight ahead. Silk, in the hallway, prayed silently. It looked like the end of the Black Bat.

Then McGrath talked.

"Well Quinn," he said, "the Black Bat cleaned up another mess. You know, I swore I'd get him some day and I shall. When that day rolls around you will walk into a nice neat little cell. However, I suppose you'll deny being the Black Bat and I couldn't prove you were. At that,

I may even be all wrong and you really are blind. Sometimes I'm not sure; sometimes I am. This happens to be one of the times when I can't figure out how you could possibly do it."

TONY QUINN'S face betrayed none of the turmoil seething within him. At any moment McGrath would produce handcuffs, slap them in place and—exit the Black Bat.

McGrath fumbled again for a match and could not find one. He slipped a hand into an inner pocket and took out two pieces of paper. He spread these out on his knee.

"Wonder what I'm carrying this junk around for?" he said in a steady voice. "A bad habit of mine, carrying notes in my pockets until they rot."

He rolled both papers into a long tapir, stepped over, to the fireplace and set fire to it. He lit his cigar and threw the still burning papers into the smoldering logs.

"Well," he said, "guess I'll be on my way. Funny thing about me. I like to pay my debts."

Tony Quinn spoke to him for the first time.

"I have no doubt of that, Sergeant. You're an honest man. Some day, I hope, you'll catch this Black Bat red-handed."

McGrath smiled. "Sure I will. He can't get away with it forever."

McGrath nodded to Silk and walked through the door. On his way to the car he was muttering to himself.

"I'm a damned fool. A stupid damned fool. I should have compared the handwriting and made sure, even if I didn't use the information. But handwriting experts don't always agree. Maybe it wouldn't have done any good anyhow. Still—Boy, I've gone soft. Soft and foolish."

He got behind the wheel of the car. His jaw dropped an inch, his cigar tumbled into his lap. Across the whole center of his windshield were Black Bat stickers.

Behind a hedge, Butch was barely able to restrain the horse laugh that surged up within him.

McGrath ground out a salty oath. He stepped on the starter and pulled away.

"Oh-h-h, what a fool I am!" he groaned. "If this ever gets out… Fool, that's me! Jackass, nincompoop—double damned fool!"

Then he frowned. "I wonder! I wonder if he is the Black Bat! Those stickers—he couldn't have put them on the windshield. And his eyes didn't show any recognition of those papers. I wonder if I could have caught him at that!"

CPSIA information can be obtained
at www.ICGtesting.com
Printed in the USA
BVHW031311230719
554111BV00001B/22/P